I0553820

Tapestries in Time

Taylor's Destiny
Christine Young

Sardinian Sunset
C.L. Kraemer

Street Dog Dreams
Genie Gabriel

Published by Rogue Phoenix Press
Copyright © 2019
ISBN: 978-1-62420-471-5

Cover by Designs by Ms G

Taylor's Destiny
Christine Young

Chapter One

1823 Sardinia

"Captain, it's real curious, look over there," Sam, the first mate on Reid's ship, pointed to a small sailboat bobbing in the water, rocking to the swells of the waves while the wind whistled, and rain bombarded everything.

"It wasn't there a few minutes ago." Reid ran his hands through his hair, wondering about the vessel's sudden appearance. He didn't like surprises, which could mean danger.

"Nothin' was there."

Reid leaned over the bow of his ship for a better look. "Someone's in trouble. There's a person on the bow who's not moving." To Reid, the figure appeared to be an almost naked lady. The hair on the back of his neck stood on end. "I'm going down."

"She's not moving, Captain."

Reid threw the ladder over the side of the boat. Stepping quickly down, he landed on the deck then strode to the lady lying face down. Sitting on his haunches he watched her, amazed at the way the sight of her seemed to give a small jolt to his heart.

"What has happened to you, pretty lady?" he asked softly, wishing she would wake up. Good lord, but she wore... He didn't have words to describe what he was seeing. A narrow strip of cloth ran between both halves of her bottom and the top covered her breasts, but in the position she was lying, in he could see her nipples and the entire swell of her breasts. He gulped a lungful of air as his body instantly responded to the evocative sight.

Touching two fingers to her neck, he felt the steady pulse. "Got to get you on board my ship before something else strange happens." Slinging her over his shoulder and striding to the ladder, he tried not to touch anything he shouldn't be touching, but the feat was impossible.

Swiftly, he scrambled up the ladder, managing to land on the deck with both feet without letting go of the woman he rescued. He didn't want the crew to see her, didn't think he should be seeing her, but there was nothing to do but take her to his cabin.

"Sam, go down and bring up any items she might have on the boat. Take Destiny Rose with you. I want everything, every bag you can find. The way it's listing, the ship could sink any minute. Set the anchor though, we want to give it a chance to keep from blowin' away." He barked out more orders as he continued to the captain's cabin.

He set the lady on the bed, studying her. Her short blond hair framed the delicate features of her face. He wondered if she had blue eyes, too, or an exotic color of brown.

After covering her body with a quilt, he poured himself a glass of whiskey and waited for her to wake up.

"Captain?" Sam pushed the door open and delivered one large bag and two smaller ones. "Here's her things."

"Did you look inside them?" Reid asked, grinning because he knew the answer.

"Of course not, Captain. Can't say I'm not curious though. You should have seen the inside of that boat. So...ah, different." Sam ran his hands through his hair, his eyes scrunching as he stared from the bags then back to him before roving to the lady on his bed.

"She deserves some privacy," Reid said, but she sparked a whole lot of curiosity he wanted desperately to understand.

"Don't know the circumstances and it's none of my business, but it seems she wants to show the world all of her."

"That's right, you don't know what brought her here in this condition. We're going to have to wait until she wakes up to find out anything." He rubbed his chin thoughtfully while Sam backed from his cabin.

"Hope it's soon." Sam pulled the door shut behind him.

Reid sat down at his desk, flipping through ledgers then making notes. His mind wasn't on his work though. He looked to the woman curled up on his bed, a slight smile on his face. Obviously, there were more questions than answers when it came to his interesting find today.

Once again, he tried to concentrate on his work. He would load tapestries in three days' time. They were headed to London. He'd delivered tea, coffee and tobacco to the residents here. And now he guessed he would have a traveling companion...or not...on his way home.

Was she a native Sardinian? If so, why was she dressed or not dressed in such a bizarre fashion. Was she a victim of some crime? More questions needing answers swirled in his head.

A small moan emanating from the direction of his bed caught his attention. He looked up. She'd moved, pushing the quilt to her waist. The tiny top she wore slipped from one breast, baring it completely. He closed his eyes, realizing he was at this moment either in heaven or hell, couldn't be sure though.

Covering her was imperative so he strode to the bed. When he stood over her, she opened her eyes. They seemed glassed over and hazy, almost as if she looked through him. He sat beside her, trying to draw the quilt to her shoulders.

She shrugged it off, reaching out to touch his face with her hand. "Sean... I thought you were dead."

The slightest touch of her fingers on his face sent a wave of desire surging through him. Swallowing hard, "I'm not Sean."

Her eyes seemed to cross. "I'm sorry, no," she shuddered. "I guess you're not but you look like him. You could be his twin."

"Who is Sean?" He was suddenly more curious than when he first saw her, with a touch of jealousy surging through him.

"My fiancé a Navy Seal, but he's MIA." She pushed her hair away from her face, the quilt falling to her waist again. When she noticed how much she bared in front of him, she gasped and pulled the covering higher before meeting his gaze once more.

He wanted to tell her he'd seen practically all of her, knew every inch except the minutest details. "What is MIA?" He had two questions but he meant to take them one at a time.

"Missing in action. Who are you? And where am I? Everyone these days knows what MIA means." She settled against the backboard, keeping the quilt high.

He mulled her words over for a second, deciding not to ask his second question but to give her an answer instead. "I'm the captain of this ship, Captain Reid Stewart. Obviously, you're in the captain's cabin of my ship, my cabin. There was nowhere safe to take you except here. I hope it doesn't make you feel too uncomfortable."

She seemed nervous as she picked at the quilt then looked at him again. "Where is my sailboat? I'm sorry. It's just that this is all so weird. If you could lend me a shirt or something to put on over my swimsuit, I'll leave."

He couldn't help but chuckle, not at her discomfort but her use of words. "You call what you're wearing a swimsuit?"

"Well, I don't wear it to swim but that's what it's called." A soft pink color rose to her cheeks. Strange that she wasn't embarrassed earlier.

"You couldn't possibly swim in it." But on second thought, it would probably be easier to swim in this suit than the ones women usually wore.

"My boat?" she persisted, a hint of anger in her voice.

"Your sailboat is anchored nearby and I suppose, when it's safe, you can sail it away. The storm persists though and I wouldn't want to leave you to navigate the churning waves and violent unpredictable winds." He paused a moment, "I'd be happy to lend you one of my shirts, but when would you return it?"

"After I dressed. You could wait on my boat."

"Your clothes are here, in my cabin. I had my first mate bring all the bags he could find on board. We were afraid your ship would capsize in the huge swells, or blow away." He turned his attention to the window and the rain pelting it. This tempest wasn't about to let up anytime soon.

"Why am I here? Or did you answer that already?" She looked to the door as if she wanted to race outside then pulled the quilt higher. "I see one of my bags." She nodded in the direction of the door where Sam had set them down. "Could you..."

4

"Would you like something to drink?" he asked, pouring her a small glass of whiskey, his drink of choice.

"I suppose so." She shrugged slim shoulders that still poked above the quilt she was hiding behind.

He handed the drink to her then sat down on the bed. "Let's start at the beginning. You're here because your boat appeared suddenly out of nowhere and you were sprawled unconscious on the bow. I climbed down to see if you were still alive. You were, so I brought you to a safe place. Now you're awake and we're having a pleasant conversation."

"I don't remember anything." Closing her eyes, she rubbed her temples. "I don't feel very well and even though I'm trying to get my bearings, the room won't stop moving." She tried to place her hands on the sides of her head but the covering dropped and she grabbed at it. "My head won't cease its pounding."

"It's the head injury. You shouldn't sleep for a while, so we're going to have to keep talking." He grinned, pleased with himself. "Talking to me."

"I don't remember," she said softly, closing her eyes and looking thoroughly miserable. "Do you have anything for a headache? Any drug will do."

"Nothing that will stop the ache."

She looked around the room for a moment, clearly distracted by something but he couldn't be sure.

"Do you want some food? Maybe that will help the pain, or water." He was lost in this situation. Everything seemed just a bit off, but he didn't know what it was. She spoke strangely and wore clothing he'd never seen before.

"Some food might help. Can you bring me my bags?"

"Do you have clothes in them? You might want to put something on. Although I like what you're wearing..." He tried not to smile.

"I would never wear this in public," she interrupted, the color staining her cheeks turning a brighter shade of red. "I thought I was alone and I was just tanning. I'm nearly naked."

"I know. I do believe I've seen nearly all of you." He couldn't help the smile that burst from inside. "You're beautiful." Truly he didn't

5

know where his two comments came from. Of course she was beautiful and he was sure she knew it. He handed her the bags.

"I need to put more clothes on." She looked at him as if she wanted something from him. "Then I want to leave on my boat."

For some reason he wasn't sure of, he didn't want that to happen. "I won't stop you if that's what you're afraid of, but I have to insist you wait until the storm has passed. I rescued you and I consider you my responsibility."

"Thank you." She continued to stare at him.

"Oh, you want me to leave." Trying for nonchalance, he crossed his arms over his chest while he leaned against his desk. It wasn't his normal behavior, but he liked teasing her.

"That would be nice," she told him, pulling items from one of her bags and inadvertently letting the quilt slip again.

Nothing she pulled out looked like normal clothing any respectable woman would wear. He didn't move for a few seconds then unable to help himself, he sat down on the bed again and picked up several items of apparel. Turning them over and letting some of the tinier pieces slide through his fingers, he decided he liked the way they felt and would have loved to see her wearing them.

"Could you leave?" She let out a breath of air it seemed she'd been holding. "Please."

"What?" he grinned, "Why? As I've just told you, I've seen nearly all of you." He wasn't sure why he was being perverse. This wasn't like him. Angry with himself, he stood. "I'll be back with something for us to eat."

"Make sure you knock," she shot at him as he left, closing the door quietly behind him.

He leaned against the door, closing his eyes, trying to absorb those few minutes he had with her. His heart pounded and his breaths seemed to have turned to small pants. He still had more questions than answers. Pushing away from the door he strode to the kitchen.

"Destiny?" He looked around but the cook was nowhere to be found.

"Captain?"

"Sam. Where's Destiny?"

"That's the strangest thing. He went down to the sailboat to make sure we retrieved everything that was important and..."

"And..." Reid prompted, a small tick in the back of his throat told him he wasn't going to like what Sam was about to tell him.

"And a streak of lightning flashed then a huge whirlpool opened up and... And everything is gone." Sam was waving his arms around, gesturing wildly. "Just like that boat appeared, it disappeared."

"So, she can't leave on her sailboat." He wasn't entirely sure why he liked that fact, but he did. He wanted her to stay around for a few more days or weeks, possibly longer. She captivated him, touched his heart in a way no one else ever had.

"She wants to leave? Where she going in a storm with no boat?" Sam's question was blunt and to the point.

"Did we imagine the boat?" he asked, suddenly needing to look in his cabin to make sure he didn't imagine the lady but decided against it. "I'm grabbing some food from the kitchen. Let me know if anything new happens or if you see Destiny."

Returning to the door, Reid paused, hand in the air. Inhaling a deep breath, and feeling suddenly insecure, he knocked. "Can I come in now?"

She didn't answer but opened the door, a smile on her face. Staring into his eyes, she asked, "What's wrong?"

"I thought you were going to get dressed?" He strode through the room to set the food he pillaged from the galley on the table. "Look at you, barely wearing anything again." He wasn't angry even though he understood he sounded that way. She could parade her curves and beautiful body around him anytime she chose and he wouldn't complain.

"I did dress." She stood beside him, picking up a chunk of bread and a slice of cheese.

Needing a moment of thinking time, he changed the direction of his thoughts, "Sorry this isn't a real meal, but cook seems to have vanished with your sailboat." He sat down, unable to stop looking at her and the lack of clothing. Indeed, he had nothing more he could possible say on the issue of her apparel.

She found a chair, sitting, the smile vanishing. Then, blinking a few times, "My boat is gone? How am I going to get back to land?"

"I'll take you when the storm subsides. Not safe now." He spoke through bites of food he picked off the platter. His gaze focused on her, on her ever so long, slender yet well-muscled legs.

"I'm going to have to pay for it and I don't have enough money for that." She downed the whiskey he poured for her earlier then held her glass out seeming to ask for more.

"Slow down, I'm not understanding anything here. You don't make sense." He downed his glass of whiskey and filled both glasses again.

"I rented the boat and if I don't return it, I'll have to pay for it. I only have enough cash for the rest of my vacation, hotels and such unless my friend, Olivia, gets the villa she's renovating to a point where we can live there."

"People rent sailboats? Around here? Since when?" he asked, settling into the chair behind his desk with a plate of food. He wasn't sure if she was sane, yet she was beautiful. He could get used to all the strange things she said and did. What she wore certainly couldn't even be considered pants. They ended just below her well-shaped derrière. And the top she wore molded to her breasts like a second skin; the neckline was edged with lace as well as the bottom, which ended above her waist.

He grinned and ate a piece of cheese before sipping the whiskey. Bloody eyes but he could see her navel. She had a tiny waist and large beautifully shaped breasts, although he suspected she'd never worn a corset a day in her life.

"Just this afternoon," she replied indignantly, hands on her hips.

"Impossible. Why don't you start telling the truth?" He drummed his fingers on the table and was surprised when he noticed tears in her eyes.

"Are you calling me a liar?" she blurted out.

"Of course not, it's just that...well, well...no, whatever you say." He was tongue-tied.

Seemingly indignant, she brushed the tears away with the back of her hands. "This is the truth. Why don't you try being a gentleman?"

"There is no place on this island that you can rent a boat, and I'd be shocked if there are any villas anywhere on Sardinia to be bought. Nothing on Sardinia needs to be renovated."

"Everything needs renovation and almost all the villas are empty. What are you talking about?" she shot back at him.

"Then we're speaking of two different places."

"I just came from the town of Ollolai. I drove down to the bay, rented a boat and was enjoying the day when the storm hit. The boom hit me in the head, and I woke up here."

He poured her another glass of whiskey then filled his. Shaking his head, disbelief in everything she told him settled in, but she spoke as if she described some other place and she sounded so sincere. He'd always been good at deciphering truth from lies but this time, with this lady, he had no idea. Everything she said sounded genuine.

"I'll take you there tomorrow if the weather is good. I don't know what you mean by drove but we'll have to ride donkeys to navigate the steep trails." The expression on her face turned to horror.

"Donkeys?"

"That's the only way up to Ollolai."

She waved her hand in the air, shaking her head at the same time. "No, we can take my jeep. I'm not riding a donkey. No way in hell."

He shrugged, at his wits end, having no idea what was left to say. The conversations they had since she woke were bizarre, and they didn't seem to end in resolution. "Suit yourself." There was no reason to argue or disagree. She'd discover the truth tomorrow when they rode into the bustling town on donkeys.

He decided to change the conversation to something that couldn't be disputed. "I'm the captain of this ship, the Aina. Aina means joy and that's what this beautiful ship gives me when it cuts through the water, dolphins playing alongside, wind filling the sails. For several years, I was in the British navy."

"I don't know your name or perhaps I forgot it." She poured herself more whiskey, swirling the liquid in the glass then seeming to study him as she peered over the rim.

He wasn't sure but she either drank a lot or she was just as confused about this conversation as he was. If he didn't stop her, she was going to wake up with a blinding headache. "Reid Stewart. Captain Reid Stewart."

"I'm Taylor Maxwell." She held out her hand.

He took it in his, felt a jolt of passion, or perhaps lust was a more appropriate definition, surge through him and quickly let it go. "You from Sardinia? You speak nearly perfect English with very little accent. Although it seems more like an American accent."

~ * ~

Taylor studied her self-proclaimed rescuer carefully. Time and again he subtly accused her of lying then distinctly told her about things that weren't true. Ollolai was not populated and one could rent a boat. Hadn't she just done that? And she drove down to the bay on a dirt road in her jeep. Didn't she?

"My home is America, Oregon to be exact," she told him, daring him to dispute that fact and he didn't disappoint.

"Oregon is a territory where only a few inhabit, besides the natives of course. I believe Lewis and Clark led an expedition there only twenty years ago. I also know there is a fort there, but I'll bet you your villa that no one wore clothes like that." He pointed to her.

His words struck her hard. Gasping for breath, she sat down. "What did you just say?"

"Twenty-two years ago Lewis and Clark settled at the mouth of the Columbia River. Is that what you wanted me to repeat?"

"Yes, something like that." She set her glass on the table hard, staring out the window a second in an attempt to get back her bearings.

He refilled the empty glass. "Are you going to get muzzled?"

"If that means smashed, yes. What year is it?" She didn't want to ask the question and she certainly didn't want to hear the answer either. She pinched herself to see if she was alive or at least not dreaming. By his math, it was eighteen twenty-three but that just wasn't possible.

"If you get drunk, I'm not going to be responsible for your actions, or mine," he told her. Regarding her lazily, his gaze rested on her, especially the space above her shorts and below the skimpy tank top.

She pulled it down. "I'll accept all responsibility for my actions. Always have and always will." Her bag was still sitting on the bed. She rummaged through it and pulled out an oversize shirt. Putting it on she said, "It's getting a bit chilly."

He looked at her as if he was saying you just figured that out. "The sun has gone down but it's still warm. You don't have to cover up for me. I like looking at your bare skin."

Was he challenging her? Well, if her guess was right, men were scum everywhere. "I felt a slight chill. Maybe it was the blow to my head. Perhaps it was the way you were looking at me." *As if he wants to devour me.*

"Maybe it's the whiskey."

"That too," she told him, abruptly sitting down. "I should probably eat something."

"Not a bad idea." Looking out the window, he said, "The rain has stopped and the clouds have cleared. Would you like to walk on the deck?"

"After I eat." She coupled a piece of cheese with a slice of bread, wishing for peanut butter or something else, anything to smear on the bread. Mustard would be nice.

"That walk?" he asked again.

"By myself, yes," she said, wondering if he would allow something like that. Yet in a way she didn't understand, he helped her forget about her fiancé. She liked this man and the way he smiled when he looked at her.

"Not possible."

"Why ever not?" She wanted to scream it's the twenty first century, but she knew first hand just how despicable men could be in that time. And she'd also guessed that she was no longer in the twenty-first century even though every part of her told her this wasn't possible. He had to be lying to her, but she could think of no plausible explanation for that.

"Not safe," he told her as his fingers drummed the table all the while he watched her. "You have to take me with you or you can't go.

It's as simple a fact as anything."

"That's autocratic."

"I am the captain." He grinned shamelessly as he stood and gallantly offered his arm to her. "I enjoy giving orders."

"Most men do," she said bitterly, remembering the man who thought he had the right to her body just because he was her boss.

"For the moment I'll ignore that, but I would like to know what makes you so jaded about men."

She picked up another piece of bread and inhaled deeply, reminded of all the reasons why she traveled to Sardinia. One of those reasons stood beside her: tyrannical men. Men who thought they could take what they wanted without asking.

"It's not your business," she said curtly, trying to get over the fact she was attracted to him. She'd travelled halfway across the world to forget that man and what he expected in return.

"As your captain it is my business. I need to understand what could go wrong and why." They stood at the door, seeming to wait for something.

"A man tried to take what I didn't want to give just because he thought he could," she blurted without thinking.

"Why did he think that? No man should take from a woman what she doesn't want to give."

"He was my boss."

"Boss? Did you provoke him?" He looked at her clothing as if suggesting it might be her fault.

She realized he would accept different standards of dress if this were the nineteenth century. "Of course not and I wasn't wearing shorts. I was dressed in very severe office clothing that covered almost every inch of me." She smiled inwardly, realizing those words might baffle him.

"Is that what you call these? Shorts?" He starred pointedly at that item of apparel. "I like them on you."

She didn't want to admit anything to him just yet, and she had no idea what he might be thinking. In any case time travel wasn't possible. It only existed in fiction. He was just acting but he was damn good.

"I don't have anything you might consider acceptable clothing. For the most part, I took the bare minimum to the sailboat. I was going to be alone for a few days. I didn't need very much." She now possessed only a few changes of clothing and minimal underwear. Her makeup was in a separate case, which had been brought aboard, as well as her purse with her ID and cellphone.

"What do you think I consider acceptable? Like I said before, I like your shorts and this top. The color suits you, and I also like to see a little cleavage. Just enough to make me curious." Gently he touched her lips with a callused fingertip.

She appreciated the way his touch sent a spiral of heat inside. "I don't know what to say."

"You said you had a fiancé. What war was he missing in action?"

She realized he wouldn't accept her answer unless he was beginning to accept the truth. "Iraq. The Iraq war." She tilted her head slightly, trying to read his reaction.

"Never heard of it, that war. Never heard of the country," he told her, implying she was lying again.

What she did know was that the country was not titled Iraq until 1922. "Well, it's part of the upper Mesopotamia and the Syrian Dessert and Arabian Dessert. Have you heard of those?" She didn't mean to be sarcastic. Slowly, she was beginning to feel differently about this man.

"The territory sounds like a British holding to me. Is your fiancé British?"

If her worst fears were correct, she truly had travelled back in time. *Just ask him what year it is, fool. Confirm what you're thinking. He might just be joking about the Lewis and Clark bit.* "Perhaps and no."

"Why would Americans fight a war on British land?"

She didn't understand his tone. She decided for the truth as she knew it in her time. "Terrorists and nine eleven."

His heavy sigh gave her second thoughts and brought her closer to her conclusion. "Can we go for that walk now?"

"I'd like that." She needed a diversion from this conversation.

"Let me send my men below."

"Why?" She wanted to hear the words from him but if her guess was right, men weren't used to seeing women's legs unless they were having sex with them.

He coughed, "Because I don't think you'd be comfortable if they were staring at you, at your, at..."

"My butt? Or my breasts? Or perhaps my navel?" Once again she snapped at him and he was only trying to be nice to her. He hadn't asked for anything from her, for the most part had only been courteous.

This time it wasn't a cough. He choked. "That was a bit graphic." Then he tossed his head back and laughed. "Are you always so blunt?"

"Just telling it the way it is. If you have something, I can...wait." She rummaged through her bag and found a skirt she used as a cover up. It was semi-shear but with the darkening night, no one would get an intimate view of her or clothing they probably never saw before. She wrapped it around her waist and fastened it.

"That's a little better." He told her, grinning. "But if you're going to be honest, I should too. I liked your clothes better without the skirt."

"Of course you did. You're a man." She laughed at his look of chagrin, which lasted only a second. Then he smiled and it touched her heart even though the grin was arrogant and all alpha male. She knew he appreciated her well-toned body and large breasts.

"I'm certainly glad of that fact. Don't believe I would do well as a woman." He opened the door for her and waited for her to exit.

She didn't know why but she accepted his arm when he offered it to her. Sean used to do that and she loved to walk beside him. "In too many ways to count you remind me of my fiancé."

"Why is that? Besides the fact I look like him." They stopped at the railing on the starboard side near the bow.

His hand settled on her shoulder and she took comfort in that small gesture. "Yes, you do look like him, and your voice is similar. I..."

"He is missing in Iraq. Does that mean you're waiting for him?" His voice turned husky and inquisitive.

She was, even when she was told he was most likely dead. "It's been over a year. All of the men with him were killed. No one, not even the Navy, believes he's alive."

"Do you?"

"Before I left for Sardinia, I came to terms with his death and I made the decision not to wait for him to miraculously be found alive." If she now lived in another century, she would never see him again. Waiting was ridiculous.

"I'm glad to hear that," he told her, his fingers gently massaging her neck muscles. "Is this alright with you?"

"The massage? It's heavenly." She liked the way he asked, the way he teased yet treated her gently. She reminded herself he wasn't anything like her boss, ex-boss. This man wouldn't take anything from her or assume he could.

"You're hard to resist. You're smart and beautiful. You make me laugh when you say the strangest things. I have more questions for you than answers. America must have very interesting women."

She felt the warm touch of his lips where his fingers had just been. Sudden heat swept through her, infusing her with hope for love and a future of happiness. It had been such a long time since she'd felt this way.

Mourning for her lost love had sent her into a spiral of despair and depression. She turned in his arms, suddenly gazing into his eyes. In the moonlight they seemed to sizzle with desire and passion.

"We should go inside," she told him, realizing if she gave in and let him kiss her, it might lead to something more than she was ready for with him. Twenty-three and a virgin, she and Sean had made a pact of celibacy until their wedding night. It had been easy because he shipped out soon after their short engagement.

Reid Stewart reminded her of her lost love and the fact they never acted on that love. It was something she regretted for the year he'd been missing. She no longer lamented that act of abstinence because she had found an instant attraction to this man, and in time, she was more than willing to give him her virginity, just not tonight.

"But the moon is shimmering and the night is warm." One of his hands wrapped around her waist, pulling her closer to him. She felt his hard arousal against her and knew he wanted her.

"I don't trust myself with you. I don't fall into anyone's bed the first day I meet them," she told him and knew there was a greater chance these impulsive feelings could quickly change to sex. Before she let him make love to her, she needed to know more about him and where exactly she was.

He chuckled softly. "Again your honesty amazes and intrigues me. I don't know any other woman who would be brazen enough to imply they wanted to make love or they were even thinking about it."

"Is it shameless here for a woman to tell a man how she is feeling?" She knew it was in any other century but her own. Even then many women did not speak of their feelings and needs. Men still assumed control.

"Americans are different," he told her. "But since you admitted feelings for me, could I plead my case for a kiss, a chaste kiss, well maybe not too chaste." He pushed her hair behind her ears, his hands settling gently on her face.

Unable to help herself, she moistened her lips and leaned into him at the same time. His mouth settled softly against hers. She opened for him, accepting the tantalizing warmth of his breath before feeling his tongue touch hers. In the back of her throat she moaned, accepting all he gave. One hand now resting on the small of her back, he drew her closer to him.

Her breaths came in short intervals. When he looked at her, she knew she craved more but also told herself she didn't want him to think she gave herself to anyone or everyone who kissed her.

In his arms, she turned in a slight effort to distance herself from him and regain a tiny measure of composure. This was happening too quickly. In a rush, she found she was falling in lust with him. She'd only felt this way once before and that was with Sean. It had been incredibly hard to remain chaste with her fiancé when she craved intimacy.

"That was enough for one night," she told him, running her hands along his arms, wishing her life was more stable.

"Never enough but I'll abide by your wishes." His hands now rested on the bare skin at her waist and she realized with the slightest invitation from her, he would explore higher, perhaps slip his large, calloused hands beneath her top.

"You told me you were in the Navy. A captain perhaps?" She needed to discover more before sex kept her from thinking rationally.

"I was, but I didn't fight in the War of 1812." He moved his hands a bit higher until they rested just beneath the swell of her breasts, "I was too young for a commission."

"Did your family buy you one?" she asked, curious about the workings of the British government and trying to find out more about the time. She told herself she had to keep her mind on the questions and not where he explored.

"No, a friend of my family bought the commission with the provision I work for him once my duty to my country was done."

"What do you do for him, this man who helped you become a captain?" She laughed, understanding he wouldn't appreciate her question.

"If I told you I'd have to kill you." He trailed kisses down the back of her neck in what she assumed was an attempt to distract her.

"You're a spy."

"I can't answer that," he said as his teeth slowly seduced, leaving an impression as they investigated. She shivered, succumbing to his seduction of her.

"Doesn't matter if you deny or confirm. I've no interest in anything secretive." If he were on a mission on this tiny island...well, she couldn't imagine unless he was after a person. Perhaps she was more interested than she let on.

"Earlier you spoke of an office and a boss. Seems strange. Women work in America?"

"Whatever I told you, you wouldn't believe me and I don't want you to think I'm lying to you." Nothing she told him about her work would be believable to him. She was a graphic artist who specialized in advertisements, emphasis on the internet and social media. She could tell him she drew pictures.

"Try me." He wrapped one arm around her and leaned against the railing with his other arm.

When one door closes, another one opens. For the first time since Sean left, she felt protected and safe. More than anything she wanted to tell him what he asked but... She didn't want to find herself committed to some insane asylum.

"You have no faith in me?"

"It's not that..." she paused.

"What is it then?"

~ * ~

Destiny Rose jumped from the rope ladder onto the bow of the sailboat. She didn't know why she was so curious about the vessel and the lady they found, but she felt from the first moment she saw her something was different. She must have known her. Had this woman been sent to her? Was she supposed to weave a tapestry for Reid and this lady? Intrigued, she had been determined to see the boat for herself and was reminded of something she'd forgotten, a life in another time.

Slowly she walked into the main cabin. No one on Reid's ship knew the cook was a girl, no one except the captain. Over the years he'd made so many concessions for her, she felt as if she owed him her independence. She smiled. He protected her privacy for years and she didn't doubt he would continue.

One reason and one reason alone forced her to masquerade as a man. Her stepfather had abused her for years. When she was old enough, she ran away. An advertisement for a ship's cook caught her attention. With the help of a friend, she wrapped her breasts, cut her hair and approached the captain to ask for a job. She never thought...well there had never been a deserving lady in the captain's presence before.

She walked into the galley of the lady's ship. The small kitchen contained things she'd never seen before. The stove was different and she opened a door to a small box. It was cold inside. A container labeled milk sat on one of the shelves as well as wrapped cheese and turkey slices.

There were others things she couldn't define or explain, yet something niggled in the dark recesses of her brain, some memory that wanted to get out but couldn't. Starting for the stairs, ocean swells rocked the boat. She scrambled to keep her footing while hanging onto a table that was bolted in place.

"Bloody eyes," she murmured. "I'm not supposed to be down

here. What if the captain finds out I'm snooping? Damn, I'm...a dream spinner."

Lightning slashed across the sky and thunder drummed in her ears. The vessel began to turn on its axis, swirling faster and faster with each passing second. Destiny Rose lost her balance. Her head hit the floor hard. She heard the crack then nothing more except a roaring in her ears.

When she opened her eyes, sunshine filled the tiny cabin. She pressed her hands to her temples, trying to ease the pain throbbing through her head. Slowly, she found her way to the deck.

The sky was a vivid blue with a few clouds lying close to the horizon. Reid's ship was nowhere to be seen although the sailboat sat in the same cove. She didn't know how to sail a boat, didn't have any idea how to get to land.

Would Reid sail without her? Good lord, she hoped not. She'd have to find another job and she'd have to find another man she could trust.

Another boat passed by and she waved at it, hoping someone would rescue her. It made a turn, heading her way. Watching the sails come closer, she held her breath, praying for her safety.

"Can we help?" someone from the boat asked as it pulled up close. "You look stranded."

"I'm lost. Yes, stranded," Destiny admitted, shrugging her shoulders as she tried to assess this man who seemed to be offering aide. "Can you take me somewhere, a city close by?" While she'd made several trips with Captain Stewart, she'd never been on the land, never left the boat. She had no idea what Sardinia offered.

"Sure thing, I'll take you to Ollolai. You know anybody there?"

"No," she was shaking her head and wondering what she would do to survive. "I can cook. Does anyone need a cook?"

"I know someone. Climb aboard."

Chapter Two

"Ah... captain? You spend the night on deck?" Reid's first mate asked while he stood over him grinning.

"No, I'm in my bed cuddled up with Tay. What does it look like?" he answered as he thought about the beautiful woman who appeared out of nowhere yesterday. Last night when they walked back to the cabin, he made excuses to Taylor before grabbing a pillow and blanket and bedding down on the deck in front of his door. Thank goodness no storms erupted to drench him.

"Well, don't get testy on me," his first mate said. "Just 'cause you didn't get any sleep doesn't mean you have to be grumpy and take it out on the crew. You could have stashed her in one of the other rooms."

"Sorry, didn't want to put anyone out. You understand they're all occupied." He grumbled, rubbing the back of his neck. Finding a solution to this tiny problem was necessary, but he didn't want to put her on the spot or make her feel threatened. Did he want to share his bed with her? Of course he did. But he knew that would have to wait and with no promises of a happy ending.

He picked up his bedding then headed the few feet to his cabin. When he stepped inside, she was once again nearly naked, only wearing a miniscule top and bottom. She turned, smiling at him.

"What are we going to do today?"

"I have to go into town and arrange for the delivery of the tapestries I'm taking to London. Can I assume you want to go with me?" he asked, watching her as she wriggled into a pair of pants that molded to every luscious curve before slipping a sleeveless top over her head.

"Yes, I'm going. I want to see the town you described to me last night. Where did you sleep?" She took a tube of something out of her bag and opening it she ran it around her lips, coloring them.

Her pointed question left him with no answer he wanted to give. "Found another place to put the blanket and pillow."

"Did you find the cook?"

His stomach rumbled hungrily. "No, I suppose I should look for someone in town. Don't want my first mate fixing the meals. He's a worse cook than I am."

"I'm a very good cook." She slipped the tube into a small container then fastened it with something he'd never seen before.

"No." He picked up the container, unfastening and fastening it again then he glanced at her.

"What?"

He watched her step back as if he hit her. "I don't want you in contact with the crew and the passenger that will join us on our voyage to London. It's really simple."

"How are you going to feed your men and that single traveler? They'll starve then he won't pay his passage."

"He's already paid and I won't let anyone starve."

She had a sound idea but he did know a few people on Ollolai, and perhaps they could put him in touch with a man who wanted to see the world and in addition could cook. "Good point."

"You're a very stubborn man." She turned her back to him, combing her hair.

"How long before you're ready?" He paced the room, picking up articles of clothing she'd dropped on the floor and the bed then neatly folding each piece and setting them on top of his trunk.

She watched him, seeming to study his actions with her head tilted provocatively. "I'm ready now, but I'm not riding a donkey."

He looked at her feet. "Do you have any other shoes? It's a steep rocky climb. While the road is wide enough for a wagon, if you wear those things, your feet will be cut and bruised by the time we reach the top. Then you still have to walk down."

"Flip flops," she told him.

"Flip." He sighed softly. "Flops. Why am I not surprised? Never heard of or seen any footwear such as these."

"I have something else." She bent over one of her bags. While she pushed things aside, some remained in the bag some landed on the floor. "Here they are, my running shoes."

"Running shoes..." He folded the items she left on the floor, setting them on top his trunk. "Why do you need shoes for running?" She was definitely a puzzling woman.

He watched her shrug as she slipped on the socks and shoes. "Exercise," she told him, smiling sweetly. "I like to stay in shape and a little cardio is good for the heart."

"Good for you," he said trying to ignore the curious statements and offering her his arm.

"I get to scale the ladder," she seemed to muse. "Is it hard?"

"Probably not for someone who likes to run and stay in shape. What's cardio?" He truly didn't know what to say to her anymore. But when he looked at her...well he was going to be hard pressed to sleep on the deck of his ship for many more nights. The clothing she wore outlined and accentuated every curve of her body, and he wanted to explore each and every one of them.

She stood at the railing, hesitant, and looked at him. She inhaled a deep breath of air then let it out slowly. "How do I..."

"Get over the railing?" he asked, bringing her a bucket she could stand on so she could swing her leg over. "There you go." He turned the pail upside down.

"Shouldn't you go first?" She stepped back, looking hesitant. "It's a long way down."

"Whatever pleases you but I don't want to have to come back up and get you if you change your mind." He wasn't sure any more about her courage and the rope ladder was precarious.

"I'm not afraid."

"Good," He was quickly over the railing and down the ladder. Shielding his eyes from the sun, he looked upward, waiting for her. She was nimble and managed to navigate the ladder to the boat with ease.

She sat in the stern of the rowboat watching him. "I could do that," she told him, smiling. "You know, row."

"You've rowed a boat before." He grinned back at her, wondering what new revelation she would make.

"It's not hard. I like canoes better though." She tilted her head, seeming to wait for him to respond. "And kayaks are fun."

He mulled her words over in his head deciding once again the best course of action was to ignore them. "We're here." He jumped from the boat, splashing through the water. "I hope you've reconsidered the way you're going to get to the top. Walking is not a great option."

She grimaced as she looked at the road then back to him. "I'm not afraid of much but..."

"You're afraid of donkeys?" He was incredulous.

"Yes," A fingertip was in her mouth. "Horses too."

"There is nothing to be afraid of. They are quite docile." He laughed softly, appreciating the conversation simply because he didn't believe she was truly afraid. "At least you have pants on and you're not trying to ride in a dress or those shorts you had on last night. It would be much harder."

She straightened, her back stiff, her chin up, "I'll do it. I don't intend to fail."

"Good girl." He didn't want to tell her but he was proud of her courage and conviction. Going up the side of the mountain was much easier on the donkeys, unless of course one was terrified of the animal.

The donkeys were corralled a few feet from the start of the trail. A man strode from a nearby shack. "Wondered when you were going to need my services."

"Need two donkeys and I'll bring a couple of carts of tapestries to the ship. I'll need a couple more dinghies to load it all."

"I'll have it ready." The man gaped at Taylor, a thin line of drool from his mouth down his chin.

"You can close your mouth anytime," Reid told him curtly, angry with the way he gaped at her.

He snapped it shut. "Sorry, sir."

The donkeys were saddled and ready. He watched the way her eyes narrowed when she looked at them. Her hands shook when she took the reins. As she glanced his way, her chin shot up.

"Do you need help?" he asked, taking pity on her and realizing she wasn't confident about everything.

"I don't know how to get on that animal," she said, her voice soft almost as if she admitted defeat. "And I also don't know how to stay on or get off when we reach town."

"I'll help and I don't think someone as indomitable as you will have any problem once you're on." He caught the chuckle in the back of his throat, realizing his laughter at her expense would not help the situation.

"Come here," he said, motioning to her.

"My heart is pounding so hard it feels as if it's going to jump out of my chest." She stepped toward him. "Are you positive riding is easier than walking?" her reluctance tangible.

"I hope this is alright." He pulled her into his arms, holding her, feeling the way her body trembled against his. Trying to lend a small amount of comfort, he ran his hands up then down her back in a feeble attempt to soothe her obviously frayed nerves.

"It is, thank you. I don't mind if you touch me and thank you for asking."

He felt the dampness of her tears soak through the fabric of his shirt then tried to encourage. "You can do this."

"I don't know."

"Well, I do." He kissed her forehead. "Let's get this done. We'll be at the top of this tiny hill in no time, and you'll wonder what you were so afraid of."

"What if he takes off?" She pointed to the donkey, her hand still shaking.

"He's a she and she won't," he said, once again trying not to laugh at the expression on her face.

"What if I fall off?"

"You won't. Now put your left foot in my hand. I'm going to give you a boost so you can throw your leg over the donkey. Hold on to the saddle horn with both hands."

She was nodding yes so many times he was again tempted to laugh. "I'm ready."

He mounted and they started up the road. "You're doing fine. Now, isn't this better than walking?"

"I'll tell you when we're at the top," she said, her voice tight. In fact, her entire body appeared rigid.

"You should probably wait to pass judgment until we're back where we started." He paused, looking over his shoulder at her. "Try to relax." Her muscles were going to be sore, not just from the riding but the way she was holding herself.

At the Ollolai stables as he helped her down, she groaned and when her feet touched the ground, he had to hold her up.

"I don't think I can stand let alone walk." She closed her eyes, leaning into him as if trying to absorb his strength.

"You're strong," he told her, wrapping an arm around her waist. "Sit here for a minute while I make some arrangements." He was not too sure he should leave her alone.

"I'd like that." She smiled at him, brushing her hair away from her face before rubbing her neck. She placed her hands on the small of her back, stretching and moving her shoulders up and down.

If she'd allow it, he'd give her a massage tonight. "I'll be right back." He kissed her forehead then whistling strode into the building feeling an unusual lightheartedness.

Quickly, he signed the last papers arranging for the tapestries and watched as the loading onto the wagons began. He needed to see how Taylor was doing. Only a half hour had passed, but he didn't like leaving her alone in this town for that long. He knew very little about her but what he was sure of on some instinctive level was that she could get herself in a great deal of trouble without even trying.

He stepped into the sunlight, seeing she still sat in the same place he left her. "How are you doing?"

"You were right about the town. It's not void of people." She made a sweeping gesture with her arms. "It doesn't look anything like I remember."

He sensed she didn't like admitting she was wrong. "I'm going to buy you some clothes. Some things that are appropriate for being seen by the public. Don't get me wrong. I love your clothes; love the way they look on you, but..."

"But I shouldn't wear them anywhere but your cabin on your ship. I understand. I've seen what the women are wearing."

"You should only put them on for me." He agreed with her and liked the way she was beginning to trust him.

"I can't pay for any clothes and I don't want to be beholden to you."

"That's not a problem. And I promise you, I won't ask for anything in return."

"No payback?" Skeptically she lifted one eyebrow. "No sex for clothes or whatever else I might need."

"I don't want or need a mistress," he spoke softly but by the expression on her face, he was sure she heard.

Then, "I'm no man's mistress. I could work off the purchase in your galley. As I told you I can cook a little bit."

"No."

She inhaled a deep breath of air. "Don't spend too much money. I'm going to find a job and pay you back."

A job? What could she do to earn money? Women didn't work. "Only the necessities, I promise." He offered his arm and they walked down the sidewalk of the bustling street until they reached a dressmaker's shop.

Inside the establishment, he could tell by her reactions to every piece the seamstress included in the stack of items to be purchased she was overwhelmed. When the lady came at her with the measuring tape, she shrunk toward the back wall, her eyes wide again. Then she stiffened her back.

"This isn't anything like walking into a store and just buying it." Her chin jutted out and she picked up a bolt of fabric then turned it over as if it would appear different on the other side.

"We're looking for anything readymade that will fit the lady," Reid said, realizing the fact this lady who could do so many things and talk a good story about events he'd never heard of was out of her element in a dress store.

"Do you know what you want?" The dressmaker turned her full

attention to him.

Watching Tay's expression change to one of confusion, he decided he would have to answer. She'd probably say a pair of pants that fit so tight they didn't leave anything to one's imagination. "A walking dress, a couple of day dresses and an evening dress. We'll also need underthings including two corsets."

"Yes..." It seemed the dressmaker was taking mental notes as she walked through the store gathering items.

"I don't want a corset," Taylor interrupted.

"You must; your dresses won't fit without one."

Taylor slanted a wicked glance at him. He shrugged his shoulders then said, "The seamstress is right you know. Unless we have time to have the dresses constructed to your figure they are all made for very tiny waists. We don't have that kind of time. We're leaving with the morning tide." But Taylor had a very tiny waist and they might fit without. He certainly wouldn't want to be laced in tight.

"As long as I only have to wear them in public," she mumbled begrudgingly.

He wondered at her reticence. Were all women in America like her? In his world there were unwritten rules and regulations about clothing, and she defied all of the ones he was aware of.

"On board ship, only when we go for walks, take some fresh air." He tossed the idea her way.

"So, if I want to go outside and walk on the deck, I have to change my clothes." Her hands were on her hips and it seemed she wanted to argue with him, yet her smile spoke a different story.

"I'm more than willing to help." He waggled his eyebrows at her. "But I do enjoy taking clothes off my lady more than putting them on."

"Sir!" The dressmaker sounded shocked.

"We're newly wed." He lied to shield Tay from the embarrassment he unthinkingly created.

The dressmaker looked to Taylor and it seemed she was more than willing to go along with his ploy. "Just a few days ago. I'm still trying to get used to the less than subtle things he says. He has this way of making me blush with just a few well-chosen words."

"A few days ago," he agreed, thinking that perhaps it was about time he settled down for real. Who would suit him better than this woman who seemed to arrive out of nowhere and who had him curious and intrigued every moment of every day.

"I like lavender and pale blue," she said. "Pink is nice but I don't really care for red."

The dressmaker pulled several gowns, as well as a corset. "Do you wish to try these on?"

When she looked at him, she appeared almost as lost as she was when standing in front of the donkeys.

"I buy online," she muttered, "and I can't lace a corset. So, someone has to do it for me."

He muttered to himself, hopefully so no one could hear him, "What the bloody hell is on line?"

"I'll explain over a bottle of whiskey or anything else you have. Perhaps when we're both drunk enough you won't remember what I tell you." She walked into the dressing room, one of the seamstresses behind her.

"I'd like to see everything I'm buying," he called out, regaining his equilibrium for a moment.

"Of course, sir."

"Are you wanting this to take the whole day?" Taylor said, looking over her shoulder at him. "With this pile of clothing then putting on and taking off everything, the process will be hours in the making, and if I have to show you..."

"We don't have the whole day." He did want to see a few things, but they had to be finished here in less than an hour. "Just try what you like on and if you want them, I'll buy them. I don't need to see anything."

~ * ~

Taylor spread all the dresses and accessories Reid bought her on the bed. Stepping back, she looked from the bed to her benefactor. "You really didn't have to purchase all of these things. I only needed two day dresses. Look, I'm beginning to learn the lingo."

"Lingo? If I help you with the corset, will you let me see these things on you?" he asked, his steel blue eyes shimmering with what she thought looked like passion. It wouldn't take much to fall for his charming and gallant ways, along with the burgeoning sense of humor.

"Are you fighting the impulse to fold everything?" She laughed, watching his fingers as they seemed to twitch above the shambles she made of the newly acquired purchases. "I promise I won't leave the clothes spread across your bed."

"No, no, I'm waiting for an answer." He crossed his arms in front of him, placing his hands beneath his armpits.

"Yes, I'd enjoy donning the dresses I liked but didn't try on. Taking a chance on their fit, I still don't want to wear the corset, but in the dressing room today I realized I would have to." She pulled one of the corsets from a bag and wrapped it around her then she turned her back to him. "I think this is where you lace it," she told him, looking over her shoulder.

"You should remove that thing, the top you are wearing, then put the chemise on first. I'll step out of the room so you can do that." He backed toward the door, his grin broad and endearing. The look on his face gave her pause and a reason to smile.

"Not necessary. I'll do it with my back toward you." Turning, she slipped out of the tank top she was wearing and pulled the chemise over her head. Once again with the corset wrapped around her, she waited for him to lace it.

She felt the tug and was reminded of Scarlett O'Hara's servant lacing her into her corset and asking for it to be tighter. Never in her life had she thought to have the same experience. But she wasn't going to ask for the crazy torture device to be pulled snugger.

"Finished," he said, brushing his hands off, seemingly proud of himself. "I'd like to see this dress." He held up a pale blue evening dress created from India muslin, ornamented with small sprigs of silver. The corsage was made to fit, with an elegant stomacher, composed of double rows of silver lace, placed diagonally from the front and continued over the shoulder. It had short full sleeves encased in bands edged with silver and a broad silver lace band around the waist. The bottom of the skirt was also decorated with silver lace.

She held up her arms and he helped her slip it over her head. More than anything, she'd never expected to dress in something this elaborate. Even at her prom she didn't wear anything this fancy. He fastened the buttons that ran the length of the back.

Stepping back, she faced him, placing her hands on her hips. "Well? What do you think?"

"Beautiful." He smiled at her then stepped toward her, holding out her arms before twirling her around. "I wish I could take you to the opera and show you off." He paused, seeming to think, "Maybe when we get to London. Do you like the opera?"

"And would I be able to show you off? What would you wear?" She needed to turn his sexist remark to something she couldn't take offense to. "Do you wear those things called cravats and a waistcoat? Would you look splendid holding my arm? You could be my eye candy."

"Show me off? Eye candy? Hmm...that's a novel idea and yes, I would dress in the height of fashion, just for you."

"Reid, we really have to talk, but you have to promise me even if you don't believe what I'm going to tell you, that you won't have me committed to some insane asylum. I am very rational and completely sane. I promise."

"You don't want to go to Bedlam? Perhaps you could try on another dress in the interim." It seemed he wanted to change the subject.

She couldn't let him avoid her or talking to her, not now, not when she had the courage to tell him the truth as she knew it about herself. "No, you can dodge this conversation, but at some time we must have it."

"Alright, but we need food first. It's been a long day and we haven't eaten since this morning. I'll be back in a few minutes."

She watched him exit the room, his back stiff. Sometime at the dressmaker's shop he must have found a cook, because suddenly there was food to be had. It could have been when she was trying on dresses. The young man must have gone ahead of them, because he had to have been on board when they arrived to have dinner ready now.

Looking in the small mirror hanging on the wall, she saw very little of herself. She sat down on a bench located beneath a window and in her mind tried to put everything she needed to tell him in order.

I come from the future was probably not the best way to begin the conversation. She could show him some of the things she had with her that might convince him, her cell phone to start. She'd tried to ease him into this conversation for the past twenty-four hours, yet she had no idea what his mindset was.

He laughed at some of the things she said, things no one in this century would say. Yet he didn't ask her questions. He'd just smile and go on with the conversation as if nothing was untoward.

Opening the door, he pushed it shut with his foot. He set the food on the table and uncorking the bottle of wine, he poured them each a drink. "No talking on an empty stomach."

"Alright." She supposed the information could wait. While he dished up the hot stew and set biscuits on her plate, she watched the ease with which he seemed to do everything.

"Wine? It's from a friend of mine's winery in Bordeaux."

"Really? You know someone who owns a winery." She always wanted to visit one in Italy. She supposed France would be just as good. The wines in Oregon were truly very good too.

"Actually, Logan owns two, one in Tuscany also." He poured the wine then sat down behind his desk as if he needed a blockade to protect him from her.

"Is that meant to be a barrier?" she asked, wondering how much truth there was in her question.

"Just trying to get comfortable," he mumbled with a bite of stew in his mouth. "Try the food." He motioned for her to eat.

"Very well." She smoothed her skirt and attempting to inhale a deep breath, she found the feat impossible. "Tell me when I can lay my heart on the table. You need to know the truth about me."

"What you have to say can't be that bad," he told her, waving his spoon in the air. "Now, you have me even more curious. Go ahead. Talk if you must." He sat back, resting his hands on his stomach and appearing more relaxed and at ease than she'd ever seen him.

While he was out of the room, she'd set the items she wanted to show him on the bench where she sat. "I know you're not going to believe me, but I hope that what I have to show you will help bridge the gap between what might be fantasy and reality."

"I've been to America. In fact, my travels have taken me all over the world. Nothing you can say will make me believe that women across the ocean dress as you do or talk and say the things you do. But that doesn't answer the most burning question. Where do you come from?"

"No, I wasn't going to say anything like that, although it's a true fact. But I'm not starting at the beginning and I'd like to do that. Despite my intentions, I've already muddled everything all up."

"By all means the beginning is always good. That way I'll understand. I do have an open mind where you're concerned, and I'd like to learn more about you." For a few seconds he drummed his finger on the desk. "You intrigue me."

Taylor held up her cell phone and pressing her finger on the button at the bottom, it lit up. She sat down across the table from Reid and handed it to him. "It's a cell phone. You use it to call people, but it doesn't work here because there are no cell towers and there is no electricity to keep it charged. Luckily, it's almost fully charged and if you are still curious, I can show you some apps." She held her breath, terrified of his possible reply.

He turned it over in his hands before pressing one of the icons on the phone. The picture quickly changed. "It's different. I've seen nothing like this before just as there are other things you have I've not seen before." Gingerly, he set it down on the table.

She moved to the bed and patted a place beside her. "Will you sit by me? And trust me?"

Seemingly reluctant, he rose, bringing the cell phone with him and sat next to her. "Show me something else this can do. I'm guessing an app are those little blocks I see on it."

Taylor held her hand out for the phone. He gave it to her as he sat down next to her. She wasn't sure where to start, something easy. She pushed the calculator icon and as the screen appeared, he watched. "I can calculate any numbers with this. What would you like to know?"

He rambled off a lengthy division problem. She punched in the numbers then the equals sign. His expression was blank as he shook his head, "I wouldn't know if it's right or not."

"It is. I guarantee it, but I'll put in numbers we both know." She added then subtracted, ending up with an easy division problem. All the answers were correct.

"Your device can calculate. I'm surprised and impressed. What else can it do?"

An epiphany hit her and she grinned. She held the phone out, "Wrap your arm around me." He did. "Now smile that handsome grin I've come to adore." He did and she snapped the picture.

Clicking on another icon, she showed him the photo. His gasp of surprise made her want to laugh, but she held the impulse in check. "Is that witchcraft? Some kind of sorcery."

That was something she'd not thought of. "No, it's technology. Just as there are all kinds of mechanical devices that are being invented in this time, there will be more to come." She remembered a picture of Sean with her before he left on his mission. Quickly flipping through her photos, she stopped on one then showed it to him.

"He could be my twin."

"I know. Sean's dressed in his navy uniform. It was a formal event we attended. He was very handsome."

"Are you trying to make me jealous? If you are, it's working. I've never had a feeling like that before."

A second thought and another memory had her flipping through the pictures again. "There. Sean's mother was into genealogy. Sean had a great, great, great something grandfather named Reid, Reid Stewart, just like you."

She showed him the photo she took one day from the notebook Sean's mother kept. "Could this be you?"

"And you," he said, tracing the line of her jaw. "We're older but that picture looks a lot like you."

"Yes, if it is you and me. It won't be too much longer before pictures can be taken in this time. I think it was the early eighteen hundreds, sometime before eighteen fifty."

"How do you know all this?" He looked amazed as well as

astonished.

"That's why we're having this talk." She pointedly reminded him. "I need to convince you that I used to live in the future."

He seemed to be thinking about what she showed him. She continued to flip through the pictures, stopping at a video of killer whales she'd taken on a whale cruise in Victoria.

"Look at this one."

"Whales and they're moving?" His voice held a touch of awe. "You promise me you're not a witch."

"No, just as confused as you are. I came here to Sardinia to buy a villa. They were offering them for one euro, but the homes had to be renovated and a timeline was attached to the price. Believe me the city was very nearly devoid of people when I arrived. It seems as time passed, there was nothing here for the children. So, they left to find work and other young people."

"What year was it?"

She hesitated, studying him, uncertain she should really tell him the entire truth. *When one door closes, another one opens.* She fought for courage. "Two thousand nineteen."

His expression turned blank. "You have anything else to show me?"

"Did you hear me?" She wasn't sure if he was ignoring her or just trying to make sense of what she said.

"I did." Frown lines creased his brows. "What's in that bag? I'm sure it's nothing I've ever seen before."

"Not a lot but..." She dumped her makeup bag on the bed, sorting through it for something to impress or convince, she wasn't too sure anymore.

"I'll see what you have here."

As he picked up things, she elaborated. "Lipstick tube, foundation, eyeliner." And the list went on.

"You don't need all this on your face to look beautiful, you understand." His words were slowly spoken. "I know women paint their faces in this time, but..."

A wave of pleasure at his words swept through her. He thought she was beautiful. While she didn't need or want constant reinforcement, a little bit never hurt. "Do you believe me?"

"Your story is a lot to take in, to absorb. Yes and no to whether I believe you or not."

"I haven't even mentioned my clothing which you've seen." She handed him the leggings she ran in. "They are made of a fabric called spandex. It stretches and makes life very comfortable. Then there are my panties and bra, which you've also seen. I wear them beneath my clothing."

"I need more wine," he rose, seemingly unable to say anything more. Returning with two full glasses, he sat down beside her, taking her hand in his before bringing it to his lips for a quick kiss.

Over the rim of the glass, she watched him. Moistening her lips, she tried to speak but could think of nothing more to say. Her pulse throbbed while she felt the steady rise of her blood pressure. Nervous energy consumed her as adrenalin pulsed nonstop. She downed the glass of wine and poured herself another. "I hope you have another bottle."

"More than you can drink." He laughed, leaning against the wall. "I could probably drink an entire bottle myself."

"I can't breathe. Will you help me out of this?" She closed her eyes as the room began to spin. "I think I'm going to faint."

He took her glass, quickly setting it on the table. She collapsed in his arms. "Reid..." She touched his face.

He set her on the bed face down and swiftly unfastened the dress then loosened the corset. She inhaled a breath of air then another. "Is that better?"

"Much. Can I take this off?" Air was flowing into her lungs now. "I don't think I'm cut out for wearing this stuff."

He helped her from the dress and the corset and she wore nearly nothing. "Are you getting used to seeing me like this?"

"Never."

She laughed, liking the way that sounded. She drew a black dress from her bag. After ridding herself of the chemise and with her back turned to him, she slipped the dress over her head. The deep V cut of the bodice had him staring but the slit up the side of her leg had him groaning.

"I'd rather wear this. Do you like it?" She turned so he could see her from every angle.

"You test my endurance. Tay, there's only so much a man can take. I want to make love to you."

"Because of the way I look or because of who I am?" she asked, knowing he wouldn't have an answer but also understanding there had to be something more between them than lust. She realized too that he'd seen most of her and she'd never seen him without clothing, not even sans his shirt.

"I don't know, both maybe. I can't think. This is a fine thing. You can't breathe and I can't think." Without a backward glance, he strode from the room, the door clanging shut behind him.

She had no idea he would leave when she tried to entice him to make love to her. She'd never been assertive like that before.

He fled.

Tears formed in her eyes and she tried to push them back, telling herself she was a fool. Even Sean had very easily agreed to celibacy. Perhaps there was something lacking in her and that's why she was still a virgin.

What was wrong with her? She tried to take a quick inventory of herself. There was nothing unique about her, but she always thought she had pleasant features. Her friends had always told her she was too thin and needed to gain weight, but her boobs were large. Were they too large?

Morose and insecure, she sat on the bed, sipping her wine. Maybe she was just too messy. He was constantly picking up after her. For that matter so had Sean. She sniffed then brushed away the last of the tears, vowing not to shed any more tears for any man.

Dangling the wine glass in one hand, she strode around the room. When she sat on the bench by the window, the sun was setting. It was going down in her century too. Her sailboat could be in twenty nineteen just as she should be. She could have been on it except Reid Stewart thought to rescue her. Had the cook gone back to the twenty-first century? Would he meet her friends?

Needing fresh air, she followed Reid's example. She didn't want to stay in the cabin either. She filled her glass with wine before fleeing the room, despite his earlier warning not to go on deck without him. The ocean, seagulls, and the setting sun called to her. She hoped he wouldn't be angry with her, because she was leaving this prison for a few seconds of dearly needed reprieve.

On deck she ended up in the same place Reid took her the night before. She sipped her wine, staring at the sun as it dipped closer and closer to the horizon. Right before her eyes it would disappear soon, vanish, just as her previous life evaporated. Brilliant colors spread across the line between the ocean and the sky.

This was not the path her life was supposed to take. She was going to be a famous graphic artist. Now, she couldn't even get a job and was totally dependent on a man. Not since she was a child had she depended on anyone but herself. She put herself through college, paid for graduate school and all her cars, all two of them.

She missed her Prius and never buying gas. She laughed softly. Well, she would never have to stop at a gas station here. They didn't exist. Leaning against the railing, she closed her eyes, trying to bring herself to her present predicament and accept her new life. She would have to come to terms with it and acknowledge a new beginning as well as a different way of thinking.

The first touch at the small of her back made her think of Reid, but something was wrong. The hand ran up her spine, but the sensation made the hair on the back of her neck stand on end. When she turned to smile at him, she saw her boss from her office in Portland, Oregon.

"No!" she cried out, tossing what remained of her wine in the man's face. "Stop."

"Bitch," the man ground out, pulling her close, his mouth descending to take hers.

She responded, biting his lip hard and when he released her, she ran for the cabin.

~ * ~

"What the bloody hell just happened?" Reid stood by his

passenger, Marcus Willoby. His fists clenched at his sides.

"She bit me." He touched his lip with a fingertip. "The little dollymop had the nerve to toss her wine in my face and bite me. I can taste the blood." He pulled a monogramed handkerchief from his pocket to wipe his face then dab at his lips.

"And why would she do something so dastardly?" Reid asked, turning his attention Willoby's way.

"Just wanted a kiss. A woman like that, dressed as she was. She was asking for a kiss and more." He stared at the cabin where she vanished. "She staying in the captain's cabin? Just want a bit of what you're getting." His face burned a deep crimson, anger simmering heatedly. He wasn't used to hearing anyone say no. The word from a woman didn't mean much. He took what he wanted.

"It's not like that," Reid spoke softly.

"What's it like then?" Willoby sneered, mopping wine from his waistcoat. "She'll need to pay for my coat."

"There was nowhere for her to stay. I don't have to explain anything to you. Don't come near her again."

"Or what? She's available and..."

Hands fisted, Reid turned his back on the man then seeming to calm himself he glanced at the smirking male animal. "She's not available to the likes of you."

"I'm a paying customer."

"You booked passage, and this ship is not a floating whorehouse."

"Perhaps you should take a closer look at your behavior. If you keep an unmarried woman in your cabin, then she's available for anyone who wants to claim her."

"She's under my protection."

"We'll see about that. I mean to have her before the end of this trip," Willoby said, sure of himself.

"If you try, you'll find yourself at the bottom of the ocean."

"Murder on the high seas." He laughed, enjoying the conversation. It was one he knew he'd win... "What excuse will you give my family when I don't return to London."

"Accidents happen; a huge wave, a gust of wind, you decided you wanted a view from the crow's nest and fell to your death. In any case, ship burials are always at sea."

Chapter Three

"Tay?" Reid placed a gentle hand on her shoulder. She was sobbing and he didn't know what to do or how to handle the situation. "That bastard's not going to hurt you. I won't let him. If I could turn around and leave him in Sardinia, I would."

When she sat up, he pulled her into his arms. "He looks just like my boss, the one who..."

"The one who sent you running to Sardinia? While I'll forever be in that man's debt, he had no right to expect something you didn't want to give. Was he going to get rid of you if you didn't succumb to his advances?" Her mistreatment by men sent an inferno of rage pounding through him.

"He didn't fire me if that's what you mean. I didn't want to give him the chance or the satisfaction, and I didn't want to see his pudgy face and slobbering mouth again." She sniffed. "I wasn't going to go back there. I quit."

Her tears soaked his shirt. "Don't cry." He still didn't know what to say. He drew farther back, wiping away the moisture with his fingertips then kissing the tears away. "I'm glad you're here with me and not in the future somewhere. Whatever went wrong in your time to send you here, I think it was fate. Perhaps your, our, destiny." He'd never before believed in fate or traveling through time. But she was living proof at least one existed if not both.

His lips gently found Tay's, taking in the essence of her, feeling as if he absorbed her soul, melding with it. She was his and soon she would understand he would never let her go. If she wanted to return to her time... He didn't believe that was possible, but he'd fight for her and try to convince her to understand he would make sure she would be happy.

He made a mental adjustment to the thought. The decision had taken him time, but he believed her story. Who could make up such a tall tale and who would have such incredible things in their bags?

"Reid?"

"What is it?" His lips explored her. He tasted the sweet exposed flesh of her neck and cleavage, slowly inching toward the tender curve of her breast.

"I want to see you without your shirt. I've never seen you." She was tugging his shirt from his pants, her hands exploring his skin, resting on his nipples. "I need to see all of you."

He shuddered, feeling the sensual pull of her fingers against him as they made their way from his waistband up his chest. It was erotic and provocative. He needed the will power to keep himself from taking her right now and here. No other woman had ever had this draw, this attraction to him.

Quickly, he lifted his arms and let her remove his shirt. She wore so little, her skimpy black dress, the neckline open to his exploration. Slowly his hands cupped her breasts. Her silken flesh tantalized every part of him.

Bloody hell. He closed his eyes, absorbing the crux of everything she gave, and trying to understand all she had experienced in her life in what seemed to him to be another world. He would never understand. All he could do was empathize.

"Are you sure you want this...me?" Making this right for her was crucial. He wanted her to accept him in every way. And he wanted to give her everything she needed now and in the future; physical, mental and emotional.

In answer, she turned her back to him, "Slide the zipper down."

He did, amazed at the fastener and the way it worked.

When the zipper was below her waist, she shrugged, sending the gown off her shoulders then seemed to shimmy out of it. She wore nothing now save a tiny scrap of material she called panties. He could see her through the thin fabric. He swallowed hard, inhaling a deep breath as if that simple movement would give him the control he sought.

He came down on top of her, closing her eyes with his kisses, no longer tasting the saltiness of her tears. She returned his passion, touching, exploring all that he bared to her.

"Reid," she spoke his name lovingly.

"Tay?"

"I'm a virgin, just thought you should know." Her fingertips raked over his shoulders then up his neck.

"Your instincts are impeccable. You seem to know exactly what to do and where to touch me." He tried to explore her with his lips teeth and tongue everywhere.

"It's the movies and the books. I've watched a lot of them." Again, she ran her hands down then up his back, then into his hair.

"Movies?" He'd ask about them later.

"Remember the whales." She sighed when his lips found a sensitive spot. "Something like that. You know that people or animals move. Movies." A tiny sound sprung from the back of her throat when he found a very enticing place.

"Explanation needed later. Not now."

He felt her nails dig into his skin as she arched against him. He was going to tell her he wasn't a virgin but decided against it when her nimble fingers rested on the fastening of his pants. She probably already knew that fact or would assume.

Hooking a thumb around the top of her panties, he pulled them off. "God, Reid, what are you doing to me?"

"Making love to you. What did you think?" He chuckled as his lips closed over a nipple then sucked the hard bud into his mouth, his other hand dancing attendance on her other breast.

Her hips moved beneath him and he delighted in the sensations he was able to create within her. He needed to feel her cream, touch more intimate places, bring her pleasure. Her hands closed around him.

"I want to make love to you."

"And you will but if we go too fast, I won't give you the pleasure you deserve." Gently, he removed her hand. "Anywhere else, touch me wherever you want except there."

"You don't like..."

"Too much." He gasped, enjoying the sweet pleasure as well as the inferno rising within. "Way too much. So very much." He found her lips again, drawing her tongue into his mouth before changing tactics and exploring her teeth and tongue then seeming to duel with her.

"Never too much." She sighed, running her nails down the length of his back to his butt then squeezed.

Wild slivers of heated pleasure wracked his body. "Tay, what you do to me." He rested his hand on her stomach, feeling her body respond to him then moved his hand lower, searching intimately, massaging, testing.

"I can't breathe," she whispered softly. "And I feel so...so...hot. Is that the way I'm supposed to feel?"

Thrilled by the tiny sounds of desire she made, he continued. "Good sweetheart, that's exactly how you're supposed to feel." She was ready for him, slick with moisture, her hips rising to meet him. He wanted to become one with her, part of her.

"Do something," she moaned. "I..."

"This might hurt," he warned before he joined with her. He pushed against the thin shield proclaiming her innocence then broke through.

She cried out, unmoving. Stopping, he brushed hair from her face, feeling the slight sheen of moisture on her forehead.

A few moments later, her hips began to move again, her walls clenching him tightly. He groaned, trying to hold back until he could feel her climax building.

Suddenly, her hips bucked against him, as he felt the spasms of her release rip through her and into him. "Reid, please." She drew him inside and he let his seed spill as his climax swept through him.

For several seconds he lay on top of her trying to keep his weight on his arms then he rolled to the side, pulling her with him. Her body glowed with a fine sheen of moisture. Her lips were swollen from his kisses, and she had this sleepy-eyed look that sent a feeling of wonder through him.

"I feel spineless," she whispered. "I don't think I can move."

He chuckled, enjoying the first time with her and praying there would be many more. "Spineless you say?"

She punched his arm. "Don't make fun of me."

"Never." He traced her collarbone with a fingertip. "I'm just feeling really proud of myself."

"Proud, why?"

"You climaxed in my arms. I felt the magic as well as the primal dance between us. You're very special."

"And that makes you feel proud? Maybe egotistical? I think I understand. I've friends who complain that they have to fake a climax so they don't hurt their boyfriend's feelings."

"You didn't fake, did you?" He was sure she had not because he felt it building and building.

"No." Her hands rested against his chest. "I can feel your heart beating. Is it always this good?"

"As we get to know each other's wishes, what we like and don't like, it will get better." His thoughts suddenly went to a possibility of pregnancy. He'd taken no precautions, never even thought about it. He always used a condom for his protection as well as the lady's.

"How can it ever be better?" She let her nails rake lightly down his chest to very low on his abdomen.

He groaned, stopping her hand from what he was sure was her objective. "Not yet. We need to talk."

She rose on one elbow, the tip of one breast resting against his chest, enticing him. "About what?" With her nail she traced his tiny nipple.

"Pregnancy. You could even now be pregnant." He had no idea how she would react.

She pulled on a corner of her mouth with her teeth before she smiled, her eyes shimmering with humor. "I won't get pregnant."

"What do you know that I don't? I was buried deep inside you. I touched your womb and my seed spilled into you."

"One minute." She rose, walking to one of her bags, which she rummaged in until she pulled out a small package.

She seemed completely at ease with her nakedness. That

surprised him for some reason, but he was heartily glad. He needed someone who would match his passion and desire.

"In here..." She drew out another one of her objects then opened the container. "...are birth control pills."

"Bloody hell," he murmured. "Those little white..." He looked at her. "...pills, will keep you from having a baby?"

"They will and when I left, I didn't know what kind of health services I'd find in Sardinia so my gynecologist agreed to give me a year's supply. I even stocked up on these." She pulled out another box. "Condoms."

"I see..." He did see. He didn't use one today because he forgot and perhaps because he wanted to feel her essence, reach to her soul. "Condoms exist in this time too."

"I've heard Casanova was supposed to have used them because of all of his affairs." She laughed.

He chose to ignore her comment. Yet the sound went straight to his heart. "I had thought that once we returned to the ship, you might like a massage but I got distracted. You confused me."

"I'd love one." She sat down on the bed, still exposed, her large breasts with beautiful rose-colored tips a heavenly image to him.

He wasn't entirely sure what to say now. "I'll get the liniment." Sounded lame to his ears. "Lie on your stomach."

When he rose, he stopped to pick up his pants.

"No, you don't. If I'm to be fully naked, you can't be wearing clothing." She had turned on her side and was watching him.

He folded the garment before placing it on the table. "You do know you're playing with fire. I'm finding I've barely any control when it comes to you."

She rested her head on her hands as he began to rub the liniment into her muscles. "And you are too, you know, playing with fire," she murmured.

He began work on her shoulders and arms, spending time there because he knew once his hands moved lower, he might not be responsible for what would happen next. Just looking at her naked back accelerated his passion to a burning inferno. He closed his eyes in part to distract himself, but the images on the back of his eyelids were of her breasts, the tiny waist he could almost span with his hands combined with the gentle curve of her hips then...

"Tell me if I do something you don't like, touch you anywhere that bothers you," he told her, making his way lower, giving attention to the small of her back then moving higher again. He stroked her sides, feeling her ribcage and enjoying every breath she inhaled.

"I like everything." She sighed softly. "I never knew a man's touch could generate the sensations or the heat and desire yours create."

He tried to remain detached from her heated words as well as her body, strained to keep his mind on the massage, not on the tender flesh of her tiny derrière and lower to the more intimate places he should ignore for now. Later, he wanted to taste her.

Turning his attention to each leg, he worked his way from the apex of her thighs to her slim feet, massaging the arch then back up to follow the same path down her other leg.

He relished the soft moan of pleasure he heard rising from her lungs. "Now turn over and I can do your front."

"Why, I'm even more of a pool of jelly than I was after we made love. Don't think I can move ever again."

"Because I don't want to forget your front." He knew with the spoken words he had ulterior motives and there was no guilt involved as long as she was pleased.

"My breasts?" she asked as she slowly turned over.

"Don't know if I can stay detached." His fingers danced across her shoulders and down her arms while his gaze remained fixed on the rosy tipped mounds that even now beckoned for his attention. He licked his lips in anticipation.

"I know I can't." She placed her hands on his chest, touching, exploring in such an evocative way. He groaned. Moving lower, she touched his heavy sex, drawing a path along his hard member.

"If you keep that up, I won't be able to finish the massage."

"I'm not sure I care," she purred. "Besides, you can always finish after the fact."

"After the fact," he mused as his fingers explored her belly then lower to find the nubbin between her soft moist folds.

"I could give you a massage. Would you like that?" she asked, her voice very nearly a purr.

"No one's ever done that." He brought her legs over his thighs, gazing at her intimately. "A massage..."

"What are you doing?"

"Looking at you." The huskiness of his voice surprised him. "You're beautiful. You know that, don't you? Every part of you." He hadn't really looked at her before. Now he was soaking in all of her. Staring at her very white belly and what must be a tan line below her navel, he focused on the soft fleece of dark blond hair covering her mound.

Her beautiful deep blue eyes shimmered with the light cast from the candles. It seemed her breathing nearly stopped.

Not a sound, not even a whisper of a sound.

Then, "I want to believe you."

He slanted her a fierce look. "You better," he growled, stroking her. His fingers lightly touched her then eased away. He was seeing her more clearly now, her full breasts, and very long, sleekly muscled legs, beckoned to him. He felt himself shudder. He needed to touch her again, taste every inch of her. He never wanted to let her go.

"Do you want me, Tay?"

"You know I do."

They made love again, the climax more intense than the first time. Now they lay together, their arms and legs entwined. "What's happening to me, to us?" He pushed hair from her face, enjoying this experience with the lady from another time. "Are we meant to be together?"

"Perhaps it's too soon to know. What I do know is what I've seen and that's the photo of the two of us together."

"We were older..." He wanted to think about that for a while, having never thought of marriage or fancied himself falling in love until this moment.

"Much older," she told him.

"How old are you now?" Age didn't make a difference to him but he was curious.

"Twenty-three. Why?"

"Just curious. I'm twenty-eight."

"Curious and curiouser, Sean was twenty-eight also." She straddled him.

"Tay..."

"Do you want me to ride you?"

~ * ~

Tay yawned and stretched before brushing a quick kiss on Reid's forehead. "Wake up, sleepy head. The sun is shining and it looks to be a beautiful day."

"Is that all I get after last night? A kiss on the forehead? Come here." He opened his arms for her.

She ignored his command, realizing she needed time. "After a night of lovemaking I wouldn't expect you'd want me again so soon. Is there anywhere to take a bath?"

"Looking at you makes me crave you." He uncovered himself and it was blatantly obvious just how much.

"A bath," she reminded him with a flirtatious smile and a wink. "Before I'm back in that bed with you doing enchanting things to each other. I'm sure you've captain things to do." For some reason she wanted to be alone, needed to think about what had been happening to her as well as her feelings for him. When she looked out the window, she realized they were well at sea, in the Mediterranean somewhere between Sardinia and the Strait of Gibraltar.

"What are you going to do while I'm doing..." He paused, sitting against the backboard, his hands behind his head, a grin spread across his too handsome face. "...captain things."

"Think," she said, not really comprehending her hesitancy in this relationship. Deep down she understood she would never return to the twenty-first century and she was trying to accept the fact. Another miracle would not happen. In any case, even if she was given the opportunity or a choice, she wasn't sure she wanted to leave.

"Me too. Perhaps a little wind and sunshine in my face will help clarify what has happened here between the two of us," Reid said, seeming to appear thoughtful.

A wave of insecurity swept through her. For her to question their relationship seemed logical, but she didn't like the idea he would do the same. She had to laugh at herself as well as her self doubts.

"You're not sure about us, either. Don't know if I'm your person?" The emphasis on *your*, she laughed at the expression on his face and she found she delighted in giving him insights into the century she came from. "Don't want you to ghost me. Of course, that would be difficult since we're on this ship together."

He rubbed the appealing stubble on his jaw, "Am I your person? Ghost you?" he asked as if guessing the meaning. "Don't answer, put something on and I'll order up some hot water for your bath."

"Alright." She rummaged through her bags and finding a pair of shorts and a top, she slipped them on before turning to him. "What I think is that I tumbled into something that I'm having a difficult time accepting and I've no clue how to proceed. What I know is that I don't want you to be a one-night stand."

"Ah, I want you for more than one night too. After that I can't say. Once we reach London, it could mean you leave me. Is that what you're planning?"

"Leave you? I don't know anyone in London or anywhere. I've no money, nowhere to live. I'm completely at your mercy."

He strode to her, pulling her into his arms. "I love the sound of that, at my mercy." Then he paused as if seeing her look of distress. "Maybe not. We do need to figure this out. From all that you've told me, I doubt if you ever want to be at any man's mercy."

"Thank you for that." Wrapping her hands in his hair, she pulled his head down then molded her lips to his. He opened for her, letting her be the aggressor. She tasted his spirit, the heat emanating from him into her then explored the inside and dueled with him. He was right. She didn't want to be at any man's mercy, not even his.

Drawing away, "I need a bath," she reminded him and some alone time.

"You started this." He acted petulant.

"And I'm ending this." She watched as he strode to the door, calling out for his first mate.

Within a few minutes hot water was brought into the cabin and a tub was pulled out. "I'll dress and give you some time. Are you hungry? For food?"

"Incorrigible, that's what you are." She crossed her arms over her chest. "Famished for food. Yes."

"Me too." He pulled on his clothes before letting the men in with the water. When they left, "I'll leave you now. But I'm coming back in about thirty minutes with hot breakfast and coffee. Make sure you're out of the bath and dressed because I can't make any promises where you're concerned."

"You have coffee?" She tossed him a grin. "I think I love you."

"Sounds like you love my coffee."

"I do but I'll have to try it first."

Tay settled into the water, closing her eyes and letting the heat encase her. She rested her head on the rim, recalling the day that dramatically changed her life. That day now seemed like a lifetime ago.

There was a storm, the howling of the wind and waves washing over her boat. She lost control of the vessel, the ropes sliding through her hands and the boom hitting her on the head. She'd been knocked unconscious.

Reid looks like Sean and the pudgy passenger was a twin to her ex-boss. Was she somewhere in an alternate universe?

The water started to grow tepid, and she knew Reid would be back in his cabin before she finished her bath if she didn't get going. If he did return before she was out and dressed, they would probably find themselves in the bed again or making love in the tub.

What was the potent and a bit primal attraction to each other? Now she wondered if what she thought she had with Sean had been real. It was nothing even close to what she felt for Reid. When he left for Iraq, she thought she was in love with him. Now she had no idea what love was or how it felt. This thing with Reid could just be lust, and she wondered too if lust could last a lifetime.

She washed her hair using the extra bucket for rinse then she finished soaping her body. Rising from the tub, she wrapped a huge bath sheet around herself.

A knock made her look at the door then Reid entered with a platter of food. "We have enough to feed us all day. Do you want to stay in the room and play?" He wriggled his eyebrows at her.

"No, I need to get a little bit of perspective on and about us. If I could go on deck later...after breakfast?"

"After what happened last night? No. Absolutely no."

"I won't let you keep me a prisoner in this room for the entirety of the trip. And being afraid of a man goes against everything I believe." Defensive she'd placed her hands on her hips trying to press home her feelings.

Frown lines marred his brow. "Perhaps you should learn some prudence where men are concerned."

"You have a pistol. I could take that with me."

"And you'd probably shoot yourself."

"I know how to use a gun. They're a bit more complicated in the twenty-first century. I had a friend who taught me." She didn't want to use Sean's name. When she did, it felt a little hollow and she didn't like the way Reid looked at her when she did say his name.

"You only get one chance," he warned. "If you miss..." He let the rest of the sentence hang, and she understood exactly what the point was he was trying to drive home.

"In my time and no matter how many rounds, when dealing with a man close up you usually only get one chance, unless it's a semi-automatic then you might get a few shots off." She understood if the first bullet missed, he'd overpower her. It was the simple truth. Despite that man's expanded girth, he was stronger.

"I don't know." He rubbed his neck. "It goes against everything I've been taught, all that I know. The man is supposed to protect."

A moment of pity for him swept through her. "I could take the sword. It would give me some distance, and it would be easier to wound him than kill him before you came along to save the day." She wanted to laugh at the expression on his face.

"It's a rapier."

"Very sharp. I'm a proficient small swordsman."

"Your friend taught you," he grit out, clearly angry or jealous.

She wasn't at all sure what the emotions she saw were, but she didn't like the tone, "No, I started lessons when I was five. My father was an expert swordsman and he wanted me to learn. I've won many championships."

"You never cease to amaze me. Truly I don't know who you are. Every time I think I'm figuring you out, you toss me something new to run over in my mind."

"So, can I take your pistol and go outside when we finish breakfast?" She tried for a sugary sweet smile, sure he would succumb to her request.

"Yes." He hesitated, scrubbing his face with his hands. "If you stay close by me. I need to be able to see you."

She sighed heavily then tossed him a huge grin. "If you insist. I can make concessions too. Thank you."

"Let's eat."

The conversation seemed to stall while they ate. Cook had outdone himself this morning. Pancakes with syrup and butter, and where the man found the berries, she didn't know. Oranges had been sliced and they were sweeter than any she'd ever tasted. She was sure there was an entire slab of bacon on the platter.

She had to admit that where she was concerned, he had to trust in a lot of things. What she understood about the nineteenth century could fit in the palms of her hands, but what she was telling him about the twenty-first century were unbelievable from someone who didn't live in the time.

Setting her napkin on the table and finishing the cup of coffee, she picked up his pistol and started for the door. "Is it loaded?" She wasn't at all sure she would be able to figure this out, but if it had a ball and she assumed gunpowder in it all she would need to do would be pull the trigger. Hopefully, all she was required to do would be point it at him if he crept too close. She didn't want to shoot anyone.

"You said you know how to use it?" He took it from her and checked. "Yes."

"I do know how to aim and fire. I just don't know how to load the dang thing. I'm a good shot too." She watched as his eyebrows drew together in question.

"I'm accepting a lot at face value." He handed it back to her.

"There are things you can teach me," she told him, tossing him a flirtatious wink. "More than just things in bed, although I like those too."

"I feel as if I've lost this verbal sparring contest. You have a way with words I don't understand. Come." He held out his arm. "I'll walk the deck with you then I'll leave you alone." He stopped, staring at her. "To think."

"Thank you." She clung to his arm, her head resting against him. She didn't realize he was so tall, taller than Sean if she remembered correctly. Or had she ever walked so intimately with Sean? Sometimes Sean held her hand, but more often they were independent of each other.

The best of everything was she felt comfortable and at ease even though she'd known this man for how long? Two days?

Heat rushed to her face as she realized what she'd done with him last night. The way she let him touch her, explore her intimately. She understood a one-night stand was something many of her friends enjoyed. Then they never saw the man again.

Now she knew why but she didn't want this to be just that, a one-night stand. She wanted it to go on...forever?

"Here, this spot will give you a pleasant view."

They stopped at the railing near the rear of the vessel. "Will you be close? Captain things, you know?"

"I'm going to...yes, do captain things." He laughed, humor sparkling in his steel grey eyes.

She watched his back as he walked away, loved the way his broad shoulders gradually narrowed to slim hips. His hair was longer than hers. At the moment it was tied back with a thin leather strap.

Her fingers closed around the butt of the pistol as she remembered the pudgy man who waylaid her last night. Reid silently gave her permission to shoot the man if he accosted her again. Well, she wouldn't kill him, but she'd make him regret assuming he could take whatever he wanted from her.

"So, stop thinking about the worst case scenario. This was supposed to be your time to figure out what you want," she murmured, turning to watch the waves lap against the side of the ship.

Sunlight sent a shimmer of light across the water, changing the ripples to a gorgeous silver blue, reminding her of the Pacific Ocean. Sea gulls followed the ship, and she hoped she'd see dolphins playing in the water or perhaps a whale.

She turned her back against the railing, watching Reid as he did captain things and smiled. Closing her eyes, she could see him naked, more handsome than the statue of David.

Her cheeks hot, she touched them with her hands, trying to cool them off.

He was beside her, caressing her heated flesh with a calloused fingertip. "What are you thinking that has turned your cheeks scarlet? Want me to guess?" He brushed a quick kiss on the back of her neck.

She turned away for a moment then decided to confront him with the truth, "I was thinking about the way you looked naked."

"Really?"

"Absolutely." She turned away though; bluffing was one thing but admitting you didn't know how you felt about a man you just made love with was not something she had experience with.

"Did you like what you remembered?" he asked, placing a finger by her chin and turning her to look at him.

Her lashes lowered for a moment. "More beautiful than any statue by Michelangelo."

"I'm so flattered." He kissed her gently, tracing her lips with his tongue.

She wanted to call him out, yet she needed to submit to his lovemaking. She opened for him, letting him inside, knowing everyone on deck watched them and judged her.

They wouldn't judge Reid. He was a man. Good lord, she'd been tossed into a time that was more repressive to women than the one she lived in before. Perhaps she could be a voice in this time of oppression. She didn't have any wild thoughts that she would change anything. Indeed, she knew from the history she'd read women were already beginning to assert themselves.

If she stayed, of course she would stay in this time, she could be another voice. Now she had a small measure of purpose. Even if this thing between herself and Reid didn't work out, she could find some degree of happiness in the cause for women's rights. And if it did work out, he would have to come to understand how real and deep her feelings were about everything including how their relationship would proceed.

"Where are you?" he asked, drawing away from her, staring into her eyes. "You're certainly not here."

"No, I was living in the future and trying to bring some of it to the present."

"I didn't understand a word you just said."

"That's why I need to think. I've been caught up in a relationship with you that I don't understand and have never experienced. I don't know what is going to happen to me or if I have a purpose here."

"You don't need a purpose. I'll take care of you no matter what happens."

"I'm no man's mistress."

"Then I'll marry you."

"I don't know if I want to wed you, Reid Stewart. Don't know if I love you."

~ * ~

Sounds of helicopters whirling as well as the sound of men giving orders then the rat-a-tat-tat of gunfire filled the tiny cubicle where Sean Stewart was being held prisoner. He strode to the tiny window in the door that had been his only view other than the room he'd been living in and saw Navy Seals infiltrate the building that had been his home for months.

"No man left behind," he murmured or it was dumb luck that had these men in this place at this time.

"Over here," he'd called out.

They rescued him, taking him to Germany then home to the US. He'd gone to Taylor's house and discovered she'd moved. After another week of hunting for her, the news of her move to Sardinia came to his attention.

Now he was on the Italian Island, staring at the home she wanted to renovate and live in. Her friends spoke with him, bringing him more bad news.

"She's gone." Olivia said with a shrug and what sounded like a sigh. "I filed a missing person's report but there has been nothing."

"Disappeared the first day she was here," the other gal said.

"How?"

"She rented a sailboat for some relaxation time."

"Instead of Tay returning, this woman, Destiny Rose strode up the hill with a strange story about time travel. Destiny insists Taylor was sent back in time to 1823 and she accidentally was transported back here."

"Do you believe her? The woman's not a nutcase, is she?" Sean asked, pacing the floor of the rundown home, his fear for his fiancée growing exponentially.

"Some think Destiny Rose killed her so she could take her place," Olivia said, "but I don't believe it for one second. I'm more than suspicious of people, but Destiny couldn't kill a fly."

"But you don't think so." Sean repeated, staring into the vividly blue sky.

"There's been no body found, nada."

"Destiny doesn't know about so many modern things. Her ignorance can't just be chalked up to living stranded on this island for her entire life. Besides, her weaving is magnificent, shades of an earlier era."

"Yeah, there are cell towers here and just like at home, all the young folks who are still here have their noses glued to their phones."

Sean mulled the conversation over in his head for several days while he continued the search for Taylor. He always met dead ends.

"I'm not giving up," he muttered to himself while he tore apart old countertops in the once well-used kitchen.

Chapter Four

On the bridge of Reid's ship, Tay stood next to him, awed by the sight. London was in front of them and he would face decisions concerning her very soon.

Drake Montgomerie strode up the gangplank with the same air of confidence Reid had come to know over the years.

"Who is that?" Tay whispered, looking straight ahead, her hand hooked around his arm.

"A friend." He couldn't confide in her. The less she knew about this man and the work he did for Montgomerie and the Crown the better. His was a dangerous life even though both men denied the peril, at least where they were concerned.

"Liar," she said, the one word softly spoken yet with an impact he couldn't refute. She saw into him in ways no other person could.

"Not so, he is a friend." And so much more he couldn't say.

"He's your boss? What you do for him that you'd have to kill me if you told me?" She gripped his arm tighter.

"You remember too much." He paused, "And yes, that was true, but I wouldn't do either."

"Tell me or kill me?"

"Right." He extended a hand and the two men shook. "Montgomerie."

"You have what I need?" Drake asked with no more niceties to be exchanged.

"Everything." Reid pulled a packet from his pocket, handing it to Drake.

Without looking inside, Drake stuffed it in his breast pocket then turned his attention to Taylor. "Who's this beautiful lady?"

"Taylor Maxwell, I met her in Sardinia and gave her passage to London." Reid knew he wouldn't pull one over on this man who seemed to know everything before it happened.

A smile crossed Drake's features and rocking back on his heels, he said, "More than a just a passage, I assume."

Reid saw the slow rise of color to Tay's face, immediately understanding her embarrassment. "More than just a fare, yes. She is that and also very important to me."

"She your mistress?" Drake pursued information that wasn't his business.

"I don't see where that's your concern." Reid stiffened, displeased with his boss as well as the curiosity directed at Taylor.

"My employees are my concern as well as those they associate with. We need to talk soon. She can't live with you if that's what you're planning. You and I both know what it could mean."

Beside him he felt her stiffen and was pleased she waited to talk to him about Montgomerie's words. "She has nowhere to live and no money. So, what do you propose?" Reid certainly didn't like the way this conversation was going. Neither did Tay by the way she was gripping his arm.

Then, it seemed Taylor could not remain silent. "I'll stay where and with whom I please. No man is going to tell me what to do, particularly one I don't even know."

Reid felt his heart stop and when he glanced her way, he knew Montgomerie was in for an argument.

"You sound a bit like my wife." Montgomerie roared with an easy laughter. "But what you say doesn't matter. You can't live in the same house with the Earl of Castlerose unless you're married."

"An earl? I should have read the genealogy charts a bit more closely," she muttered.

Inside, Reid grimaced, hoping to hide the reaction. "What would you suggest? Taylor has no family here and no matter where I put her up, it will be considered a violation by the ton. They will call her my mistress."

"The two of you are talking as if I'm not here. I see no reason to care what this so-called ton says about me. I simply don't care. Where I live is up to me."

"But the earl should care. He does have a family reputation to uphold which it seems you do not." Montgomerie spoke directly to her this time and not around her.

She tried to smile through the anger seeming to be building within. "No, you're right. I'm a peasant. Of course I don't care what they think nor do I care a fig about his or my reputation."

"You don't talk like a commoner," Drake mused thoughtfully. "You don't even sound like an Englishman. Your accent is clearly American."

"You're right and we both know what the English think of Americans," she shot back.

"Feisty piece of baggage." Drake laughed again, seeming to enjoy the sparring contest. "I can see there is nothing common about you."

"If we want to solve this dilemma, I suggest you stop goading my friend. She has an argument for everything."

"I'm beginning to see the drift of your meaning."

"As well as a way with words that can leave you wondering what the bloody hell she is talking about." Reid was enjoying this. He rarely saw Drake at a loss for the right words that would end the debate.

Drake bowed low, seemingly conceding. "What would you want then? If I can come up with a place for you to stay and also see Reid without tarnishing his reputation, would you consider my suggestion?"

"I couldn't say." Her lips thinned.

Drake turned to Reid. "Would you be willing to court her properly? That is if you truly don't want her as a mistress." Drake still pursued that venue, seeming to realize they were lovers.

"I'm no man's mistress," Taylor said with force. "And never will be," she finished. "I'll find my own way if you two keep arguing about me as if I'm not here or I'm a lesser person since I'm female."

"Well, you found a handful of woman; maybe two handfuls. Think you can survive the relationship?" Drake asked, grinning from ear to ear.

"She keeps me guessing about what's in store for me around the corner. Now what do you have in mind?" Reid needed to figure out what he wanted from Tay as soon as possible, and he was sure he had a lot of explaining to do about his title.

"I do have a cabin in Scotland you could use if you haven't figured out what you really want," Drake said.

Reid remembered the stories about Montgomerie and his bride. They were squashed when his wife didn't get pregnant before the nine-month waiting period after their wedding.

"That wouldn't help. We need time to figure out what is right for us," Reid said taking Tay's hand and squeezing, trusting the gesture would tell her he cared about her and hoped she was willing to work with him about this.

"The carriage is waiting. I've an idea." Then he looked at Taylor. "My wife's aunt has taken all of her sisters and cousins into her house and under her wing, so to speak, to help them find suitors. I'm sure she'll be more than willing to be your chaperone and confidante." Drake paused briefly. "If you're willing, of course."

"The Duchess." Reid couldn't stifle the gasp rumbling up from inside his lungs at the news. He certainly didn't like the idea of Tay looking for a suitor when she had a perfectly good one standing next to her, one who knew her intimately. No one else was going to have that privilege, not as long as he lived.

"Yes, a formidable lady but good-hearted," Drake said.

"Who is this duchess? I don't think I like this idea." Tay tried to give her opinion. "I don't want or need a chaperone."

"I'll introduce you to her then you can decide," Montgomerie said chuckling. "I believe the two of you will be a good match for each other."

As Reid helped Tay into the carriage, he realized he didn't like any of this, especially since Tay's future had just been yanked from his hands. The only way out of this was to propose marriage and even though that seemed inevitable, he wasn't ready to spew the words.

"You promise I can decide. What if I say no? What then?" Tay asked.

"The Duchess is the most formidable lady in the city, although I do believe that over the years she has softened. You really have no choice," Drake said. "Here is the carriage. Let's continue this little chat on our way to meet The Duchess."

"And why is that?" It seemed she had stiffened and was averse to most anything. "There is always a choice."

"I didn't want to bring this up but it's really quite simple. If you don't choose The Duchess then you choose to whore," Drake spoke harshly.

"Never. I can work."

"At what?" Drake shot back, seemingly tired of the conversation at hand and needing to end it.

Reid had been left out of this discussion. He prayed she'd pick The Duchess, because he didn't have one doubt Montgomerie would make sure he never saw Tay again if she chose the other living space Drake offered.

"Don't let your pride get the better of your decision. If you don't choose The Duchess, you'll never see me again. Whether you'll end up in a brothel is up to debate, but I would never put anything Montgomerie threatens aside as not fact." Reid tried to caution her.

"He has that much power?"

He watched her swallow then moisten her lips, wishing he could see inside her mind. "He does."

"Glad to hear the two of you are agreeing to the best possible solution to your problem. And Reid, if you don't decide to do the right thing with your paramour, I'm sure someone else will steal her heart. The Duchess seems to have a way of pointing everyone in the right direction."

"Bloody hell, Montgomerie, do you hear yourself? If I remember correctly, you defied all the rules of the ton when you courted your wife."

"Ella." He smiled, seeming to recall those days when he courted her not so long ago. Then, "I'm sure you'll find a way to solve any problems that might arise from your forced abstinence. There is always another country if that's your proclivity." Drake feigned boredom, gazing at his nails before stifling a yawn.

"Men always do," Tay said softly but both men heard.

Montgomerie let out a low belly laugh. "And you are so right.

How did you become so smart about men at such a young age?"

"Movies." She suddenly put her hand in front of her mouth.

"Movies?"

"Nothing, just a word that has no meaning." She quickly pointed out.

"A code word," Reid said.

"Ah, here we are. Hope Charlotte's at home." Drake jumped from the carriage then strolled up the front steps. The door opened with the first knock. "Scarlett." He pulled the older woman into his arms for a quick hug and a kiss on the cheek. "Is Charlotte at home? I've a new charge for her."

"Oh, well...who? Well, David is here too. Yes." Scarlett turned, letting them into the home.

"Charlotte, the Duke is here," Scarlett called out. "Should I get some refreshments?"

"What duke? We seemed to have a couple of them in the family now." A slender older woman entered the foyer, a smile of greeting on her face, a tall man behind her.

Over the years Reid had heard a lot about The Duchess, and he knew she'd recently wed a Scottish Laird, David McLellan, if his memory served right.

"Drake, how are you? Is everything fine with Ella?" She hugged Montgomerie who seemed to take on a slightly more subservient air in front of this woman.

"Ella is just fine. She is enjoying the new baby. You can come see them anytime. We are at the townhouse for a few weeks more."

"Who are these people? Oh, I recognize you, the Earl of Castlerose...what brings you here to my home?" she asked. "Do we have business together?"

"Duchess, I'm honored." Reid kissed the back of her hand.

"Pshaw." She waved her other hand. "What is it you need?" But it seemed she couldn't keep her gaze from Tay.

"I need your help. Reid had the privilege of bringing this young woman from Sardinia. She's an American but she has no family there or here. She needs someone to present her to the eligible suitors in London."

Montgomerie seemed to enjoy the exchange.

"No," Reid said. "Tay is not going to be presented to anyone. She is no debutant."

Taylor spoke up before anyone could reply to Reid's abrupt and emphatic no. "I'm too old for a season and I really don't want to be paraded in front of eligible bachelors. As Reid just said, I'm not a beginner in anything."

"It seems I keep hearing that story," The Duchess cackled. "I think you've already found your eligible bachelor, but I can teach you a few things and you are certainly welcome to stay in my home while your suitor labors over jealousy and indecision. Soon he will come to his senses. Together, my dear, we will make sure of it."

"I'm afraid I'm as much the problem as he is. I don't know what I want." Tay sounded deflated to Reid.

"Well, I've heard that tale before too. You and I will do well together." The Duchess took her arm and strode with her into the parlor. "Scarlett, are there any lemon bars?" Then she turned to Tay, "Brandy or tea?"

"Brandy," Taylor said, appearing completely overwhelmed by The Duchess' attention.

Reid wasn't sure about a lot of things but what he did know was that he didn't like giving Tay up to The Duchess and her matchmaking skills. He wanted her where he could be with her when he chose.

"You must try a lemon bar. They are quite delightful and my favorite afternoon snack." The Duchess held out the plate to Tay. "There is a ball tomorrow evening. By the way, your dress is beautiful. Did you pick it out?"

"I did," Reid interjected, now feeling as if everyone spoke as if he wasn't in the room. "I think it's too soon after our long voyage for Tay to attend a ball." His feelings of jealousy were escalating at an alarming pace, but he didn't seem to be able to tamp them down.

The Duchess tap, tapped her cane on the floor before waving her hand in the air in a dismissive manner. "Nonsense," she said then leaning toward Tay who was sipping her brandy, "you're not too tired for a ball. Are you dear?"

It didn't seem to Reid that Tay had been listening but she managed to say, "No, ma'am."

"Don't ma'am me," The Duchess said. "Either call me The Duchess or Charlotte, whichever suits your mood. That way I know how you're feeling."

Drake roared with laughter but Reid said, "Don't see the humor in that."

"By the time you finally come to your sense and marry Miss Maxwell, you'll understand my laughter and you'll be heartily glad you've done the right thing by her. The Duchess can be quite formidable."

"Then the gossip about her is true?" Reid asked, gaining what seemed to him new insight into this woman.

"Most of it," Laird McLellan said as he strode into the room. "There are times though where she is really quite sweet."

The blush appearing on The Duchess' face didn't go unnoticed. "No one except you has ever called me sweet."

"Back to the ball," Reid said. "I'm afraid she won't know how to act or what to say."

"You give this woman, your soon-to-be fiancée, no credit. She seems quite learned to me and capable of figuring out what to say."

Reid choked when The Duchess used the word fiancée, but when he thought about it, he was becoming used to the idea.

"I'd like to go the ball," Taylor said as she seemed to regard him. "But I'm going to have to avoid the dance floor. It seems I've two left feet. It would be nice to meet some people."

"Not too many," Reid spoke up, thinking only women but refusing to bury himself any deeper.

"I'd like to find work. Can you help me with that?" She turned her attention to The Duchess. "That way I can take care of myself and I won't have to depend on anyone to survive. When I've a job and money I'll pay you room and board."

"Why ever would you want to work?" Reid asked, stepping into the conversation before The Duchess could find another way to yank Tay away from him.

"My dear, don't listen to him. He doesn't know what's best for you, just what's best for him. Now," she paused, seeming to take stock of Tay, "what can you do? Can you read and write?"

"Of course." Tay seemed to take offense at the question but smiled. "I'm a very good artist."

"Can you sell your work? I've an idea. What is your middle name?" The Duchess asked.

"This is all nonsense," Reid said after downing the glass of brandy and pouring another one.

"Allison," Tay said. "I do watercolors mostly but I like to work with India ink and sometimes a combination of both."

"Good then, we can market your work as T. A. Maxwell, and I know just the places to showcase it. When do you want to get started?"

~ * ~

Thrilled with this notion and for the first time since Drake Montgomerie came into her tiny circle of people she knew in London, Taylor felt some hope for her future. "As soon as possible. If you help me purchase the materials I need, I'll pay you back the first second I sell something," Taylor told The Duchess.

"I'll pay for your materials," Reid said, his voice gruff.

Tay looked to The Duchess, "Would that be proper? I really have no idea about etiquette." Eager to begin work she still wanted to make sure she didn't screw things up for Reid.

"Of course it wouldn't be proper and Reid knows it. He's feeling the man thing and wants to control what you do." The Duchess picked up Tay's hand, holding it in hers for a moment. "I will be proud to help you out with this endeavor. It will be fun. We can shop tomorrow before the ball, and if you don't have an evening gown, I'll take you to my dressmakers."

"Reid bought me one. I don't suppose that was proper but no one needs to know that do they?" She sounded way too submissive and didn't like what she was becoming, but what could she do?

"No, we don't talk about our private business. Reid would only buy a dress for a mistress or his wife," The Duchess said, pouring Taylor another drink.

"When he found me, I didn't really have anything to wear."

"Found you? Now you've set my curiosity spinning," The Duchess said, laughing. "You're an intriguing woman, my dear, and I'm sure that's why Reid is so attracted to you, but I've a feeling the story is a long one."

"It is. I accidentally ended up in Sardinia and I didn't know anyone. I only had a small bag of clothes that were entirely inappropriate. That's the short story."

Another woman swept into the room. She was so beautiful the sight nearly stole Tay's breath, "Drake, why didn't you tell me you were going to see Aunty?"

Montgomerie's demeanor changed dramatically as he drew the tiny woman into a hug and a quick kiss on the lips. "Because I didn't know I was going to visit her."

He stepped back, arms crossed on his chest. "Ella, what are you doing out of bed? You just gave birth."

"I was bored. You seem to think that giving birth is a sickness and that I need to be molly coddled for months afterwards. I left the babe with Alma so I could have a few hours out of the house. And I didn't just give birth. I've been fine for two months now."

Tay wanted to laugh outright but settled for a tiny smile. In this circumstance she didn't dare say anything.

"You went against my direct wishes." Drake seemed to be angry but his features didn't show the emotion. If it was possible, his eyes seemed to shine with love and desire as well for the woman.

The Duchess was tapping her cane on the floor again. "Hush, Drake, you know she is fine and you two can continue this discussion at another time. A time when you can end the argument in the bedroom where the two of you always end up."

Drake cleared his throat, motioning for Ella to sit. "Very well," he said gruffly.

"Who is this?" She looked to Tay. "You're very beautiful in a haunting sort of way."

Tay didn't know what to think about the woman's words. She knew her features were a bit unusual but haunting? "I'm Taylor Maxwell and I suppose one could say I'm the reason your husband had to visit your aunt. I don't know anyone in London, and I needed somewhere to stay. So, Mr. Montgomerie volunteered The Duchess."

"Lord Montgomerie," The Duchess corrected. "You must remember when we're out and about that nobility must have the word Lord or Lady in front of their name."

"I didn't know."

It seemed Ella didn't hear the brief exchange or for that matter perhaps she didn't care. "Well, of course Aunty would help you out," Ella said. "What can I do? Introduce you to a few people maybe?"

"Really nothing," Tay said, "I think Charlotte and I have everything under control." She looked to Charlotte. "Don't we?"

"Yes, yes, and we're going to start tomorrow." The Duchess sat up straighter. "Besides keeping David happy, you've given me another purpose in life. I miss having girls in the house. You all have kept this old woman feeling young."

"And who is this? I've seen you before," Ella said, turning her attention to Reid.

"Reid Stewart, Earl of Castlerose," Reid said.

"Ah, you work for Drake. That's where I've seen you. I suppose you met Taylor on one of your missions. I hope this all works out for the two of you," Ella said, looking from one to the other. "If you ever have anything you want to talk about, you can come to me."

"Thank you." Taylor felt overwhelmed suddenly. This woman was more awe-inspiring than The Duchess.

"I'm beginning to think I'm getting your gift of sight, Aunty. Can't you just tell they're in love with each other by looking at them. They don't know what to do about it either. Probably been denying the fact."

"Life would be so much easier if the two wonderful people in love with each other would just say the words each of them is waiting for the other one to say," Drake said as if he knew everything also.

The Duchess cackled delightedly, offering Ella a lemon bar,

which she declined. "You just can't tell young folks anything. They think they know everything. Saying I love you is just not that hard."

"Tay and I know how we feel." Reid spoke stiffly as if he tried to defend himself. "No one needs to butt into our business."

Ella took Taylor's hand in hers. "Come, let's get you settled upstairs. It's getting late and I'm sure you're very tired." Then she turned to Charlotte, "Is that alright with you?"

"Of course, dear, I'm sure Reid and I still have some things to talk about and some rules to address. Go on." She shooed them away. "Give her your old room and make sure she is snug and cozy."

"I suppose Taylor needs to learn some of the house rules too." Ella laughed then, "How to break them."

"I doubt if she needs lessons in that," The Duchess said quietly. "She seems very astute and willing to learn. Breaking rules however... I'm sure she knows everything and might be able to teach you, dear."

"Tay doesn't like rules." Reid seemed to regard her closely.

If she had thought finding herself on a ship in the nineteenth century was strange, she could not have dreamed of anything like this. They were all crazy. Rules of the ton, house rules, and now what was Ella going to tell her? How to break said rules.

Up the steps then down the hallway, Ella showed her the way. When she opened the door, Ella grinned at her as she waited for her to walk by.

"You're not from around here." Ella sat down and motioned for her to do the same. "Tell me about yourself."

"What do you want to know?" She wouldn't believe the truth, and Reid had pounded it into her head she needed to keep her secret between them. He believed her but others would not.

"You're not English and I've two sisters who married Americans." She seemed to be waiting for a confirmation.

"I do come from America." Taylor fiddled with the lace on her dress, trying to think up a plausible lie. "A part I'm sure you're not familiar with." If you stick to the truth, you don't have to remember the lie, she repeated to herself.

"And where exactly?" she prodded. "I haven't been though. I

suppose you're probably right. I've really only heard of the major cities."

"You wouldn't believe me if I told you," Taylor said, wishing this lady, as nice as she was, would leave and quit asking questions she couldn't answer.

"I want to say try me, but I'm going to move on. You obviously don't want to say anything, and I plan on respecting your privacy."

"It's not that. It's just that you won't believe me and I don't know how to explain." Taylor was sure this conversation was going to end badly. Yeah, she didn't know how to clarify she was now in a different century than the one she came from. The place where she'd lived wasn't even founded yet.

"I see."

But Taylor knew she didn't and she was eager to change the subject. "If you want to know about the project Charlotte and I are beginning tomorrow, I'd be happy to talk about that."

A knock on the door stopped the conversation for a brief time. Ella opened it and a platter of cheese, bread and meats was handed to her as well as an opened bottle of wine.

"Aunty always knows what we would like, but I'm sure you'd rather be sharing this food with Reid. Do you love him?" Ella prompted, seeming to take on the role of matchmaker. "We all assumed you do and we talked around the two of you."

"No offense, I would rather share this with Reid, but it seems that's not allowed any longer." Taylor didn't want to lie to Ella but it was becoming increasingly clear she would need to if she were to survive her time in this century.

Picking up meat and cheese before pouring two glasses of wine, Ella asked, "What's the project? Perhaps I can help you with it. I do get so bored, and Drake is so overprotective."

Taylor closed her eyes, sipping the red wine and thinking about all the changes in her life. Perhaps this one would be a good one. "I'm going to make my way, by myself and without a man. The Duchess is helping me to earn money so I don't have to stay here and I can buy a house, put food on the table and pay my other bills."

"How?" Ella asked, smiling and seeming as if she appreciated

Taylor's position. "I wanted to do something productive with my life too. I'm teaching orphaned children how to read."

"I'm a graphic artist, an artist," she amended quickly. "And The Duchess has said she thinks she has a market for my works." The blush rising on Ella's face surprised Tay. "What are you thinking?"

"Well." Ella plucked at her skirts then inhaling a deep breath, "I'm very good at sketching." She paused then her grin was broad, "My naked husband."

"You what?"

"It's true but don't tell him I told you. Only one other person that I know of has seen my drawings." She giggled, placing a hand over her mouth as if she needed to stifle the sound. "I bet I could make a small fortune with those drawing. Every member of the ton would want a copy."

Ella laughed so hard she was doubled over. Tears started rolling down her cheeks. The laughter seemed to be contagious. Taylor started laughing, too, thoughts of those drawing in elegant frames to be bid on by Drake's peers.

"Perhaps it would be fun to sketch Reid. I'd always have something to hold over his head." Taylor was wiping away tears of laughter.

"Don't tell Drake I told you," she repeated.

"I'd never dream of that. It's way too private just as I'm sure you would never frame them."

"I also sketched us making love. He adores the drawings but keeps them hidden away. I think his greatest fear is that when he dies someone will find them." Ella brushed tears off her cheeks, sipping more wine, her laughter finally becoming a bit more manageable.

"Anyway, I'm going to do a combination of water color and India ink drawings. Don't know if they'll sell or that I can make any money from it but The Duchess is willing to help."

"So." Ella relaxed on the chair, her glass of wine in hand. "What will you do if you earn enough money to move out?"

Taylor didn't have a single idea other than. "I'll buy a house, something modest and unassuming."

"Will you continue to see Reid?" Ella asked, once more seeming to probe for more information than Tay wanted to give.

"If he wants to see me, then of course I would like that." Taylor had not really thought about not being with Reid until today when everyone made the fact blatantly clear it was not acceptable.

"If you are still seeing the earl, people will believe you're his mistress and he's purchased the home for you. No one will believe you are paying for it or your other bills. It's just not done that way here in London and Europe."

"Why ever not? Just because it's not done that way doesn't mean I can't."

"Because unwed women don't have that kind of money. Not in England anyway. The jobs women can obtain would not garner any money, certainly not enough to buy a house. They can sell flowers, bake bread, maybe a seamstress might be able to earn that kind of money without a man helping them, but they would have a shop and people would be aware of their work."

"There's so much I don't know," Taylor mumbled, wishing for some type of equality. "I'm so out of my element here." Immediately, she regretted the last words spoken.

"You either have to become his wife or give him up altogether. Are you ready to do either of those things?" She downed the wine then poured herself one more. "You know, it's really sweet of Logan to keep us supplied with his Bordeaux and Chianti as well."

That was one more thing she didn't need to know or understand right now. She assumed one of the girls was married to the man who brought wine. "As to making a commitment to Reid, I don't know if I love him."

"Do you miss him right now?" Ella asked.

"So much even though I know he's probably still downstairs," Taylor replied to the question, understanding she didn't want to spend this night or the next one or the next without him.

It seemed Ella read her mind. "Do you want to spend every night for the rest of your life in his bed and in his arms?"

She grimaced a little. "Yes...the weeks on board his ship weren't enough to last a life time, and it made me understand what I'm missing even now while we talk."

"The questions you have about loving him and marrying him have just been answered." Ella set the glass on the nightstand.

"You think so? It can't be that simple."

"Of course I do, and yes, it is that simple," Ella said with an all-knowing air about her that could not be denied.

"Deciding about something as serious as marriage with one question can't possibly be that straightforward." Taylor had always thought the feelings would be so intense and hot they'd knock her socks off. But her feelings for Reid were slow and strong, even fierce at times. Thinking about him warmed her deep into her soul. Sex with him though was so hot and so fast it did knock her socks off.

"It was for me, but I knew I loved Drake almost the first moment I saw him. He stole my breath and made my heart stop for a second. I can't sleep at night if I'm not in his arms."

"That's how I felt when I opened my eyes and Reid was sitting beside me. Is that what love feels like? I'd always thought that emotion was lust."

"Both, it's both. One has to lust after the person they love, don't you think?" Ella appeared pleased with her answer.

"Lust and love, I would hope so," Taylor murmured, mulling over the words and whispering, thinking only she could hear what she was saying. "When I'm with Reid I can't keep my hands to myself, don't want to for that matter."

Ella leaned forward, her hand resting on top of Taylor's. "That's the way I feel about Drake."

"You do?"

"And I'm not ashamed of showing Drake every time I get the chance, which is pretty much every night and sometimes during the day, how much I want him."

"I think I need more wine."

"Help yourself. There is more downstairs, I'm sure. I'll have Scarlett bring another bottle to the room. Now, I probably should go. Drake will be up here telling me how I need to rest, and I'm sure the nanny is ready for me to return. I need to nurse Lizzie." She stood then left the room after giving Taylor a quick hug.

Taylor sat on the bed, nibbling on the food that was brought to the room and sipping the excellent wine. She did want to be with Reid but did he feel the same about her? He'd certainly agreed to this solution more quickly than she would have expected. Now she wallowed in an uncertainty she never felt before.

She discovered that her clothing had been brought to the room. Rummaging through the bags, she found her nightshirt and quickly put it on. So much to think about, she couldn't sleep. She contemplated everything Ella had spoken about, especially the part about love and lust.

Missing Reid, she pulled a pillow to her and held onto it. Knowing if they'd stayed on board the ship, they would be in bed together, making love. Just thinking about sex with Reid left her wanting him even more.

She closed her eyes, remembering every touch of his hands, his lips, teeth and the way he felt when he was on top of her, his huge body covering hers. She groaned, as her body responded to her thoughts.

"Reid," she whispered, "I need you."

"And I need you too, sweetheart."

"Reid?" She opened her eyes, seeing him, feeling his touch against her flesh then lifting her arms as he swept the nightshirt from her body.

"Yes, just who did you expect?" He laughed as he hooked his thumbs around the waistband of her skimpy shorts, pulling them off and tossing them on the floor.

"Just you. Only you." She sighed, hungry for him and hoping he'd find some way to spend the night with her.

Eager to feel his skin against hers, she drew his shirt over his head as he lifted his arms to accommodate her. His lips found hers, drew her into him, melding his mouth with hers to become part of her.

"Truly, I didn't expect you, wanted you though. How?"

"Hush, we may not have much time." His lips explored her, touched her, found a nipple and sucked the sensitive flesh into his mouth. "God, your breasts are beautiful. They are so large and you're so tiny."

He sat back straddling her, gazing at her lovingly, lightly touching the objects he just spoke of.

"You have no time." Drake's voice pounded in her head while Reid covered her with his body.

"You have no shame," Reid said while he pulled her shirt from the bed and covered her front.

"No, you have to learn to follow the rules. The Duchess knew you would try this, so she wanted me to escort you home before you could..."

"It isn't like I'm a virgin," Taylor said indignantly, holding her shirt to her breasts. "My reputation doesn't need to be guarded. It's already tarnished. So, what difference does it make?"

Reid slipped his shirt over his head. "You could have waited for a few more minutes before intruding."

"No one in London knows you are, as you say, tarnished." Drake laughed. "What the two of you need is to decide what you want for each other. The sooner you decide the easier this will all be for you. You're different, Taylor, and it won't take long for those you meet to see that difference too. There will be questions that need answering, and I have this gut feeling you won't answer them."

"You can leave any time," Reid said, his voice harsh with warning.

To Taylor it seemed the two men fought for the superior position, and it was clear to her Drake won this round.

"Not until you walk out of this room in front of me."

"Perhaps I'll sneak out and go to Reid tonight. Ella forgot to tell me how to break the rules, but I'm guessing that might be one of them."

Reid ignored Drake and sat down beside her. Pushing her hair from her face. "You can't go to my home in defiance, at least not tonight. You don't know where I live or even the address. Obviously, I can't give it to you now. Stay here and I'll see you in the morning."

~ * ~

Marcus Willoby watched the house most of the day and was surprised to see Drake Montgomerie escort Captain Stewart and the little whore into the home of The Duchess. Then only a few minutes later Montgomerie's wife entered the house.

He wasn't going to let the captain ruin his ideas for the girl. She was perfect for his plans, and he didn't want to look any farther. Putting his thoughts into action was going to be more difficult than he thought if she had the Duke of Richmond's protection, and of course he'd have to find a way to get rid of Reid. He knew things about Reid Stewart, incriminating things. He learned a lot during his short stay on Sardinia.

Ah, but there were ways if one was creative. All he really needed was to get the girl out of the house and somewhere she wasn't protected. But that wouldn't take care of Reid, which was his first order of business. The girl was just a pleasant after thought.

"Boss, what you think?" A large burly man stood next to Willoby. "This going to go off without a hitch."

"I certainly hope so, and I think we've got our work cut out for us, but we will persevere. She's only a dollymop after all. We just have to offer her something more than Stewart will be able to give her." And he's a spy, Willoby reminded himself, understanding the very real problems that could be encountered. He'd have to stay one step in front of them.

"What would that be, Boss?"

"I think perhaps her independence. Look there, Montgomerie is leaving with Stewart. I wonder why?"

"They don't look really friendly."

"No, they don't. In fact, Captain Stewart appears ready to kill if I'm understanding his expression," Willoby said laughing and thinking this new development might be in his interest.

"Think Montgomerie interrupted a tryst?"

"I do, which gives me more reason to believe I'm right about this girl." Willoby purchased the house before he left for Sardinia and on his maiden voyage of another ship, he'd met with many diplomats and royalty who would love to have a warm willing woman when they spent time in London. They'd also promised to pay for her services handsomely. There were also secrets to be learned from these men. He wasn't sure yet how he would use any information coming his way, but he'd figure it out in time.

"What is that, Boss?"

"She's going to be our ticket to a better life along with the tapestry, if we can find it. One where we no longer need to work. And I'll sell Reid to the highest bidder. There are some, who would like the information he has and will stop at nothing to obtain that knowledge."

Chapter Five

"The Earl of Castlerose, Reid Stewart, is here." Reid's gut clenched as he was presented at the ball then bowed slightly while searching the room for Tay. He knew she was here. He'd stopped by the house hoping to escort her only to discover they had left.

Spying her in a far corner of the room sitting next to The Duchess, he set off across the dance floor, circumventing revelers until he stood in front of Tay. "May I have this dance?"

"No." To his dismay, she was shaking her head, a desperate cornered expression on her beautiful face. "No, no...not at all possible. Can't dance a step."

He was taken back slightly by the rebuff then remembered her saying she couldn't dance, had two left feet. Perhaps she couldn't. "Would you like something to eat or drink then?" he asked with ulterior motives dancing through his head.

As if asking permission, she looked to The Duchess and David McLellan who nodded their approval. "I am hungry. I've been busy all day, and now I'm so nervous my stomach feels as if it's going to jump out of my body, but food might calm it."

He was floored by her comment. "And you want to eat?"

"Since you arrived, I feel better, a bit more secure. I'm not terrified of every shadow. This is not something I ever dreamed of doing. All this royalty..." She waved her hands in the air. "Lord this and Lady that, when to curtsy or let someone kiss my hand. I don't want anyone kissing my hand except you," she finished dramatically.

Then her expression changed and she looked totally forlorn and even more endearing to him than ever before. He wanted to figure out a way to take her home with him tonight but was at a loss. "I'm glad to hear that. Let's get a plate of food and a glass of champagne then we can find a spot on the balcony where we can talk."

"I'd like that."

A few minutes later Reid pulled out a chair for her. "Tell me what kept you so busy today."

For a few seconds she looked at her plate then, "I painted and I actually finished two pieces. The Duchess said when I completed ten or so, she would take them to the gallery. I'm going to paint as T. A. Maxwell. She thinks if I pretend I'm a man, they'll sell better. Figure that."

"Can I see your work, T. A. Maxwell?" he asked, picking up her hand and holding it in his, his thumb rubbing gentle circles on the underside while he contemplated other parts of her he'd like to see and touch right now.

"Of course, but it's not going to sell. The Duchess is wrong on that score. Besides what would I do with the money when I can't buy a house with it?"

"I'm sure your paintings are amazing and you could do anything you wish with your earnings. Come, let's go to the balcony. Perhaps I can steal a kiss or more."

"They are really very different, the paintings. They don't look like anything you'd see in this time."

"Different, you say." He pulled her into a darkened alcove, his lips claiming hers, his hands on either side of her head.

"Hmm..." she whispered into this mouth.

Drawing away. "I've waited all day for this, thought about it all day, longed to taste you again." His hands rose on her ribcage to just below her breasts as she leaned into him, silently asking for more.

"I need you, Reid."

The hard and very rapid thumping on his back surprised him and sent all his fighting instincts into play. He turned rapidly, grabbing the instrument then let go just as suddenly. "Duchess."

"I won't have you taking advantage of my charge," The Duchess said, grinning as if she was delighted to have found them.

How Montgomerie strolled by with Ella on his arm at that exact time baffled him until he realized Montgomerie must be the informant that sent The Duchess his way.

"Don't worry, old man. It just means she likes you. The more thumps you get the more pleased she is that you're courting her charge." He let out of roar of laughter before leaving them.

Reid understood then, he would have to become more assertive and take charge of the relationship and how it played out. Tay's reputation was important but so was figuring out what they should do with their lives and if they should spend it together.

Turning to The Duchess, "If it's alright with you, I'd like to take Tay riding tomorrow, well, no for a carriage ride." He remembered her fear of Donkeys and assumed it carried over to horses.

"A carriage ride in Hyde Park would be acceptable," The Duchess told him, her eyes gleaming as if she'd won this round. "And you will keep your hands to yourself. I'll expect you home by four o'clock sharp."

They might ride through Hyde Park for appearances sake, but they weren't staying. "I'll be there at noon." Then he turned to Tay, "If that's alright with you. I can look at your paintings."

Charlotte and David left about an hour later, asking for Tay to leave with them but with Reid's encouragement, she refused. It was either abide by her wishes or make a scene, but The Duchess chose to leave her at the ball.

"Do you think I did the right thing?" Tay asked, holding on to his arm and leaning into him.

"Don't worry, she left Montgomerie as the chaperone and it seems he's taking a delight in the title." Reid intended to make the most of this time with her. He was going to take her home, ride in the carriage with her and hope noon the next day would come soon.

The Duke of Richmond, AKA Drake Montgomerie, dogged their steps for the time they were at the ball, and he watched as Ella left the ball without her husband. That fact didn't bode well for them.

When Tay asked to leave, he was more than happy to have a few minutes of private time with her. The carriage arrived and while Reid was trying to close the door, Montgomerie jumped inside.

"Wouldn't be doing my chaperone duties unless I saw Taylor home." He tapped on the roof to tell the driver he could go.

"You didn't have to do this," Tay said, staring at the man as the carriage began to move slowly at first. "We are, after all, adults and we can make decisions about how we spend our time together. I don't need or want a chaperone. It's archaic."

"Oh, but I did have to do this." He smiled, leaning back and stretching his arms out. "It's not just your reputation at stake here but national security as well."

"You don't trust me?" Reid asked, irritated with Drake.

"Not in this matter. I know what I would have done and it's not take Ella home. I would have spirited her off to a private place to make love to her. In most cases I would have applauded you. But I promised The Duchess, and it's so much more fun to watch your pain."

"You're a very evil man," Tay said. "A woman should also have some say in this but all of you just ignore my wishes."

"Yes, at times in my life I've been evil but not now. Trust me," he told her. "This will all work out the way it should."

"And what way is that?" Tay asked, clearly displeased with the men and their conversation. "That the two of you don't think I've a say in anything." She pounded on the roof signaling to stop before trying to get out of the carriage. Her skirts caught in the doorway and it stalled her for a moment, but it seemed she was determined and reached the ground before Reid could stop her.

She was five feet in front of him when he touched the ground behind her. Running, he caught her, stopping her. Whispering, "It's not safe. You have to do what Drake asks just as I do. But I promise you, we'll find some privacy tomorrow. And I'll make love to you."

Tears slipped down her cheeks. With his thumb he brushed them away. "I don't like this century we're living in. It's so suppressive. I want to scream and scream out all of the unfairness."

"It's for your protection. A woman must have her virtue guarded until she weds," he told her, understanding why she was so angry. The time she'd lived in before was nothing like this. "Get back in the carriage."

She pushed away from, him shaking her head, seemingly still determined to set her own course. One she could control, but it wasn't going to happen, not for her, not now.

He caught up to her, lending her his arm, Montgomerie behind them offering no words, just following as he was asked to do and the carriage behind him.

"I'll walk you the rest of the way. It's not very far," Reid said, wishing she could be the same here as she was in her time. Wishing they were alone on his ship with no one to gainsay them.

"You don't have to, you know." She sniffed yet at the same time picked up her pace. "I can walk by myself."

"You want me to leave you to walk home, with Montgomerie dogging your footsteps?" he asked, hoping she would see some humor in the words. By her expression, she didn't.

"I'm a big girl," she told him.

"Not so very big." He laughed softly.

She yanked her hand from his arm and stopped, turning to stare at him, her expression hard. "I didn't mean it literally. I'm old, old enough to make decisions on my own. Old enough to walk a few blocks by myself if that's what I want."

"So, you can decide to put your life at risk by walking alone at night. I'm sure there are predators in your time also. Would you do this at home in Oregon? Would you risk your life to defy a man?"

Her jaw clenched. "No." She reluctantly accepted his arm again. "I'm just so confused."

"You two going to get back into the carriage, or do I have to walk all the way with you?"

"Walk," Reid said without turning around. This was the only part of the moments at hand he enjoyed, Drake's discomfort. If he could increase it, he would. But he meant to find something to appreciate.

"You really mean that?" Montgomerie asked. "You want to walk?"

"The night is beautiful, the stars bright." Reid was strangely happy at the moment.

"Are you trying to be nice?" she asked Reid as she leaned into him.

Her soft curves molding against his hard chest always felt so right. She was a perfect fit, her body against his. "Always, think this evening we should make the most of the extra minutes we have together. Pretend Montgomerie isn't a few steps behind us."

"Then you should kiss me." Her head tilted upward. "Pretend the chaperone isn't watching. What do I care?"

When he gazed into her eyes, they shimmered where the moonlight touched upon them. Her lips were moist and inviting, calling to all his baser cravings. Needing to taste them, he lowered his head, running his tongue along the seam, his hand pressing on her lower back, drawing her as close as possible against his arousal.

Behind him, he heard Montgomerie clear his throat. "You two can't wait until you get to the front porch?"

Lifting his head for a moment. "Nope." He returned his attention to Tay, enjoying the physical closeness more than Montgomerie's eagerness to return home to his wife.

To his wife...

He could change these untenable circumstances with two simple words, I do. He'd have to ask the question first and she'd have to agree. But...

He would propose, but it had to be perfect and he needed help. The Duchess, of course would know what to do.

He drew away from her, framing her face with his hands then gently pushing her hair behind her ears, "It's getting longer," he murmured, searching for the right words. But now with Montgomerie following them waiting impatiently with little grunts and groans then shifting from one foot to the next, "We should get home. It's late."

"And getting later but I'm spending as much of the night with you that I can and I don't want it to end. Montgomerie can go to hell for all I care."

"Neither do I, want it to end. Too bad there's no way to ditch the big guy behind us." Reid struggled with some way but could come up with nothing short of hitching a ride in the carriage that was still following them without Montgomerie beating them to the vehicle.

"Can we do something tomorrow, something that doesn't involve our indomitable chaperones?" she said, walking again. "I'm not going to be easy to get along with if I don't get to see you more privately."

"I'll pick you up at noon. We'll tell The Duchess we're going for a ride in Hyde Park."

"Can't do that. We've a meeting..." It seemed Montgomerie listened to their conversation. He wondered what else of their unguarded conversations he'd heard.

"It's not going to last all day." Reid couldn't help the irritation sounding prevalent in his voice. He was annoyed and frustrated and he bloody well needed time with Tay.

"No, but I can't say how long right now. This situation with Taylor wearing on you?" Drake prodded them. "Well, I'm getting tired of it too. I wasn't built to be a chaperone."

"Then bring Ella. Tay and Ella can talk while we're having our meeting. When it's over—"

"No," Drake interrupted. "If you were thinking with your head instead of your cock, you'd realize that's a horrible idea. You know we don't mix business with pleasure. It's too dangerous."

"The next day then," Reid said, feeling as if Montgomerie punched him in the gut. "I'll take you for a ride." Now that he made up his mind to marry Tay, he wanted to get on with the rest of his life.

Behind them Montgomerie cleared his throat before speaking. "Don't count on it. I might need to send you out of town for a few days, perhaps a week. I'm running short of help."

"I quit," Reid said quietly. "I've more important work and the rest of my life to live."

"You can't. This is your case and England needs you." Montgomerie played the loyalty to the crown bit. He didn't do it that well, but Reid was through with espionage. Montgomerie was going to have to get used to the idea and find someone else.

"I won't be there." Reid was blunt and he meant what he said, but he was also afraid Montgomerie had something else to hold over his head.

Tay was his only weakness. So what on earth could Montgomerie be thinking he could blackmail him with? There was nothing... Only Tay, but he couldn't know anything about her. She had no past and barely a present. He wouldn't just announce to the world she was from the future. No one would believe him. So what then?

"You will, if you want to see Taylor again."

Tay whirled on the man, her hands fisted at her sides and for a moment Reid thought she might hit Montgomerie. "Are you threatening me?"

"No, I'm telling Reid the way it is going to be. I need him one more time then he can quit, and the two of you can resume your lives however you want. God knows I'm not going to chaperone again, even for The Duchess. This situation is untenable."

Reid clenched his jaw, his heart pounding fiercely while his nerves seemed to explode.

They reached the house and the front porch. "I promise you this will end. Montgomerie means what he's saying. I've known him a long time and when necessary he can be ruthless. I don't doubt for a minute he would take you somewhere I'd never see you. I'm going to do this one thing for him."

"I don't understand any of what is going on here, and I'm also not sure I want to understand."

"If I told you—"

"You'd have to kill me," she finished for him.

"Work on your paintings and sell as many as possible. "When I get back, I'll take you to see my summer home. We can talk about our future." He kissed her on the forehead, his nerves more on edge than they'd ever been.

He watched her disappear into the house. This was not how the evening should have ended, not the way he planned. He needed to be with her tonight and was afraid something sinister was happening.

"Are you coming?" Montgomerie asked, sounding impatient.

"That was underhanded," Reid said as he climbed into the carriage. "You threaten a helpless woman to get what you want?"

"Only doing what was necessary. You've got to learn to put your emotions in their proper place or you won't survive," Montgomerie warned.

"Like you do with Ella?" Reid shot back, deciding the less he said the better, but he couldn't erase his parting words.

"That's why I retired from the field." Drake sat back against the seat, his hands folded in front of him. "It would put Ella in too much danger and I couldn't have that."

"But you won't allow me the same privilege."

"Not tomorrow. This investigation pertains to you as well as your visit to Sardinia and the tapestries you brought back. I need to find out where Taylor came from. If you would tell me right now, this might all be over."

"I don't know the answer to that."

Montgomerie implied more than he said, and Reid wondered how much of this had to do with Tay's sudden arrival in Sardinia and on his ship. The only people who had any idea what happened that day were his crew.

~ * ~

"You've had a long wait," The Duchess said as she sat down in the drawing room, watching her paint. "Reid will be back soon, I'm sure of it."

"It's been a week. It's not fair you know, but then I learned a long time ago that life isn't fair." Tay and The Duchess were going to the gallery today. A check was waiting for her which she hoped would be sizable. She didn't know for how much, a few pounds maybe more, but anything would be nice.

"Of course life's not fair," The Duchess said, sipping her tea, "But this time away from your man has been good for both of you. I just know it."

Tay put the finishing touches on another painting then stepping back, observed her work. She'd heard reviews: different, intriguing, imaginative, over the week. The owners of the gallery had sent Charlotte many of the written reviews and Charlotte handed them over to her. People actually liked her paintings, but did they buy them all?

"The separation has not given me more insight into myself or Reid's and my relationship, if that's what you're implying." Deep inside she was angry and frustrated. Ella visited a few times, but Tay resented the visits knowing Ella went home to her husband.

"Separation is good for the soul, makes you appreciate what you have." The Duchess snacked on a lemon bar in addition to her cup of tea.

"Don't know if I agree with anything you're saying but you're welcome to your beliefs." Taylor stared out the window for a few seconds, trying to rid herself of the encroaching depression. She couldn't even go outside and run. Instead, she was relegated to running through the house and up then down the stairs.

"That's quite diplomatic of you," The Duchess said, watching her intently. "Everything is very different about you, Tay. Why? And those clothes you run through the house in..."

"Don't know why, maybe my mom and dad played a role in shaping my behavior. I like to run and Reid told me not to go outside in my running gear." Tay wrapped the finished paintings and stacked them one on top the other.

"If you've made a significant amount of cash from your sales, we should visit the bank and set up an account for you. Something that's not easily transferred to your husband when you wed," The Duchess said. "That is if Reid was to request them."

Tay had not thought of that horrific factor. When she arrived here, she had nothing, so she never considered the fact that her husband would own her and everything she possessed.

"Do you honestly think I've made some money with these?" She pointed to the assembled paintings. "I can't imagine people buying them. They didn't before..." She caught herself just in time.

"From what my friend at the gallery has implied, the short answer is yes," Charlotte said. "What are you smiling about?"

"You're starting to talk like me." Tay quickly gave Charlotte a hug. "Thank you for doing all this for me. No one has ever been this nice."

"You have an air about you and a way of creating chaos in my head, but yes, some of the things you say make sense even though I've never heard certain phrases. Are you ready?"

"No." She sat down, hands folded in her lap. "Terrified I've failed, anxious to see what the people of London think about my work, and so many more emotions. My stomach is churning, but I understand the sooner I discover the truth the better I'll feel. The unknowing is harder than anything else."

She did want to earn a living and be self-sufficient, but from what Ella told her, when she purchased a home everyone would believe Reid bought it for her. And, she told herself, berating her feelings, why should she care what people thought about her. She never cared in her time, so why now? Truth was the important factor here.

"I'm sure, dear, you haven't failed but we won't know how much you made until we get there. The owners are waiting for you, and they told me they were eager to obtain more of your paintings. So, I'm glad you've got a nice stack to take to them this afternoon."

She inhaled a long deep breath, wishing Reid was going with her, wishing he was back from the mission Drake sent him on, knowing Reid tried to quit. And why was it so important that Reid go on the assignment?

Something could have happened to him. She knew espionage in any time was dangerous. Well, she couldn't and shouldn't dwell on that fear. And she took solace in the picture of them taken in the future. Time to stiffen her spine and get on with the day.

She stepped outside, paintings in hand. The day was extra warm with little to no breeze. A few clouds dotted the sky. It hadn't rained for so long. She was used to rain even in the summers. August had turned into September. Where was the year going? Heavens, it would be Thanksgiving before she knew it then Christmas. No Thanksgiving in England, but maybe she could have a little influence and cook a turkey on that day.

"All you need is a hat, Charlotte. It's hot out here." The carriage waited for them. If she had money, the first thing she meant to do was hire one and go see if Reid had returned home, preferably without Drake to dog their steps.

The driver helped them both inside. Tay sat back, her heart

pounding while nervous energy surged within, her foot tapping on the floor, feeling as if every nerve she possessed had snapped.

"It is hot." Charlotte waved a fan in front of her face as she made small talk.

"You don't have to think of things to say. I'm perfectly comfortable with silence and my thoughts." She didn't mean to discourage Charlotte, but the conversation was turning senseless.

"There you go again. While there is nothing absurd with what you're saying, it's just unusual. Comfortable with your thoughts?"

"Don't you like to just sit back and close your eyes while enjoying the peace and quiet and silently talking to yourself?" Tay sat back and shut her eyes as if she meant to do just that, but she had a strong feeling Charlotte wasn't going to let her.

"You truly are a strange woman, and I don't mean that in a bad way. With my nieces I needed to talk to them about men and what men wanted and how they thought, but you seem to understand men better than most young girls."

Tay wanted to tell her it was the psychology classes she enjoyed in college but knew that wouldn't work to her advantage, so she shrugged her shoulders instead. "I don't understand men at all. They are just too different, but I do love the differences."

"See, no woman of this time would say something so outrageous, not even Ella," The Duchess said. "And Ella can be most shocking."

"What seems like a long time ago, I was engaged to a man. He was in the Navy. I thought I loved him." Tay held back from mentioning the Navy Seal bit. She didn't need questions from Charlotte she couldn't answer.

"What happened? Did one of you call it off?" Charlotte appeared concerned, her brows drawing together while her light blue eyes sparkled with what appeared to be curiosity.

"He's missing in a ridiculous war and presumed dead," she spoke bluntly. "He was ordered on a dangerous mission, and he was the only one who didn't come home in a casket."

"You don't want to wait for him?" The Duchess looked appalled at her statement.

"He's been missing for a very long time. I was told he wasn't coming back, ever. That he was most likely dead just like the rest of his team." Of course Tay couldn't say that she was living in a time before he was born.

"I see and Reid knows about this man?"

Reid is his great, great something grandfather wasn't something Tay could tell Charlotte so, "He knows and understands that even if Sean returned, I would end the relationship. I've discovered, with Ella's help, that I never loved him."

"How did Ella help?" Charlotte rearranged her skirts then stared out the window for a few seconds before casting her gaze back to Tay.

"Probably something you passed on to Ella. Some of your words of wisdom, I would guess."

"And what was that?" Charlotte asked. "I always like to hear that what I've told my nieces did not fall on deaf ears."

"Simply asked if I could live the rest of my life without Reid in my arms." Just thinking about making love to him sent a wave of heat through her.

"And..."

"I don't want to live without Reid. I suppose I could but I would have lost an important part of my heart as well as my soul. And after thinking about Sean, I never felt that way about him."

"That's good for you, dear. I do believe we're here." The carriage rolled to a stop and the ladies were helped from the vehicle.

They stood in front of the door, Tay's feet seemingly frozen to the ground. "I have to do this, don't I?"

"There is nothing to be afraid of, dear. Just good news awaits you, I'm positive. Take a deep breath and proceed. Look as if you deserve all the good fortune waiting for you."

"That's always good advice." She did as Charlotte suggested and stepped, head held high, through the door ahead of Charlotte.

"Let me do the talking. They don't know T. A. Maxwell is a woman. They're about to find out, and they're probably not going to like it at first."

"Monsieur Gerrard, how are you?" The Duchess smiled,

extending her hand in greeting.

"You're here to collect what we owe Mr. Maxwell I assume. Where is he? We can't give the money to anyone except Mr. Maxwell."

The Duchess cleared her throat. "T. A. Maxwell is a woman and while I don't have any proof, I would suggest my word should be good enough. She is standing right behind me. Come here, dear." The Duchess turned, waving her hand for Taylor to move forward.

"I'm not sure." The man sounded hesitant, bordering on disbelief.

The Duchess tapped her cane repeatedly on the floor. "I still have favors I can call in. There are things I know about you and your mistress that I'm sure your wife would like to know."

"You're threatening me?"

"Of course not, just making a suggestion about your future. This is T. A. Maxwell, and she has completed more paintings. If you refuse to believe us, I'll take my business elsewhere."

Tay had known The Duchess could be formidable, but this was amazing. She defied the carefully constructed female roles in this century. "I'm T. A. Maxwell." She held out her hand, which the man ignored. "I believe we might have a lucrative business between us, but as The Duchess suggested, we can go elsewhere." She didn't know yet if her paintings had sold or if this was lucrative for both of them.

His back stiffened as he turned, striding toward the counter and where Taylor assumed would be her money.

Behind the counter, he pulled out an envelope and handed it to her. "Now, I assume you have more paintings per our contract. I'd like to see them. They must be just as good as the ones we sold or I won't take them on consignment."

Taylor unwrapped each one, setting each in a place where Monsieur Garrard could step back and look at them. "How many of the previous batch did I sell?"

"All of them and we got an amazing price for each one. It seems as if we didn't ask enough for them. I'm going to raise the price for these pieces." He looked at her, staring hard. "Difficult to believe a woman could do these. I assume you signed these with the same name."

"I did. How much?"

"Your commission came to a total of ten thousand pounds. As I said a moment ago, we'll put a higher price on these paintings, and I'll assume you will continue to supply the gallery with work. It's profitable to us all."

At the mention of ten thousand pounds, Tay's hand went to her heart and she gasped, surprised by the amount. "Ten thousand pounds..." she murmured.

"I did tell you..."

"That I'd made a lot of money. Did you have any idea it was this much?" Taylor still couldn't breathe. Her work would never command this price in her time. This was difficult to imagine.

"The price tags were evident when I brought more paintings a few days ago. Now, my dear, you can do whatever you want. You won't have to fall victim to the rules of the ton. You can live outside the aristocracy and you can be as singular as you want."

She turned to Charlotte, tears of happiness sliding down her cheeks. "What I want is Reid. This is all nice but..."

"Let's set up an account at the bank. If Reid is half the man I think he is, he'll allow you this account when you are married to him."

"Charlotte, I don't really care anymore. I've changed so much in so little time. It's as if I've learned what is important in life and what is not. A life with Reid is what's important."

They spent the rest of day running errands and setting up that account with the name T. A. Maxwell on it. They arranged for the profits coming from her paintings to be sent directly to her private account.

"Every woman should have money of their own. Most of the wealthy men of this time give their wives an allowance. The simple fact now is that Reid will not need to do this. You have what we call pin money that you've earned. It is what you wanted."

"Probably way more than most as long as my work keeps selling." Tay knew how whimsical patrons of the arts could be, and she didn't miss the words from Charlotte, *in this time.*

Did Charlotte suspect something, for that matter did others suspect she was not from the nineteenth century?

"Shall we go home now? Scarlett would love to hear this news, and I'm sure Cook has something spectacular made for dinner. I'm very proud of you, dear. You're very talented."

Very talented. She'd been told that before, but until now she'd never really been appreciated. The Me Too movement was taking over her time, but perhaps she could play a small part in this time.

"Women should be able to speak their mind and should be treated as equals to the men around them." Her thoughts suddenly shifted to Marcus Willoby and what he'd thought to take from her.

"Of course they should," The Duchess said. "But this isn't the century for that. If I had a crystal ball, I'm sure I would see it in the future. Do you know anything about that?" The Duchess questioned.

Taylor wasn't all that sure who was questioning her, The Duchess or Charlotte, but her entire being craved to tell the truth. "No, I don't," she tried for the answer Reid would have liked her to utter.

"Don't suppose you or anyone would, but I've seen things change in my lifetime. Another hundred or two hundred years could prove quite interesting," The Duchess said, appearing almost wistful. "I'd love to see those changes."

She agreed but she wasn't sure if Charlotte was challenging her or if she suspected anything. In another hundred years women would have the right to vote in the United States. She didn't know about England. Perhaps some of the things she did now might help women earn that privilege. Even in her time, despite all the progress, women were still not treated equally.

After clearing her throat, Taylor continued, "I'm sure everything will continue to change."

"Yes," she sighed softly. "What are you going to do with your money? I could help you invest a portion."

Taylor perked up with that question. "I'd like that. Do you have any ideas?" She never thought of investing but then she'd never had money. Now there were ten thousand pounds sitting in the bank in her name with the possibility of more to come.

"Real estate is always a good investment," Charlotte said quietly. "Now, before you wed Reid, would be a good time to purchase land or a modest cottage. I'd seriously think about continuing the idea of using T.

A. Maxwell as your name."

"British law doesn't allow married women to own or buy land independently of their husbands?" Taylor was sure she knew the answer but needed to hear it.

"It does not but there are ways around it. I'm sure Reid will have no problem with granting you some independence from him," Charlotte said.

"You've jumped the gun, Charlotte. He hasn't asked and I haven't agreed to a marriage."

"But you are, my darling. We both know it and you told me you loved him."

"He hasn't asked," Taylor persisted, feeling the rush of heat to her face. "Maybe he doesn't love me."

"It's just a matter of time."

"Do you know something I don't?"

"Pshaw." Charlotte waved her hand in the air. "Let's take a look at the Times and see if there is anything that looks exciting for you to see. You could buy a home to live in until Reid decides to ask you to wed or you could rent it out. Which would you like?"

"For now, I'd like to stay here and I'd like to pay you."

"Never. I've more money than I can spend in a lifetime, and my son has more than me. Let an old woman enjoy what is left of her time."

Chapter Six

"Tay, what are you doing here?" Reid turned his attention from the men gathered in his study to that of the tiny woman who created such a burning passion in him he was aroused just seeing her.

"I've news, good news and it's..." She tried to look around him. "I guess telling you can wait."

Reid stepped aside, motioning to the men. "We're done here. You know what you need to do."

When the men were gone, she asked. "How long have you been back?" Her voice held a myriad of accusations.

"Don't be angry, sweetheart. About an hour and I'm sorry but the men were waiting in the study. I had no choice but talk to them. Drake told them when I'd return." He paced the room, massaging the back of his neck and wishing his headache to vanish.

"So, he could tell your men and not me? Didn't he think I had the right to know?" She sounded indignant and angry.

He drew her close, his lips descending to meet hers. She tasted sweet and hot, opening for him as his tongue initiated a foray of its own. When he pulled away, her breathing spoke to him in tiny little gulps of air. "I don't want to waste any time, any longer. You're going to stay here, with me."

"I don't think so."

Shocked by her answer, a sudden terror of losing her swept through Reid. "Why?"

She looked away but he wouldn't allow it, gently moving her chin so he could see into her eyes. "Given our marital status, it's not proper."

"You don't follow rules." Annoyance set in but he meant to get to the truth. "So why?"

"My good news." She sat down on a sofa, smoothing her skirts and seeming to study the floor for a few minutes before meeting his gaze.

He needed to listen to her. "Tell me." He poured them each a brandy, somehow feeling he needed a drink.

"My paintings have sold and now I've money and independence. The Duchess helped so much." She held the crystal glass in both hands.

"And..."

"I made ten thousand pounds and will probably make more. I gave the gallery ten more paintings to sell."

He nearly choked on his brandy when she said ten thousand pounds. Her paintings were truly unique, but that kind of money was not easy to come by. "You must have made a thousand per painting."

"Monsieur Gerrard said they would sell the next batch of paintings for more money. The Duchess wants me to invest in real estate. I agreed and I plan on buying a house and maybe some more land somewhere to rent." She watched him, her eyes wide and questioning.

He didn't know where this was leading, and he couldn't think of a thing to say to her. He'd meant to ask her to marry him this evening, now they were discussing investments and a potential large source of income. He didn't want her to think he would take her money. He wouldn't. But a proposal at this time wasn't exactly appropriate.

Bloody hell. "That's nice." He sipped his brandy, wishing cook had prepared a platter of food for them. He needed something to do with his hands besides drag her into his arms and make love to her.

"That's all you can say?" Her voice sounded cold. "I thought you'd be proud of me, maybe gush over my talent."

"Congratulations." Well, that did seem in order. He needed distance from his thoughts as well as his cravings. "Would you like to come with me to the kitchen. I'm hungry."

"The kitchen?"

"Well, yes, it will be fun." He didn't want to wait and he didn't want to hear her deny the possibility of a tryst in the kitchen as not being fun. With long strides he headed for the kitchen, hoping she would follow. He wasn't disappointed.

She did trail behind and now she leaned against the doorframe, studying him. He wished she'd say something. The silence ate at him, stripping his nerves. He'd been in tighter situations but this was a hell he'd never encountered.

He rummaged in different areas of the pantry and brought meats and cheeses as well as grapes. She still watched him, her arms crossed in front of her, pushing her breasts up so he couldn't ignore them if he wanted to.

"Are you going to say anything?"

As if she just made up her mind. "I'm going to buy a house. Charlotte and I looked through the paper today. We found a small cottage just outside London that would suit my needs."

"I don't believe what I'm hearing," he muttered, tossing a grape in the air and catching it in his mouth. He chewed thoughtfully. "Is it something I did? Or didn't do?"

"Of course not." Her voice was brittle.

"Tay, talk to me. You sound miffed and I'm not understanding this new side of you." Sweat beaded on his forehead. He wiped the moisture away with his shirtsleeve.

"What I'm about to say might sound a bit pretentious." Now instead of the emotions flitting through and changing her features, she looked terrified.

"I'm not going to hurt you. You can say anything you want." This when all he wanted to do was sweep her off her feet and make sweet love to her. So much time had passed since they'd been together.

"Since I have money now, with the possibility of more, would you take it for yourself? If we wed and I know you haven't asked, might not ever ask, but I have to know." Her words seemed to explode from her as if the questions had been heating to a boiling point and needed to detonate.

Now he fought the urge to smile, understanding the seriousness. "Do you feel better? Now that you got that off your chest." Once again he pulled her into his arms, his kisses tenderly placed on all her exposed skin. The day dress she wore had tiny little sleeves, ones he could slip off her shoulders and down her arms.

It seemed as if the short argument never took place. Her head was back, allowing him access to her neck and as he pulled the bodice further, her breasts were exposed and he feasted his gaze on the beautiful ivory globes and pink buds. Deep in the back of his throat he groaned.

"May I?" he thought to ask a little late but she'd made no objections.

In answer, she tugged his shirt from the waistband of his pants then ran her fingers up his chest. "Reid," she whispered. "I've missed you so... I don't care if you take everything for yourself."

"I haven't asked you to marry me yet." He wanted to do this on his terms and when the question felt right.

He picked her up then set her on the table in the kitchen. "We can eat later. I've found I'm hungry for you." His hands were beneath her skirts, hooking his fingers around the tiny panties she liked to wear, pulling them off and letting them slide through his fingers to the floor. He ran his hands up her well-muscled and long legs, enjoying the silken flesh he encountered.

When he touched her intimately, she was moist and ready for him. He craved her breasts and while she unfastened his pants, he sucked a tender pink bud into his mouth, laving then biting gently, enjoying the movement of her hips against him. He was lost in the mystery and the magic surrounding this beautiful woman who came to him from the future, a gift he could never refuse.

He slid inside, craving the intimacy he'd been denied for so many days. In seconds they both climaxed. Her skin was flushed with a sensual sheen that captivated him and her hair was in beautiful disarray. The lovemaking was primal and enchanting, everything he imagined and remembered. He craved a lifetime with her.

"I can't move," she said her voice barely a whisper in the waning light of the afternoon. "I'm drained of all energy."

Sweeping her into his arms and picking up a bottle of wine and two crystal glasses that he let her carry, he strode up the steps, taking them two at a time until he was in his bedchamber. Kicking the door shut, he slowly set her on her feet, reveling in the feel of her curves against his body.

She shimmied from her dress and underclothes, standing in front of him with nothing on then watched him as he undressed.

"I see you with clothes on and I need you, but seeing you naked I can't keep my hands to myself. I need to feel all of you, touch you, take you into my mouth," Tay moistened her lips.

At the sight of her tongue against her soft pink lips, he felt as if they didn't just make love on the kitchen table. "I feel the same," he said, his breathing hard and labored, his body throbbing with sexual need.

She smiled at him, reaching out to touch him. He pulled her into his arms again, his hands on her buttocks then tracing a path up her spine, drawing her closer, her breasts against his chest an aphrodisiac to his heart and soul.

In his arms her body shivered with need. Again, he swept her into his arms and together they landed on the bed. His body resting lightly on top of hers, no words were said but once more they made love.

When they finished her lips were kiss swollen, her entire body touched by him. "I'm spineless," she murmured, but they made love again and once more he lost himself in the beauty and enchantment she wove around him.

He pulled her into his arms, his hands resting on her belly they were spooned tightly together.

"I want to marry you, Taylor Maxwell. I don't want to spend one more night without you in my arms."

She rolled over, touching his face lightly. "Neither do I but I'm not sure why you're asking now."

"It has nothing to do with your good news. Nothing at all, I promise." Convincing her might be more difficult than he thought at first. He rose then and poured them both a glass of wine. Walking naked across the floor, he sat down on the bed, handing her the drink.

She grinned at him, "I will never be tired of looking at you."

"And I you but that's not the most important factor right now. I want you to know I've more funds and investments than I can spend in a lifetime or two lifetimes for that matter. I don't need your hard-earned money nor do I want it. You and Charlotte can spend the money from your paintings or invest the funds anyway you please."

"You wouldn't try to confiscate it by saying you could manage it better than me?" she asked, gazing at him over the rim of her glass.

"I'm sure The Duchess has more knowledge in that area than I do. It's rumored her late husband, the Duke, not the man she's wed to now, had a sizable fortune which is now ten times what it was when he died." He laughed at the change of expression on Tay's beautiful face.

"Really? How?"

"I certainly can't say. But if you want to ask her, please do. She might tell you everything she knows. I wouldn't mind at all if you were the richest woman in England."

"She might. I think she likes me and likes taking me under her wing so to speak," Tay said. "Don't know why."

"Enough said about The Duchess and art work or even financial investments. Will you marry me?" He needed to hear yes but he craved words of love. Did she love him and did it really matter?

She hesitated for the longest time. Then, "Yes, I don't want to spend another night without you, and I don't want to ever be considered your whore or your mistress. I need to be your wife."

"Then, let's get married tomorrow?"

"Tomorrow? IDK."

"IDK?"

"Short for I don't know," she said sheepishly. "Texting, something we do on the cell phone I showed you what seems like a lifetime ago."

"What's standing in the way?" He thought he might laugh or cry or maybe a little of both seeing the horrified expression on her face.

"A girl has to get used to the idea of being engaged before she gets married. While I don't really care about all the falderal of flowers and dresses and of course I don't know anyone to be attendants..."

"We can do whatever you like, but if we don't get married tomorrow then there might be a long wait and we will be living in different houses. Is that what you want?"

"No, of course not. But..."

"But?"

"Let me think for a few minutes. Maybe we can eat now."

"Thinking is good. I'll go get us some food." He pulled on a robe and left her alone in the bed to mull over what they talked about.

What was there to ponder? He laughed. At least she was considering his idea. And he had to admit any other woman would have probably given him an emphatic no. She wasn't any other woman.

In the kitchen he piled a platter high with cheese and fruit, a few slices of summer cucumbers and tomatoes. Rummaging in the pantry he found slices of bread and a few berry tarts cook left in a container.

"You having a party?" Drake leaned against the stair railings, studying his fingernails.

Reid jumped, startled by the voice behind him. "And you're not invited." Reid wasn't about to let Drake intrude on this night. He had too much to gain and everything to lose.

"Is Taylor upstairs?" He started up.

"I wouldn't do that if I were you. I've put up with your autocratic behavior where Taylor was concerned far too long."

Drake stopped with one foot on the first step. "Perhaps you're more deserving of her than I thought."

"What do you want, Drake?" Reid asked, impatient and angry. "I'm in the middle of an important discussion, and I'd like to get back to it."

"About what?" Drake grabbed a berry tart from the platter and popped it into his mouth. "Delicious," he murmured. "Charlotte will be worried. Just tell me if she's safe and where she wants to be."

"Of course she's safe and she'd rather be here than anywhere else."

"You sure about that?" He grabbed a slice of cheese.

"Get out of here, Montgomerie. I've quit the business and there is no reason for you to be in my home disturbing me." Reid started up the steps, intending to ignore the Duke.

Reid didn't know if the odious man left but he assumed he did since Montgomerie didn't follow him. He opened the door hoping to see Tay naked on his bed. Instead she was dressed in one of his robes, completely covered. Well, one could dream.

"I've food." He set the tray on a small table near a window.

"Was that Drake Montgomerie I just watched leave?" Taylor asked.

"Thank God he left. I thought he was going to follow me upstairs." Reid dished up a plate of food wondering why Montgomerie's departure had been so easy and what the man might be up to.

"Perhaps you should lock the door," Taylor said. "I remember another time when we thought we were alone. It was the most embarrassing moment of my life."

He strode to the door and did as Tay suggested. "It's locked."

They ate in silence and he was on edge, needing an answer but afraid to pursue the question of marriage. His heart in his throat, "Did you have time to consider my proposal?"

"I didn't think you would ever ask." She smiled at him, wiping a way a small crumb of food from his lips.

"I'm terrified."

"Really? I am too but probably for a different reason."

"Well?"

"I want to marry you and tomorrow is fine with me, but I want Charlotte and David to witness the marriage. I'd also like David to give me away. I'm hoping they'll agree to this."

His sigh was long and dramatic but the relief he felt was tangible.

"Since I've no living family, that would honestly be wonderful. If they agree..."

"That's settled. So, where is this church?"

"In the country. It's charming and I grew up with the pastor. We went to Oxford together. My father bought me a commission in the navy and he became a priest. He will be more than happy to marry us."

"We should talk to Charlotte and David tonight if we want to do this tomorrow," she said, sipping the wine he poured but seeming to ignore the food.

He groaned, knowing that meant she wouldn't stay the night. "Then we'll go see them now."

"I think we have to do just that. I really want Charlotte at my wedding. It's all I really care about."

~ * ~

The carriage ride to Charlotte's home was met with silence, Tay's body shaking with nervous tension. It seemed Reid had nothing to say, as it was with her.

Inside, Scarlett met them. "Are Charlotte and David home?"

"Charlotte is here, but David is not. I don't know when he'll be home," Scarlett said, clearing her throat before taking Taylor's shawl and draping it over the coat stand. "May I ask why?"

"Reid and I have news and need to talk to her about her part in it." Taylor peered into the parlor, expecting to see Charlotte sitting there but the room was strangely empty.

"She was napping but she is up now. I'll tell her you and Lord Stewart are here." Scarlett departed quickly up the steps.

Tay still had trouble getting used to the formality of saying lords and ladies. It seemed so strange, foreign. When they were married, would she be a lady, in name only. Inwardly she laughed at the notion. "We'll wait in the parlor."

"Would you like brandy?" Taylor asked, holding the decanter. "I know I do and I'm hoping it will calm my escalating nerves. Every synapse seems to be stretched to the breaking point." She closed her eyes for a second, trying not to stop breathing. One slow breath at a time, inhale slowly, exhale slowly. Meditation before this would have been nice. People must meditate in these times.

"Please," he said, pacing the room then staring out each window as if he were looking for someone or something. He picked up a figurine then turned it over several times before setting in down.

Tay brought the drink to him. "Thank you. Do you feel as if all this is a dream?" Reid asked.

"I'm sure Scarlett will show up with a plate of lemon bars," she laughed. "Charlotte loves them and cook must have a standing order."

"I do believe I've noticed the penchant for the treat. They must have a calming effect. Think I might try one this time," Reid said, wrapping an arm around her shoulder then nuzzling her neck. His lips sent sensations of delight through her and for a moment she forgot the trepidation she'd experienced ever since she said yes to Reid.

She felt the shiver all the way to her toes, her body heating with passion for this man. "Let me do the talking."

"Is that the way they do it in the future? You emasculate me. It's my job to ask if I can have your hand in marriage." For a moment, Reid sounded angry.

She made herself think before she responded, "It's considered polite and gentlemanly, but I always thought I could answer for myself." She wondered if Sean would have asked if her parents had been alive?

"Do you want to take charge here? I'll abide by your wishes if that's what you would prefer."

Moisture formed in the back of her throat and she pushed it back, thinking she was acting childish. "On second thought, I'd like it if you asked Charlotte for my hand. Sometimes a girl likes her man to take care of her."

Reid appeared shocked but he quickly schooled his emotions, "Thank you. I'm honored."

She leaned into him, resting her head on his chest, closing her eyes while she wondered about their future together. Charlotte announced her presence by tapping her cane on the floor.

They turned. Taylor's breath caught in her throat. She was on the precipice of something that would change her life even more than it had already been changed.

"You two look just like two cats who swallowed the pet bird." Charlotte waltzed into the room. "What news?" she queried. "And do I want tea or brandy?"

"Brandy," they both said.

"That's the way it is then." She poured a glass then sat, motioning to them to find a seat also. "Good or bad news, or perhaps a little of both?"

Reid stood, seemingly unable to remain still. He looked at her then back to The Duchess before clearing his throat. "We came...I came to ask for Tay's hand in marriage. She has said yes."

Moments ticked by while Tay held her breath. She truly didn't know how she'd feel if The Duchess said no.

"You know about her windfall?" The Duchess tapped her cane, a stern expression gracing her features. "The two of you need to talk before I can give an answer of any consequence."

"Charlotte, we have talked. He won't confiscate what I earn. I have his promise." Since she turned eighteen, she'd never had to explain herself to anyone in a position of authority. While Charlotte wasn't exactly that, a position of authority, Taylor respected her.

"She has a bank account where her profits will be deposited. Does she have your promise not to take that?" Charlotte continued as she sipped the brandy Tay poured for her.

Reid cleared his throat. "I don't have to explain anything but the short answer is yes. I don't want or need her money, and she has told me you are going to help her wisely invest what she earns from the sale of her paintings. She has my blessing even though she doesn't need it."

The Duchess waved her hand in the air, "Of course she does and well, you know that fact. If you had the urge, you could take everything from her. The good news for you is this way she doesn't need an allowance."

Tired of being talked over and around, Taylor spoke up, "You haven't answered Reid's question, and we're getting married tomorrow with or without your permission. We don't need it, just wanted it." She had the immediate feeling she overstepped her bounds.

"Tomorrow you say?" Charlotte's tone softened. "Of course you have my blessings, but we can't have the banns read or plan anything special. Tomorrow is just that, tomorrow. You won't even have a dress."

"I have a beautiful evening dress Reid bought me and..."

"You wore that to the ball. You can't possibly think of wearing the same dress on your wedding day. No, I'll have to figure this out. It's just that I don't have very long to do that."

Taylor lifted her shoulders, smiling at Charlotte and understanding the lady liked to have everything perfect. But her wedding would be perfect for her. It didn't have to be perfect for Charlotte.

"I don't need or want a wedding dress. All I crave is to spend the rest of my life with this wonderful, caring and very sexy man." She stopped, gritting her teeth, knowing that wasn't a phrase used in this time. Then she shrugged her shoulders again and with a small grin said, "Well, it's true. He is sexy. That's what women say in America when they appreciate the way their man looks."

Reid was grinning at her, "Very sexy man? I'd like to explore that later when we're alone."

"Well, that won't happen tonight. If your wedding is going to be tomorrow, you won't spend this night together." The Duchess tapped her cane as if trying to add emphasis to her words. "You must be celibate for at least one night."

Except for today they'd been celibate for what seemed like weeks. At least they had this afternoon, and she was infinitely glad she hired a carriage to take her to see Reid even though she'd not been invited.

"We, Reid and I, would like you and David to attend the wedding and witness it," Taylor said, truly hesitant now. "If that wouldn't be too much to ask."

"Of course we'll be there. We'd be honored to witness your marriage. Where exactly is there?" Charlotte asked.

"In a small village church east of here. A friend of mine is the priest. I sent a message that we would be there tomorrow," Reid said.

"Sure of me, were you? How long will it take, the carriage ride, not the wedding?" Charlotte asked.

"Not more than an hour. We'll leave at noon," Reid said. "I'll drop by and pick up Tay."

"You must ride in separate carriages. Give me the directions and we'll meet you there. Bad luck to see the bride before the marriage."

Taylor watched Reid's hands fist and wondered at the anger she saw. "Not superstitious but I'll abide by your wishes. After all, I'll have a lifetime to gaze at my wife. I will not look, but my carriage will follow yours. David can ride with me."

He was trying to make concessions and she knew how hard giving in to any of The Duchess' mandates must be. David strode into the room, tossing his hat on the coat stand. "We've company."

"The best news, David." The Duchess clapped her hands

together. "Taylor and Reid are getting married tomorrow and we're invited. I hope you don't have anything major planned that might need cancelling. Brandy?"

"No, I'd love to attend a wedding. Would I be the gentleman to give the bride to the groom?"

Taylor rose, "I'd love for you to walk me down the aisle."

With open arms Taylor hugged the older man, wishing she'd had a father who could have loved her or even cared more for her than being a pawn in his wishes and life. Even barely knowing this man, she knew he had tender feelings for her.

She stepped back, "Thank you."

"David, open one of those bottles of champagne we have in the pantry," Charlotte said. "It's time for a bit of a celebration and perhaps a toast or two for the lucky couple."

"Of course, my dear, I'd be happy to get the champagne." Before he left to find the champagne, he kissed his wife.

If she'd married Sean, his family would have taken over the wedding. Now Charlotte would probably do the same, but in this case she liked the feelings of a surrogate mother and father. Charlotte could do whatever she wanted.

The Duchess tapped her cane several times, affectively getting everyone's attention. "Now, despite your protests, you are going to have a wedding dress. I have figured this out. You and Ella are much the same size. Except for your bust line, we might have a problem there." She fell silent then but strode to a small desk and taking paper and pen out wrote something.

"Scarlett," she called out.

It seemed Scarlett had been close. "Charlotte?"

"Have this delivered to Ella and tell her to bring herself here post haste no matter how much Drake might protest. It's imperative she comes as soon as possible." She paused a moment. "Tell Drake he is also welcome."

ASAP What on earth did The Duchess plan? It was getting late and the day had been outstanding and overwhelming all at the same time. Exhaustion seemed to claim her body. She'd gone from poor damsel in distress without a dime to a woman of means, small means, but means. In addition, she'd gone from spinster to a woman with a fiancé.

She would be a married woman tomorrow. Her breath caught in her throat.

David returned with the champagne and crystal flutes. "This is such a delight. Our last wedding was Aidan's and Blade's then of course our own. The wedding night..."

Charlotte sent him a glance that stopped his monologue and gave her a reason to smile.

"Isn't that what all couples are looking forward to? The wedding night?" Reid spoke up. "It should be a night to remember."

"Those were my thoughts," David said, unable to hold the grin back "And you were a lovely bride, just as lovely as Aidan."

"And you, my husband, were just as handsome or should I say just as sexy as Blade." The twinkle in Charlotte's eyes surprised Tay. "I like your American lingo."

The older woman was passionate and understood so much more than she let on, yet she'd been the person who held her family together over the years.

With the champagne poured, David held his glass in the air. "To the beautiful bride and the handsome—"

"Sexy," both Charlotte and Taylor interrupted then broke out into laughter while they held the crystal flutes in the air.

David appeared a bit out of his element. "Sexy groom," he amended, turning a little red then grinning seeming to become more himself. "My daughters would not recognize their dear father."

"Dinner is ready if anyone is interested." Scarlett stood in front of the dining room door, hands clasped in front of her.

"Of course we're interested. David, be a dear and bring the bottle of champagne with you." Charlotte stood, glass in hand and led the way into the dining room. "With all this wonderful news, I'm famished."

The dinner began with a serving of soup then progressed to several more servings. Tay felt as if she ate enough for three people. Actually she felt as though she just finished Thanksgiving dinner. Now she wanted to watch a bit of football and take a nap.

Half way through dinner Drake and Ella joined them. "I brought the dress, Aunty. What do you want it for?" She sat down, sipping on the champagne Drake poured for her while he piled her plate with food.

"The dress is for Tay, if you approve. She and Reid are getting married tomorrow, and she has nothing to wear except an evening gown she wore to a ball."

"I assume we're invited to dinner even though we're a bit late," Drake said as he pulled out a chair for his wife.

"Fashionably late," Ella amended. "Now about the dress?"

When she glared at him, he shrugged his broad shoulders, "You need to eat more. You've lost weight."

"How would you know?" she shot back then seemed to wish she hadn't said that.

The twinkle in his eyes bordered on wicked. "You really want to know? Probably a conversation we should have in private, but if you insist." He kissed her forehead.

"No," she quickly said. "I'm sure I don't really want to know the answer to a question I shouldn't have asked in the first place."

"I'll tell you tonight." He sat down beside her. "Or if you prefer, I'll show you."

"So, why did Charlotte ask for you?" Taylor said, hoping it wasn't because Charlotte wanted more people at the wedding. While she didn't mind if Drake and Ella attended, she had not planned on inviting anyone.

As if Ella guessed at her look of distress, she leaned forward. "Don't worry. Drake has so much to do tomorrow. We came because it was obvious that Aunty doesn't want you to have a wedding without a dress."

She couldn't stop shaking her head and trying to say no with her eyes. "I don't need a special dress," she repeated for what seemed like the hundredth time.

"Of course you do and I've brought mine. It's only been worn once, and it's so beautiful it should be worn at least a second time. Aunty thought it would almost work for you except for your..."

"Bubbies..." Reid said, grinning while at the same time looking well pleased.

The word was close enough to boobies she knew exactly what he spoke of. In another time she wouldn't have been embarrassed, but right now in the nineteenth century in front of people she barely knew, she was mortified and prayed Reid had not just finished the sentence. Yet when she stopped to think about it, she'd always been a little self-conscious about the size of her breasts.

"I can't believe you said that." She sent Reid a look that she hoped would tell him she didn't appreciate what he said.

Instead, he laughed then as if realizing he overstepped, "Sorry, but it's true and if you can talk about sexy men, well..." He wisely left the sentenced unfinished.

"Point taken," she said, conceding defeat in this verbal spar at least. "So, you've brought me the dress you wore at your wedding. Do you really want a stranger wearing it?"

Ella laughed and the sound was musical. Tay understood why his wife mesmerized Drake. "You are a bit different but I feel now as if I've known you my entire life. I want to be part of your wedding even though I'm going to assure you again, Drake and I cannot come. Now a reception later might be nice."

"Maybe a few days later. I've something planned for after the wedding, and I don't want to change those plans," Reid said.

"You should try it on and see how beautiful you'll look in it. After dinner we'll go upstairs and see what needs to be done. Ella has agreed that she's fine with changes, didn't you Ella?" The Duchess spoke, seeming to watch her and Ella closely.

"I would love to have someone else wear my beautiful dress," Ella mentioned again. "I left the box in the sitting room. Your soon-to-be husband cannot see the dress."

With the meal finished, the women took the dress upstairs and the men retired to the parlor.

In Taylor's room, Ella pulled the dress from the box. Tay felt as if her eyes bugged out of her head. It was not in the fashion of the twenty first century, but she'd never seen anything so beautiful; the lace, the fabric, the beading...

Her hands on her chest and barely able to breathe, she said, "Are you sure you want me to wear this? I know the seamstress will have to change the bodice."

For an answer and with tears in her eyes, Ella hugged her. "I'm positive. You should have something beautiful for your wedding day. It only happens once in a lifetime," then looking at Charlotte, "well, if you're lucky."

"That's alright, Ella. I mourned the loss of my Duke and now I was blessed enough to find another loving man. Yes, I had two weddings but I will truly always remember both with such fondness."

"You need to put the dress on. The seamstress will be here in a few minutes, if she got my message, and this will fit you tomorrow."

"Like a second skin," she murmured.

~ * ~

"Willoby has been following you and stalking Taylor. You should be cautious and very careful not to let Taylor go anywhere by herself," Drake said.

"Bloody hell, what does the man want?" Reid asked, thinking the mission had gone off as planned and all the documents delivered.

"Rumor has it he thinks there is something woven into one of the tapestries you transported here. I've also heard he has plans for Taylor as well as a grudge against you."

"The tapestries?" Reid asked, shocked by the information, trying to recall everything that happened on the island. Truth be told, Tay's appearance there had sent him into a tailspin. "If there was information, I didn't know about it and the merchant didn't say anything."

"You need to figure it out. Are all the tapestries in the warehouse?" Drake asked, pushing for a definitive answer.

"No." Reid had taken one for his summer estate and had planned on hanging it in a guest bedroom. The figures reminded him of Taylor and himself. "I was taken by the beauty of one of them and it's in my home in the country."

"We'll need to examine it. If there is something of value to the ministry, I'll have to confiscate it," Drake said.

"Whatever is necessary, but make sure you go through the ones in the warehouse before they are sold. I don't want to fear for Tay's life. Willoby needs to be restrained."

"Where is the tapestry?" Drake asked, "I can do what needs to be done while you're getting married and have the tapestry out of your home before you return with your bride."

"In the guest bedroom in the south wing of the house." Reid massaged the back of his neck, a very real fear for Tay racing through him. He remembered the words Willoby spoke on the ship. The odious man assumed things about Tay that weren't true.

"My men we'll be out of the house by the time the two of you are married," Drake said, seeming to finally relax.

"I've pie and an after-dinner drink?" Scarlett brought a tray into the room, setting it on the sideboard. "Lady Ella says they will be finished in about ten minutes. She wanted me to tell you."

Drake nodded, gazing up the stairs as if he meant to kidnap his wife and spirit her home. "The baby is probably up and crying."

"You have a wet nurse? Not that it's any of my business. Just curious for when it's my turn at parenthood." Reid felt a pang of emotion at the thought of a child, something he'd never experienced before.

"We do have a wet nurse, not that Ella will use her unless it's necessary. Tonight will be one of those times. Lizzie can only go a couple of hours without being fed."

"A few hours? What about sleep? Do you get any?"

For a moment a look of chagrin crossed his face. "I get more than Ella does," he reluctantly admitted then shrugged his shoulders. "I can't feed the baby. She goes a bit longer at night, usually four hours."

Chapter Seven

Reid picked up David the next day at noon, resisting the urge to look out the window so he could see his soon-to-be wife.

"Nervous?" David asked, as he stepped inside the waiting carriage then tapped on the roof to signal the driver it was time to go.

"Does it show? My knees are even shaking. The crazy thing is I want this more than anything I've ever wanted in my life. I crave a lifetime with Tay." He was so sure of what he wanted, he didn't understand the anxious energy surging inside.

"Doesn't show at all," David laughed. "You'll feel better as soon as it's over."

"You wouldn't tell a lie, would you?"

"Maybe you're just a little anxious, but it's normal and when you see your beautiful bride, you'll understand how wonderful the rest of your life will be. This is going to be a day you'll never forget."

"Well, if the rest of my life is as interesting as the last few months, I'll be a very happy man." Reid sat back, closing his eyes while he listened to the sound of the carriage bumping along the road.

His body tightened as he thought of the night to come and the following days. They had a lot to talk over. He was waiting to tell her about the move to the summer home. Living in the city was not to his liking. Used to life on the ocean in his ship and the wind at his back, he needed to be away from the throngs of people inhabiting London.

Moving to his ancestral home in the country seemed at times bittersweet yet also necessary. Since his parent's passing, he'd not been there. When he made up his mind to ask Tay to marry him, he completed arrangements for the home to be updated to his liking. The renovations should be finished now.

The day of their passing was only five years ago, but he remembered the visit from the constables telling him his parents had died in a carriage accident. It had felt surreal and for days he existed in a blind haze. The funeral seemed to make their deaths real, giving him a small measure of closure.

He'd found he couldn't breathe as he realized he knew very little about Tay's parents. They still needed to learn a lot about each other. He planned on doing just that the next few days.

"You alright?" David's voice held a hint of concern. "You look so serious."

"Just remembering some things better left in the back of my mind today. I was thinking about my parents. Wish they could be here."

"My girls..." he paused, "lost their mother when they weren't very old. Aidan was only about five. Can't remember exactly. I'm having a hard time for you. Losing both parents must have been devastating."

"It was." He leaned against the backrest, closing his eyes. "Time to think of happier things. I'm getting married today to the most beautiful and intriguing woman I've ever met."

David popped a bottle of champagne. "Should have done this sooner but I didn't want you to be tighter than a boiled owl by the time we get there."

Reid opened his eyes, laughing at David. "I don't get drunk easily. It would take two or three of these bottles of that fancy wine to do the trick."

"When was the last time you ate?" David asked as he poured the bubbly liquid into the glasses he pulled from a nearby basket. "There's cheese and crackers too. Charlotte didn't want me to starve."

"Point taken. It was last night's dinner and my stomach was churning so bad...well, I didn't eat much." He downed the glass, "One more won't have me staggering into the church. But it's already relaxing me." He looked into the basket, bringing out a few of the proffered snacks and downed them.

David obliged, refilling both glasses and continuing to chat about inane things but passing the time.

The carriage drew to a stop. "We must be here," David said, peering out the window. "We need to give the ladies a chance to go into the church ahead of us so you won't see the bride."

"I didn't tell Paul who was coming, just that I was getting married. Shouldn't we do this the other way around?" Reid was worried about this arrangement. His need for control seemed to surmount the rest of his worries, and he didn't want any problems confronting his bride.

David patted his hand, "No worries. The Duchess sent word this morning just who would be coming for your wedding. I'm sure Paul will allow the ladies to come into his church and find a spot for them to get ready. "

"The Duchess," he smiled. "I see even her husband refers to her with different names considering the situation. I wondered at how easy Tay seemed to pick that habit up. Most the time she calls your wife Charlotte, but there are those incidents when she refers to her as The Duchess."

"The Duchess is in action as we speak. You know she learned this when she married her duke. Before that, she was more like her sister, my first wife."

"And how was that?" Reid was genuinely curious.

"Just that she was naïve. One might call her innocent," David said, "But I wouldn't change Charlotte in any way. When she lets down her guard, she's the sweetest woman alive."

"Sweet you say?" Reid wanted to laugh but looking at the expression on David's face, he forced himself to remain silent.

"The wedding party is inside, Reid. The two of you can come in now." Paul had opened the door of the carriage.

Reid stepped out and after a handshake and a pat on the back with Paul, "I'm so glad you're going to marry us. It's like bringing a tiny bit of my past into my future."

"Can't believe after all this time you finally found the woman for you. She must really be something special." Paul spoke from the heart. "I didn't think you'd ever settle down. I kept up with your shenanigans through mutual friends and the rumors that have a way of circulating. I'd say your life has been a bit like butter upon bacon."

"At times I've been extravagant, but now I'm ready to settle down and hopefully start a family."

"Again, this lady must be really special to have snagged you," Paul said as they made their way around the church.

"She is one of a kind." Reid realized how very true the words were. He'd always believed them but when other people put his thoughts in perspective, it reinforced just how special and unique Tay was.

"Come on, we'll go in the back way. If we don't go through the front doors, we'll be taking no chances. Bad luck you know." Paul was laughing as he was leading the way to the church and its back entrance.

Reid inhaled a long deep breath. This was it. He made his decision and she accepted. Now he was about to embark on another life, a different way of living but with the woman he loved... Well that was a new thought. Maybe he should tell her how he felt. Telling Tay he loved her would make him too vulnerable.

Stepping inside the back room, nervous energy once again seemed to consume him. When he picked up the glass of water Paul offered him, his hand shook. He ran his finger around his collar, sweat beading on his forehead. Bloody hell, he'd never expected his nerves to be at a boiling point.

"Since I'm serving as the father of the bride as well as the best man, I need to see what the ladies are doing." David slapped him on the back. "I'm sure Charlotte will let me know when the ceremony should begin, but I like to keep up on things."

"I'll make sure he behaves. No running out the back door to escape what he set in motion. My wife is seeing to the needs of the bride. She'll tell me when everyone is ready."

"Why aren't they ready now?" Reid thought he'd walk into the church, say his vows then leave. He didn't count on waiting.

"Brides, they have to look beautiful for their grooms. She has to get dressed; her hair done as well as her face. You wouldn't want her to show up without everything perfect, would you?" Paul asked.

"I never thought of that." He seldom felt out of his element, but he'd never married anyone before.

"She should be ready soon." Paul laughed. "I was the same way the day I said my vows. It's a life changing event."

A beautiful red headed woman poked her head in the room. "She'll be ready in five minutes."

"You never told me your wife was beautiful. For that matter you never invited me to your wedding," Reid said with a bit of sarcasm.

Paul grinned. "It wasn't conventional. Indeed, the ministry wouldn't be happy if they knew the truth."

"You had to marry her," Reid said, suddenly shocked but knowing his friend Paul it shouldn't come as too great a surprise.

"We were, and I always wanted to wed the love of my life, but it was a bit sooner than we planned," Paul said. "We should go inside the sanctuary."

Reid followed his lifelong friend into the church and took his place beside Paul at the altar. Paul's wife played the organ. The church was so empty. Was this what Tay would have really wanted? Shouldn't she have friends and family in attendance? *Fool, she doesn't have friends and family in this century.*

Surprisingly, Drake and Ella sat in the front pews, smiling at him. It was just like Drake to do something like this, show up when he said he wouldn't. He was a hard man but underneath his thick skin he was as soft as a kitten.

Charlotte stood in the doorway, holding a bouquet of yellow flowers, slowly walking down the aisle. She stopped at the altar.

Inside Reid laughed at the notion Drake could be soft in any way. Now he only had eyes for the woman who stood framed in the doorway. His heart caught in his throat. Tay was so beautiful he could barely breathe.

David and Tay walked slowly down the aisle, her dress flowing behind her. He held his breath, his stomach churning. He prayed David still had the rings. Wanting this over was the best thought he could have.

"Who gives this woman to this man?" Paul asked.

"I do," David said. "While I'm not her father, I've come to love her as if she were my daughter." He handed her over as Reid took her hand in his.

Taylor gave her bouquet to Charlotte and David stood beside him.

The music ceased and the ceremony began. Vows were exchanged and Reid wasn't sure he was really present for any of this.

Suddenly and after repeating words he truly didn't remember, "You may kiss the bride," rang in his ears.

He looked to Paul for affirmation and after Paul nodded, his lips met hers. The security he suddenly felt overwhelmed him. She was his now and if he thought about it, he was hers, but the last part didn't really matter to him.

Tempted to take the kiss to another level, he stopped himself. This wasn't the time. He had to wait for the wedding night which would not be far behind if he had any say in the matter.

As it turned out, he didn't.

Then Paul spoke, "May I present the Earl of Castlerose and his new wife, the countess. Now we have a cake for the bride and groom and a small feast for the witnesses of their wedding. I know that you wanted the ceremony private, but I've taken this opportunity to invite a few of your friends who were just as eager to see you settled down as I was."

"You did what?" Reid didn't know if he wanted to strangle his old friend or bless him. There had been something missing for him and perhaps Paul had understood. He needed his friends and he wondered if Tay felt the same, but her friends could not be here. He wasn't going to complain.

Outside in the foyer a handful of old friends and their wives gathered in greeting. Reid shook their hands, welcoming them, talking about old times. He introduced Tay to everyone. Unfortunately, she didn't seem quite as pleased as he was. She was going along with him, but it seemed to Reid she wanted to run as far and as fast as she could from this situation.

He wrapped an arm around her shoulder. "Are you alright?" he asked, hoping the answer would be yes but knowing if she spoke the truth it would be no.

"If you're happy, I'll persevere. Your friends are important to you as mine would be to me. I've thought about my two friends I left behind in Sardinia. I miss them and they would be so happy for me now." She spoke so softly he was sure no one else heard.

He held up the glass of champagne that had just been handed to him. "To all our friends, old and new as well as the ones who could not be with us. We love you all."

"Shall we eat?" Paul asked, smiling at them.

"Of course. I see your wife has prepared enough food for an army." It seemed everyone conspired against them and their private celebration in their bedroom. But he determined he would enjoy this.

Eating and laughing about old times seemed to be the order of the day. One hour led into two then three.

Paul's wife stood, tapping a spoon on her glass. "I believe it's time to cut the cake. I'm thinking the happy couple would like to leave for their honeymoon and some well-deserved privacy."

"Are you going anywhere?" Paul asked. "If not, we don't need to rush."

Reid sent him a glare that made his old friend laugh. "We wouldn't tell if we did have a specific destination."

"So, you're not going anywhere," Paul persisted.

"Would you like to cut the cake, Tay?" He turned to his wife, touching her hand.

"Absolutely," she said standing.

He placed her hand in his and walked with her to the cake. "Here we are. Don't get any ideas," he whispered. "If you do, you'll pay dearly."

"I'm not a fan of smeared cake on my face. Don't worry." She grinned wickedly at him.

With her fingers she fed him a small bite and she shivered when his tongue met her finger and his lips closed around it. Then he did the same to her.

"Everyone enjoy. I for one am ready for privacy with my wife."

His words were met with cheers and applause, a few lewd jokes following. Sweeping Tay into his arms, he strode quickly to the carriage before anyone else could waylay them. "I want you all to myself," he told her, his tongue touching her earlobe.

"Finally," she said, her hands wrapped around his neck then running them through his hair. He was able to open the door and set her inside before hopping in behind.

When they were both inside and the carriage underway, he pulled her onto his lap.

"You are now my countess, Mrs. Reid Stewart." Their lips met for a long passionate kiss.

When he pulled away, "I'd like to be Mrs. Taylor Stewart. In my time many women keep their maiden name. Or perhaps Mrs. Taylor Maxwell Stewart, what do you think?"

"You'll still be T.A. Maxwell." The disappointment he felt was tangible, but he wasn't going to let it ruin this afternoon. He wanted her to be proud of his name.

"Where are we going?" she asked, running a delicate fingertip along his jawline.

"The Castlerose estate, our summer home. I hired a staff a few weeks ago. They should have the place cleaned up and ready for us to live in."

"I didn't know you had another place to live, another home."

"There are probably a lot of things you don't know about me. Except when we were on board my ship, we haven't been able to spend a lot of time together." He meant to remedy that in the next week, having made sure he had no business to attend to during this time.

"Admittedly, we didn't talk much." She pulled his head down to meet her lips.

He always enjoyed their lovemaking when she became the aggressor. His hand closed over her breast, knowing this was just another way to torture himself. Making love in this carriage was not something he intended to do.

"Ah, Tay, such sweet torment. I wish we were home now, not in another hour."

"Is that how long it will take?" Her breathing labored from the sweetest of kisses, and her lips were swollen from the pleasure they shared.

He leaned his head back. "Maybe we can talk. Any more of this, I'll have your skirts tossed and I will make love to you here. I wouldn't want to ruin the dress since it's not yours."

"What do you want to talk about?" She rested her head on his chest while he stroked her back as if that gesture would calm her. He knew it wouldn't.

He thought for a few seconds. "Would you rather be in your own time?"

"I want to be in the same time as you. Would you like to see all the wonders of the future?" she asked, gazing at him as if searching his eyes for the truth.

"Seeing all the things you've talked about would be too overwhelming. I'm happy in this simpler time. So, no, I don't want to travel forward to the future even though I am curious. I will be quite satisfied with the stories you weave."

"Good, you're right about the time being simpler. It's not so fast paced. If we had a car, we'd probably be at your home now. Do you know that there are people who still complain about all the time it takes to get somewhere?"

"They must take a lot of things for granted."

"Too many."

"Look, we're here," he told her, opening the window curtain. "I gave the staff the night off with the promise they would have the master chamber ready for us."

~ * ~

He carried her up the porch steps and into the foyer. Setting her down, she gazed into his eyes. Her hand settled on his cheek as he slowly lowered his mouth to meet hers. His hand resting at the small of her back, he pulled her closer.

"Well, would you just stop and stare. Look at the two lovebirds. I say, ain't that just so adorable?" Marcus Willoby stepped from the shadows. "Too bad we couldn't find the tapestry. Where did you put it?"

"Don't know what you're talking about." Reid set Tay behind him. "Do as I tell you," he whispered to her.

Maybe. "I won't argue with you." From the corner of her eye she saw movement down the hall just before she was grabbed from behind.

"Over here." Willoby waved his gun, motioning for Reid to sit down.

"So you can tie me up? Don't think so." Reid's hands were fisted at his sides.

"If you give me the tapestry, I'll leave the two of you alone," Willoby said, eyeing her. "Or I might have to hurt your pretty little plaything."

Her heart thundering in her chest, she watched as Reid rocked on the balls of his feet, readying himself for a fight. She knew Reid wouldn't like it, but she'd have to defend herself, and she meant to do that as soon as the second man made the first move.

"Damfino! Drake took it. Could be anywhere by now." Reid slowly stepped nearer to Willoby.

"Don't come any closer." Willoby waved his pistol in the air, his hand shaking.

It seemed Willoby wasn't used to confrontations such as this. Tay had never seen Reid fight, and she imagined he was capable of taking care of himself. But Willoby held a gun. Perhaps if she could create a diversion, Reid would be able to overpower the odious man and grab the gun.

She hoped Reid wouldn't also be taken by surprise when she decked the man holding her. Slowly, she began to pull her skirts away from her legs. Thankfully, the skirt was made of a lightweight fabric and it wasn't a mermaid gown. For a moment, she smiled at her thought.

Without giving any suggestion of her plans, she head butted the man holding on to her. Even while the man let out a roar of pain, she turned and pulling the skirt nearly to her waist, kneed the man in the groin. While he was doubled over in pain, she side kicked him, sending him to the ground. One down, two more to go. She looked around for the man she'd seen earlier.

She heard the scuffle and Willoby's grunts as Reid's fists hit him in the face. The man still held the gun, but the weapon dangled uselessly at his side while Reid delivered the punch that sent him backpedaling then to a sprawl on the floor.

Another ruckus on the front porch by the doorway sent her

attention in that direction. It seemed Drake and Ella had followed them. Drake shoved the third man into the foyer.

Ella rushed forward, taking her by the arm. "I saw what you did. Can you teach me?" She was nearly breathless and excited at what she'd seen.

"Why did you do that? You could have been hurt." Reid hovered over her while two of Drake's men hauled the three intruders from the room.

"No more than you could have been hurt." She shot back, indignant at his overprotective nature.

"Why?" His hands were fisted once more, his anger simmering in his eyes.

"Isn't it obvious?" Taylor didn't want this conversation. What she needed was acknowledgment that her actions helped him. She needed to hear a thank you.

"Never mind them, they're just men and they're going to posture and pretend you didn't just knock that man out. I want to know how you did it?" Ella stepped between Reid and Tay.

"I've trained..." She didn't know how much she should divulge, knowing it wasn't something women did in this century.

"Show me on Drake. Show me exactly what you did," Ella persisted, seeming to be overly excited about the prospect.

"Yes, knock me out." Drake stepped forward, a smug grin on his face.

She was looking at him, sizing him up and shaking her head. "I couldn't."

"Because you don't want to hurt me?" Drake let out a roar of laughter. "I'll wager my wife one hundred pounds you can't send me to the ground."

Taylor looked to the floor then Ella. "Go ahead and make the wager." She intended to pay the bet if she failed, but she didn't expect to lose the wager for her friend.

"You're just as foolish as my wife when it comes to fighting a man. She thought she could down me several years ago but found she couldn't even move me an inch."

"Well," she paused. "I can't do it the same way as I did the other man. You see he was short and Drake is not." She was speaking to Ella. "It's a matter of physics."

Drake took his waistcoat off. "I'm ready."

"How much do you care about this dress? I might tear it. If you want it in one piece, I'd like to change my clothes, but if I truly want to make an impression on your husband, it might be better to actually be wearing women's clothing rather than my pants." She was suddenly excited about the prospect of sending this arrogant Englishman to the floor.

"I'm sure it can be repaired if you actually rip it. I'm eager to see this." Ella stood, her hands folded beneath her chin and her eyes wide.

Drake surprised her by grabbing her then. She inhaled a deep breath then assessed his position and with a quick move, easily flipped him over her head. Now he lay sprawled on his back, a look of shock painting his handsome features.

"I've laid you low, sir Lord or sir Duke. I'm not sure the proper name to call you." Then she turned to Ella, "In truth, if this was a real fight, he would probably be on his feet right now rather than lying on the floor staring at the ceiling. I doubt I could fend him off. He is much bigger and stronger than I am."

Drake rose, dusting his hands off on his pants. "She's right, you know."

"The other man was short and weak. I came pretty close to knocking him unconscious with the first blow." Taylor was smiling now and when she turned her attention to Reid, he looked just as surprised as Drake.

"Why didn't you do that with Drake? Hit him in the head with yours then..." Ella asked, appearing confused by the conversation.

"Drake is too tall, much taller than me. I would have succeeded in head butting his chest and unless the hit was so hard it stopped his heart, he would have let out a grunt and I would still be his prisoner."

"Remind me not to get you angry," Reid murmured.

"Taylor is right on all counts. How did you learn to do that?" Drake asked, drawing his wife into his arms. "You cannot defeat a man.

123

Remember what Taylor said."

Taylor wanted to make light of the accomplishment. "My father wanted me to learn how to defend myself, and I used to practice with my ex-fiancé." And... she knew she'd said too much.

"She's also an accomplished swordsman." Reid seemed to speak the words with pride.

"Thank you, but don't exaggerate. You defeated me quite handily every time we sparred."

"Only because my reach is so much longer. You're much quicker on your feet, and I think you might have more stamina."

"It's the running," Taylor said. "Cardio...well," she waved her hand in the air. "Never mind."

Drake groaned. "Don't put any ideas into my wife's head. She has enough to do taking care of the children."

"Don't you want me to be able to defend myself as well as the children?" she shot out clearly, meaning to continue the confrontation.

Drake silenced her with a kiss then, "We should leave. It's going to be dark by the time we get home, and I don't want to spend unnecessary time on the roads. Highwaymen you know. Besides, the newlyweds," He looked at Tay and Reid who now stood with their arms around each other. "I'm sure they have things they'd rather do than listen to this argument which, I might add, you'll never win."

"Of course I will." Ella's smile was smug as if she knew she had her husband wrapped around her little finger. "Wait." Then turning to Taylor, "I left a wedding gift on the bed. Don't let Reid undress you. Take it into the changing room and wear it for your new husband. Promise me."

"Alright then, I promise."

"No, I won't allow you to learn any of this nonsense. Now let's go," Drake said looking over his shoulder.

Ella tossed her husband a look that Taylor could only guess promised reprisals if he didn't give in to her wishes, but she doubted Ella would stay strong by the way she let Drake's arm settle around her shoulder, his hand so close to her breast. There would likely be shenanigans during the carriage ride home.

"Shall we go upstairs?" Reid asked, kissing her neck while he swept her into his arms again. "I want you naked."

"You first." She tilted her head, knowing he would have her dress removed before she could blink, but she wanted him to know how she felt. "No wait, I'm going to do what Ella has suggested."

He growled low in his throat, his voice suddenly husky and whiskey smooth. Striding up the steps, he kicked the bedroom door open then closed it the same way.

"What if I don't want to wait?" he said, laving more kisses on all her exposed flesh and undoing some of the fasteners on her dress.

"You're going to have to. I mean to see what Ella has left for me. I'll bet it's something provocative, silky lingerie perhaps." Taylor would have received a lot of sexy night things at a wedding shower if she'd been in her time.

"It will result in the same thing. You naked and in my arms."

"But it might be more fun this way. I don't know what it is, but if I put it on, I want to see your eyes. You were too far away to see them when I stood in the doorway of the church."

He held her close, her tiptoes just touching the floor. His lips closed over hers. "You taste damn good, Tay." His hands rested on the small of her back. With a hint of pressure, she moved closer to him, feeling him hard against her.

"So do you," she murmured.

Tay didn't say anything more. She needed this kiss so she opened for him. Good Lord, but he tasted so good, as he explored the inside of her mouth. Teeth, tongue, lips; everything to taste left her breathless with longing, almost changed her mind about the gift that sat on the bed, but she promised.

Unable to pull away from him, she met his tongue with her own, danced and played with it until she heard the small sound of pleasure emanating from within.

Pushing away from him, her hands resting on his chest, she smiled at him. "I'm going to put that on now. Why don't you pour us some wine?"

Lord she was hot and the desire for him nearly overwhelmed her.

She picked up the package, disappearing then into the dressing room. The gift was wrapped in beautiful hand painted paper. She was careful to untie it without ripping anything.

She gasped when she pulled the present from the package. In her hands, she held two pieces of the sheerest lingerie she'd ever seen. They were both a pale rose color. This would leave nothing to his imagination. He would see every curve, every part of her.

A seduction tool Tay was sure Ella used quite often. Maybe that was how she was planning on getting her way with the self-defense lessons. She made a mental note to thank Ella for the gift and perhaps learn a few more things she could surprise Reid with from this impetuous and passionate lady.

Struggling with the fastenings on the gown, she was finally able to undo the garment. She didn't want to ask Reid because she knew if she did, she wouldn't make it back to the dressing room. The wedding dress had fit her too thin form perfectly so a corset had not been necessary.

She laughed, thinking of Reid in the other room most likely wearing all his wedding finery when she entered the chamber in this confection. She slipped the first garment on, tying the straps at her shoulders then put on the robe, which was just as sheer. He would see all of her.

She meant to make him wait for at least a few minutes before he took the garment off and made love to her and she wondered just how long they could wait. Perhaps a glass of wine long or a few pieces of cheese long. For some reason, she needed to drag this out for as many minutes as possible. It was her wedding night, and she didn't want to spend the entire evening in bed even though that's where she planned to end up.

She stepped into the room. His back was turned. "Reid?"

The glass he held slipped to the floor, spilling the wine. "My God, I never expected anything like that. You're..."

"Wearing a nightdress and a robe but really very naked?" she breathed softly. "Is there another glass?"

"I'll get one as soon as I clean this up. You should sit by the fire. I don't want you to catch a cold." He picked up the pieces of broken glass then strode through the door but was back in a few minutes with a third glass.

When he returned, she was sitting by the fire on a plush white fur rug. The platter of food rested on the hearth.

He sat down next to her, seeming to feast his gaze on her. "To my beautiful wife." They clicked glasses. "I love you," he murmured.

With his words her heart caught in her throat. "I knew from the first time I saw you and I never thought I would fall in love but I have. I love you so much. You're my destiny. Taylor's Destiny."

"As you are mine."

With that Reid took the glass from her and after setting both on the hearth, he showed her how much he loved her.

Sardinian Sunset
C. L. Kraemer

Author's Note

Sardinia is considered a state within the country of Italy. However, the primary language is Sardinian, with Italian being a close second. Only those communities hosting international tourists might have people who are English speakers. Much of the dialogue in this story is written in either Italian or English for the ease of the reader. My Italian is passable. My Sardinian—non-existent.

Prologue

USA Today, Feb. 1, 2018
Ollolai, Italy, is selling homes for $1.25. That's cheaper than a cappuccino.

Ollolai, a hillside town toward the center of Sardinia, a large Mediterranean island west of Italy, is offering crumbling dwellings for 1 euro (about $1.25) in an effort to boost the shrinking population of the mini-metropolis, which dates back thousands of years.

The catch? You have to spend about $25,000 to renovate the home you buy and do the work within three years. You can sell it after five years.

Over the past half-century, as reported in official figures, the town's population has declined from 2,250 to 1,300, leaving hundreds of abandoned homes.

According to Britain's *Independent* newspaper, Ollolai sits on the slopes of Monte San Basilio Magno, and is one of the few remaining Sardinian towns where a local martial art, S'Istrumpa, is still practiced. It also keeps up traditional artisan crafts such as the weaving of baskets.

Chapter One

Keys winging through the air, accompanied by an exasperated, "I have HAD IT!" announced the arrival of Olivia Francesca Porcu Martin. The unintended target, a replica of an ancient, Italian, wine container, shattered into shards on the floor. "I always hated that vase."

Traffic on the way home from work had her wondering if the State Mental Hospital had freed all the patients with keys to new cars, releasing them on the unsuspecting public. Her briefcase thunked to the floor, and she dropped to the sofa. Toeing off her high heels, Olivia sighed as she lay her head on the back of the cushion. "What I wouldn't give to fly away to a quiet Greek island and disappear."

Working was a distraction, nothing more. Years of living in the fashion her friends referred to as, *monk-like*, she had invested her earnings wisely, wanting for very little in the way of material items. Why couldn't she fly away? She huffed. "Where would I go, and what would I do?"

Sitting on her laurels didn't appeal. Her finance degree opened the door to a world of fast and furious; leave your emotions in the lobby. Another wistful sigh escaped her lips. "Something will show up. Just a matter of time." Leaning forward, she snagged the remote from the coffee table and turned on the local news.

"In other news, today… On the island of Sardinia, the mayor of a small village in the mountains is offering approximately two hundred abandoned and crumbling homes for sale for… are you ready?" The newscaster peered into the camera lens and waited an appropriate length of time. "…one Euro. That's right, one Euro. There is a catch, however," he chuckled, "Isn't there always? The purchaser must sign an agreement to refurbish the home to a livable state. The mayor figures it will take $25,000 to $30,000 and the new owners have three years to reach that goal."

Olivia was on the edge of the couch cushion, waiting for more information.

"We'll be right back."

She groaned. "Of course."

When the broadcast came back live, the newscasters moved to another story without divulging the name of the town. She knew she had some research to complete as soon as possible. "Comfort first." Olivia struggled from the couch and traded her work clothes for jeans, t-shirt and tennis shoes. She snatched the laptop from its resting place on her dresser and walked to the sofa. Folding her legs beneath her as she flipped open the laptop, she powered it up. "If this story isn't a con, I'm outta here. If not...well, can't hurt to check it out." The sound of fingers maneuvering computer keys muted the rest of the news. Olivia leaned against the cushions, folding her arms. "I'll be. They're serious." She tapped through the photos, stopping when she'd located the place in which she was most interested.

Decades old stones tumbled into a courtyard. The layout shown suggested the previous owners of some wealth at some point. *I wonder what could have happened to make them move?* Olivia scanned the rest of the pictures and noted the number assigned to the property.

"Tomorrow, I'm taking a vacation day and doing as much research as I can. I believe I hear the call of Mediterranean sirens. No point in ignoring their songs."

Chapter Two

Salvatore Lucchesia, current mayor of Ollolai, Sardinia, Italy stared at the pile of correspondence covering his desk. The center was full of envelopes containing letters and money. To the right was a pile of phone message forms needing answers.

"What the heck have I done to myself?"

A dark head peeked around the corner of the open office door. "*Un attimo?*"

"*Si*. What do you need, Angelica?"

Angelica Porcu was the receptionist/secretary/office manager of the small city office. Nothing in the town of Ollolai happened without her knowledge.

"We have someone holding on the phone who wishes to speak with you."

Salvatore sighed. "Right now, it seems the whole world wants to speak to me. Why is this person any different?"

"You know the house at the end of SP29?"

"The old Porcu place, *si*."

"Well, Olivia Francesca Porcu Martin is on the phone and interested in buying it."

Sal's eyes widened. The story of the Porcu family at the end of SP29 was a tale spun right out of the movies in Rome.

"Francesca Porcu?"

"Olivia Francesca Porcu Martin. Please, Sal, she's calling from America."

"Okay, but no one else. I need time to sort these requests out."

Angelica scurried to her desk. "Hello? Thank you for waiting,

Signorina Martin. I will connect you with *il sindaco* now." Angelica pushed the connect button and heard the telephone in the mayor's office ring. *Just a matter of time now.*

~ * ~

Olivia spent most of the evening researching Sardinia and the surrounding islands. She knew her heritage included Italian, as her grandmother spoke the language to her during childhood. In fact, when she started school at five, her mother, Anya Martin, was quite irritated at having to reteach her daughter English. It was the incident that pushed her to restrict Olivia's visits to her Nonna.

Pictures of the island pulled at Olivia's sense of adventure. She was not tethered to the Northwest. Her one act of rebelliousness was to leave New York and move to the West Coast for college. The move proved prophetic for her life. Graduating summa cum laude from Stanford, Olivia accepted a position with a financial agency in Portland, Oregon. Her professional life was a roaring success. The only fly in the ointment was when she'd tried a relationship once and still smarted from the fallout. *Nope. Not for me.* Why shouldn't she move to Sardinia? She'd wisely invested funds set aside from her checks and didn't need to work. A villa, albeit small, on an Italian island in the Mediterranean? What was not to like?

Livy set her sights on the two-story building. She quickly figured the time difference and set her alarm to call as early in their morning as she could. By the end of this week, she was going to be the proud owner of a home in Sardinia. She could only hope it wasn't just a pile of rocks.

The following day, Olivia made the call to the Mayor's office in Ollolai. It was listed as the contact point. She spoke with a very nice lady who put her through to the man himself.

"This is Salvatore Lucchesia. To whom am I speaking?"

Livy had to stifle a giggle. He was not comfortable speaking English as was evident by his stilted, proper use. She figured she would try her Italian, as rusty as it was, and see how far she could get. "Yes, Mr. Mayor. I hope you will bear with my feeble attempts at Italian."

"That's not Italian."

Oh, no. Here it comes.

"You are speaking Sardinian. If I had any doubt as to your identity, this has wiped away all my hesitations."

"Sardinian? But, how…?" Livy was confused.

"You must have a family member who was Sardinian." the mayor commented.

"I'm not sure about Sardinian, but my Nonna said she was Italian. She's the one who taught me to speak this language."

Salvatore knew the tale of the lost love was true. "I must say, you do the language proud. How might I be of assistance?"

Livy barreled forward. "I'm very interested in the property you list at the end of SP29. I'd like to put a bid on it."

"Okay. You do understand you must sign paperwork that obligates you to make the property livable within three years? After that time, if you wish to sell, you may, but we will need an affidavit stating your intentions."

Olivia smiled. "Of course, sir. I have no intention of selling should I get this property. I'm moving and staying. I was under the impression that was your purpose in selling these homes."

"Si. We welcome new people to our community and hope they will bring or start families here. I believe you have the attitude we want in Ollolai. Once I have the signed paperwork, and your one Euro, I'll take the picture from our website."

"Great. Please send the paperwork to my fax number, 1-503-222-4141. I'll sign it, fax it back, and send a payment to the bank. I'll need to set up an account if I'm going to live there, anyway. Will that work?"

Salvatore finished writing the number on his notepad. "Yes. The paperwork will be in Italian. Do you have resources to have it translated?"

"I'll find a way. Thank you for your time. I hope we meet soon. *Ciao.*"

"*Ciao*, Signorina Porcu Martin."

The fax machine Olivia used as part of her computer started beeping and spitting out paper. *They are fast. I just hope everything else will go as quickly.*

Chapter Three

Olivia tucked the last personal item into her briefcase and snapped the lid shut. *There.* There was little to indicate this office belonged to anyone.

"Olivia?" Taylor poked her head in the doorway. "Where are your personal things? Pictures, plants, all the little do-dads you used to have here?"

Olivia thought about lying but why? Taylor was a friend, a good one at that, and she deserved to know the truth. "My last day is Friday."

"What? Where are you going? Did you finally start the company you were planning?"

Livy put up a hand to stop the deluge of questions. "First…no, I didn't start a company—yet. Second, I'm leaving the country and moving to Sardinia."

Taylor, her mouth slightly opened, stood, disbelief on her face. "I guess congratulations are in order."

Livy could see Tay was struggling to wrap her mind around something. "Tay? What's the problem?"

Tears threated to cascade down Tay's cheeks. "What am I going to do? You're the only one who has even a small clue as to what I'm dealing with; the only one I trust enough to tell the truth to. If you move to another country, I'll have no one!"

Olivia looked at the waterlogged eyes. "Taylor? It's the 21st century. We can email, text or call each other. Distance can't break our friendship. You will always have a place to stay, or live if you want. I've seen the pictures of the place I've bought…"

Taylor's eyes widened. "Bought?"

"Yes, bought. Anyway, there is enough room for plenty of guests." Livy's face brightened. "A bed and breakfast. Yes!"

"Bed and breakfast?"

Livy sat at the computer and pulled up the pictures of the home she owned in Ollolai. "See? Plenty of room." She smiled.

Taylor lifted a brow. "Sure, if you're into camping. What in the world have you done?"

Olivia leaned against the back of her chair. She waved her hand at the seat opposite. "Have a sit down. This is going to take more than five minutes."

Tay sat and waited for the story to begin.

"It's been about a month now since I started down this path…"

Half an hour later, Taylor had all the details of Olivia's new adventure. "What I would give to be able to go with you."

"The invitation is always open. You can stay a day, a year or to the end of your life. I'd love to have you close. But I know you have an agenda of your own. I hope it works to your favor."

"I've taken steps to start the process. We'll see how well the system in place works."

Chapter Four

Clusters of thoughts crowded Olivia's brain clouding her insight to the hovering presence to her right. When she tried to move that direction, a wall of humanity stopped her motion. Returning to her situation of the moment, she turned to stare at the impediment. "Excuse me?"

She stared at a face she'd not seen in several months. "Brian. How?"

"Were you really going to leave town without telling me?" His blue eyes appeared so earnest she almost believed him. Then she remembered to whom she spoke.

"I was under the distinct impression you didn't care and, frankly, I don't give a damn whether you know or not. You closed the door on—us—several months ago."

"Wow. You're going all *Gone with the Wind* on me. I've come to my senses and thought maybe…"

"Don't think. Don't what if, if only, or all the things you suspect will work to sway me right this moment." She pushed past him. "I'm leaving the Northwest. Goodbye, Brian." Olivia bolted to the gate for the pre-flight security dance. *If that jerk made me miss my plane, I swear, I'll kill him.* She arrived at the waiting area noting she had twenty minutes to spare. After checking in with the airline personnel, she sat watching the tarmac and planes ferry people in and out of the Portland airport. There were things she'd miss about Oregon, but Brian Froeschner was not one of them.

The only time she'd taken down her self-imposed, emotional wall, the guy turned out to be a philandering letch. She'd tired of feeling as though she were an observer in her own life. His ministrations to con her into thinking he was interested in her while he was trying to mine her for financial, i.e. insider information, to plump his portfolio wore her out. Early in the relationship after yet another lunch spent pretending he wasn't ogling every female in the place, Olivia decided to end the charade.

"Brian, I think we need to end this, this whatever it is, we have. You aren't interested in me, and it's painfully obvious to everyone in the room; including me. Don't call again."

She got up and left him, mouth gaping. Stepping into the mist of a winter's day, Livy reveled in the sensation of sunshine. She hadn't realized the weight of the deception he was attempting to pull off was so heavy. She smiled at a passerby and hummed all the way back to the office, pulling his file, and trading portfolios with Liam, a burly Rugby player and fellow broker, for a sedate, retired couple only interested in *safe* stocks.

He swept into her office around two the same afternoon, bearing a single red rose and the specialty coffee she liked so well. Accepting the coffee, she directed him down the hall, commenting that Liam would love the rose. Later, Liam would ask why she was willing to give up such a lucrative client. Her mumbled comment spoke to downsizing her risk factors. She asked him to inform her when the client was to be in the office for a conference. It was pure coincidence her outside appointments seemed to coincide with these visits.

Livy sighed. "And that's why I have no use for romance or men in my life."

When her flight was announced over the speaker, Olivia Martin stoically marched down the boarding corridor to one of the planes flying her *home*. Taking her seat in business class, she tucked her purse beneath her feet, having stowed her carryon overhead. She allowed the muscles of her neck to loosen.

"Ma'am?" The attendant gently touched her arm. "You need to bring your seat back fully upright and buckle up. Once we reach altitude, the lights will go off and you can relax."

There was a sudden kerfluffle at the entry door. The voice of an excited female was speaking rapidly, met by a response, presumably from the attendant, which seemed to calm the late passenger. The routine for departure from PDX continued, albeit a few minutes late.

Now what? Olivia felt annoyance starting to build behind her eyes. *Just chill. You have all the time in the world.* When the attendant escorted the person toward Olivia's row, she cringed and turned her gaze to outside the window. The last thing she needed on a long flight was some over-apologetic person babbling away.

The soul sat next to her, placing an item beneath the seat, and buckled in as instructed. Olivia continued to stare at the scenery until she heard the engines ramp up. A bumping motion let the passengers know they were rolling away from the terminal. She watched rainbows created by moments of sunshine through summer showers. Her departure was bittersweet. Portland had been good to her, but the time had arrived for Olivia Francesca Porcu Martin to start living. Imagining sunshine and the dulcet sounds of oak trees whispering in warm Mediterranean breezes helped her settle for the flight to a new life.

"Is the invitation to stay at your new home still open?" The familiar voice jolted Livy from her reverie.

"Tay! You made it!"

"I thought about it and decided there was no time like the present to get myself together. I hope you meant what you said about me staying with you."

"Of course, but right now, the place is in dire need of repairs. You're welcome to share my hotel while I work to make a part of the house livable."

"I may take you up on that if they don't have any rooms open. In the meantime, I think we might consider napping a bit. It's going to be a long few flights."

Olivia and Taylor waited until the seat belt sign was turned off. They swapped ideas on the future of Livy's new home and giggled with excitement over their adventure. When they stretched out their seats, both quickly dropped into a light slumber.

~ * ~

The flights were uneventful, thankfully, and Olivia was glad Taylor decided to accompany her on this journey. Customs, luggage, and car rental moved along without a hitch. Tay opted to rent a vehicle for herself to explore on her own while Olivia was dealing with the business of hiring a construction company to begin repairs on her home. Driving along the west coast of the island from Alghero Airport toward her destination, Olivia observed the landscape change from commercial tourist to local inhabitant. The more local-inhabitant towns and farms she witnessed, the more she felt her body relax. This was better than she hoped. She opted to turn off the air conditioning and roll down the car window to experience the island in all its glory.

Salt air and petrol fumes were replaced by the aroma of green; green fields of hay, grapes for wine, and vegetables. The animal farms provided their own essence depending on the livestock. She continued to check the rearview mirror, keeping Taylor's little Fiat in her sights, when she realized her driving speed had slowed compared to her habit in the States. Why not? She wasn't in a hurry to get anywhere fast. Turning into the driveway of the inn where she was staying until the home was finished, Olivia parked her rented vehicle then checked in.

Taylor parked next to Olivia and followed her into the reception area. She was in luck. There was a room available two doors down from Olivia's. Taylor paid for a week in advance. She'd decide at that time if she were going to stay longer.

The pair grabbed their keys and headed in the direction of their rooms.

"Meet me in the bar for a glass of wine?" Olivia stopped at her door.

"Half an hour?" Taylor set her suitcase on the sidewalk.

"Sounds good to me. I'll see you there." Olivia opened her door, and situating her belongings, changed to a comfortable pair of jeans, t-shirt, and sandals. Realizing the half hour was nearly up, she stepped outside her room and waited for Taylor.

The pair meandered to the small restaurant and ordered glasses of the local alcoholic delicacy, slipping to the outside patio to enjoy the evening. The air whispered of new beginnings. Warblers darted around the sky chatting and bringing a happy end to a long journey.

I've come home. Olivia sighed and took a sip of the local wine. The fear she'd carried since making this decision evaporated into the cooling night air. She looked at her friend. "Tomorrow, Ollolai."

Taylor took a sip of the wine and allowed the liquid to soothe her soul. "Yes."

Chapter Five

The day dawned with an azure sky teasing voluminous white clouds from the horizon. Olivia opened the drapes to take in the view. She wanted to smell the air and feel sun on her face, so she opted to have her breakfast on the restaurant's veranda. The service was quick, and the hotel guests appeared caught up in plans to explore the island, leaving her to her thoughts. She'd opted to allow Taylor to sleep this morning and would check on her before leaving. After all, this was her home and her journey of discovery. Taylor was here to relax and try to recover from the situation back in Portland.

"Thanks for not waking me up, friend." Taylor sat at the table.

"I thought you might enjoy exploring a little. After all, this house stuff is my thing and, from what I hear around me, there is a lot to do on this island."

Taylor chuckled. "I won't do anything until I get some coffee." Magically, a full cup of coffee appeared before her. She looked up into a pair of dark brown eyes smiling her direction.

"*Buon giorno, signorina.*" He whisked away only to return with a menu. "When you are ready." And off he went.

"Wow. They are amazing here." Taylor scanned the items and made her decision. As the menu touched the table, the waiter was at her elbow.

"What may I bring you?" His eyes twinkled and a warm smile lit up his face.

Taylor ordered her meal and sat drinking her coffee. "Livy?"

"Hmm?"

"I think I'd like to go to the beach and walk on the sand, maybe

145

do a bit of sailing. The wind on my cheeks and sun in my eyes will help clear my head. I hope you don't mind."

"No. Just make sure you take your phone. That way if anything happens you can contact me. Okay? Safety, girlfriend, safety."

"You got it." Taylor's food arrived and silence descended on the table as the pair were lost in their thoughts.

When they finished, paid the bill and headed back to their rooms, the girls ran over the schedules they hoped to keep on this day, promising to check in often. They hugged and headed their separate directions.

Olivia had only one discovery in mind—her home. After checking at the front desk to verify the route into Ollolai, she started the journey to her new incarnation. She was in no hurry to arrive at the town center, but the trip was less than a mile from her hotel. She cruised the narrow streets at a respectful speed and, quickly, located a parking spot at the town square.

Strolling along the avenue, she passed a couple restaurants emitting the most enticing aromas. Somewhere close by was a bakery. The fragrance of freshly baked bread was making her mouth water. *Living here could be dangerous to my waistline. Maybe it's best that I don't cook.* She checked her map, noting the *Uficio Postale*, post office, and realizing the city hall was a few steps away.

She entered city hall. The building, while new-ish, still smelled of history and stories yet to be told.

"*Si. Come posso aiutarvi?*"

"*Parli iglesi?*"

"A little." The dark-haired woman behind the desk leaned back in her chair. "What do you wish?"

"My name is Olivia Francesca Porcu Martin. I believe there are some papers I still need to sign to get my home? And I need directions."

"*Oh, si, si. Un atimo.*"

The woman left the room, returning with a manila file folder and a pen. She put the folder on the desk and motioned to Olivia to have a seat. "I will need you to sign, here," she pointed to a spot on the official document, "and here. Then I will provide you the keys to your home and a map."

Livy looked at the document. "May I have a copy?"

"*Naturalmente.*"

She signed in the spots indicated and put the pen on the desk. "I don't know why I'm being so OCD." The woman stifled a giggle. "I mean, I'm not planning on going anywhere and everyone will know where I live. *Siamo spiacenti.*"

"My name is Angelica Porcu. We are distant cousins, so, *si*, I will know where you live. Allow me to make a copy for you. I'll bring it back along with the key and address of your home. I can give you clear directions to get there. Any other *informazioni* you require I'll be able to provide if you call."

Angelica returned with a manila envelope bulging with documents and a very old iron key, then walked Olivia to the sidewalk. She pointed west and provided Olivia with detailed instructions on how to travel the quarter mile to her home.

Olivia turned to her distant cousin. "*Grazie.*"

"Welcome home, Olivia Porcu."

Livy waved and, wearing a large grin, went back to her vehicle to find her home. The directions she'd been given were spot on. She realized once she drove up the earthen driveway that walking might have been faster. A nervous giggle escaped her. All her worries evaporated the moment she set eyes on the home. It was not a mansion but not a ruin, either. The walls still stood and, apparently, the doors and windows were intact, but all she could see was the front of the building and property. The lot butted up to a small hill at the end of SP29. Far enough from town to be private but close enough to walk, if necessary. From the looks of the surrounding area, she would probably be able to get cell service.

"Olivia Francesca Porcu Martin, get your butt out of this vehicle and inspect the area, you ninny. You can speculate until your brain blows up. Feet on the ground will verify what and how much needs work."

She got out of the car and walked to the front of the building. She noted that, unlike most of the homes in town, this house sported a porch on the front. *Unusual.* The other buildings in town abutted the narrow lanes. She only noticed balconies on the second floors which made sense if you took into consideration the front of the home was right on the busy street. Olivia tried the door and felt chagrined when it was locked. She pulled out the key she'd been given and used it.

"Surprise! It works." A quick survey of the rooms before her showed a simple layout. Immediately in front of her was the area she presumed to be the living room. A stone fireplace took up one wall. The rocks were local and probably had been taken from the very lot where the house was built. At one time, the interior had been whitewashed, but time and neglect left everything in a layer of fine dust. She could see where pictures had been placed on the walls and there were still a few tattered rugs on the floor beneath a layer of dirt. Scuff marks indicated furnishings had been sparse. When she thought on it, the last inhabitant of this place had been here until about 1955; nearly three quarters of a century ago.

A double doorway opened into the kitchen and dining area. Unlike the states, there were no built-in cupboards. However, a hand carved hutch was pushed against the wall. She could see where the pots had been hanging near a wood stove—a real stove using wood for cooking and heat. *Well there's the first expense.* About three feet to the left of the stove stood a square box with two handles. *Oh, a small cupboard.* She opened one of the doors. "I don't believe it. A refrigerator. Good lord, it must be nearly a hundred years old. I wonder if it works."

Only time and better wiring would tell. Livy found a staircase at the end of one wall in the kitchen and took it to the second floor. She drifted through bedrooms, one bathroom, and a water closet, taking pictures on her phone for reference. *That's going to have to change. Especially if I want to have a B & B.* She took in plumbing done in the twenties and thirties as well as wiring of about the same era. Everywhere she looked the euros added up. *Oh, well. I couldn't buy a modular back in the states for what it will cost to get this place into living order.* She descended the stairs and walked to the counter. Over the large sink was a window. Surprisingly, the glass was still in place. Livy peered into the back area noting a three-sided wooden shed. She was only guessing but thought the family might have had sheep, chickens or, in this area, donkeys. After all, Sardinians, her people, were very self-sufficient. They'd lived on the island since the Neolithic age. With all the pictures she needed of each room, Olivia left the house, locking the front door, and stood on the porch gazing at the surrounding hills. The scent of Mediterranean scrub brush and a hint of oak filtered by on the breeze.

"I need to eat. I'm starved. I haven't heard from Taylor yet. That worries me. I hope she just lost track of time… Maybe, I'll call after I order dinner to see where she is." She took the few steps off the portico and got into her rental. A garage was going to be a necessity too. What she thought was a garage had been nothing more than a storage shed off the kitchen. *Phew. More money.* Starting the engine, Olivia put the car in gear and headed back to her current lodgings.

"I only hope it doesn't take three years to finish the job."

Chapter Six

Olivia tapped a finger on the windowsill. "Come on, Taylor, pick up the phone. Where the hell *are* you?" She'd dialed the number from her table at dinner, but the call went to voice mail. She was trying again this morning. If she didn't get any answer, her next stop before going to her house would be the mayor's office in Ollolai to make a missing person's report. Okay, maybe she was overreacting, but Taylor was her friend. News reports from the last couple years weren't encouraging for single American women in foreign countries.

This was unlike her. A quick trip to the front desk to ask them to do a welfare check had proven her clothing was just the way it had been when she left yesterday. The bed had not been slept in.

Livy's stomach soured. "Oh, god! What have I done to my friend?"

She drove directly to the town center and the mayor's office. She opened the door to the office, finding Angelica at her desk.

"Good morning, cousin. What can I do for you today?" Angelica smiled.

Olivia wrung her hands. "My friend, Taylor Maxwell, decided to take a vacation here. I offered her a place to stay, and she took the offer. Yesterday, when I first came here, she opted to do some sightseeing while I checked out the house. I haven't seen her since around nine in the morning when we went our separate ways." Olivia put up a hand before Angelica could say anything. "She is not the type of person to go off with some handsome lothario and party the night away. She is engaged and waiting for her fiancé to return from—the war zone. I'm very worried. What do I need to do to file a missing person report?"

Angelica thought and pulled open a drawer. "Let's start here with this paperwork. I'll do some investigating and contact the American consulate. Just leave your number with me, and we'll do all we can to try to find your friend." She hesitated for a moment. "It's what families do for each other; even, distant cousins."

They sat and completed a mountain of paperwork with Olivia filling in as much information as she could remember. When she walked out of the mayor's office two hours later, her stomach hurt as well as her heart. At this point, she needed to stay positive.

Chapter Seven

Lightning slashed across the sky and thunder drummed in Destiny's ears. The strange vessel began to turn on its axis, swirling faster with each passing second. Destiny lost her balance. Her head hit the floor hard. She heard the crack then nothing more except roaring in her ears.

When she opened her eyes, sunshine filled the tiny cabin. She pressed her hands to her temples trying to ease the pain throbbing through her head. Slowly, she found her way to the deck.

The sky was a vivid blue with a few clouds lying close to the horizon, Reid's ship was nowhere to be seen, although the sailboat sat in the same cove. She didn't know how to sail a boat; didn't have any idea how to get to land. Would Reid sail without her? Good Lord, she hoped not. She'd have to find another job, and she'd have to find another man she could trust.

A boat passed by, and she waved at it, hoping someone would rescue her. It came about and headed back her direction. Watching the craft come closer, she held her breath, praying for her safety.

"Can we help?" someone from the vessel asked as it pulled up close. "You look stranded."

"I'm lost. Yes, stranded," Destiny admitted, shrugging her shoulders as she tried to assess this man who seemed to be offering aid. "Can you take me somewhere close by?" While she'd made several trips with Captain Stewart, she'd never been on the land, never left the boat. She had no idea what this island had to offer.

"Where are we?"

"Sardinia. I'll take you to Ollolai. That's where I'm staying. You know anybody there?"

"No," she was shaking her head and wondering what she would do to survive. "I can cook. Does anyone need a cook?"

The man chuckled. "I've heard another guest at the hotel mentioning her need. Climb aboard."

~ * ~

Destiny Rose groaned. "Where the hell am I?" Her head pounded and, she surmised, she must have hit it on one of the many rocks covering the interior of this—what the hell was this anyway? She must be in a newer century than the last. Her head throbbed and she placed a hand on the back of her head, flinching at the pain. Oh, right. Boat, water, storm, floor. And a rescuer, not a pirate, assisting her to the shore. How the heck did she get from the coast to this, thing?

She could only bide her time, of which she had plenty, to discover her final destination. A jet keened overhead giving her the hope this was the 20th century. *Well, of course it must be, you ninny. You were brought to the center of town in a motorized vehicle. I must have walked here. But why?* She tested her limbs by stretching; waiting for the inevitable pain of something broken and was pleased to find her parts in good working order. She sat up and observed the three-sided structure. "Hmmm. Manger? Could have been much worse. I've a covered refuge, for now. This will give me time to explore where the fates have landed me."

Cloaking herself in a cover of wariness, she peeked around the corner of the stone shed. The small out-building was placed at the back of a home two-stories in size and encompassing some area. She noted a path leading around the side. If the shed where she currently stood was a home for animals, they'd been gone for a long time. No fresh hay or *presents* littered the rocky ground. She listened carefully but detected little movement in the surrounding hills. *The area is not heavily peopled.*

A movement caught her attention. She noted a face appear in one of the windows on the ground floor. Destiny pulled back into the shed. She stilled her pounding heartbeat, afraid the soul inside the building would hear and chase her away. *Don't be such a ninny.* Subterfuge was not her strong point. *Doesn't need to be.* Standing against the back wall, she was sweating profusely. Her 19th century clothing was hot, scratchy and, with the help of a gentle breeze, alerted her to the smell of brine and oily cooking clinging to her person. *Fates be cursed, I need a bath.* An abode with four walls and water close by would be deeply welcomed. There may not be creatures seeking her for a midnight dinner, but she wasn't about to tempt the fates any more than necessary.

A motorized sound reached her ears followed by crunching fading into the distance. Hope she might explore the bigger structure blossomed. A familiar tickle spread across her scalp. This had to be her new assignment. Destiny scratched her head then stepped into the open. No sounds assaulted her ears. The person inside the structure must have left. Marks about the size of a supply wagon showed a vehicle moving toward a faint line down the hill, which must be a road.

She inched her way across the back of the house checking each point of entry. Window—no, unable to open. Second window—same result. Bloody hell, was she going to have to stay in that little...place tonight? Not the optimal choice. She sighed and pulled up tall. One more window. Pulling on the bottom of the frame resulted in movement. The squeal of swollen wood on swollen wood caused her ears to ache. In one quick movement, she pulled up, swung over the frame and landed on smooth stones.

Sliding down the sturdy wall, she blew out a breath. Allowing the span of a few minutes to pass in which she steadied her pounding heart, Destiny stood and closed the window. Pulling *in* the frame didn't seem to have the same effect. No screeching. Now to do a quick surveillance of the property. She poked her head into an area she presumed to be the sitting room. Down a long hallway to a sleeping room on the first floor complete with a bathing room. *Thank goodness.*

She peered around for a bucket to fill the white horse trough she thought must be for said purpose. There were some fancy knobs on one side. Her curiosity pushed her to twist them. Nothing. *Well, what are they for then?* There must be a well close by. Opposite the horse trough was a funny looking chair. Destiny was puzzled by this bit of furniture. It didn't face a mirror but the trough. *Why would people wish to place a chair in that spot? Bugger.* There was so much catching up she needed to do before the end of the week. The sands of time were slipping through her fingers. She had the sensation this task wasn't meant to be but a brief interlude into the life of the assigned.

She poked around some of the other rooms on the first floor. A quick jaunt up the stairs and a brief inventory of the remaining rooms, including another bathing room with the same weird set up of funny chair facing a horse trough. *Why would people bring their horses up to the second floor and watch them drink? Were they that valuable?* All the exploration in a house covered in decades of dust and dirt was taking its toll on Destiny. Trudging down the stairs to the first floor, she decided if she was going to stay here for the night, it might prove to her advantage to stay near the ground. Recovery would be easier with bumps and bruises as opposed to broken bones should she need to leave in a hurry. Traveling back to the kitchen, she spotted a narrow door at one end of the room. Opening the closure proved to expose storage for cleaning equipment. Thank goodness the broom appeared to be the same, whatever time this was. She grabbed the tool and determined she'd pick one of the rooms and give it a dust up.

The chamber, second opening off the hallway, was her choice for tonight's slumber. She couldn't recall peering inside this door. The window beckoned. She jimmied it open to allow fresh, cool air to enter and escort some of the dust motes to the exterior of the house. Using skills she'd been called upon to employ at her last location, Destiny dry-swabbed the floor with the broom. The center of the room was covered with a patterned carpet. Once she shuttled the dirt into the hall, she turned to view her chosen sleeping chamber. The sun shone on a carpet of such quality Destiny gasped. She dropped to her knees, ignoring the fine dust marking her dark britches. Gently, reverently, she reached out her hand and caressed the quality fabric. The weaving was the finest she could recall seeing—ever. Much as she hated to admit it, the finished product rivaled her own. This night she would experience the pride of Sardinia. Maybe a good night's rest might help her come up with a plan to help this assignment—person. She really was going to have to speak to the boss about a vacation. Too many assignments in too short of a time were dulling her ability to relate to them as people.

Twinges slicing through her forehead drew a moan from the traveler. "Not now. I don't have time for this." The warning was a precursor to a raging headache rivaling a drunk's hangover. It was her recompense for time travel. *Bed. Sleep will chase away the demon.* Destiny lay on the magnificent carpet and easily slid into a deep slumber.

Chapter Eight

A night of rest knowing there was a roof over your head and enough barriers to discourage an attacker helped Destiny's plan drop into place. Upon opening her eyes in the morning, she noticed a rucksack next to her makeshift bed. She opened the bag to find a treasure trove of items to assist her with this assignment. A small blue booklet with a fair resemblance to herself sported several official seals from different locations about the globe. A booklet with papers held together by a curved wire had a title of *Research* handprinted on the front. Once she opened the cover, she read a few lines and realized the information was about the Nuragic structures of settlers living in the area three thousand years ago and still standing today. In writing visible only to her dream weaver eyes, she noted her cover story was she was a student studying the ruins for a degree in Archeology, specifically ancient weaving.

The last items placed in her bag appeared to be clothing of the current era. Items she recognized her rescuer wearing. An instruction sheet was included giving her the accepted way to wear the articles. She quickly stripped out of her 19th century wear and into the new clothes. She quite liked the pants; they were comfortable, sturdy, and covered her entire legs. The shoes were a tad confusing, but once she mastered the short stockings, she realized these foot coverings were going to provide her more flexibility than the oversized boots she'd grown accustomed to wearing. Rays of warm sunlight brightened the room.

Destiny hastened her movement. She quickly repacked the rucksack and made her way to the kitchen area. Lifting and pushing out the window, she peered out as far as possible to ascertain if others were close by. A relieved sigh slipped past her lips on discovering she was alone. The rucksack dropped to the ground followed by her body. She closed the window and scooted along the side of the house to the front corner. Her plan was to wait on the front steps until the owner returned. She was certain once she spotted the assignment—owner—what she was to do would be obvious. Covertly she made her way to the steps of the home, pulling out her booklet to read the material within the covers. Best to know what she was supposed to be studying.

The crunch of vehicle wheels coming up the drive alerted her to the arrival of her latest dreamer. She faced a 20th century vehicle similar to the one driven by her rescuer. *Thank goodness. Maybe, they'll be able to find where to pump the water.* She was in sore need of bathing. The vehicle slowed; the occupant not exiting nor turning off the motor. Destiny resisted the urge to look up wondering why the driver hesitated. She concentrated on the book but opted to change her tactic. Looking up, she smiled. The simple act seemed to work. She heard the click and watched as the door opened and the driver exited. The young female approached Destiny.

"Can I help you?"

Not British or Sardinian. Maybe American? "Morning, Miss. The lady at the mayor's office said I might be able to find temporary work and, maybe, lodging here."

Olivia allowed a frown to cover her face. She wasn't accustomed to people knowing her business. *Hold it. Small town. Everyone knows everyone else's business. Get used to it or go back to the states.* "What are you looking to do?"

"Whatever needs doing, Miss. I've picked up a great many skills on my travels."

"You're British?"

"Yes, ma'am. I'm taking a year sabbatical from Oxford to get in some field study to do research for my Masters' thesis on ancient civilizations. One of the oldest civilizations was from this particular area of the Mediterranean."

"Really? I didn't know." Olivia was warming to this brave traveler. "I'm afraid I haven't much work in the way of housekeeping or the like. I'm sure you can see my residence is in dire need of repair.

Maybe the hotel where I'm staying will have an opening."

Destiny could feel the situation slipping from her control. "Beg pardon, Miss?"

"Oh, sorry. Olivia Martin."

"Destiny Rose."

"What a beautiful name."

"Thank you. Will you be making repairs to your home?"

Olivia puffed out a breath. "Yes, but I'm feeling a bit overwhelmed. While I have a reasonably long amount of time to complete the repairs, I want to live in my home as soon as possible. It will save money that I can invest back into my house. I just don't know where to start."

Destiny knew she had to tread lightly here. "What if I act as a watch guard? You can feel certain your home will be protected, and I'll be able to study without worrying about my budget being broken. Inns are nice but can be very noisy if one wants to concentrate. I can swing a hammer with the best of them. I would just need some floor space to sleep and study. I'm capable of cooking my own meals."

Olivia's eyes lit up. "You cook?"

"Fairly well, if I say so myself."

Livy worried her bottom lip. "Okay. But if I feel the least bit threatened or sense things are not as they should be, I have no problem calling the *Polizi* to come haul you away and lock you up."

Destiny slowly released a breath she'd been holding. "As my Aussie roommate at Oxford would say, fair dinkum."

The two shook hands. Destiny followed Olivia through the front door. Something about the young lady tugged at Destiny's memory. Maybe it was her voice or the hazel eyes, she wasn't sure. She knew, eventually, whatever was triggering her memory would come forward.

Olivia stopped suddenly, only moving when Destiny bumped into her. "Someone has been in the house." There was no question; it was a statement full of consternation and concern.

Destiny ventured to ask. "How can you tell?"

Livy turned toward Destiny and slowly raised a brow. "The air in this room doesn't smell sixty years old. Someone has come in and aired out the place or *Le Janas* [faeries] have invaded my home thinking it completely abandoned." She crossed her arms, eyes narrowing.

Destiny swallowed hard. "I, uh, I, uh, oh, bloody hell. It was me. I found a way through the kitchen window and stayed in one of the ground floor rooms. I wanted to find a way to thank the owner."

Olivia continued to stare at Destiny, letting her squirm beneath her glare. "Thank you. Don't you have any lodging set up?"

Panic crawled up Destiny's throat. She had the good sense to blush. "I'm studying the Nuragic ruins in the area and got so caught up in the amazing architecture, I lost track of time. Sunset was quickly darkening the area, and this was the closest dwelling. I didn't wish to sleep in the donkey shed for fear of wild animals. I'm really sorry." She lowered her eyes and affected a sorrowful expression.

Olivia wasn't sure if she wanted to believe this young student or not. She'd been honest enough to wait out front but neglected to mention her stay the previous night. "As I said, if I don't feel comfortable or suspect any felonious actions on your part, I've no hesitation to so what is necessary to keep my home and myself safe. Are we clear?"

"Yes."

"Good. Do you want to stay at the house while you complete your research?"

"If you will allow me to."

"Yes. A presence in the home might deter unwanted visitors of the two-legged and four-legged kind. As far as the crawly, slithery type? You're on your own."

"Thanks."

Olivia pulled a notebook from her bag along with a tape measure. "Destiny? May I ask you to help me get measurements?"

"Of course." She placed her rucksack on the floor in the kitchen area.

Livy sniffed the air and wrinkled her nose. "It smells like dead fish in here. That odor wasn't here yesterday. I would've remembered."

Destiny straightened up. "I'm sorry. It must be my clothing. I've been so busy researching and writing, I've reverted to an older era for cleaning. I find the nearest natural water and go in with all my clothing on. The last time was on one of the local beaches. I didn't realize it would smell."

"Uhm, okay." Olivia found the idea very strange. Her schooling had been in Finance, not Archeology involving field work. "When we finish here, we can take your stuff to the local laundromat and give it a good cleaning."

Panic flooded Destiny's chest. Her 19th century clothing would not hold up well to the modern-day cleaners. "As you wish. You're the boss."

"Lord, *please*. Don't all me that. I'm just Olivia or Livy."

"Of course."

For the next hour and a half, the two women measured all the windows, floor space, and pretty much anything not moving fast enough. When Olivia mentioned burning the carpet from the room where Destiny spent the night, she turned, horror showing on her face.

"Please don't do that. Allow me to do my best to clean it. Sardinian carpets are rated in the same class as Persian carpets."

Livy looked skeptical. "Right…"

Destiny cleared her throat. "You have found me out."

Olivia waited.

"My bachelor's is in Archeology. I'm researching my master's in ancient textiles, weaving specifically."

"You weave?"

"Uhm, yes. Why?"

Livy's face lit up. "I have something to show you." She bustled down the hallway to beneath the stairs, waiting for the college student to follow. Once Destiny arrived next to Livy, she opened a door built seamlessly into the stairwell, exposing descending steps. Her last visit had revealed this entry. She'd leaned against what she thought was solid, only to experience a cool breeze tickling her ankles. A gentle push on the wall, and the hidden door opened. Venturing as far as the light would allow, she glimpsed the large item languishing in the corner venturing a guess as to the item's purpose. Turning on a torch, Destiny couldn't remember her having, Livy gingerly took the steps to the bottom. She shined the light around a stone walled cellar, stopping on a large item in the corner wearing a cloak of spider webs and years of dust. "Is this what I think?"

Destiny felt the flush of her skin from head to toes. She walked to the wooden loom and touched one side. The machine was made from the local oak trees and expertly carved. Even with the dust of decades, the parts glowed with warmth. The shuttle hung from a post. She ventured closer to look at the surface worn smooth by the diligent hands of many weavers.

"This is a magnificent work of art. Do you know how to weave?" She turned to face Olivia.

Livy shook her head. "I'm afraid that skill died when my grandmother left Italy."

A tug of memory struck the weaver. *That's it. This is the completing of this family's circle.* She realized she'd been here previously. She was the weaver who'd fulfilled the wish of a young Sardinian girl to leave an island steeped in sorrow. She turned and grasped the fine wood. Memories roared at her, overwhelming and filling in the gaps.

Olivia watched as Destiny's eyes rolled back in her head. She emitted a groan and slumped to the ground. Olivia panicked. *What now?* She sprinted across the room, leaning down to feel for a pulse. The girl's skin was clammy and cool to the touch. *I wonder when was the last time she ate?*

"What happened?"

Olivia jumped then offered a hand to Destiny, allowing her to sit. "I don't know. You touched the loom, groaned, and, well, passed out. Have you eaten lately?"

"I don't recall. Blimey, but my head is swimming."

The women cautiously raised from the cool floor.

"I'll know where to go this afternoon when hell decides to open its doors."

"Wow. That's colorful." Olivia slipped her hand around Destiny's waist. "Time to put some food in your stomach."

"But there's no food in the house."

Livy encouraged Destiny up the stairs. "No, but there are several restaurants in town."

"But I smell!"

"You won't get an argument from me."

"Thanks."

"We'll find a way. Now out to the car with you."

Destiny struggled to reach the front porch. She dropped to the step and pulled deeply of the vanishing morning's air. Memories were returning with a vengeance. The horse trough was a bathtub and the funny chair, a toilet. This house, too, was coming back to her memory. There'd been wondrous times and heartache. When the young Francesca had lost her love to the fighting in North Africa during the second World War, she was gutted. No amount of ancient wisdom could begin to heal her heart. She pleaded with her mother to be sent to an aunt living in America, but Annemarie would not hear of it.

The great grandmother tightened the house rules and restricted Francesca's movements. In so doing, the inevitable occurred. Destiny was sent to keep the young woman from doing something completely rash.

Young Daniel Kilkenny was an honest, sweet man who wasn't looking to leave his mark on Europe. He was in Sardinia to do his duty to his country and return home in one piece—alive.

Destiny chuckled. Everyone knew when she stepped into the picture, all bets were off. The two young people met, fell in love, and as soon as Danny was able, he paid for Francesca to sail to New York. She willingly left knowing she would never see the island of Sardinia or her family again.

How ironic her granddaughter would return the family back to the island.

She realized she'd woven a tapestry for another pair of lovers but had to put it aside. The woman in the tapestry was born two centuries later than originally planned. Someone in the planning department had fallen asleep on that assignment. She thought she'd never hear the end it.

This time turbulence could put right what a clerical error had created.

Chapter Nine

Olivia locked the front door and spotted Destiny on the steps. "Why aren't you in the car?"

"I smell?"

"Oh, right. Come on." She helped her new resident up and guided her to the passenger side of the vehicle. Opening the door, she grabbed Destiny's rucksack. "I think it would be best to keep this in the trun…boot, for now. The smell won't be quite so overwhelming."

Destiny nodded and let go of the bag. She quickly surveyed the inside of this automobile. Changes made during the time she'd been elsewhere left her confused; almost as confused as she was the first time she'd seen a gas powered vehicle.

Olivia entered the driver's side and buckled her seat belt. "You too. This car doesn't move until everyone is belted in."

Destiny blanched. A belt for a seat? "I'm sorry. Back home I drive an old car that doesn't have—seat belts. Please show me?"

Livy leaned over Destiny and pulled the metal clasp attached to a—rifle strap—from the retainer across her body, snapping it closed in the silver buckle on her left. "Now we go." She put the auto into gear and the vehicle lurched forward. When she looked past Destiny to see if the road was clear to enter, she noted the young woman's face was devoid of all color. "You okay?"

"Uhm huh." A weak nod accompanied the answer.

"I called my, cousin, at city hall and asked for a recommendation of where to eat that might allow us to sit outside. She gave me the name of a couple pizzerias. Oh, and she told me where we can go to wash clothes. She's going to have the water turned on at the house, so we can do a more thorough cleaning." Livy looked at her passenger. "And be able to bathe."

Destiny's hands were grasped tightly on the seat edge. Absolute fear emitted from her body in waves.

"Are you scared?" Olivia's brow corrugated in concern.

Destiny cleared her throat. "These roads are so narrow. It gives me pause... and yes, scares me a bit."

"I'm driving the best I know how. Would you like to drive?"

"No, good heavens, no. I can honestly say I've not driven any of the new automobiles and don't wish to start now."

"I guess it's a good thing we're here then, right?" Livy parked the car in front of a building displaying a pizzeria sign.

Destiny hesitated.

"We'll go inside, decide what we want to eat, then go to the patio out back." Livy smiled. "Fair dinkum?"

"Fair dinkum."

The pair took a moment, once they were inside, to adjust to the darkened atmosphere. Destiny was slowly regaining her memory of the language but opted to allow Olivia to take the lead. *No sense in tipping my hand just yet.*

A medium sized, deep dish pizza pie was ordered with the local goat cheese for topping. They walked through the *ristorante* and out the back door, where the order would be delivered to them on the patio. A few folks sat at tables eating and conversing, but neither woman paid attention to them. Rumbling stomachs were demanding food.

Olivia felt the hair on the back of her neck prickle. *Someone is watching us.* She grabbed her mirrored sunglasses and slipped them on.

Destiny watched this action with interest. "I didn't think it was that bright in here."

"It's not. I just have the distinct feeling someone is watching us. Wearing these give me the advantage of being able to see without being seen."

Destiny shook her head. "I know we've just met, but...have you lost your mind?"

Olivia huffed. "Maybe, but I'd rather be safe with a plan of action than not."

Destiny took another bite of the warm pizza. It beat the heck out of hard tack or moldy bread. This assignment might not be so bad, after all.

~ * ~

"Oh, come on, Rafaele. She's a real beauty. Must be a tourist, cause I've never seen her in town before."

Rafaele Sonna grabbed the pepper flakes and liberally added them to his lunch. He concentrated on the food in front of him. His friend and co-worker, Paolo Manca was a notorious lady-killer always on the lookout for a new conquest. However, this girl he'd set his sights on must be something for Paolo to call her a beauty not a babe.

He raised his eyes above his food to sneak a peek. She was leaning over the table to grab something near her plate. She looked up right before donning a pair of mirrored glasses.

He stopped, mesmerized by the hazel eyes. Her clean hair bounced with energy. Something about her manner set her apart from the summer travelers who wandered through town on their various pilgrimages.

"Hot, right?"

Paolo's garlic breath blew across Rafaele's nose. He dropped his eyes to his dish again. There was so much to do to get ready for the Autumn festival. "Paolo, we don't have time for you to try putting another notch on your bedpost."

The man let loose a belch that shook the rafters. "Good pizza. Why not? If, as I suspect, she is a tourist, she'll be gone by the end of the week."

"You assume too much. If she's not a tourist, then what?"

Paolo shrugged his shoulders. "*E la vita?*"

The two men continued in this vein until they'd finished their lunch. They cleaned their table and left.

~ * ~

Destiny watched the soap opera unfold before her eyes. All the players in this drama had been introduced. It was now up to her to start the opening act.

"You've been rather quiet. Sorry if I snipped at you. Guess I was hungrier than I thought."

The dream weaver allowed silence to descend on the table. "Were you snippy? I didn't notice. I was too busy tucking in to this amazing food. Next a bath and getting my clothes clean."

Olivia eyed her with suspicion. "Uhm, right. I agree with you about the bath. I want to check back at the city hall to see if my," she used her fingers to make quote marks, "cousin can help me find a construction company. I hope they'll be able to get the house in living condition before winter hits. I've heard it snows sometimes."

Olivia and Destiny cleaned their table and left the pizzeria.

"The office is just down the street. Let's walk." Setting a brisk pace, Destiny found she was scurrying to keep up.

"What's your hurry?"

"Time is of the essence here."

"Amen."

"What?"

"Nothing."

Angelica expressed surprise at seeing Olivia so soon. "Maybe I should hire you to work here?"

The pair exchanged smiles. Olivia pulled out her phone. "Angelica, would you be able to direct me to a local contractor who is honest, reliable, and fairly priced? I know that is a lot to ask, but I have no idea where to start looking?"

Angelica pulled her round card file toward her and quickly rifled through the small cards. *"Ecco.* These guys are local. They work on all our town festival buildings and live in the district. Oh, when you contact Rafaele, have him call me."

"Thank you." Livy entered the information into her cell phone. She and Destiny turned to leave.

"Oh, yes. I wanted to let you know I contacted the American

Embassy to file a missing report on your friend. Also, the water company will be out in a couple days to hook up your pipes. The electric…" she shrugged her shoulders and held her hands palms up. "It might take a bit longer."

Olivia thanked her and herded Destiny outside.

Having done what she could for the time being, Livy decided she and Destiny would return to the hotel where she was temporarily staying. A shower and washing her clothes would be a priority for the traveler. "Let's go to my hotel. You can freshen up and wash your clothes while we set a plan in place."

"Sounds heavenly."

The pair climbed into Olivia's rental vehicle and made the brief journey to the hotel.

When Destiny had showered and cleaned her "modern" clothing, she tossed the 19th century garb into a rubbish bag then carried it out to the community can.

They took bottles of water out and sat beneath the oaks in the yard.

"I'd like to ask, if I may, to refurbish the loom in the cellar. Weaving relaxes me after a day of digging in the dirt and tromping around the landscape." Destiny waited anxiously for Olivia's reply.

"Sure. It looks to be in fairly good condition. Letting it rot would be such a waste."

Destiny breathed a relieved sigh. "Thank you."

"Do you have anything specific in mind to weave?"

A smile snuck across Destiny's lips. "I do, but it's a gift so, don't ask any more questions. You'll spoil the surprise."

"I love presents!" Olivia's eyes sparkled.

If you only knew…

Chapter Ten

Olivia's finger hesitated over the number. *What if he thinks I've lost my mind?*

"You can what if yourself to death but that won't get the house in shape." Destiny slung her rucksack over her shoulder.

"Where are you going?" Livy's forehead furrowed.

"It's just a jaunt down the road and unless you've locked the house, I'll be going to work on the loom."

"I did lock the house. Let me drive you. I can call from there just as well as here." She grabbed her purse and the ever-present notebook, moving to the door.

"You don't really have to go if you don't want to. Just let me have the key, and I'll make sure to lock up when I leave to go to the ruins."

"No. I don't know what I would do here. Sitting and drinking all day is not my idea of a good time. Besides, this is my home now. I need to start considering it as such. The sooner I dive into making repairs and establishing myself in the community, the sooner I'll be accepted as an Ollollain."

Destiny agreed. "You have a point."

The pair walked to the car and were at the house before they could engage the air conditioner. Creeping up the driveway, Destiny noted Olivia stiffening at the sight of a pickup truck parked in front of the home. The ladder racks and toolbox implicated builders of some sort, a logo with R & P Construzioni on the door.

"Who the…?"

Clambering out of the vehicle, Olivia strode to the steps to question the two men seated and drinking coffee. "Who are you and what are you doing at my home?"

Paolo looked to Rafaele. *"Che cosa ha detto?"*

Rafaele held up a hand. "My name is Rafaele Sonna and this is Paolo. I'm sorry for not contacting you first, *signorina*. Signora Porcu at the mayor's office called me yesterday and told me you might be in need of a builder. She was wrong?"

Olivia shook her head. "No. I do need a builder, but I thought… Wait a minute. You speak English."

Rafaele smiled. "Some. It did not escape my attention, as a young man, just how many visitors to our small island spoke the unfamiliar tongue. I knew if I was to be successful, I would need to learn this language."

Destiny stood a couple steps behind Olivia watching the scene unfold. *This is going better than I'd hoped.*

"I do need a builder to bring the house to a livable state, but I'm not looking to change the basic format."

Rafaele turned and translated to Paolo what had been said.

"Oh, great. An American who wants to *live like the locals*. She'll probably be looking for a husband and bambinos too. She's all yours." Paolo rolled his eyes and drew circles in the dirt on the porch.

"For your *informazioni, signore*, I have no need for a husband." Olivia watched the swarthy man's cheeks drain of color. "Yes, I know some Sardinian. My nonna taught me enough to understand more than I can speak. If I decide to use your services, please keep your comments to yourself."

Livy stomped up the steps and unlocked the door. She swung it open and powered through to the kitchen area. Destiny hung back to overhear the conversation between the two men.

"You are such an idiot, Paolo. If we lose this job because of your mouth…" Rafaele shook his head, following Olivia into the house.

Paolo tagged along behind his enthusiasm visibly lacking. He muttered beneath his breath and huffed his way into the house. *If I didn't need this job…*

Destiny caught up to Olivia. "I'm going to head to the cellar and assess the loom. I brought your torch and will be able to see with it. If you need me," she turned and looked at the young men, "for anything, just call." She set off for the basement. As the sun rose in the sky, the temperature followed suit. While the upper house was currently at a comfortable temperature, it would soon begin to drift upward to stuffy and hot. Being in the cellar suited the weaver just fine.

Olivia watched Rafaele walk the kitchen, testing light switches, faucets and windows. He wrote in a notebook similar to hers.

"This house is in remarkably good condition. I think you will only need to update the plumbing and electrical to make it livable. I would recommend replacing these old windows and considering new doors."

"And how much is this basic work going to cost me?" Olivia allowed skepticism to creep into her answer.

Rafaele wrote a figure on his notebook and showed it to her.

"Are you serious?"

"*Si*. Is there a problem?"

"No, I just, well, it's very economical."

"*Si*. Why would it be otherwise?"

"Because I'm American?"

"How does that help me? I live in this community too. We would see each other at the festivals and shopping. If I were to disrespect you, your cousin would have my head on a stick."

"Ah, Angelica."

"Yes. She is but one of the *many* Porcus in this city and region."

"Including me."

"That is what she tells me."

"Well, I guess she's right."

Rafaele looked at Olivia. He was having a difficult time trying to understand what it was she wanted. Of course, these were the rates he charged all his customers. He bit back any negative remarks. "If you wish to consider other builders, I'll be happy to provide names for you."

Livy shook her head. "No, no. That's not what I meant. Listen," she pushed an exasperated sigh through her lips. *Sometimes I'm such an idiot.* "Would you walk through the other rooms with me to determine if there are any other major changes needing attention?"

"Of course." He waved his hand for her to lead the way.

Paolo looked over the room, opening a cabinet door or two, then hurrying to catch up with Rafaele and the American woman. This would be money in the bank for very little work. Just what he liked.

Destiny closed the basement door, feeling the handset catch. "Lock." She flicked on the torch and followed the beam of light to the corner. She had ripped up her 19th century shirt to use as a dusting rag. "Wind." Blowing through her lips cleared the majority of cobwebs, but there was still work to be done to get the loom ready for use. Destiny found a wooden crate. She set the flashlight on it facing toward the loom. "Bright." More illumination brightened the corner occupied by the large tool.

She took her rag, the one imbued with her scent, and wiped all the wooden pieces of the loom. With each swipe, the warmth of the creation sprung to life. Destiny grabbed the torch from the wooden box and slid the box to the machine. She climbed up, hoping against hope it wouldn't break, and continued to gently, lovingly clean the rug creator. "Pray tell, my beauty, what is your name?"

"*Sogno tessitore.*"

"Dream weaver. We have a connection. I would ask you to help me unite two people who need each other. One is returning home, the other needs his own home. You and I can make this happen. Will you help?"

"*Si.*"

"Thank you." She stepped back and gazed at the loom before her. The mastery of work applied to it required her to do her best work. "And that I will."

The sound of rattling broke her reverie, and she realized someone was trying to come into the cellar. "Open."

"Destiny?"

"Yes?"

"Are you alright? I couldn't get the door to open."

"I'm fine. Door's probably just a bit swollen from the early morning damp."

Olivia and Rafaele entered the basement and moved to Destiny. "Wow. My flashlight really puts out a lot of light, doesn't it?"

Destiny silently cursed. "Yes. Must be lithium batteries."

"Could be." Olivia faced Rafaele. "See? Isn't this amazing? I don't understand how this thing could survive all these years of neglect." She moved to the loom and touched the recently cleaned wood. "Oh, my. It absolutely glows." Her hand stroked the uprights and she stepped back to look at the complete machine. "I almost wish I knew how to weave."

Rafaele stood watching the American marvel at something he'd always taken for granted. "You don't have a loom in your home?"

Olivia shook her head negatively. "America is the land of throwaway. Most of those who weave, at least where I'm from, do it for art. Not for clothing." She stepped back. "I think it's time to set this plan into motion. Destiny?"

Olivia ambled to the steps. Rafaele following with Destiny close at his heels. When the trio exited the cellar, Rafaele looked around in an attempt to locate his co-worker. "Paolo?"

The man entered the front door, exhaling a stream of smoke. *"Si?"*

Olivia froze in horror. "Please. No smoking in the house; *per favore, non fumare en casa."*

Rafaele watched a shadow of annoyance pass over his friend's face.

"Mi dispiace. I'm sorry." Paolo tromped out the door and flicked his cigarette off the porch.

Rafaele smacked his forehead with the palm of his hand. *"Idiota."* He marched out the front door, found the butt, and ground out the lit end before picking it up and putting it in his pocket. He walked back to the house, commenting as he passed Paolo, "We'll talk about this."

Paolo huffed. "Yeah, whatever." He strode to the truck where he lit another cigarette and blew smoke upward. "Americans."

"Please excuse my co-worker. While we work on your home, there will be no smoking in the house. Will that be acceptable?"

Olivia nodded a yes. "I'd appreciate if you didn't smoke around the porch either. Please."

"Of course, *signorina.* I need to go to my office and complete an estimate for the work to be done on your home. May I call you when it's complete?"

"Sure." She opened the notebook and pulled a business card from the left side pocket. Scribbling on the back of the card, she added her cell number. "This is my phone. Please call me as soon as you have the numbers. I'll need time to consider the costs and make my decision."

"Si, signorina." Rafaele took the card and placed it into his top shirt pocket. He walked to his pickup truck where Paolo stood puffing away on another cigarette. "You know, you really are an idiot? Are you trying to lose us this job? I was under the impression you needed the money."

Paolo glared at Rafaele as he pulled in deeply of the cigarette. "What makes you think I need this job?"

"I've had to pay off your tab at the pizzeria—again. This is getting old, Paolo."

He shrugged his shoulders. "I didn't have a papa who sent me away to school. I couldn't afford a college education. You've got the money, and I'll pay you back."

"Not likely. You had the grades and the brains to go to school. I know they waive fees for those who don't have the funding in some cases. You just didn't want to leave Ollolai because of Genisse."

"So?"

"What did it get you? She married D'Agostino anyway. Let's go. I have work to do."

As the pair opened the doors to the pickup, they heard their names being called. Rafaele watched Olivia sprinting to the truck. When she arrived, she stopped, leaned over and placed her hands on her knees as she tried to catch her breath.

"Please...wait a minute." When she'd recovered, she stood and leaned against the truck fender.

"I wouldn't..." Rafaele started but failed to stop her action. "It's really dirty."

Olivia smiled. "No biggie."

The odd expression received raised eyebrows from the pair.

"What did you need, *signorina?*" Paolo attempted a neutral tone to his voice.

"I wonder if I might ask you to do me a favor?" Her hazel eyes hooded with worry.

"We will try. What would that be?" Rafaele lay an arm across the open door of the truck.

"Well, my friend Taylor is missing."

"Your friend is a tailor?" Paolo was puzzled.

"No." Olivia could see the language barrier causing a problem. "My friend's name is Taylor. Here's her picture." She opened her wallet to a picture receiving a great deal of attention lately. It was Olivia and Taylor leaning against the railing along the Willamette River in Portland during Fleet Week. The sun was highlighting the pair, and they were giggling about some private joke. It was before the news Taylor's fiancé was MIA. "She came along on this trip with me but…"

The men could see something was bothering the American *signorina*. She straightened and started speaking again.

"About a week ago, we arrived and settled at the hotel. I knew I wanted to see the house as soon as possible, but she wasn't as excited. After all, this is *my* home. She was only considering staying. Not important now. She decided to take the day and go sailing. She took her rental car and left. I've not seen her since that day. The local police have been notified, and my—cousin—made out a report for the American Embassy. She's just, disappeared. If you are on the east side of the island, will you please keep your eyes open for her? If she's hurt and can't remember her name or something, I'll drop everything I'm doing to come get her."

Rafaele pursed his lips. "You say she told you she was going— sailing?"

Livy nodded. "She wanted to see the Spanish watch posts."

"Last week in the afternoon." He turned and gave Paolo a knowing look. The pair responded in tandem. "Mediterranean Mist."

"What?"

"In the summer, our beautiful ocean hides a secret known only to those living in the area. The sky is blue, and clouds appear white and fluffy. Around two or three o'clock, a storm blows in and steals unwary sailors from their vessels. They disappear and are never seen again. We call it the Mediterranean Mist."

"Oh, please." Olivia scoffed at such an idea. *Mediterranean Mist.*

"Does not your country have the Bermuda Triangle?" Paolo tilted his head slightly.

"Yes, but…"

"Is it not the same there? People go in and don't come back?" He lifted a brow.

"Uh, I, guess."

"I'm afraid your friend has become one more person to disappear in the Mist."

"We'll look for your friend, as requested," Rafaele answered. "But I think she has arrived at her destination already; wherever that may be." The men crawled into the truck and drove away.

Olivia returned to the house, mindlessly roaming through the rooms. She pulled the old broom from the closet in the kitchen and went to the furthest room. She started her campaign there. Every cobweb, dust mote and foreign object was cleansed from the area and escorted to the outside by the broom. As her mind tumbled through the ideas implanted by the men, Livy experienced a deep, unfamiliar ache in her chest.

A hand gently touched her shoulder. "Are you alright?" Destiny seemed to sense the turmoil roiling through Olivia's mind.

"I guess." She walked to the front porch and sat on the top step. "Taylor is the closest thing I have to a best friend. I'd really hoped she would decide to stay on in Sardinia. I don't know too many soldiers who return from the battlefields, alive, after being listed as missing in action."

Destiny took a seat next to Livy. "It does happen occasionally, but not often. Could she have opted to return to the Colonies without her stuff?"

Olivia contemplated the thought. "She might have, but her passport is in the room. I suspect traveling without one isn't easy."

The weaver patted her benefactor on the shoulder. "Why don't you go back to the hotel, get a meal and wait to hear from the contractor? I've a feeling he'll bring some good news. I need to get into the field, again, for my research. I'll be sure to lock the door any time I leave. If you allow me to keep the torch, I'll have some light when it gets dark…if I stay awake that long." Destiny graced Olivia with a smile.

Olivia stood. "I could sure use some good news about now. I think I'll have the staff let me into Taylor's room to gather her items. If she comes back in the next day or two, we can double up in the bed. Otherwise…" she allowed the thought to die. With luck, tomorrow would be the start of reconstruction of the Porcu villa in Ollolai.

Chapter Eleven

Paolo asked Rafaele to drop him in the center of town. "I'll walk home."

"You sure?"

"*Si.* Call me when it's time to work."

"Okay."

Paolo watched the truck rumble down the street and disappear around a corner before he pulled out his phone. He punched in the number and waited.

"*Pronto?* "

"Genisse?"

"*Si.* "

"I need two drops, as soon as you can. I've business in Nuoro."

"Problem?"

"Not if you make the drops in the next thirty minutes. Otherwise, yes."

"*Capisco. Caio.* "

"*Caio.* "

Paolo jogged the five blocks to his house. He quickly threw together clothing for a weekend away. Locking his home, he used the stairs from the kitchen to the garage. Opening the door, he stepped out and scanned the road. Determining there were no other vehicles utilizing the street, Paolo backed out his Fiat 124 Spider. He turned from the driver seat and used the remote to close the garage. Once secured, he put the vehicle in gear and maneuvered the back streets to No. 129 straight into Nuovo. If Rafaele called him for work, oh well.

~ * ~

Olivia spoke with the front desk and notified them of her plans regarding Tay's things. It was the height of tourist season. She surmised they would have no trouble filling the vacancy. Her task filled but half an hour as she checked the room and adjoining bathroom twice hoping against hope Tay would walk in and get pissed at her "rummaging" through her things.

Olivia meandered to the *ristorante* and ordered the lunch special with a local wine. She opted to sit outside and consider the current situation. It really wasn't like Tay to walk away without explanation. That was why Olivia was so worried. Tay said she'd be back. But her things now resided in Livy's room. As completely ridiculous as the local legend seemed, it was the only explanation making any sense at all.

~ * ~

Rafaele ran the numbers twice. He was ready to give Signorina Martin an estimate. He called her cell and received the voice mail. "Hate this thing," he muttered. "Signorina, please contact me when you get my message. I have an estimate I believe will work for both of us. Caio." There was nothing else he could do but wait.

~ * ~

Olivia took a sip of wine and glanced at her phone. "Damn. I have a message. Maybe from Tay?" Her heart started pounding as she hoped. The message was from Rafaele with a quote on the remodel. "That has to be wrong. Maybe it's without building a garage. I'll need to talk to him for clarification." She dialed the number he left. He answered after the first ring.

"Pronto?"

"Rafaele? It's Olivia. I have a few questions regarding this quote."

"Si. How can I help?"

"I don't wish to sound ungrateful, but these prices are so reasonable I'm wondering if they include the garage I wanted to have built?" Olivia heard the groan at the other end of the phone.

"No, *dispiace*. A garage would be an additional $5000 Euros."

"Hmm. How about a three-sided carport?"

"*Que cosa?* Sorry, what?"

Olivia sighed. "I think we really need to get together. I'll explain what a carport is when you bring a contract for me to sign; at the house around ten in the morning?"

"I will have the paperwork ready. We can talk about this…carport at that time. *Ciao.*"

"*Ciao.*"

Olivia breathed relief. She had a contractor for the refurbishing and a—cousin—willing to ride roughshod over him if he considered committing fraud or presenting inferior work. She couldn't help but wonder why her grandmother had been in such a hurry to leave this place. *No matter. I'm back and planting my roots in this Sardinian soil.*

~ * ~

Rafaele pushed back in his chair. He needed to call Salvatore's Supply and see about setting up an order. The supply line to Sardinia was sometimes…more relaxed than he would like. He picked up the phone and dialed the familiar number.

"Salvatore? It's Rafaele. *Bion giorno.*"

"*Bion giorno.*"

Rafaele was taken back. Salvatore was normally jovial and chatty. Today, he seemed—reticent.

"I would like to order some supplies for a job I have coming up. Can I do that through you?"

"I'm sorry, Rafaele. I can't preorder supplies any longer."

"May I ask why?"

"I've had issues with some of my accounts not paying in a timely manner…"

"But I always make sure Genisse pays you first."

"I know. However, I can't make an exception. As small as this town is, well, you understand. Yes?"

Rafaele didn't understand completely, but it was Salvatore's business, and unless he wanted to go all the way to Nuoro to buy supplies, he'd abide by the man's decision.

"Si. May I write you a check? I know there is plenty in the company account. You can contact the bank before they close today. Will that work?" He felt the hesitation on the other man's part.

"Okay. I'll take the check and call the bank. If it is verified…"

"When…"

"When it has been verified, we can go from there."

"Fine. I'll be at the shop soon. *Ciao."*

"Ciao."

Rafaele experienced the hair on the back of his neck bristle. "What is going on?" He grabbed his checkbook and headed to Salvatore's. Maybe the man would be more forthcoming in a face to face encounter. He'd calculated the cost of the initial work would run around $2000 EU. He was owed money from a couple other jobs completed in the last month, so liquidity was not an issue.

Pulling in front of the store, Rafaele parked his truck and ambled inside. He headed for the electrical department to check if the modern switches would work with what he suspected was ancient wiring. *Won't know until I open an electrical box.* He was examining several other wiring necessities when Salvatore approached him.

"Rafaele."

"Salvatore."

"How much do you want to write your check for?"

"I'd like to make it for $2000 EU and have what I don't use immediately put on my account. Is that doable for you?"

The storeowner nodded affirmatively. "I do want to check with the bank."

Rafaele agreed. The man's insistence at making sure his check was covered was becoming irritating. They'd been doing business for the last ten years. What had suddenly changed? He wrote the check. "Here you go." As Salvatore trundled to the back office, Rafaele wandered to the plumbing section of the store. He was examining new designs for the toilets when Salvatore appeared at his side, check in hand.

"I'm sorry, Rafaele, but the bank says this is not covered." He watched disbelief cover his client's face.

"But, how?"

"I don't know. The lady at the bank just said there was not enough to cover the check."

Rafaele stiffened. "Will you be open for the next hour?"

"Yes."

"I'll be back with cash. Will that work for you?"

Salvatore nodded.

"Good. Oh yes. Don't work with anyone but me until I tell you otherwise. No Paolo, no Genisse; just me."

"Understood."

"Thank you."

Rafaele walked to the bank and drew from his personal funds. He brought the money to Salvatore. "Remember, I will be the only contact you work with from R & P Construction."

Salvatore sighed as he shook his head. "Yes, just you."

The short ride to the offices of R & P Construction only exacerbated Rafaele's anger. *How could this happen?* Exiting his vehicle, he slammed the door and stomped through the entry. Genisse looked up from her magazine. "Everything all right, boss?"

"No, it's…" Rafaele halted. *Calm. Until you have all the facts, stay calm.* "Just a trying morning. That's all."

"Okay." She didn't sound convinced but seemed hesitant to inquire further. "Paolo called to say he has some personal business that will keep him away from Ollolai until Monday."

"Fine." *Whose wife is garnering his attention, now?* "If he calls back, let him know I'll contact him when there is work to be done."

Genisse set the magazine on the desk. "Of course. Do you wish me to stay?"

Rafaele turned abruptly, several words crowding his thoughts, and slowly breathed out. "No, thank you. I have a few minor tasks to complete, but there really is no need for you to be here. I can grab the phone myself. Have a good weekend, Genisse."

"You, too, boss." She gathered her purse and left the office. "I believe something is going to explode, and it won't be Vesuvius this time."

Chapter Twelve

Paolo babied the sports car through the back streets of Ollolai, easing it into the garage. Tonight, the door slid quietly on the track to the closed position. So far, everything was going smoothly, except for the panicked call he'd received from Genisse.

"Paolo, he knows! I swear. I just stepped out for a cigarette…"

"I thought you quit."

"Well, I didn't. D'Agostino has no issue with it."

"Whatever."

"Anyway, by the time he'd come in the back door and left again, I was just finishing my smoke. I didn't really see him but when he returned, he was fuming."

"Did he say anything?"

"No, but he was clenching his teeth."

"Look, if he didn't question you, I wouldn't worry. It's when he starts asking questions that we need to panic." Paolo convinced her things would work out to their advantage. It was after this panicked call he made the decision to slow his plan down. By Monday, the situation would be no different than it was the prior week.

He was getting ready to crawl into bed when his cell phone rang. He checked the readout. *Good Lord, now what?* "Hello, Genisse. What do you need?"

"Rafaele told me to pass along this message. Don't come into work. He'll contact you when there is a job to do. Goodnight, Paolo."

Before he could respond, she'd hung up. This wasn't like Rafaele. Paolo realized now was probably a good time to start worrying.

~ * ~

Destiny fit the final piece into the loom. Standing back to admire the beauty of the pieces, she pulled the fine yarn from her bag to begin the process of setting up the machine for weaving. The threads held no color and shimmered in the light of the flashlight. Having done this for several lifetimes, Destiny was aware the color would tint the tapestry as the assignment, and weaving, neared the finish. "I'm going to need more thread."

A whisper answered. "You'll have all you need. Just ask when you are close to running out."

"I'm taking a leave of absence after this assignment."

"Mmm. Not so fast."

"What?"

"There is another—client—right there on the island. Since you are so near…"

"You're joking, right?"

"We don't joke."

"Fine. Then I want half a century vacation at a location of my choice."

There was a long silence. Destiny began to think she might have pushed her luck.

"Fine. Until…"

"I also want the finest wool, spun and ready to weave, without any red tape attached."

Again, the long silence.

"Alright. We'll be in touch."

She grumbled lowly. Anything louder would have brought unwanted attention her way. *Not what I need.* She checked her bag and, just as promised, new, finely spun threads waited for her to apply to the loom. She closed her bag and grabbed the light. A tickling sensation at the back of her neck alerted her to the fact Olivia might appear. *Best not tempt her.* Opening the door, she saw lights flash across the room. If it wasn't Olivia, they'd be very sorry. She might not have powerful magic, but what she did possess, she knew how to manipulate to her advantage.

A timid voice called out. "Destiny? It's Olivia. I brought dinner. I thought you might be hungry."

"On my way."

They met in the living room and opted to eat out on the porch to enjoy the evening's temperate atmosphere.

"You know, I'm going to have to buy a dining table and chairs. Until my furniture arrives from the states, there really is nothing to sit on or use for eating. I can't imagine trying to write your thesis on the floor."

Destiny grinned. "No, but we archeology-types tend to make-do with what we have. You never know where we'll wind up digging. Hmm. Something smells heavenly."

Olivia giggled. "You can't beat the Italians at their own game. Pasta from heaven; fettuccini. I think I'm in love."

As the pair dug into their meal, conversation lulled. Once they sated their hunger, Olivia began.

"I wanted to let you know what's going to happen. I have a meeting with Rafaele tomorrow around tenish to sign a contract and get the work started. We might walk the house one more time, so we can agree on a working schedule."

Destiny wanted to jump up and down. This assignment was finally moving forward. "Do you need me to do anything? I've a site I want to explore down the road. I'll need to get an early start to avoid the heat of the day."

"Do you want me to drive you there?" Olivia picked up the paper plates and plastic silverware. She put them back into the bag to dispose of when she returned to the hotel.

"No, thanks. After this scrumptious meal, I really think I will need to walk it off."

Olivia chuckled. "Too true. Well, it has been a very long day, and I'm bushed. Do you need anything before I take off?"

"No. I guess I'll see you sometime tomorrow?"

"Yes. Sleep well, Destiny."

"You, too, Olivia."

The pair parted ways; Destiny returning to the inside of the house as a watch person and Olivia heading back to the hotel less than a mile away.

Destiny slid down a wall and blew out a sigh. She really was in need of a vacation.

Chapter Thirteen

Rafaele rose with the sun. Years of working construction had ingrained the early to bed, early to rise ritual. He made coffee and breakfast. The newspaper was full of the usual political government misdeeds. *So glad I opted not to live on the mainland.* Once he cleaned up his dishes, he went to his home office and printed out the contracts he would need to have Olivia sign. His plan was to check with the bank first thing this morning. He wanted a copy of all the business transactions for the last year. If the account had errors, he wanted to see if it was a one off or if this was a pattern. If it was the latter of the two, he wanted to track it and find out why.

He was the first in the lobby and first at the teller window. "Morning, Cecelia." As with many of the businesspeople in Ollolai, Rafaele and Cecelia had attended school at the same time.

"Morning, Rafaele. How can I help you this morning?"

"I'd like to check the balance of the company account, please."

"Give me a minute to look it up." She ran the name through the computer and brought up R & P Construction. "Here you go. Would you like me to write down the balance?"

Rafaele nodded.

"Okay." She took a notepad and put the number showing on the bottom line. She slid the paper across the counter to him.

Heat flooded his face. "Are you sure?"

Cecelia motioned him to come closer to the counter. She turned the computer toward him so he could see the screen. "As you can see, the number here is the one I put on the paper for you."

Rafaele straightened up. "Would you please print me out all the transactions for this account during the past year?"

She waved toward a seating arrangement facing the town square. "Of course, Rafaele. It might take about ten minutes or so to get the year's business. I'll bring it to you in the sitting area. Will that be sufficient?"

He realized he must have looked quite dour because she was speaking rather formally. Rafaele smiled. "Yes, that will be perfect. Thank you so much for your trouble."

She returned his smile. "Not a problem."

He took a seat and watched as the small-town center began to come to life. The numbers she'd written and shown him were more than sufficient to cover the amount of supplies he'd wanted to purchase from Salvatore's. The bank, and for that matter, Salvatore, didn't make mistakes as obvious as the one from Friday. The whole situation irritated him to no end. Keeping the accounts up to date and current was part of Genisse's job. Was it time for an office overhaul?

He sure hoped not. Cecelia brought out a manila file folder containing a healthy amount of paperwork.

"If you need anything else, call me." She handed him a card with her number and extension listed. "Have a good day, Raffy."

He grinned at her. The nickname from school hadn't been used in many years. Signing the contracts with Olivia was his next step. He placed the bank paperwork in his briefcase then left the bank. Much as he hated paperwork, it appeared he was going to be forced to perform a complete audit of his business—alone.

~ * ~

Olivia moved the stone next to the esparto plant to find the key right where Destiny stated she would leave it. As the door squeaked open, she sensed a calmness about the house she'd not noticed prior. Destiny must have opened windows to allow the fresh air to permeate the rooms. Whatever it was gave her a sense of welcome.

The few people in the Northwest she considered friends had been aghast that she would leave a successful career and move to "a foreign country." They didn't really understand. She was the daughter of a daughter of an immigrant. When her mother was at her wit's end with Olivia, she would never fail to remind her of said fact.

"Do not get uppity with me, young lady. I'll ship you back to Nonna's homeland in the blink of an eye. We'll see how you like it there!"

Well, here she was wishing her mother had made good on the threat. What she had witnessed so far was more of the lifestyle she would have preferred. Puttering around the kitchen area, Olivia heard a vehicle crunching up the drive. She peeked out the front window to witness Rafaele's pickup parking. She had brought some cleaning items with her to get started on removing the first decade or so of dirt. Using a rag, she cleared a spot on the hutch. "That should work."

Rafaele parked his truck. He grabbed the briefcase and walked to the porch of the home. Before he could lift a hand to knock on the door, it opened. Olivia smiled and invited him inside. She directed him to the kitchen area and indicated he should place his items on the sideboard.

He opened his case and retrieved a sheaf of papers from the interior.

Olivia's eyes widened. "Wow."

He held up a hand. "Please don't panic. I have two sets of paperwork; one for you and one for me. I've also made sure to print the contract in Italian AND English. All legal papers here are in Italian. I don't wish to have any misunderstandings between us."

"Thank you. I appreciate your honesty."

The pair spent the next forty-five minutes going over the specifics of exactly what was to be repaired, projected time schedules, and the days and times work would commence. During this review, Rafaele did his best to explain the idiosyncrasies of Italian laws and how they would affect the work. "If you wish we can go to the bank and I'll resign while Cecelia witnesses and verifies the signature. She is a *notaio pubblico. Capice?*"

"Public notary?"

"*Si.* She is that."

A grin tugged at the corners of Olivia's mouth. "I believe we can both agree to honor the contract as stated. After all, we live in the same town and will see each other at town events and while shopping."

"This is a truth. Now…I'd like to inspect the electrical outlets again. Would that be acceptable?"

"Of course. I'm wanting to go over some of the house and rethink the possibilities. Maybe, with a bit more funding, I can have some modifications made. Maybe…"

Olivia made her way to the second floor. She'd been thinking about the house layout and wanted to keep the bedroom facing the town for herself. If she could convince the contractor to put in a small balcony, it would serve as a perfect place to enjoy a glass of wine in the evening and watch the sunset. The current windows were swollen in place, and she was afraid if she forced them open the old timber frames would split. It seemed simple enough to just cut to the floor level and put in French doors. Considering the improvements in the design and installation of the modern windows, she should be able to have the view and the heat in wintertime, too.

She slowly descended the stairs, consciously testing the railings. They were solid. *One less item to worry about.* On the ground floor, a trip to the kitchen informed her Rafaele was still inside. His briefcase was open, papers scattered. She fought the urge to inspect the documents. Out of curiosity, she stepped to the sink and turned on the faucet. The ensuing screeching brought Rafaele from his location at a run.

"What the…?"

Livy blushed. "I just wanted to see if the water had been turned on. It would make cleaning a great deal easier." The pipes shuttered and hissed, red dust pouring into the basin. After several minutes of excruciating noises, the liquid flowing began to clear in color. The cloud of dust settled, and dust became mud, which became water. Still retaining a hint of red, the liquid sputtered as pipes not utilized in seventy years were, once again, employed. Olivia allowed the pipe to stay open until the water ran clear. Once there were no longer particulates in the stream, she cupped her hand and sipped. "That is heavenly. I can't remember tasting water so—sweet."

Rafaele nodded. "We are very fortunate to have the best water in the region. The rocks over which the streams pass act as filters, taking out the bad taste and giving us this bit of heaven."

Olivia held her hands beneath the faucet, rubbing her thumbs over her fingertips. "This is so pristine. My hands feel soft." She turned off the kitchen water. "I need to check the bathrooms."

She darted off. Rafaele could hear the same screeching noises then a prolonged period of water running. The next half hour followed in the same manner. When he saw Olivia next, she was smiling. "Everything okay?"

"Yes. I'm one step closer to moving into my home. Oh, Rafaele, I'd like to ask you about a small change I'd like to have made upstairs. Do you have time?"

"Of course, *signorina*. What are you thinking of doing?"

As she led him upstairs to what was to be the master bedroom, she launched into her idea about the balcony and French doors. "You'll see. It has the most amazing view…"

Chapter Fourteen

Destiny could hear the conversation from above but wasn't interested enough to snoop. Olivia and Rafaele were probably just putting finishing touches on their contract negotiations.

"Light."

The room brightened, and Destiny took her place at the loom. She picked up the shuttle, running her fingers over the fine wood. "Best get started." Continuing where she'd left off the previous day, she slipped the tool between layers of the finest spun wool fibers the mortal world had seen. Right to left, left to right, repeat. After every two lines of weaving, she would use the beater to batten the threads against material already created.

The routine took on a rhythm. Right to left, left to right, right to left, left to right, batten. She'd been weaving for half an hour when she noticed threads in the material nearest her were breaking. Not completely ripping away from the body of the tapestry but unraveling ever so slowly.

"Oh, goddess. What's happening now?"

About the time she set the shuttle on the beater, she noticed the same threads reweaving into the design. "If this continues, I see I'll need to step in and set these two straight. The sooner they start on the path chosen for them, the sooner I can move on to my other assignment, then…a much needed break."

The end of her sentence was punctuated with the slam of a heavy door followed by skittering of rocks in front of the house. She sighed. "Why couldn't an assignment be easy, just for once?" Back to the loom she trotted to see if she could repair the damage and get ahead of things. It wasn't until her stomach growled, echoing through the cellar, did she decide to stop for the evening. A loaf of bread with a bit of cheese would, should, quiet her system. She recalled hearing the clanging of pipes earlier and surmised the water must be usable and flowing.

Shuttle between the weft, she spoke two words. "Secure," then "Dark." The candles flickered out plunging the cellar into darkness. Destiny skulked about the hallway, peeking around corners and listening for sounds of others. When she stopped to view the living area, the only movement was the dust motes waltzing across sunbeams streaming through the windows.

Paperwork scattered across the hutch caught her attention. Two signed contracts were opened to the material breakdown and cost pages. "He may verbally deny his attraction but the extra steps he's taken to ensure she understands the contracts show his true feelings." The two sets of papers were in Italian, the legal language of Sardinia, and English.

She moved to the sink and turned on the faucet. Waiting for several minutes, she was rewarded with cool, clear water, which she used to wash off the dust collected in the cellar. As the day was quickly warming, Destiny chose to dry off on the front porch. She picked up the key from the handy hiding place. By the time she sat on the step, her arms were dry, and her eyelids were heading toward her cheeks. A nap seemed a very good idea.

~ * ~

Olivia pushed into her room. "That man!" He could be a charming devil one moment and an argumentative ass the next. "I'm not sure I'm going to make it through this remodel without killing him." There were few options, though, so she was going to have to find a way to control her temper and tongue. She flung her body on the bed and stared at the ceiling. "Hmm. Maybe a skylight?" She allowed her mind to play with the idea. She was sure Rafaele would nix it citing building regulations, money and time considerations. And what was all this nonsense about bearing walls? Weren't all the walls bearing the weight of the roof?

Okay, so she wasn't totally construction savvy. He still didn't need to get so…excited. Guess it was just his Sardinian blood, but, wait a minute. She was Sardinian too. His face turned a funny shade of red when she mentioned putting in a Romeo balcony. How frigging difficult could it be to knock out a portion of the wall, hang a balcony and support it? As far as she could see, not very, however, he went on about a bearing wall, and scaffolding to hold up the workers, and time, and money, and on, and on.

She really wanted to go over that contract again. She was having second thoughts about hiring him. Livy traveled back to the car to pick up the paperwork. Once opening the door and facing the empty seat, she realized she'd left the paperwork back at the house. "Damn it."

Walking seemed to be a logical solution. It wouldn't kill her and might just soothe the irritation she was currently feeling. Halfway to the house, the sweat beads rolling down her back had her thinking she'd made a mistake deciding to hike the short distance. The house rose up on the horizon and Livy let out a sigh of relief. At least she'd be able to sit in the shade and cool down before heading back to the hotel. She spied a form on the porch. *Who...?*

Trudging up the driveway, dirt crunching beneath her shoes, the mysterious person took on a familiar look. *Why is Destiny sleeping outside?* Olivia's big city fear meter kicked in. *What if...stop. This is Sardinia. Everybody in town knows, and most likely is related to, the next person.*

She sat on the step and gently touched the young student's shoulder. "Destiny? It's Olivia."

The weaver woke with a start. "What? Where am I?"

Livy gawked at Destiny. "I thought you were English?"

She cleared her throat. "I am. Why?"

"You said something when you opened your eyes, but I have no idea what it was. You were talking in some weird language." Olivia watched the woman flush to her toes.

"Sorry. My parents were from Eastern Europe. We spoke Chechen at home."

"Oh. Why were you sleeping on the porch?"

"I walked in from the main road after spending time at the new, to me, site, and was just intending to sit for a few minutes. You saw what happened." The pink color creeping up her neck matched the embarrassed look on her face.

Livy bit her lip to keep from smiling. "I did, indeed. What say we go inside so I can pick up the contract and go over it with time to check out the fine details? Afterward, pasta?"

Destiny stood and stretched. "Sounds wonderful. Have you connected the stove to a power source?"

Oliva groaned. "No. I guess it's a good thing there are a couple good restaurants in town. We'll head to one of those."

"They are, after all, the experts. Oh, here." She handed the key to Olivia.

The pair entered the house where Olivia retrieved the paperwork left on the sideboard. She examined the stove, realizing it was a wood burning unit. "Another expense." While her grandmother might be able to cook on such a stove, she could not. Hell, she didn't have the wherewithal to make food in the microwave. Destiny would be leaving for home at the end of the summer and taking her cooking skills with her. "Come on, Destiny." They hiked to the hotel, working up a ravenous appetite. They opted to eat in the on-site café. When the food had arrived and both had eaten their fill, Olivia decided to broach a delicate subject.

"Uhm, Destiny?"

"Yes?"

"You really don't have any money at all, do you?"

"What do you mean? Of course I have money."

Livy smiled. "You are very thin, even for a student, and while you've not said as much, I believe the only times you eat are when we dine together. Can you really cook?"

The student bristled. "Yes, I can cook."

Olivia thought she may have stepped over the line until she saw the sag of her lunch mate's shoulders.

"You have discovered my secret." She sighed. "I had just enough money to get here. I figured I would get employment in a fast food restaurant or on a local cruise ship. I'd get my meals as a bonus. Then we bumped into each other and things took a different tack. I'm sorry for the subterfuge." She slumped into the chair.

Olivia offered a smile. "Don't worry. I had to work to get my degree too. Well, now begs the question of, can you cook and bake on a wood stove?"

Destiny brightened. "Oh, yes. My mum was from a small village in her country. They still used that type of unit. When she came to England, it was all she knew. They didn't have a lot of money, so they let a small house in a village outside Oxford. It was very similar to the one where she lived in the old country. I learned to cook on one."

"Well, we'll just have to secure a cord of wood, some kindling, and make sure you have plenty of matches." Livy's phone trilled and she answered. A smile blossomed and she sat up in the chair. "Of course. Tomorrow? Great." She grinned at Destiny. "My belongings will be in port tomorrow. I'll have to contact my cousin about getting a moving van to bring them to the house. This will solve the issue of a table, chairs and so many other items.

"I guess you will be protecting more than just the house, now. I'd like to go back and do some basic cleaning. I can try to get rid of a few more decades of dust before my household arrives."

Destiny stood. "Let's get going."

Olivia beamed. She stood, peeled off enough bills to pay for lunch and provide the server with a hefty tip. This time, they used the car.

Chapter Fifteen

Rafaele opened the office in his home, plunking his briefcase on the desk. He grabbed a blank manila folder and marked the address on the upper tab, sliding the signed contracts inside. Sitting in his comfortable, old chair, he unlocked the drawer and pulled out the monthly reports given to him by Genisse. He reached into his briefcase and pulled the stack of the same reports he'd just retrieved from the bank. The size difference was shocking. He would need to go through each month. The prospect gave him indigestion.

His desk phone rang. Automatically, he picked it up. *"Pronto?"*

"Raffy. What's up?"

It was Paolo; the last person he wanted to speak with at the moment.

"Did you get the contract with that snooty American?"

"I'm still working on it. What do you need, Paolo?"

"I just wanted to check and see if you had any work for me. I'm going to need cash pretty soon."

"Like I told Genisse to relay to you, when I have work, I'll call. Can't you borrow from one of your lady friends?"

"Things are a little dry right now. Seems husbands and boyfriends can only be lied to for so long before they get wise…and angry."

"So, I've heard. Since I have a mountain of paperwork to do, I'll talk to you later. *Ciao.*"

"Ciao, Raffy."

Rafaele couldn't quite put his finger on what it was about his conversation with Paolo, but his old friend seemed—guarded. He'd heard through the rumor grapevine his *amico* was driving a brand-new Fiat

Spider. Raffy knew he wasn't paying him enough to afford that kind of vehicle. A 500C maybe; not a Spider. In the last couple years, Paolo had pulled away from him and effected a more reclusive nature. Oh, sure, he was jovial at work, but the boys' nights they used to share no longer happened. Finally, the truth dawned on him. It hadn't been just the last few years. Paolo had been pulling away since he'd returned from University. He really was angry at Rafaele for choosing to take his father's offer of education over their friendship, as Paolo saw it.

"I may choose to spend my life in Ollolai, but on my terms." He pushed back in the chair. It was too bad his nonna had passed away this last winter. He could really use her advice. In the meantime, he'd attempt to make some sense of the pile of reports from the bank.

~ * ~

Olivia had perused the contract between herself and R & P Construction. It was no different than one from the US. There were more restrictions laid down by the local government agencies, but for the most part, it was a contract to make repairs to a home she owned. The timeline was set to have all the work completed and inspected with passing marks in three years.

The more she thought about it, the more she decided she wanted a Romeo balcony and a skylight. Since she was funding this adventure, Mr. Sonna could just get over his objections and make it happen. She stretched in the bed, having dropped in around 9:00 pm last night. She wasn't particularly a night owl, and nine o'clock was early, even for her, but she and Destiny had morphed into cleaning tornadoes after lunch yesterday. She swore they mopped the floors three times, and they were still pulling up dirt. Maybe in three years, her house would be clean.

Destiny let her know she was at the crux of important research this morning and wouldn't be around until noon. That was fine by Livy. After her phone call from the shipping lines, she'd called her cousin.

"*Ufficio del Sindaco.*"

"Angelica?

"*Si.*"

"It's Olivia."

"Oh, good afternoon. What can I do for you, *cugina?*"

Olivia smiled. *Guess I'm being accepted.* "My belongings will be here at Cagliari tomorrow. Do you know of a moving company that can bring them to my house?"

"Si. Leave this to me. Then maybe you can invite me to dinner for payment, *si?*"

Livy laughed. "As long as my new friend is here, *si.* I don't really know how to cook."

There was a noise at the other end of the phone. *Sounds like tsking.* "When she leaves, I will teach you myself. Every woman should know how to cook. If not for someone, just for herself!"

"Then I accept your offer. Will you call and let me know when to expect things to arrive?"

"Naturalmente. Ciao."

"Ciao."

A short time later, Olivia's cell rang, and Angelica announced two good pieces of news.

"The moving company is another *cugino* you will meet tomorrow around three o'clock. The people with the electric company said they would be at the house *around* noon. If they are not there by the time the movers arrive, call me. I will give them a piece of my mind in a language they can understand."

Olivia laughed. "I will. *Grazie,* Angelica, *mil grazie."*

"Anything for *famiglia."*

So here sat Livy on her front step—yet again. She realized she was still thinking in business mode. Since she had nothing but time, however long or short it took, would make little difference.

She made her way to the back of the house and looked over the area enclosed in a simple split wood railing fence. There were a few trees and bushes scattered among the boulders. A flash of sparkle pierced her right eye. She followed the light to a large rock and bent to investigate. A small cross with a red center stone lie at the foot of the stone. She picked up the delicate jewelry and turned it over. On the back in a small intricate hand, the initials FP were carved. *Could this really be?* Nonna once mentioned, in passing, that the only piece of personal jewelry she'd taken had been lost between the house and the road where she'd caught the bus to Cagliari.

Olivia held the cross to her heart. She would put it on and never take it off. A crunching sound in front of the house distracted her treasure hunt. She trotted around the side to see Rafaele's truck making its way up the drive. Once parked, he exited and moved toward her.

"Buon giorno, signorina."

"Buon giorno, signor."

"I received a call from Angelica asking me to arrive a bit early. She wants to have a native speaker here to intercede, if needed."

Olivia lifted a brow. *"Grazie.* I think I can handle this." She continued to look into his warm brown eyes and noted the tiny lines at the corner. *Hopefully, from laughing.* "I'll feel more confident knowing there is someone here who will tell me the truth of what is being said."

Shaking hands, they entered the house. They'd not been inside but ten minutes when a delivery truck arrived. Rafaele recognized the truck from Salvatore's store. "These will be supplies for working on the house. Is there someplace we can put them?"

Livy took his hand and led him to the back of the house, pointing out the lean-to. "Will that work?"

"Perfetto. Grazie."

"With Destiny here at night, there will be someone to keep an eye on things."

"Oh, that's not really necessary but I know it will make you feel better."

Rafaele dashed to the front and directed the driver up the narrow path to the shed. After several trips, the two men shook hands. The driver took off to be replaced by the moving van.

"Looks as if today is going to be busy." Rafaele nodded to the incoming van.

Olivia turned to watch the mid-size delivery van rumble up the drive. "I sure hope so. I want to start living in my house. I enjoy the hotel, but it's not really home."

Rafaele agreed. The driver of the van automatically approached

Rafaele to ask where he wanted the items.

Olivia watched as Rafaele told him the delivery was for the young lady.

The guy turned to her and gave her the once over. He broke into a smirk. *"Italiano?"*

She caught a quick glance from Raffy who smirked. Olivia decided to play the dumb American. *"Un po."* She saw the wheels turn in the driver's eyes.

He turned to Rafaele and spoke in the local dialect. "This is a really small load; kitchen table and chairs, a few living room items, and a bedroom suite. There are some boxes of other things, but I believe I can make this stretch out for a couple days." He winked and jauntily headed to the truck. He maneuvered the vehicle to put the ramp on the top step and roll the large items directly into the house. When he exited his side, the passenger door opened and a thin, reedy young man jumped out. The pair conferred, returning to the back of the van to open it up.

As they started, Livy moved next to Rafaele. "When would you like to tell him I understand Sardinian quite well?"

Raffy scratched his day's growth. "Right after they take your bed to the master bedroom and set it up. Why don't I ask him to do that first saying you'll want to sleep there tonight?"

Olivia smiled. "Okay." She wandered to the kitchen area to wait for the electric company men while the movers put her furniture in the house.

Rafaele ambled to the van. "Gentlemen. The lady of the house asked if you would get the bedroom furniture to the master suite on the second floor. She wishes to stay in her home this evening."

The men traded grimaces. "Of course." They found the frame for the queen-sized bed and each grabbed one side. Rafaele directed them to the room where the furniture was to be set. During the hour it took for the pair to move the bedroom suite in, the electric company workers had come, turned on the juice, and left. Raffy had made quick work of the visit and went to locate the movers, finding them inside their van smoking.

"Gentlemen. The lady prefers you not smoke in her house." He started to walk away catching them rolling their eyes. "Oh, yes. I wanted to let you know, while Signorina Martin speaks minimal Italian, she is fluent in Sardinian." He watched the driver's cigarette stop mid-way to his mouth.

"So, she…"

"Yes. She understood what you said to me. I would suggest you unload her items with as much care and speed as possible and be on your way. One more thing…she is a Porcu." He watched the men stub out their cigarettes in the vehicle's ashtray and bolt to the back. The rest of the furniture and boxes were unloaded within two and a half hours.

Olivia was impressed. "What did you say to them? I can't say I've seen American movers get done that fast."

Rafaele shrugged his shoulders. "I told them you wished for them not to smoke on your property, that you were fluent in Sardinian, and, this was the catalyst, you are a Porcu."

"Is Nonna's family really that connected?"

Raffy looked at the hazel eyes searching his face. "Yes. It would take a few hours to explain how and why but know the Porcu's are very important to this community, to this island."

"Wow. You have your furniture."

"AHH!" Olivia whipped around to face Destiny. "Where'd you come from? I didn't hear you."

"Uhm, the field?"

Livy was clutching her chest. "You scared the daylights out of me. Yes, I have my furniture. I'll need to go to the hotel and collect my stuff from there then check out. I suspect a trip to the grocer will be in order."

"The refrigerator works?" Destiny walked up the steps toward the house.

Olivia stopped. "I don't know. Guess we need to find out." She followed Destiny into the kitchen. They wiggled the old box away from the wall, groaning at the collection of items stashed behind it by some small furry creature.

"We know what we'll be doing tomorrow." Destiny groaned.

"Yep."

Locating a plug and socket that looked as if it should be in the Smithsonian Institute, Olivia connected the two. There was a sigh, cough producing a puff of dirt, then the old machine began humming. The girls looked at each other and smiled.

"We have refrigeration." Olivia said.

"Guess a trip to the grocer is in order," Destiny replied.

"Did you see it on your way through town?"

"No, I wasn't really paying attention to that when I came through. Maybe we should ask Rafaele?"

They dashed out the front door to see the cloud of dirt behind the truck exiting the driveway to the road.

"Darn it. I guess we'll just have to go to town and do a short tour. I'm sure it won't take us long to find the grocery. If we can't, I'll just visit my cousin again. You know, she's probably going to put me to work if I keep showing up at her doorstep."

Destiny giggled. "Would that be so bad?"

Olivia thought for a moment. "No. Not really."

Chapter Sixteen

The move in was relatively smooth. The ensuing renovation…a nightmare. Destiny was close to asking for another dream weaver to finish this assignment. Olivia and Rafaele argued about *everything.* She swore they did it just to aggravate each other. The result, however, was making her doubt her ability to keep her cool under fire.

"All you need to do is cut a small hole in the ceiling and…" Olivia pointed to a spot near the joist.

"You don't just cut small holes near a joist. It's a bearing beam; just like the wall over there," he pointed to the window where she'd wanted a balcony, "and the wall in the kitchen and…"

"BASTA!"

Olivia and Rafaele jumped. The shouted command echoed around the nearly empty house.

"You two will follow me. NOW!"

Looking at each other in surprise, they trailed behind Destiny into the kitchen.

"Sit." She pointed to the table and chairs. Olivia took one side of the table, Raffy the other, crossing his arms in defiance.

"Every single day, you two find a way to disagree on—something."

"How can you know? You're out doing your archeology study." Olivia frowned.

"I have my ways. You will get along while I'm here, so I don't have to worry when I leave the house. Olivia, what do you know about Rafaele?"

"I know what I need to. He's a licensed contractor that was

recommended by my cousin."

"Uh-huh. Rafaele, what did Olivia do in America before she moved here?"

He shrugged. "I don't need to know the history of my clients. I just need to do the work in their home and get paid."

"Fine. But how is that happening here? All I see and hear is arguing. You two will not move a muscle until you discover a bit of personal history about each other, starting now. First question will be; did you go to university and, if so, what did you study? The next question will have to do with family." She glared at the pair. "Get started." She turned and disappeared under the stairwell.

Rafaele cocked his head slightly. "Did you go to university?"

Olivia nodded.

"What did you study?"

"Finance."

Rafaele uncrossed his arms. "Finance?"

She nodded again.

"So you can do auditing?"

Olivia indicated she could. "Yes. That is part of the finance program, but my specialty was stocks. I was a stockbroker."

"Wow. I would never have guessed."

"Most people don't. Your turn. Did you go to university?"

"Yes."

"Did you get a degree and in what?"

"I got my bachelor's in Engineering...civil engineering."

It was Olivia's turn to be floored. "An engineer. I would have thought there were dozens of jobs in the big cities. Why did you come to Ollolai?"

Rafaele shifted in his seat. "My father wanted me to have an education, so being a dutiful son, I went to college to study. What I really wanted to do was work on my uncle's sheep farm and stay on the island. I was glad to have the opportunity to attend university. I took a job in Italy, Rome to be exact, and hated every minute of it. I guess I'm just a small island person. I missed the quiet at night and knowing the people in the restaurant when you go out to eat. I hated the traffic and pollution.

So, when my nonna became ill, it was a good excuse to move back to Ollolai."

Olivia had been worrying her lip between her teeth. "I owe you an apology. I was judging you by your job."

Rafaele graced her with a rare smile. "I, too, am guilty of such an act. Shall we begin once more?"

She smiled. "I'd like that."

They sat and talked for an hour, sharing family stories and life experiences. When Rafaele felt comfortable, he broached a subject he was unsure of.

"Ms. Martin."

Olivia's eyebrows rose. "So formal. What do you want?"

He cleared his throat and shifted in the chair. "I have a situation which makes me very distressed."

Olivia nodded. She could see whatever it was that Rafaele needed made him very uncomfortable. "Rafaele?"

"Si."

"Why don't you just say what the situation is and don't worry about me judging you?"

He sighed and clasped his hands together. Pulling in a deep breath, he started. "I went to the supply store to order for this job. I've been working with them since I came back to Ollolai. But the owner informed me I could no longer put my supplies on account."

"Oh."

"This has never happened. I pay my bills and don't abuse the privilege, so I'm very confused. Would you audit my books to see if there is a—problem—I don't know about? I asked Cecilia at the bank to provide me with the account history. When she came back with it, I was floored. What I receive from my secretary at the office is but a page long. The bank provided nearly three times the papers."

"Will this affect the work here?"

"No. I am a professional. I will do my best work no matter the outcome."

"Okay. Bring the papers tomorrow and I'll get started."

"Grazie." He reached across the table and grasped her hands in

his.

His touch sent an electric current blazing up her arm. She looked into his brown eyes and felt the flutter of her heart. *Oh, no. I can't let this happen again.*

"*Prego.* No promises."

Raffy pulled his hand back and held one up. "No promises. I understand. I need to continue the work upstairs. I will investigate putting in a skylight and attaching a balcony. But..." he smiled at her, "...no promises."

"Fair enough."

Destiny watched the scene with growing hope. *This is how it is supposed to be.*

Chapter Seventeen

Olivia spread the papers across the tabletop. There was no way she could immediately see how his secretary was finding the numbers she gave to him. From her quick perusal of the accounts, there was a great deal of money not accounted for in Rafaele's monthly reports.

She tracked more money going out than coming in, creating a loss. How could Rafaele be solvent with so much missing? She would need to ask him the following day when he came to put finishing touches on the master bedroom. They had sat down and discussed her "want" list, coming to an agreement on the two items she had desired. He'd been very patient and explained why the skylight would be more of a burden than a delight. Seems if it was installed when the building was put up the first time, accommodations were made to ensure the window was sealed tight. Afterward, there was always the chance of leakage of both moisture and heat.

Olivia agreed the idea was just a fancy, but she was adamant about having a small balcony off the master bedroom. She and Rafaele had batted the particulars back and forth for a week or so until Destiny put a halt to their bickering.

They sat at the kitchen table, this time with coffee, and went over the idea and construction for installation of the balcony. Livy compromised on the size, and Rafaele agreed to install the additional tier. Olivia was happy, Rafaele was happy, and Destiny was happy.

~ * ~

The knock on the front door was subtle. Olivia knew immediately it was Raffy. "Come in, *signore. Buon giorno.*"

"*Buon giorno, signorina.* How are you this morning?"

"I'm doing very well. Come. Sit and have coffee before you go to work. I need to speak with you for a moment."

A worried look crossed Rafaele's face. "I hope it's not bad news."

Livy poured coffee made from a new cappuccino machine she'd bought herself as a housewarming gift. "Maybe yes, maybe no."

As he picked up the coffee and took a sip, he smiled. "This is *molto bene.*"

"Thank you. What do you do when the bank or the store says there isn't enough money to cover a bill?"

Rafaele sputtered. "That is a bit personal, don't you think?"

Olivia sipped her brew. "You asked me to find out about your account. Unfortunately, knowing this information is important to the direction I need to take."

Silence descended on the pair. Rafaele twisted in his chair. "I cover it with my own money."

Olivia's eyebrows rose. "Okay. I won't ask."

Raffy quickly recovered. "It is not what you think. I still take on projects for the mainland and receive payment from the large companies who employ me."

"So you do this…"

"… because I want to."

"I'm sorry. It was a necessary piece of information. I have to go to the store to buy a toaster. You are on your own. If you leave before I get back, please put the key in the niche outside."

"Of course."

~ * ~

Rafaele took his cup with him and headed to the second floor. Despite the small hiccups, the job had been easily accomplished. Besides, the more time he spent with Olivia, the more he liked it. He was becoming quite fond of this American transplant. Maybe when the job was completed, he would ask her out. *No.* That was Paolo's style, not his.

The thought of his friend brought a stab of pain to him. He'd not seen nor heard from the man since the day they'd been granted the job. What could be so important he wouldn't even call? Rafaele would find out; after the job was over.

~ * ~

Olivia loved going into the stores in Ollolai. They were different than those in Portland; more homey. She was standing in front of the toaster display when the bell at the front door rang.

"Salvatore!"

Shuffling from the back brought the owner to the counter. "Paolo. What can I do for you?"

"I need you to return these electrical supplies. They aren't quite right. The house is so old, and the wiring is turning into a pain to upgrade."

"No can do, Paolo."

"Why not? You did it last time."

"Since you came in last time, Rafaele has changed his purchase policy. He told me no one but he is allowed to buy and return supplies."

Olivia heard a muttered swear word.

"But these are the supplies he purchased. He asked me to return them and get the money."

"I can't. Unless he is standing here with those supplies in his hand asking, no more cash for returned supplies."

This time the swear word was loud and vulgar, followed by the slamming of the door and jangling of the bell. Olivia decided she would get a toaster later. She moved to the store window and watched as a flashy Fiat Spider smoked the tires down the street. This was a situation where Rafaele would have to do the investigation.

She drove the car into the driveway and parked. The carport was a project that would be put on the back burner. At the end of this week, she was to turn in the rental. Afterward, she wasn't sure what she would do. First things first. Entering the house, she put her purse on the sideboard and took a deep breath. Walking up the steps to the second floor, she wasn't quite sure how to present her suspicions to Rafaele. Paolo was the man's best friend. Most men would believe their friends over any woman.

She pushed open the door and watched in awe as Raffy put finishing touches on the balcony railing. "Thank you. I will enjoy every moment I spend out there."

Rafaele smiled. "Just don't go out for at least one day. The paint needs to dry." He set his paint brush on the rim of the paint bucket and wiped his hands on a rag. "What brings you up here now?"

Olivia looked at the floor then into his eyes. "I think I know what has been happening to your business account, but you'll need to put the final piece to this puzzle."

"Can't you give me a clue?"

"I would rather you come to your own conclusion. If I'm wrong and tell you what I think, our friendship will fall apart. I don't want that to happen."

"What is it you need me to do?"

"You need to ask the storekeeper for his records on your purchases and returns for the last year. I believe you will have your answer. If it is what I think, you may not like the resolution."

"That may be, but I have to know what is happening to my company. I'll talk to Salvatore tomorrow."

"Salvatore? Like the mayor?" Olivia was surprised.

Rafaele chuckled. "Yes. This is a very small community and we cannot afford to have a paid mayor. Salvatore gets a small salary and the honor of casting the deciding vote on town issues."

"Hmm. Not sure I would want that responsibility."

"I told them no when they asked me to run."

Olivia burst out laughing. "Smart move." She turned to leave then stopped and faced Rafaele. "Will I see you tomorrow?"

A sly grin began to creep over his face. "Try and stop me. I'll get the paperwork from Salvatore and we can go over it together. No arguing."

She nodded. "Right. I really don't want Destiny yelling again. I thought the English had good manners. That woman could out yell a drunken football player."

Rafaele laughed. *"Domani."*

Olivia impulsively blew him a kiss, blushing after having done so. He smiled and returned the gesture.

~ * ~

Rafaele walked into the shop, the bell announcing his arrival. "Salvatore!"

"Si. Hold your britches. Oh, *signore Sonna. Come stai?"*

"Buono. I would like to have copies of all the paperwork from my account for the last year."

"A year? I send all this to Genisse. Why do you need it?"

"Per favore."

"Okay, okay. It might take a minute or two. I have to ask the missus to make the copies. She's going to want to go out to dinner for this."

Rafaele smiled. Yes, that would indeed be Aurora. "Tell her *grazie."*

"Yeah, yeah." Salvatore mumbled into the back area of the store. He came back out behind the counter. "I'm sorry the electrical items didn't work for you. If you bring them to me, I can find replacements."

"What are you talking about?" Rafaele stiffened.

"Paolo came in yesterday and wanted to return a bucketful of electrical plugs and sockets for cash. Didn't you send him?"

Raffy's jaw muscles tightened. He finally said, "Not that I recall. Maybe I told him before we spoke."

Salvatore opened his mouth to reply but his wife hollered.

"E fatto."

"Excuse me." He retrieved the paperwork and delivered it to Rafaele. "Here you go. See you soon?"

"Si, caio."

"Caio."

Rafaele was tempted to search through the records but the way he was feeling would not make it safe for him to drive should he do so. He took his truck straight to Olivia's. He knocked then entered, finding her at the kitchen table with paperwork in neat piles.

"Good morning."

She looked up. "Oh, this isn't good. You spoke to me in English. What's going on, Rafaele?"

He put the stack in front of her. "I would like us to go through this together."

"Coffee?"

"Do you have anything stronger?"

Olivia looked at the tense expression on his face and opted not to mention it was only ten in the morning. "I think so."

She found a small bottle of whiskey and set it in front of him. "Whiskey. Not sure of the quality, but probably has a hefty kick."

"Thank you." He opened the small bottle and drained the contents. "I think I know what you might have witnessed yesterday."

"Oh?"

"Yes. Salvatore mentioned a visit by Paolo to the store to return merchandise for cash. Right?"

Livy sighed. It was difficult to let someone know they'd been betrayed. She was a first-hand witness to the feelings of anger. "Yes. But let's go through the account ledger to see if maybe this was just a one-time happening. Maybe he was running low on funds. There could be many explanations."

Rafaele humphed.

The audit took three hours of finding, cross referencing, and double checking to come to the conclusion Olivia had hoped wouldn't be. Rafaele's best friend was stealing from him to the tune of hundreds of thousands of dollars. It had been happening since he'd first opened the company.

"I hate to believe this, but the proof is in black and white. Tell me, did you see him leave in a vehicle?" Rafaele looked up from the mass of papers.

Olivia pulled in a breath. "Yes. A new Fiat Spider. He burned rubber all the way down the street."

Raffy frowned. "Burned rubber?"

"Yes. Spun the tires so much there was smoke." Olivia said.

"Ah, yes. That would be a Paolo action."

"What are you going to do, Raffy?" Livy's forehead corrugated in concern.

"I'm not sure. I must think about this. May I come by tomorrow?"

"Of course." Olivia walked him to the door and watched him leave. Her heart hurt for him.

"Is everything okay?" Destiny appeared at Livy's elbow.

"No. Rafaele just discovered his best friend has been stealing large amounts of money from him for a very long time." She went to the sink and rinsed out the cups they had been using.

"Would you like me to fix lunch?"

"Thanks, Destiny. I really don't have an appetite. Say, when are you leaving for school?"

Destiny stopped and turned to answer Olivia. "I have about two days of wor...research to do then I'll be leaving here. I meant to say something but have been so busy putting together my paper."

Olivia looked stricken. "Two days? Are you sure you can't stay? You really are the only friend I have here."

"I don't think that's true. You have Rafaele and your cousin. You'll find others who will help you to fit into the community."

"Maybe so. First, Taylor; now, you. I'm beginning to wonder if I made the right decision."

Destiny moved to her side and ran a hand across her back. "You did. I can tell, you did."

Chapter Eighteen

Destiny finished tying the knots of the tapestry. It was really quite beautiful. She rolled it up and set it aside. "Now to the other." The second weaving had hit her with such force, she'd fought a headache for a week. The background was quite unusual. There were stars but she didn't recognize any of the constellations.

In the middle was a town, but it appeared to be deserted except for the two people looking up at the buildings and several dogs peeking around corners. She didn't understand it, but she was not going to question her assignments.

Putting the smaller tapestry into her knapsack, she tucked the Ollolai one under her arm and headed to the stairs. At the foot of the stairs, she turned and bid the loom goodbye.

"You have given me such pleasure. I hope our Miss Olivia chooses to learn to weave and takes the opportunity to work with you. Goodbye, friend."

She climbed the stairs and closed the door for the last time. Rounding the corner, she stopped and stepped back. Olivia and Rafaele were entangled in a very serious kiss. This was exactly what she had been sent to do. She cleared her throat.

She heard the shuffle of feet and came around the corner. "Hello. Rafaele. I'm so glad you are here. I have finished my gift and wanted you both to see it." She unfurled the tapestry and listened as the pair inhaled surprise. The picture showed the house, plants growing, garage built, and a couple bicycles in the drive. A man and woman stood on the porch arm in arm looking very happy. Two little ones were chasing each other.

"I have enjoyed my time here, but I must go. Please take care of each other." She moved to Olivia and gave her a hug. She shook Rafaele's hand. Opening the door, she hiked out the front and to the street. She wasn't worried about transportation. There always seemed to be a vehicle to get her to her destination. The only thing she knew about the new destination was there were many unoccupied buildings and the stars played into this story. Oh, there were also a few people and lots of dogs. She whistled as she moved toward the main road. Another assignment then vacation.

~ * ~

Rafaele pulled Olivia into his arms. "Tell me, how did you meet your friend, Destiny?"

She shrugged her shoulders. "She just sort of showed up here a day or so after I arrived."

"Really?"

"Yes. Why?"

"I happened to be at one of the sites she was supposed to be working, on the day she was to be there. The place was empty."

"Raffy. Don't be so cynical. Maybe she went somewhere else."

"I don't think so. Do you remember her telling us she knew when we were fighting? Even if she wasn't here?"

"Yes, so?"

"Come look." He took her hand and let her to the tapestry. He pointed to some areas at the bottom of the weaving. "These spots here have been...repaired."

"She made a few mistakes. She did say she was a novice."

He looked at her and smiled. "Does this really look as if a novice has woven this? I don't think so. I think your friend, Destiny, is exactly what her names implies."

Olivia exploded in a laugh. "Oh, Raffy. Don't be superstitious. All the stories about the fates, and destiny, and those types of things are myths. None of them are real."

He smirked. "If you say so."

"I hate to change the subject, but what are you going to do about

Paolo?"

"Nothing."

"WHAT?"

He crossed his arms over his chest. "Nothing. I called Genisse into the office yesterday and presented her with all the evidence of their thievery. She broke down and told me the story. Paolo has a gambling habit he has been feeding with my money. He promised to take Genisse away from here and her abusive husband, but that never came to fruition. When he went out and bought the Fiat Spider, she knew she had to extricate herself from the situation or be taken down with him.

"I never gave him any financial information like the bank number or passwords to accounts or computers. He wasn't interested. It may just have saved my hide. Genisse will be dealing with her husband, a rather nasty character, so I don't see the point of adding to her misery.

"Paolo has the gambling syndicate to answer to, and they don't take lightly to people who rip them off. Personally, I don't think anything I could do would be anywhere near as punishing as what the syndicate will do."

Olivia thought about what he'd said. "You're right."

Rafaele raised an eyebrow. "Can I mark that on the calendar?"

"What?"

"You said I was right."

"Go ahead. I'll just tell people you had too much wine and heard me wrong."

He laughed. "And they would believe you. May I take you to lunch, *Signorina?*"

Olivia smiled. "Lead the way."

Street Dog Dreams
Genie Gabriel

Dedication

To all the dogs I have loved.

Chapter One

What if Dogs Were Royalty and Humans Were Their Loyal Servants?

"Pre-paw-sterous!"

The Canine Queen looked up from her search for possible homes for their dogizens at her mate's exclamation. When he resorted to punny canine-isms, she knew something had raised his hackles. "Why do you watch these human news shows if they upset you?"

"I must keep informed. After all, I have a planet to run–" Her mate stopped in mid-sentence as a hang-dog expression claimed his face, making it sag like a bulldog rather than the sleek, ninety-pound hound he was. "Well, I used to have a planet to run."

"We'll find another dogdom. I'm looking for possible locations now."

"I hope something comes up soon. I'm grateful we found humans like Horace and Maddie to let us stay at their castle, but I'm doggoned bored."

"Fortunately, caring for our pups has taken up most of my time."

"They aren't puppies any more." Reynaud glanced out the leaded glass windows of the modern day castle where the Royal Canines had been staying since their space craft had crash-landed on Earth. Though mid-summer, this part of Oregon was still green with tall trees shading much of the grass growing on the generous grounds surrounding the castle.

Their three eighteen-month old pups–equivalent to human teenagers–played near the spaceship where their host and creative inventor, Horace Ainsworth, was working to finish repairs that would make the craft functional again.

"Time for our pups to learn more responsibility," the Canine Queen agreed. "If our planet, Canid, had not been destroyed, they would be learning how to run a dogdom by now."

In companionable silence, they watched their offspring for a time. Then Reynaud asked, "What have you found for possible homes?"

"Most intriguing so far are homes in Italy and Sardinia selling for one euro. Maddie tells me that is almost giving them away."

"What's the catch?"

"Most need extensive repairs." The Canine Queen paused, then decided her mate might as well know the rest of this story. "These small towns are looking to increase their populations because most of the young people are moving to cities to find jobs."

"So they are looking for humans."

"This is a human-dominated planet. We were fortunate to find a home with Maddie's family, who not only can communicate with us, but treats us with respect and dignity. Unfortunately, that is not the case in many places on this planet."

"Including this Sardinia?"

"I've read there are many of our kin who are dumped on the streets and beg for scraps of food to survive."

"Ri-dog-diculous!"

"A golden opportunity to save these fellow canines if we can find humans such as Maddie and Horace there."

"I'm going to see if Horace has made progress on our paw-gloves. Having opposable thumbs would mean I could be of more help."

Chapter Two

A Human Connection in Sardinia

Dressed in a dog suit, Chiara Caddu stood near the street that local Sardinian animal rescue organizations despondently called Corso Randagi or Street Dog Boulevard since so many dogs were dumped along its narrow edges. Her bone-shaped sign read, "Streets are not for dogs."

"Then get off the road, bitch!" A passing motorist shouted, throwing a basket-ball sized item at her.

Reflexively, Chiara lifted her arm to deflect the flying object. When she realized it was a small dog, she scrambled to catch the critter. The impact of the furry creature landing in her arms unbalanced Chiara. As she tried to regain her balance, the snow-shoe-sized feet of the costume tangled together. She stumbled and weaved, desperately hanging onto the precious fur bundle in her arms. The heavy head of her costume further threw off her balance as she grew dizzy. Chiara figured the easiest way to stop this crazed dance was to fall on the ground. But how to do that without smushing the dog in her arms?

Was there anything less hard than concrete or less prickly than cactus to land on? It was hard enough to see out the mouth of her dog costume, let alone to actually tell one whatchamacallit from another while her head was spinning.

Closing her eyes to try to stop the dizziness, Chiara aimed toward a scrubby form and hoped it wasn't cactus. Then she held the doggie in front of her and turned slightly so her side would hit first.

The ground, when it rose to meet her, didn't seem as hard as it should have been. The head of her costume flew off and rolled toward the road. Chiara relaxed a moment and took a deep breath. Then gagged as the smell assailed her nostrils. Slowly, she opened her eyes and realized she had landed on a pile of garbage.

The little dog howled in protest. Chiara set the pup on the ground and tried to stand up. However, the feet of her costume were still tangled together. She finally managed to flail herself onto her hands and knees among the garbage, coming face to face with the little dog staring at her with an almost awestruck expression.

"You could have given me a hand here."

The pup sniffed at her a couple times and backed away.

"So I'm on my own?" Untangling those snowshoe-sized feet proved difficult but not impossible, and finally Chiara rose awkwardly to a stand. "Don't you tell anyone about this."

A car honked as it sped away, the passengers yelling, "Thanks for the show!"

Her face flushed red with embarrassment, Chiara bent to pick up the little dog and the head of her costume before limping toward her vehicle. Some days just didn't go as well as others.

~ * ~

Chiara drove up winding roads edged by scrubby brush. After about a half hour, she turned onto another road that was little more than a dirt track leading to a farmhouse built of granite blocks, historically used by shepherds in the area.

Fortunately, this one had been remodeled to include modern conveniences such as a bathroom and numerous kennels to house dogs rescued from the streets.

A chorus of barking greeted Chiara's arrival, which subsided into excited sniffing of the puppy she brought. In the way of many in this region, the woman who came to meet her was tall and slender with longish dark hair. However, rather than the stylish women who walked the street of the cities, Gabriella's hair was pulled back into a ponytail which stuck out the back of a billed cap sporting the logo of her American husband's favorite baseball team.

"Brought you another recruit." Chiara handed the puppy to Gabby.

Gabby automatically ran her fingers through the dog's fur, doing a quick check for wounds, weight, growths, anything abnormal. She took him to their "intake" area–a smaller stone building that had once housed both sheep and shepherds. The two-room building contained a thick slab table now used for exams, a tub for bathing the dogs–braced in what was formerly a manger, and a row of stalls that had been transformed into kennels.

Gabby bathed the little dog while she and Chiara talked.

"How long are you going to stay home this time?" Chiara handed Gabby a bottle of dog shampoo.

"Going back to the States next month when my in-laws celebrate their anniversary. Planning to stay about three weeks so I have time to tour a couple animal rescues. Don't know which is worse. Constantly begging for money as the nonprofits in the United States seem to do or seeing criminal organizations take over the shelters here for the per canine money from the government."

"Does either way keep dogs off the streets?"

"That's what's frustrating." Gabby sighed as she rinsed the shampoo off the little dog's fur. "The U.S. has more shelters and are better organized, but dumping an animal isn't uncommon there either. At least more Americans seem to think of dogs as pets, and support spay-neuter efforts. I'm hoping to bring back ideas that might help our locals change their attitudes."

"In the meantime, we rescue the ones we can." Gabby dried the little dog with a towel. "This guy seems fairly healthy, but we'll separate him from the rest of the pack for a while just to be sure."

She settled the dog in a small enclosure by himself, then brought food, water, and a soft pad for a bed. The little guy paused in gobbling the food, cocked his head and looked at the two women.

"You get to stay here," Chiara said. "Gabby will take good care of you, and soon you'll be able to play with other dogs."

The pup finished the food, rooted under a blanket and curled up on the bed.

"He's settling in quickly," Chiara said.

"Yes." Gabby paused, then frowned. "You seem to bring us another dog or two every time you stand on the road in your dog suit."

"It feels good to be able to help the dogs."

"Or maybe people are counting on you being there so they have a place to dump a pet they no longer want."

Disbelief mingled with disappointment in Chiara's chest. "I hadn't thought about it that way."

"You might also be putting yourself in danger–"

"I'm used to people throwing things at me. Like this puppy."

"I was thinking of more than thrown objects. I've been told Brutto has moved into the area."

At this statement, Chiara frowned. Brutto's real identity was a mystery. He was linked to a number of criminal activities but seemed to operate on his own with a small cluster of cronies. When setting up dog shelters became profitable because of the per canine payments from the Italian government, this of course attracted the criminal element interested in making money rather than humanely caring for the dogs as had been the intent of the law.

Brutto quickly became one of the top money-makers in this area. He just as quickly earned the disdain of legitimate animal rescue groups that wanted to help the dogs, and humanely deal with the problem of dog overpopulation by running spay/neuter campaigns while educating people to change their attitudes that dogs and cats could survive on the streets without human care.

"Mr. Nasty himself? Did he offend one of his criminal cronies on the mainland?"

"Expanding his operations is what I heard. He's gathering up not just street dogs, but those with owners who let their dogs roam freely."

"Anyone know where he's set up his dog warehousing operation this time?" Chiara asked.

"Not for sure. We have a number of people scouting the area as they go about other business."

"Well, let me know and I'll do what I can to help shut him down." Still dressed in the body of her dog suit, Chiara turned to go. "Thanks for taking the little guy."

"Think about what I said." Gabby waved as several of the dogs barked and she went off to check on the ruckus.

Chapter Three

Street Tactics

When Chiara pulled up to her family home, her dog suit still smelled of garbage, in spite of driving with the windows down. She sighed. No way was she going to avoid questioning by her mother.

"Mamma, I'm home!" Chiara closed the door behind her. Large windows on two sides of the room allowed the August sun to gleam on polished hardwood floors where Chiara used to set her stuffed animals and assure them that they would always have a home with her.

"I smell you." Ginevra Caddu wrinkled her nose as she examined her daughter. "What did you get into this time? Why didn't you take that smelly thing off?"

"The zipper is stuck." Chiara turned around to allow her mother to help free her from the costume.

Ginevra clucked disapproving sounds as Chiara related a cleaned up version of her experience on Corso Randagi.

"Why can you not be more patient like Alessandro and work within the system to help these dogs?" Ginevra scolded her only daughter as she stepped out of the dog costume.

Chiara gripped the fabric of the costume in her fist as frustration bubbled at the lack of concern about the treatment of pets by the local *comune* council, as well as being compared to a childhood friend who seemed perfect in her mother's eyes. "While Alek is chasing the bureaucracy in circles, dogs are dying."

"And being a trouble-maker is saving these dogs?"

Chiara scowled. "I'm making a point."

"Maybe you should focus on making progress rather than making a point."

After her mother left the room, Chiara went to her bathroom and vented her annoyance on scrubbing the smell out of her dog costume. The entire day brought a frustrated flush to her cheeks. Having a poor dog dumped into her arms. Being laughed at as she stumbled around like a clumsy idiot in her dog suit. Finding out Brutto had moved his abusive operations right into their midst.

She was trying to change conditions for the dogs to give them better lives, yet she was the one being labeled as a trouble-maker. More than once in recent months, and now by her much loved mamma.

She just could not abide the cruelty with which dogs were disposed of in her country. The puppy today was lucky in some ways. When she closed her eyes, visions of other dogs–skinny and injured– haunted her. Rescues were making headway in how animals were treated, but shelters like the ones Brutto set up were canine jails where the government funding was clearly not used to care for the dogs.

No fresh water for the dogs or perhaps no water at all. Fights over what little moldy food was tossed into a pen with dozens of dogs. Illnesses and injuries that went untreated.

Then there were stories of hidden rooms where no one of the public was allowed. She wasn't sure even staff members went there–until the stench became unbearable.

Shutting down Brutto's facility would be quite satisfying. But that would dump these poor animals on the streets again. The real need was a safe place for these beautiful fur babies to become sleek and healthy as well as spayed or neutered so the population could be brought under control. Of course, people also needed to be educated on taking care of their pets and not treating them as disposable when they grew out of the cute puppy stage.

How can I not be angry in the face of such inhumanity? Chiara wondered. Perhaps she could start by finding out what progress Alek was making.

She retrieved her cell phone and sent her childhood friend a text message. Much safer than trying to stay calm in the face of his reasonable attitude.

When Alek didn't respond within five minutes, Chiara almost sent him a terse follow-up message.

I can be an adult, Chiara reminded herself. She waited another five minutes before sending a reminder message to Alek.

~ * ~

Alek pulled off the street a short distance from the woman in the dog suit and stared at the girl he had loved since he was a little boy in primary school.

Chiara used to be such a quiet child. Until she saw a dog hit by a car and the vehicle didn't even stop. The little dog died in Chiara's arms and a soul deep determination was born to stop this travesty.

While Alek attended veterinary school, Chiara often visited the government-funded shelters, sneaking in treats for the half-starved dogs.

Her impassioned pleas to friends and family to adopt a dog or two or three had resulted in many she once considered friends ignoring her phone calls and relatives avoiding family gatherings where she might show up.

Often, Chiara could be found dressed in a dog suit and standing near a busy road where many dogs were dumped, as she was again today.

"Streets are not for dogs," her sign read.

Ironically, Alek shared Chiara's frustration at the treatment of these beautiful souls. However, he also knew being labeled a trouble-maker would not help the dogs. So he funneled his energy and his professional status as a veterinarian into working with rescues that could save at least a few of these canine friends, lobbying lawmakers, and educating communities on better treatment for pets. Most nights he laid in bed with his heart aching until exhaustion claimed him in restless sleep.

Yes, he understood Chiara's frustration, but he didn't agree with her tactics.

From inside her canine costume, Chiara watched Alek walk slowly toward her, as if fearing she might bite him. From her terse message to him yesterday, she could understand how he would be rather wary. How had she grown so distant from the boy she adored in primary school?

"*Ciao*, Alek."

"*Ciao.*" Alek stood several feet away. "I brought you a sandwich."

Remembering her mamma's disappointment upon learning of her escapade yesterday, Chiara didn't even rant at Alek about eating when dogs were starving on the streets. "Thank you."

She took off the head of her costume and sat on a patch of dirt and dried grass on the side of the roadway. Chiara had barely unwrapped the sandwich when a stray dog slunk from behind a broken board of a nearby fence and inched closer.

"I brought extra." Alek tore off a hunk from another sandwich and tossed it to the dog. Quickly gobbling down its prize, the dog warily glanced up, hoping for more. Alek tossed it another chunk of sandwich before glancing at Chiara. "What?"

"You aren't such a bad guy after all."

Alek tossed one last chunk of food toward the dog. "Thanks. I think."

By this time, another dog had slunk through the broken fence and stared at Chiara's food. She tore what remained into chunks and fed it to the dog, then stood up.

"Crazy bitch!" a punk in a passing car yelled, then laughed and tossed a bone at Chiara.

"Watch out!" Alek stepped in front of Chiara and deflected the flying object with her sign, so it boomeranged against the back window of the car as it sped away. "That could have hurt."

With both of them holding the sign, their noses were mere inches apart. As the musky scent of Alek's aftershave teased Chiara's nostrils, she closed her eyes and remembered the first time he kissed her. The day of her sixteenth birthday. Just a whispery touching of lips, followed by an awkward silence.

But today, no kiss. Just a soft question from her childhood friend. "Why would you risk your life out here?"

Pretty much the same question her rescue friend, Gabby, had asked her. Tears filled Chiara's eyes. Of disappointment. Of frustration. Of feeling hopeless in the face of so much that seemed wrong. "I have to do something. I can't just sit home in comfort while there are dogs on the streets suffering and starving."

Chapter Four

Street Dogs: Introducing Ludovica's Ladies

"I'll bet they have soft beds there." Bianca shook back her dirty white fur and settled on her belly amid the shrubby bushes. The hill overlooked acres of luxury accommodations tucked around a bay of crystalline turquoise water on the northern coast of Sardinia, Italy. Bianca often dreamed of staying in one of the gleaming stucco buildings with an adoring and very wealthy owner who cruised the sparkling clear waters in a private yacht.

"Wouldn't let dogs on the beds anyway." Ludovica laid down beside her friend and lifted her canine nose to the wind, hoping to catch the scent of a special treat left by the tall, skinny kid with a protruding Adam's apple who worked in one of the restaurants. He seemed to know Ludovica or one of the Ladies in her pack would stop by after darkness fell. Other humans made fun of him, but their dog pack of girls knew he was a friend. At least as much of an ally as a *randagi* could have in a human.

"If we had a pedigree, humans would let us sleep on the beds." Bianca rubbed her face with a paw.

"Lots of street dogs have pedigrees. Doesn't make them any more welcome than the rest of us."

"We just need a bath and our fur brushed. Think we can sneak into the pool after dark?"

"Too risky. We're lucky to get scraps out of the garbage without the catchers getting us."

Bianca sighed as her eyes drifted closed.

"Hey, we have to stay alert." Ludovica nudged her furry friend. "The rest of the girls are expecting us to bring dinner."

"Just a short nap, 'Vica. I'm so tired."

"Are you going to have more puppies, Bianca? Why don't you stay away from that cur?"

"He brings me food. Makes me think I can be with a family again."

"We'll never be with a family again. We just have to make the best of what we have."

"I'm not strong like you, Ludovica. I need to believe someone will want me enough to take care of me some day. That my fur will be fluffy and white again. That I'll have a soft bed and my food bowl will always be full. That I could stay in a resort like this one."

Ludovica sighed. "I got part of a sandwich earlier today from the human in the dog suit. It's for you, but don't tell the other girls."

"Oh, 'Vica, if you were a stud I'd kiss you."

"After you licked your butt, no doubt."

"Don't...be...crude," Bianca said between bites. She tried to nibble the sandwich to make it last longer, but her hunger insisted she wolf it down.

"Did you see the signs about mandatory castration some new group of humans is pushing?" Ludovica's tummy rumbled a protest as Bianca finished off the sandwich.

"Too late for me again." Bianca burped, then touched a paw to her mouth in mock consternation.

"Maybe the human in the dog suit can tell us more. For after the puppies are born, you know?"

"I want to take a nap."

"Not here. Go back to the old *aeroporto* so the catchers don't find you. Tell the girls I'll be back after dusk."

Chapter Five

A New Misadventure for Maddie & Horace

As the airplane banked to come in for a landing, Madelaine Ainsworth stretched her nearly six-foot frame in the seat to see the airport of Olbia on the northern coast of Sardinia, Italy. This trip marked her first adventure with her beloved husband. After years of traveling by herself, her last misadventure had convinced Horace not to let Maddie travel alone.

Unfortunately, the dear, sweet man didn't seem to be enjoying the journey so far if the white-knuckled grip on the armrests were an indication.

Once the plane touched down, an announcement over the loudspeakers asked passengers to please stay in their seats. Among the muffled groans of the other passengers, Horace asked, "Is this normal?"

"Better than a crash landing with ants in my hat." Maddie took Horace's hand as he relaxed his grip on the armrest.

From her seat she could see airport security swarming around a jumbled mass of baggage and broken animal kennels lying on one of the runways.

Amidst the chaos, a woman with long, dark hair gestured expansively, her distress obvious even to those watching from the airplane.

"Omigosh," Maddie whispered to Horace. "Looks like the rumors of animals not being treated well by the airlines are true. I wonder what happened?"

"I don't know, but I'm glad our canine friends took the spaceship to meet us nearby. At least we don't have to worry about them being in the debris of the kennels," Horace said. "By my calculations, they should have arrived by now."

"The woman seems really upset. I hope those poor dogs are okay."

When the passengers were finally allowed to deplane and claim their luggage, the contingent of security had moved inside the terminal building, trying to calm the still shouting woman. "What do you mean my Greta was in the belly of the airplane? She only flies first class with her handler."

"We're still putting together the pieces of what happened, Signorina Rossini. But it appears your poodle may have been dognapped."

The woman pressed her hand flat out on her chest. "How could this have happened? Where is Greta's handler?"

"She was discovered tied up in the restroom at the airport in Rome. Said she was attacked by three men when she entered the terminal."

"Where was security? And where is my Greta?"

"We are searching for her now. It seems she ran away when her crate was damaged among the other baggage."

"My Greta cannot be on her own. She always has her people with her. You must find her immediately."

"Our searchers are highly trained and very successful in tranquilizing stray animals—"

"My Greta is no stray! She is a champion at international shows around the world."

"We're doing all we can—"

"And what is this tranquilizer you use? I do not allow any foreign substances in her body that could affect her status as a champion."

Another security officer appeared with a man in cuffs, interrupting the woman's tirade. "We found this man near the runway with two mongrel dogs. He stepped in front of the runaway mutt or we would have had her."

"That's Charlie." Maddie nudged Horace. "But he wasn't

walking funny like that when he left in the spacecraft. And where are our Royal Canine friends?"

~ * ~

"What did you do with my Greta?"

The woman was screaming at him, but Charlie couldn't understand all of what she was saying. The test flight of the Royal Canines' space craft had gone smoothly. He landed the craft near the Sardinian airport as agreed to meet Horace and Maddie. However, his canine king, Reynaud, spotted broken kennels and dogs running loose at the airport, so insisted on investigating.

The last thing Charlie clearly remembered was seeing men in uniforms pointing rifles at Reynaud, the Royal Pup Thor, and a punk-looking dog. Of course Charlie jumped in front of the guns to save his king. That's what the humans who served as Royal Canine Guards were trained to do. However, instead of bullets he was struck by something that felt like the vaccines he got as a child–magnified a hundred times. When he pulled the darn thing out of his butt, it was a dart.

Charlie was grabbed by security, but Reynaud and the other dogs were able to escape.

Security dragged him to a building where the angry woman yelled at him, but his brain seemed to be drifting outside his head and only partially functioning. Maybe he could hear her if he was standing closer. Besides, she was pretty and she smelled good. So he tried to step forward, but his left leg wouldn't work. Kinda collapsed when he took a step. If not for the guy holding him up, Charlie would have met the polished tile floor with his face.

Charlie tipped his head to one side and squinted at the woman. *Yep. Definitely hot.*

"Is your Greta the dog with part of a pom on her head?" Charlie slowly lifted his hands. If he narrowed his eyes and concentrated, he could kind of form a round shape over his hair.

"What do you mean part of a pom?" At least the woman had stopped yelling and was now only glaring at Charlie.

Oops! Faux pas, Charlie thought. "Well, poodles sometimes have these silly haircuts..."

If anything, the woman's glare deepened.

Charlie searched his fuzzy brain for just the facts and what little he had noticed about this dog before the dart hit his butt. He patted the air on the right side of his head. "Pom on right side."

Then he smoothed his hand over the other side of his head. "Left side shaved short."

The woman gasped. "This cannot be. My groomer would never do that to my beautiful Greta. Would not make her ugly."

Charlie tried to fight the fog closing off his peripheral vision. "Well, it kind of fit with the pink and purple swirls on the dog's sides."

Kinda like the swirling of this room...

"This cannot be my Greta!"

As the woman yelled at him once more, Charlie's eyes drifted closed and he sank onto the floor.

~ * ~

"What's wrong with him?" The woman stared at the man on the floor. What good was a tirade toward an unconscious man?

"Um, when he stepped in front of the dog, the tranquilizer dart hit him in the butt."

"He saved my Greta?" Her anger softened a bit. And he was rather gallant-looking in a bad-boy way dressed all in black as he was.

"And allowed her to escape."

"He may have been involved in the dognapping," another guard said.

"Now wait a minute." Maddie straightened her hat and stepped into the discussion. "We know this man. He wouldn't steal a dog."

"Why would we take the word of an American tourist?"

The dark-haired woman waved her hand in a chopping motion. "Because I am Ilaria Angelica Eleonora Rossini, world famous actress and singer, and I want to hear what she has to say. Besides, she is wearing a hat."

While the security officers exchanged puzzled looks while mouthing "A hat?" Maddie hurriedly said, "Charlie has been devoted to dogs all his life. He would give his life for his Queen and her Mate."

At further odd looks from those standing around, Maddie tried to clarify. "His canine, um, companion's name is Queen's Mate...otherwise known as Reynaud."

"Um, Signorina Rossini, we found another man." A third security guard approached the dark-haired woman, hauling forward a nervous little man with a weaselly face.

"You!" Ilaria pointed toward the little man. "I have seen you skulking around the shows with that Carlotta and her bedraggled beast. What do you know of my Greta?"

The little man visibly trembled in the face of Ilaria's anger.

"Go on, tell her." The security officer nudged the little man none too gently.

"Carlotta...um, said she would do anything to win the show." The little man spoke hesitantly. "And she would too. If your precious Greta would disappear or be disqualified."

"Tell her the rest."

"Carlotta offered a large sum of money to anyone who made sure that happened."

Ilaria gasped and lunged at the little man, who shrank behind the security guard.

"Signorina Rossini, let us get the rest of his statement before you scratch his face off."

As the security guard officer dragged off the little man, he seemed to gather a bit of foolish courage and shouted over his shoulder, "Your precious Greta was with some big bruiser of a dog. Flashy collar with neon lights. Bet he ruins her for sure."

With a shriek, Ilaria threw a bag of dog treats at the little man, bouncing it off his head.

"That must be Reynaud," Horace whispered to Maddie.

"What do you know of this-this...bruiser of a dog?"

"Reynaud is of royal blood and would treat your Greta with greatest respect." Maddie held out her hand to Ilaria. "I'm Maddie

Ainsworth and this is my husband. Charlie has been one of our guests while searching for a suitable new home. We hoped to find a place here in Sardinia, perhaps near my cousin's village."

"Then you have Sardinian roots."

"With a deep love and caring for our canine friends, as you seem to have for your Greta."

A tear rolled down Ilaria's cheek. Then another and another. She wiped ineffectively at her eyes to stop the flow.

"Perhaps we can find some privacy and plan together how best to rescue our canine friends."

Maddie gently took Ilaria's arm and steered her toward a room indicated by another of the airport security guards. Horace followed behind them as two security guards dragged a still passed out Charlie to the room.

Settled in the room with cups of espresso and the door firmly closed, Ilaria swigged down the drink like a shot of bourbon. "I really do love her, you know. Greta's not just an accessory for a publicity stunt.

"Greta wouldn't be safe if anyone knew how much I love that dog." Ilaria dabbed at her eyes with a tissue she pulled from a small purse, then blew her nose. "Dognappers and such. But it's happened anyway."

"Perhaps it's not such a bad thing that love cannot be hidden," Maddie said.

"That sounds very innocent. Naive. I haven't lived in that kind of world for a very long time." Ilaria paused. "I'm not sure I ever did."

Then she drew a deep breath and squared her shoulders. "Enough tears. We must plan the best way to rescue our beloved ones."

Chapter Six

Royal Dogs on the Run

"I-I cannot go much farther." Greta stumbled over her own paws as her pace slowed.

Reynaud paused in their full-speed gallop away from the airport to look at the Earth dog who had escaped with them, now panting heavily. No humans chased them any longer, but where would they be safe? He was in a strange country on this human-dominated planet with his pup and a lady dog to protect.

If they could make it back to the spacecraft, at least they would have a means to connect with Horace and Maddie, as well as find out what happened to their pilot and human guard, Charlie.

At a more cautious pace, Reynaud led the way back to the airport where the spacecraft sat invisibly cloaked. For long moments, they huddled nearby in scrubby undergrowth, watching for signs of trouble.

Seeing nothing but a plane flying overhead, Reynaud said, "Can you make one more short run to our craft?"

The partial pom-pom on Greta's head moved as she frowned. "I don't see a craft."

"You'll have to trust me on this."

Like a good sport, she found one more burst of speed and followed Reynaud and the pup. With his nose sniffing the air, the big hound paused in front of what seemed to be nothing and said, "Quickly, inside here."

The teenaged pup scampered in and hopped onto the co-pilot's seat. Greta followed cautiously, with Reynaud bringing up the rear and settling in the captain's chair.

"Do you know how to fly this thing, Dad?"

Reynaud straightened the paw-gloves on his front feet. "Well, it can't be that difficult. You just tell the computer what to do."

I hope. Reynaud didn't understand all the adjustments Horace had made that allowed the spacecraft to make short flights as well as interplanetary travel but crossed his paws the computer would take care of that also.

"Computer, prepare for take-off." The spacecraft purred to life. Reynaud grinned at his offspring. "There, you see. Nothing to it."

"Please state the coordinates of your destination."

"Uh..."

"Ask for a map of Sardinia, Dad, and just point to where you want to go."

"Right. Right. That's what I was going to do."

A map appeared on one of the monitors, and Reynaud pointed to their location with one of the fingers on the paw-glove. "We're right here now. If we stay close by, we can try to contact Horace and Maddie to rendezvous with them in the morning after all the ker-fluffle has died down."

"There's an abandoned airport a short distance away," Thor suggested.

"Good idea. Computer, take us here." Reynaud slid the robotic finger across the map. Not as easy to work these finger things as humans made it seem.

"Whoa!" Thor gripped the armrests. "Shoulda buckled in first."

Almost immediately, the spacecraft stopped. "Destination accomplished."

"What now?" Thor asked.

"Let's make ourselves comfortable until morning."

"Are we safe here?" Greta's voice quivered.

Reynaud glanced at Greta. "We should be good until morning. There are blankets in the cabinet behind you."

Greta sighed as she dug out a blanket for each of them to nestle into, then silence fell for a few moments.

"Um, Dad? I gotta pee."

"Serious-dog-ly?"

Looking sheepish, Thor nodded.

"I kinda do too." Greta sat up slowly.

"Okay. Let's see what's out there first." Reynaud activated the outside monitor. The spacecraft sat between a rusted metal gate and what must have been a hangar at one time. Now the windows were broken, staring like huge, empty eyes over the concrete runways, dotted with overgrown shrubbery and a few trees standing sentinel.

"Let's just go to the corner of that building. Not much privacy, but we're safer sticking close together."

Thor and Greta nodded. Reynaud commanded the computer to open the ramp door, then cautiously looked around before he motioned with his paw-glove to go out.

While Thor and Greta did their business, Reynaud continued to scan their surroundings. He caught only a quick scent of another canine before what looked like a giant version of an African Wild Dog pounced in front of him and began to circle. "How did you get in here? And what are those weird things on your feet?"

Flew in on a spaceship with robotic hands an inventor made. Yeah, that would go over well. Instead, Reynaud said, "We simply need to rest for the night. We'll be gone in the morning."

The other dog scowled at him for a few moments and seemed to make a decision. "I'm Ludovica and this is where my lady pack hangs out. Don't make any trouble or we'll rip you to shreds."

"No trouble. Just need to rest."

'Vica glanced at Greta when she reappeared from behind the old hangar, then did a double-take. "Girl, I don't know who does your hair and make-up, but you need to find someone else."

With a deep sigh, Greta sank onto the remains of a broken-down cardboard box.

"What happened to her?"

Reynaud briefly described what he saw at the airport of her crate being crushed and how they barely managed to escape. "We have not stopped long enough to hear the whole story."

~ * ~

As Greta drew in deep breaths to calm herself, the other girls came out of hiding to gather round.

"I was the best of show. The champion." Greta stared at the paint staining her fur and whispered, "Now I am ruined."

"Hair will grow out," one of the girls said.

"Not in two days." Greta dropped her head to rest on her paws.

"And not if you have mange," one of the other girls quipped.

"I've never even known a dog with mange." Greta wrinkled her nose.

"Most of us didn't have mange either–until we were dumped on the streets."

"Used to have a home too."

"And someone who told me I was beautiful–until I wasn't."

At the whimpers of agreement and other comments, Greta roused herself to look at the pack of dogs gathered around her. Some had tufts of hair missing. Some had healing wounds on their heads and bodies. Others had red and swollen skin. "Who are you?"

"Dogs like you who once had people. Until they didn't want to bother with us."

"Or were going on vacation."

"Or found a cute puppy."

"Or just got tired of us."

"Then we got dumped."

"My Ilaria would never do that." Greta shook her head so her ears whispered against her face. "She loves me."

The knowing looks on the faces of the other dogs frightened Greta more than she wanted to admit. "It's true."

"Some of us still want to believe we'll have family again. Like Bianca." She indicated a dirty white dog sitting a short distance away, yawning widely.

"On our planet, Canid, the dogs were Royalty and the humans were servants." Reynaud gestured with one of his robotic paw-gloves.

Most of the girls giggled. "Did the dogs all have funny paws like you?"

Reynaud glared down at his front feet. Horace's paw-glove invention seemed like a good idea. If he could only get the darn things off and on by himself. At times like now, they certainly brought his dog-hood into question.

"What happened to your planet?"

"It was destroyed, but–"

"Well, there you go," one of the girls said. "Too much of a good thing and Murphy's Law will strike you down. I'm going back to sleep."

"We will build another dogdom," Reynaud insisted. "One that won't fail."

"Let me know when that happens. In the meantime, I'm going to catch a cat nap." She stifled a giggle. "Another hungry morning will come too soon."

"We have a place picked out here on Sardinia. Our human friends are making the deal. Soon my Queen will arrive and we can move in–"

"Because humans are so reliable." A big shaggy dog shook her head. "Night, all."

Soon most of the pack drifted off to find a hiding place to sleep. Even Ludovica left to stand guard until only pregnant Bianca remained. "Do you mind if I bunk with all of you? I haven't had a blanket for a while."

Reynaud ushered them back into the spacecraft and closed the ramp. As Greta and Bianca settled on their blankets, Thor looked up at Reynaud with hope shining in his eyes. "Tell me again how our new home will be, Dad."

Reynaud settled Thor in the curve of his body and talked to him as he fell asleep. "It will be better than before, my son. Plenty of food and soft beds. Humans who love us will be partners in treating all beings with respect. We will watch out for each other and play in the sunshine..."

~ * ~

Reynaud's first indication of trouble the next morning was

Ludovica's warning growl. Instantly wide awake, Reynaud left Thor cuddled in the blanket and crept softly out of the spacecraft and toward the sound.

"You're not welcome here, Cur."

A laughing snarl answered. "Got no quibble with you, Ludovica. Heard you got fresh recruits last night. Want to work a deal to try them out."

"No deals."

"Let the little lady decide."

By now, several of the girls were stirring. Edgy. Waiting to see if they should run and hide or if this was a no-big-deal encounter.

Bianca stretched and sauntered out into the morning sunshine. "I'm up for you, Cur."

"Not interested." Cur didn't even look at the dirty white dog who carried his pups. "Call out the new girl."

Reynaud figured it was time to make his presence known. Cur sized him up and dismissed him with a single glance. "This is a new recruit for Ludovica's Ladies? With those clumsy paw things, I can see why no real dogs would keep you around."

Cur's gaze roamed to the spaceship, quickly spotting Greta cautiously appearing on the ramp. "Even with the punk look, she's a babe. Give her up or I'll rip up your pack and take her anyway."

As the other girls slipped out of sight, Cur advanced toward Greta. "I'm all yours, baby."

"Ew!" Greta's lip curled in reaction to the smelly, slobbery canine who lumbered toward her.

"You heard the lady." Reynaud stepped between Greta and the cur.

"Think you can take me, Miss Sissy Paws?"

Cur charged Reynaud, who did a doggie version of martial arts.

"Kee-ah!" Reynaud jumped, executed a one-two kick with his back feet, and landed on all fours in a lithe movement.

"What was that?" one of the girls whispered from her hiding place.

"Ninja canine?" another one suggested.

With a roar, Cur charged again, only to be met with a flying scissor kick that rolled him several yards away in the dirt.

His next charge wasn't quite as strong, and he almost immediately landed on his side with a dull thud. He lay unmoving for several moments before struggling to his feet to slink away. Warily, several of his most loyal cohorts followed. "You're gonna regret this, Sissy Paws."

As the girls cautiously crept out of their hiding places again, they looked at Reynard with more respect. Thor sat proudly by his sire as one of the girls said, "Tell us again about this dogdom you have planned."

Chapter Seven

The Search

While Chiara donned the dog costume and stood on her usual street, Greta's wealthy dog owner had searchers combing the streets for her beloved canine. Though worried about their canine friends, Horace and Maddie let the searchers do their job while they respected the Canine Queen's wish to move ahead in finding a place for a new dogdom.

So they journeyed to the advertised one dollar house. Though disappointed in that place, a short distance beyond they found an entire abandoned city. Crayon-colored houses marched shoulder to shoulder up the hillside crowned by a castle-like fortress. Although many of the stone structures were crumbling, a large number were mostly intact and could provide shelter while repairs were underway in the rest of the city.

Maddie marched from house to house, snapping multitudes of photos to send to the Canine Queen. At the same time, Horace tagged along behind, juggling a measuring wheel and his new computer tablet to calculate and record the size of houses, the width of streets, and how large the entire town was.

"Do you think the Royal Canines would like living here?" Maddie asked.

"I can think of many ways to make life easier for our doggie friends." Horace frowned thoughtfully as he touched the screen of the computer tablet. "They won't all need the robotic gloves with human-like thumbs if we automate the doors to open, have pedals to operate refrigerator doors, build self-driving vehicles to transport puppies and older dogs–oh my! So many possibilities. I'll be busy tinkering to help our friends for quite some time."

"Maybe you can take on an apprentice," Maddie suggested.

Horace scratched his head, encouraging his spiky white hair to stand up even more. "Maybe I could if the right person–or dog–was interested. Maybe I could."

"Don't forget your rolling measure, dear," Maddie said as Horace began to wander down the narrow cobblestone streets, rubbing his chin thoughtfully. Horace kept walking, so Maddie shrugged and tucked the instrument into the wheeled cart that contained several other tools and a picnic lunch.

Maddie easily caught up with Horace and took his arm as they resumed examining the houses.

When they neared the top of the hillside city, Horace paused to take a deep breath. In spite of the joy of being with his beloved wife, Horace missed his basement laboratory at home in their modern day castle. He also wasn't sure how much of this adventuring his out-of-shape body would tolerate. Maddie seemed tireless and fearless while he...well, he was much more cautious and ready to go home. Well, at least back to his host's home.

"Have we seen enough for today?" Horace asked.

Maddie looked toward the top of the hill just a short distance away. "Let's go see what's behind those rock walls. Maybe it's a castle like ours."

"Or just crumbling stones."

"Come on, where's your sense of adventure?"

"Down the hill a ways, I think, along with most of the soles of my shoes."

With a laugh, Maddie said, "You've been such a good sport for our first adventure together. A quick look at the castle, then we'll go back to my cousin's house."

Horace took a breath, then marched the rest of the way to the top of the hill with Maddie.

Indeed, the rock walls did seem to be crumbling in many places, with stones scattering down the hillside. However, inside the walls, the structures were more solid.

"This building seems to be in good shape." Maddie pushed open the door of a two-story stone structure.

"Not as new as our castle back home." Horace scanned the building.

"And without most of the conveniences you have invented for us, I would imagine." Maddie smiled before she stepped inside.

"Be careful, my dear. There may be rodents or rotting floors."

"Oh, my." Maddie stopped just inside the doorway.

Not expecting her abrupt halt, Horace bumped into her. "Apologies, my dear."

"Horace, look at this!" Maddie whispered with awe.

She stepped closer and examined a scene of the village spread out below them with stars twinkling above. Several people stood in the narrow streets and dogs peeked around corners of the houses. "It's a tapestry."

"Two of these dogs look like Reynaud and the Canine Queen." Horace squinted, trying to see the detail through glasses that insisted on slipping down his nose. "And I believe those are their puppies playing in the courtyard."

"A dog in every house." Maddie's grip on Horace's arm conveyed her excitement. "This is the new dogdom."

"How can you be so sure just from a picture?"

"It's not just a picture. This is a sign—an omen. The Canine Queen will be so pleased."

As they hurried out of the stone fortress and back down the hill into the city, a woman watched from inside the stone structure, smiling.

~ * ~

When Chiara arrived home that evening from standing on the street in her dog suit, she told her family about a large dog who sat and stared at her almost all day. "He wasn't scary, but seemed determined, like he was trying to tell me something."

"Did he stand about waist high?" Maddie asked. "Reddish-brown with a collar studded with jewels? Have a smaller dog with him?"

250

"That sounds like him. Didn't notice any jewels on the collar. It was kind of dirty..." Chiara's voice tapered off as her thoughts connected. "You think these are the dogs you've been looking for?"

"Was there a poodle with them? White, standard size, pom-pom cut on her head and legs?"

"I didn't see a dog like that," Chiara said. "But some of the dogs hang back or hide behind the fence."

"I'm going to call Ilaria. This may be the break we've been waiting for."

Ilaria, the owner of the show dog who had been lost when the kennels had been damaged at the airport, insisted on going to the street with a team of searchers. Though they spent several hours combing the area, they didn't find Greta or the Royal Canines.

Chapter Eight

Royal Canines Captured!

Reynaud paced the perimeter fencing of the abandoned *aeroporto*, sometimes silently cursing the clumsiness of the paw-hands on his front feet. He knew Horace and Maddie would be looking for them and had been trying to send telepathic messages to Maddie of their location. Was telepathy here in Sardinia as unreliable as the radio in the space ship? Neither seemed to be working.

Soon they would be discovered. But when and whom? The cur pack continued to linger within howling range, and Ludovica's Ladies told him of the constant danger from the catchers, who made regular sweeps of the area to round up any *randagi* who might upset the tourists.

"Do you smell them?" Ludovica appeared silently beside Reynaud.

"The cur pack?" Reynaud nodded.

"They are always around before a sweep by the catchers who come through to clear the streets of dogs before another boat of tourists come. So be especially alert. I'm going to visit our restaurant friend to see if he left any special treats. Bianca needs more nourishment as the time for the puppies draws near."

"What will happen to the puppies?" Reynaud didn't want to think about what might have happened to his own pups if they hadn't found Horace and Maddie.

Ludovica simply sighed. "We will do what we can."

Frustrated, Reynaud swished his tail. Perhaps their dogdom would be ready for new dogizens by the time Bianca's babies arrived.

He had just rounded the corner of the fencing when searchlights flipped on with blinding intensity. He howled the signal for danger–run for those who could and hide for those who were slower.

~ * ~

"I-I can't move very fast," Bianca panted. "My belly..."

"As quickly as you can, get to the spaceship and activate the cloaking device." Thor urged Bianca in that direction.

"The others won't be able to find it."

"Everyone who was going to hide there will already be inside. Hurry now, while I distract the catchers."

"Be careful, Thor!"

Thor peeked around the corner of the old hangar, then dashed toward the gates, figuring the movement would draw the catchers away from accidentally bumping into the cloaked spaceship.

"There's a little one!" One catcher tried to tackle Thor but came up empty-handed, then tripped over his own feet and tumbled over and over before landing against the old hangar with a ker-thump.

"I'll get him!" Another catcher with a bow-legged gait came running with his catch pole out in front of him. But as he swung it down toward Thor, the pole stuck in a hole in the ground and the catcher went flying through the air before landing in a patch of overgrown thorn bushes.

Thor zigzagged toward the gates, figuring he could slip into the underbrush and hide until the catchers went away. However, he had not counted on the blinding lights used by the catchers. He stumbled as he neared the gates and crashed into the metal mesh rather than streaking through the gap.

"Got him!" One of the catchers snagged Thor with a long pole with a noose at one end. A strangled cry emitted from Thor's throat as the noose cinched and pulled him off his feet. Blackness danced in his vision.

He heard his father's roar and barely caught his breath as the noose loosened and he crashed to the ground, the catcher falling against him.

"Get the big one!"

~ * ~

Reynaud bucked and dodged the catch-poles that swung around him while trying to reach Thor and free him.

"Drag the little one and the big beast will follow!" one of the catchers shouted.

And follow he did. Reynaud grabbed the handle of the catch pole in his jaws, chewing the wood desperately in an attempt to break it.

Not soon enough! Thor was dumped into the back of an oversized van with Reynaud still attached to the catch pole by his teeth. No way would Reynaud desert his son, though he knew he might be signing his own death warrant.

The metal doors slammed shut, leaving Reynaud and Thor crammed in the space with other dogs who had been captured that night.

Silence settled over them all as the vehicle jerked to a start, jostling them against each other.

"I'm sorry, Dad. The lights blinded me and I missed the gates." Thor fell into silence for a moment before he said softly, "At least Bianca and some of the others weren't found."

Silent in his anger for a few moments, Reynaud glared at the hand-paws on his front feet. They had been of no use during the struggle except to get in the way. At least now they were tattered enough for him to pull off with his teeth. "We both violated the rule that the Royals must be doggone safe at all costs."

"Why is that, Dad? Why are we more special than the others?"

Reynaud gazed around at the others in the back of the van. Some shivering with terror. Others lying in resigned defeat. *Why indeed?*

His recent experiences with the Geeks in Green, who drugged him and planned to use him for experiments, and now with most humans and the catchers showed him how horrendous life can be when each being was not valued. Perhaps the Royals' greatest value was to give hope to those who had lost their way or to offer a dream to fellow canines who never had one of their own.

Over the next days in the shelter, Reynaud refused to join the fights over moldy scraps of food. Instead, he organized others to share what was tossed into the cages. As one of the bigger dogs, the sneering humans expected him to bloody the others and supply entertainment for the staff. To their disappointment, Reynaud carried pieces of food to the smaller and weaker dogs, then stood watch to be sure they ate. Through this experience, Reynaud's determination to build the dogdom strengthened.

And he and Thor began to plan an escape.

In the bowels of the concrete shelter where dogs were cast to die, close to the incinerator, Thor found a weakness in the wire fencing. From the marks on the concrete flooring, this potential escape route had perhaps been scratched by others who had nothing to lose. The dogs took turns scratching and working at this weakness, until nails were broken and paws were raw.

Chapter Nine

More Than Just a Pretty Fur-Face

"I hope they come back today." Chiara arrived at her usual street the next morning with Ilaria, Horace and Maddie. Yesterday, the large dog who matched Reynaud's description had spent a good part of the day staring at Chiara, as if trying to convey a message. Unfortunately, he skittered out of reach when she tried to grab his collar.

Today, no reddish-brown hound or small dog, but what looked kind of like a poodle peeking from behind the fence. Until Ilaria, the show dog's owner, began calling her name.

"Woof!" Greta bounded toward Ilaria, her tail held high and wagging. But she never expected the stunned expression on her beloved human's face.

Someone who told me I was beautiful–until I wasn't. Until they didn't want to bother with us. Or were going on vacation. Or found a cute puppy. Or just got tired of us. The words of the other girls echoed in Greta's memory and her steps slowed, her tail drooped and the smile faded from her face.

Then Ilaria enfolded Greta in her arms. "What have they done to my baby? I will beat them senseless with their own body parts. Oh my girl. My beautiful girl. You will have a full spa treatment. No one treats my Greta like this and gets away with it."

As Ilaria's tears and kisses rained on Greta's face, her tail began to wag again and she licked the tears off her human's face.

"Come, *mio bebe*. We will go to the spa."

Greta entrenched her feet and shook her head. *We must save the*

256

others, mio mamma. *There are others who need our help.*

"I don't understand." Ilaria frowned. "My Greta has always been so compliant."

"She is telling us there are others who need our help," Maddie said. "Like Bianca who is near to having her puppies. Greta wants to help them first."

Ilaria frowned, clearly not liking anything that would delay pampering her beloved dog. With a dramatic sigh, she said, "Very well. First, we save the others, then we will go to the spa."

When the humans arrived at the abandoned airport, Greta led them to the cloaked spacecraft and sat in front of it, smiling expectantly.

"What trick is this? There is nothing here but overgrown shrubbery and crumbling buildings." Ilaria gestured around the bleak space.

"I think I know where our canine friends may be hiding." Horace reached out and tapped on the side of the cloaked spacecraft until he found the open door and ramp leading inside.

Ilaria gasped as he disappeared step by step. She seemed even more aghast when the cloaking device was deactivated and a silvery spacecraft appeared in front of her.

"My Horace is an inventor, after all." Maddie gestured for Ilaria to follow Greta inside.

They found Bianca laying on blankets, surrounded by several other girls.

"It is time for the puppies."

Like the experienced mamma she was, Bianca applied herself to the birth process and, before long, four healthy puppies were cleaned up and nursing from their tired mother.

Ilaria wiped a tear from her eye. "The miracle of birth always moves me. What do you think, Greta? Would you like to share our home with this brave mamma and her babies?"

Greta nodded. *And there are more.*

"More puppies?" Ilaria asked through Maddie.

"Not puppies," Maddie relayed the dog's thoughts. "But those taken by the catcher."

Chiara shook her head. "It's nearly impossible to find a dog once they disappear into those hell-holes."

"Do you know where they were taken?" Maddie asked the show dog.

I circled back and followed the truck as far as I could before they outpaced me. I can take you to where I lost them.

~ * ~

They did indeed locate the "shelter." A somber stone structure surrounded by metal fencing. No human responded to their repeated calls for attention, just occasional howls from inside.

In frustration, they left. After flying the spacecraft to what they hoped would become the new dogdom in the abandoned village, they enlisted the help of Maddie's cousin to rescue Reynaud and Thor from the shelter. Of course, Ginevra knew everyone in the area and was related to many of them. As her cousin, Maddie was part of the family.

After several days of "persuasion" by Ginevra's relative in the mayor's office, Horace and Maddie were allowed into the shelter to adopt one dog only. However, tired of Chiara stirring up the local *comune*, the mayor's office had its own condition. She must no longer stand on the streets in her dog costume.

The padlocked chain link gates and frowning guards were a far woof from the landscaped entries and smiling staff Maddie had seen at animal shelters in her neighborhood back home. However, she reminded herself she was not here to critique their public presentation, but to rescue their Royal Canine friends.

In spite of the officials' attempts to steer them toward the dogs most likely to die, Maddie resolutely marched through the shelter, following instructions relayed telepathically by Reynaud. Though a piece of her heart cried with every pair of begging eyes that watched them walk by, Maddie soon stood in front of the cage that contained Reynaud and Thor. "We want those two dogs."

The officials vigorously shook their heads and insisted, *"Uno cane."*

Reynaud said, *Take Thor. He won't survive without my protection.*

Realizing they were not going to win this battle, Maddie finally agreed with great reluctance. "Very well, the smaller of the two."

Thor looked mutinously at his father.

Remember our plan. You will be needed on the outside to guide the others as they leave here, Reynaud said.

As reluctant as Maddie, Thor walked away from Reynaud, promising his dad, *We'll be back.*

When they were outside and away from the shelter, another surprise awaited Thor.

"Mamma!"

The youngster ran to the Canine Queen and gratefully received her kisses, then somewhat reluctantly endured her examination of how he had changed in the time since she had last seen him. "Thinner but wiser. You are no longer a pup."

"We can help our fellow dogizens here, Mamma. They need us and they can help us build a better place for dogs and humans."

Chapter Ten

Operation Rescue

As part of the deal to keep Chiara in her dog costume off the streets, the mayor's office had pushed through the purchase of the abandoned hillside village. Details were kept vague, saying only they had plans that would make tourists happy, which in turn would make Sardinian officials and business owners happy.

With tourists becoming increasingly vocal about starving dogs on the streets, Chiara reasoned giving dogs their own dogdom with plentiful food and shelter would make everyone happy. Why mention the dogs would be running most of the show with only enough humans to seem like any other normal village?

They set up the Royal Offices in the fortress at the top of the hill in the structure where the tapestry hung on the wall and christened the building the Tapestry House.

Another pleasant surprise was the weaver of the tapestry and lover of animals, Destiny Rose, had recently returned to the area, and was willing to act as receptionist for the dogdom. Her duties included being the lookout to signal dogizens to act dog-like if strangers came around.

Leading the others through the stone wall of the fortress were Bianca and her puppies, becoming the first dogizens of their new home. Some of Ludovica's Ladies also arrived to stay in the Tapestry House until homes in the village were repaired. Local workers were eager to help retrofit the houses with Horace's ideas for automation that would allow the dogs to live almost independently.

However, Ludovica felt the need to stay on the streets and guide other doggie girls who were dumped. She could bring street dogs to the abandoned airport to fly to the new dogdom. She promised to come when most of the streets were empty of *randagi*.

Though the Royal Canines and their human friends wanted to rescue Reynaud from the shelter immediately, he felt honor-bound to free the dogs in the shelter. He feared without someone to feed their dreams conditions would revert to fights over moldy scraps of bread.

They finally agreed on a plan to bring food to the shelter each rescue trip, then transport several shelter dogs out with dogs rescued from the streets. With only a few dogs out of hundreds disappearing at a time, the rescue crew hoped staff at the shelter wouldn't notice missing dogs for quite some time. They also insisted if Reynaud's life became endangered, he would evacuate the shelter immediately.

They quickly installed double rows of kennels in the spacecraft to transport several dozen dogs at once. The craft's ability to make short flights as well as outer space travel would be quite valuable in these rescue efforts.

The rescue crew consisted of a quartet of dogs and humans. Charlie, a top-notch pilot, was determined to redeem himself for losing Reynaud and the royal pup. Horace went along to provide tech support in case something malfunctioned with the spacecraft or the cloaking device. Thor went because he promised his dad he would be back. And, of course, Chiara was determined to put Brutto out of business. In addition, she had much information about the workings of the shelters since she had been banned from several of them.

Buckled into the spacecraft, the rescue crew took a collective deep breath to calm their jagged nerves. Within seconds, they landed at the abandoned airport to pick up the first contingent of *randagi*.

As promised, Ludovica and the strays waited in the abandoned hangar. Many of the dogs cowered on the cement floor when the spacecraft materialized. But 'Vica had been inside several times, so woofed in encouragement and walked up the ramp. Cautiously—and most likely drawn by the smell of treats inside the craft—several of the dogs made their way up the ramp.

Horace invited them to choose a kennel and let them know they would make one more stop before flying to the new dogdom in the formerly abandoned village.

"What if it's a trick?" one of the dogs whispered.

"You can stay on the streets," Thor said. "No dog is being forced to go. If you come with us, you can help build a dream where all of us are well-fed, have soft beds and, most importantly, are respected. You choose. If you don't like our dogdom, you can leave."

"We have a choice?"

"Yes," Chiara said. She was wearing her dog suit, since many street dogs knew her by reputation. "But you have to decide now. We have one more stop to rescue the first of the dogs out of Brutto's shelter. There's limited time to be in there and out."

"I-I don't want to stop at the shelter. Dogs don't come back from there."

Others whimpered in agreement.

"The choice is yours," Thor repeated. "Stay here or take a chance on something better."

"I'm getting old. I don't have anything to lose by taking a chance." A shaggy shepherd mix lumbered toward one of the larger kennels.

Though a couple of the dogs decided to stay, most of them picked a kennel and settled in for the ride.

"Ludovica, we'll be back tomorrow," Thor said.

"Ciao, my little friend."

Some of the *randagi* put their paws over their eyes as the ramp closed up like a clam shell and the spacecraft purred to life.

Within seconds, they arrived at Brutto's shelter. The rescue crew looked at each other.

"The moment of truth," Chiara whispered.

They left the cloaking device activated and the engine idling with Horace at the controls.

"In and out fast," Charlie stated. Like all the Royal Canine Guards, his first duty was to protect the beings who were considered pets, at best, here on Earth. Quite a change from life on their recently destroyed home planet, where dogs were the rulers and humans did their bidding.

Charlie set his laser pistol to "stun" and slipped it back in a shoulder holster. Dressed all in black, he seemed to disappear into the night as he walked soundlessly down the ramp, with only a slight limp on his left leg where he took the dart to the butt cheek.

Thor trotted out and Chiara in her dog costume brought up the rear.

"Not a sound that will give us away."

Unfortunately, within moments a stray cat decided to examine the strange opening that allowed humans and dogs to appear and disappear into the night.

Almost in unison, the dogs inside the spacecraft erupted in a cacophony of barking.

"Quiet! Quiet!" Horace shouted, though he couldn't be heard over the noise of the dogs.

Inside the shelter, dozens of dogs answered the alarm of their kind.

"What is going on?" Charlie yelled into Horace's earpiece.

"Cat. Should we abort the mission?"

"We're on our way back with Reynaud and a swarm of others who ran for the opening when the barking started."

Then spotlights flashed on and alarms screamed.

"Run!"

"I'm stuck!" Chiara cried. "My costume is caught in the wire."

Thor tore at the fabric with his teeth, ripping it enough Chiara could crawl out of the costume.

"Come on, Chiara, we have to hurry."

Chiara scrambled to her feet, taking one last look at the dog costume flopping in the fence. It had served her cause well. Time for a new phase in life.

Although some of the dogs headed for the streets, most of them followed Reynaud and had already reached the spacecraft when Thor and Chiara ran up the ramp.

Horace closed the ramp as Charlie powered up the craft for take-off. "Hang on. This could be a rough ride."

The thrust from the spacecraft stirred dust and gravel as it lifted off. Cloaked as it was, the *polizia* simply stared at the blank sky with baffled looks. What had caused the mini-tornado?

However, they couldn't miss the dog costume in the fence that pointed out the escape route from the shelter.

~ * ~

When the spacecraft touched down inside the walls of the fortress surrounding the Tapestry House, those who stayed at the dogdom came out to greet the new arrivals.

What was intended to be a small contingent of *randagi* for their rescue test run turned into an outpouring of dogs who had packed into the spacecraft...and one terrified cat who huddled in Horace's arms.

Amid the joyous reunion of Reynaud and the Canine Queen, the story of the narrow escape from the shelter unfolded with much excited yelping.

When the doggie crowd calmed down a bit, the Canine Queen insisted everyone head for the showers before eating. Before howls of protest rose above a whimper, Aunt Maddie announced there would be steaks for everyone afterward.

In spite of a few initial spurts and rumbling pipes, Horace's invention of solar hot water showers set up rather like a car wash settled into the perfect spray. The dogs walked through getting wet, sudsing up with a naturally medicating and good-smelling shampoo, a thorough rinse, and blow dry.

Considering the unexpected number of doggie guests, the planned health checks were put off until after their late dinner.

Royal Canine Reynaud was the first to bring up the furor their unexpected escape might stir in the comune.

"Brutto will not be happy," Chiara agreed. "Nor will my mamma and her cousin in the mayor's office."

"We should plan for angry visitors," Reynaud said. "It would be in-dog-itably beneficial if our canine guests were not visible when they arrive."

"I think I might be of help in that area." Destiny Rose, who had been mostly quiet while helping serve dinners, spoke up. She had woven the tapestry foretelling the new dogdom. She also had a great love of animals, so stayed to help build this dream.

"What do you suggest?"

"There are legends of cities dug deep in these mountains, accessible through portals."

"Is there truth in these legends?"

"I believe so," Destiny Rose said.

"How do we know where these portals are?"

"I have a gift, shall we say, of being able to open portals."

As Destiny Rose predicted, the portal did indeed lead to an underground city hidden in the mountain. So they spent the rest of the night moving masses of bedding and food stuffs through the portal into a beautifully secure and hidden paradise.

Chapter Eleven

Risky Dreams

When visitors showed up early the next morning, they found Chiara, Horace and Maddie—with their one dog, Thor, helping a crew of repairmen work on one of the houses. The cat had attached itself to Destiny Rose, who was weaving its feline likeness into her latest tapestry.

Since Maddie was experienced in dealing with buffoonous officials through numerous run-ins with their mayor back in the States, she assumed the role of guide for the group of visitors.

Furious, Brutto declined a tour. The cold, hate-filled expression in his eyes clearly said he suspected more was going on in this village than it seemed.

Instinctively, Chiara moved close to her childhood friend, Alek, who had arrived with the group. The *comune* officials frowned at Brutto, then took a short tour, with many praises for all the work being done.

When the officials left, Alek stayed behind to confront Chiara with the remains of the dog suit.

"This is yours." It wasn't a question. "What are you doing with these dogs?"

Chiara couldn't deny his statement nor could she look Alek in the eyes and lie to him. Could she trust him with their dream to build the dogdom or would he destroy them by telling the local officials the real purpose of the village?

"Saving them. Much faster than working with officials who throw up roadblocks with double talk and favors to their cronies."

Alek took a deep breath and clenched his fists into the fabric of

266

the dog suit. "I'm doing what I can without being labeled a trouble-maker so no one will even try to work with me."

In that moment, Chiara finally looked deeply at Alek. Weariness bracketed the firm line of his slightly full mouth and sadness dulled his eyes. "You really do care what happens to these dogs."

"Of course I do. After all the years you've known me, *bellamissa*, how could you not know how I feel?"

The way he looked at her, Chiara knew Alek wasn't just talking about the dogs. She had risked her life on the streets to rescue dogs. Could she risk her heart? "Do you love me too, Alek? Like I've loved you since I was a little girl?"

Alek reached out and traced the line of Chiara's jaw with his fingertips. Tipped up her chin. And claimed her mouth with his. The kiss probed and melted Chiara's bones so she clung to Alek to remain upright. When he finally lifted his head, the kiss lingered between them. Forever changed the way she would look at this man.

"Yes, I love you."

Several humans cleared their throats and Thor howled, reminding Chiara and Alek they weren't alone.

Looking a bit embarrassed, Chiara stepped away from Alek. "Come meet the Canine Queen and see what we have planned so far."

Inside the Tapestry House at the top of the hill, the Canine Queen and her mate, Reynaud, sat on their haunches beside a banquet-sized table–though the legs were short so it only stood about a foot off the ground.

When Chiara introduced Alek to the Royal Canines, he sank to one knee and bowed his head. "I am honored to meet you both."

The Canine Queen considered Alek for several moments. Alek didn't flinch and waited for her to address him. "So it seems we have another human ally in this man."

"I believe I might be of service to the cause of our canine companions on Sardinia."

"Please, sit with us while we consider our next steps."

Chapter Twelve

Meanwhile, Back on the Streets

A Leonberger-like dog with shaggy hair over his eyes and a Chihuahua mix sat on their haunches off to the side of the street where the human in the dog suit usually stood with her sign. They watched a car slow down, dump a dog, and speed off.

"Ouch! That must have hurt," the smaller dog said.

"I'll go get him." Big Dog lumbered over to where the dog shivered in terror beside the road, dazed and wondering what had just happened. He was so excited when his human said they were going for a ride and then...

"We gotta get you off this road."

The scruffy little dog looked up and up and up at the hairy beast standing over him. "I can't leave. My people will be coming back."

"They won't be back, kid. I've seen this before."

"They'll be back. They just had to–um, well, go to the market. That's it. They went to the market to buy me treats."

The little dog scrunched his eyes closed as a warm, slobbery mouth grasped him gently by the scruff of the neck and carried him to a scraggly patch of grass where a small tan and black dog sat watching them.

"I'm Little Pal. Welcome to our pack. What's your name?"

"I'm Scruffy, but I don't need another pack. My people will back. This is all a mistake..."

The pity in Little Pal's eyes was unmistakable. *Surely what they said couldn't be true.*

"Happens several times a day, kid. You're lucky Big Dog and me were here. Little dogs don't usually last too long on the streets."

"Wh-what are you doing here?"

"Living a fantasy life."

Scruffy was pretty sure Big Dog was kidding, but he had to ask. "What kind of fantasy?"

"What if dogs dumped humans in the streets and drove off in their cars?"

"Except we'd need two dogs," Little Pal added. "One to steer and one to work the pedals."

"Yeah. Give it some gas. Not that much! The brakes–hit the brakes. Ke-rash!"

Big Dog and Little Pal doggie-laughed for a few minutes. Until their chuckles turned to whimpers, seeming to forget their new companion.

"I'm hungry, Big Dog. Will we ever not be hungry?"

Big Dog curled around Little Pal amid the garbage that kept the wind from stinging the places where their fur had fallen out. "Let's just go to sleep. Then we won't notice so much."

Confused but grateful for his new friends, Scruffy cautiously settled next to Big Dog and watched the street. He didn't want to miss his humans if–when they came back.

Little Pal fell into a restless sleep, dreaming of finding a few bites of pasta in the restaurant garbage can in the morning. But Big Dog stayed awake, watching. How long could he protect his Little Pal and their new friend from the Cur Pack that roamed this part of town? Or from the catchers who dragged their doggie friends off to prisons called shelters, never to be seen again?

Finally, exhaustion claimed Big Dog, and he too fell asleep. That's when Little Pal slipped away to investigate. What had happened to the human who dressed in a dog suit? She usually had a lunch to share and kept alive Little Pal's hope for something even more miraculous: a home.

Little Pal closed his eyes and scrunched up his face, searching his memory for what a home felt like. *A vague feeling of warmth settled around him when he thought of a giggling little boy who smuggled him into bed and under the blankets.*

That didn't last long. Soon Little Pal was relegated to the back yard. For a while, he still got a few pieces of pasta tossed on the ground to ease the rumbling of his belly. Then nothing.

The house was empty. The humans were gone.

His hunger finally drove him in search of food. That's when he met Big Dog, who protected him from the Cur Pack and humans who threw bottles at him and tried to kick him. Big Dog seemed mean when he growled and showed his teeth, but Little Pal knew the truth. Big Dog shared what little food he scrounged and curled around Little Pal to keep him warm.

But without much food, Big Dog grew weaker and had been hurt the last time he fought with the Cur Pack to protect Little Pal. He didn't say anything, but the limp gave away his injury.

Time to repay Big Dog for saving his life. Time to see what he could find out about the human in the dog suit. He didn't have to search far. Red Hound lay in his usual gossip central spot near one of the restaurants. "Go to the abandoned *aeroporto* and ask for Ludovica if you want to know what's going on."

"So what is going on?" Little Pal asked.

"Haven't been out there myself. It's a long trip and I'm doing okay here. Have a human friend in the restaurant who makes sure I get food and I can curl up in the doorway if it gets really cold at night."

The big old hound closed his eyes and soon was snoring, so Little Pal made his way back to Big Dog and their new friend, watching cautiously for any of the Cur Pack.

If the hound thought it was a long way to the abandoned airport, the journey would probably be tough for Big Dog with his injured leg. However, Little Pal was determined to convince his shaggy friend to make the trip. He knew in his bones this was their ticket to a new home.

"Do you know where the abandoned airport is?" Little Pal asked.

"A long way." Big Dog closed his eyes again.

"Even if it meant a new home with soft beds and plenty of food?"

Big Dog opened one eye. "Who told you that?"

"Red Hound over by the restaurant."

"He's a gossip."

"He was the first to tell us about the human in the dog suit."

"Um." Big Dog closed his eye again.

"What if he's right about this, Big Dog?" Little Pal lowered his voice. "Scruffy won't last long on the streets, you know, even with us to protect him. What do we have to lose?"

Without opening his eyes again, Big Dog responded, "I'll think about it."

Rather than go back to their usual hideout, the three dogs spent the night nearby, hoping the human in the dog suit would show up the next day. When lunchtime came and went with no sign of her, Little Pal tried again to convince Big Dog to take them to the airport.

The screech of vehicle brakes brought all of them to full alert. "Dump 'em here."

The humans in the car pushed a box out of the back of the vehicle and sped off amid a squealing of tires.

Big Dog sighed. "I'll go take a look."

Little Pal heard growled curse words as Big Dog dragged the box away from the road. "Just babies. In bad shape."

"Red Hound could scrounge some food for them," Little Pal said. "And his restaurant is on the way to the abandoned airport."

Big Dog stared at his Little Pal for a moment. "You and Scruffy take turns helping push the box while I pull it."

~ * ~

"We have to go back," Thor the Royal Pup insisted. "We promised Ludovica. If we don't show up, we will have violated the trust of the *randagi*. We might as well shut down our dream."

Though the muddled rescue at the shelter put all the humans and dogs on edge at the dogdom, they saw the truth in what the young Royal dog said.

"Thor is right," Canine King Reynaud said. "We can't go back to the shelter right away, but we can continue to save our fellow dogs from the streets. We'll just be extra cautious."

So for the next week, the rescue team made stealth transports of street dogs from the abandoned airport. As word spread among the *randagi*, the spacecraft kennels had been full on every trip, sometimes with dogs lying on the belly of the craft between the rows of kennels.

None complained. They were just grateful to be going to a safe place with food and others who cared about them.

~ * ~

"Come on, Big Dog, I can see the old hangar. We're almost there." Little Pal jumped up high trying to see over weeds grown up around abandoned building.

Big Dog panted. His feet were sore, and his back leg dragged. If not for the puppies, he would have insisted Little Pal and Scruffy go on without him. But they couldn't have dodged the Cur Pack and pulled the box of puppies also.

Calling on reserves of strength once more, Big Dog hauled the box of hungry puppies through the gate of the abandoned airport. "Where are we supposed to meet Ludovica?"

"In the old hangar." Little Pal pointed his nose that direction.

"It's awfully quiet," Scruffy whispered. "Are you sure this is the place?"

"That's what Red Hound said."

"He'd better be right. I don't have another mile left on these old paws." Big Dog dragged the box of puppies up to the old hangar and pushed at the door with his nose.

The door creaked open and a pair of red, glowing eyes stared at them. "What's the password?"

"Red Hound sent us." Little Pal's voice trembled a bit when he answered. "Said ask for Ludovica and she could get us to the new dogdom. The puppies aren't doing too well."

"This transport filled up by noon. We've got *randagi* waiting for tomorrow's trip."

"At least take the pups," Big Dog said. "They may not make it another night."

Ludovica's answer was interrupted by the arrival of the spacecraft, stirring up dust as it landed.

Little Pal watched in amazement as a disk-shaped object became visible on the concrete pad beside the hangar and three humans emerged from inside. To his further amazement, the humans seemed to engage in a conversation with Ludovica. Something he didn't know was possible. All of the humans he had contact with didn't listen to dogs at all, let alone have respectful conversations with them.

One of the humans peered into the box of puppies and frowned. "When was the last time they ate?"

"We started our journey yesterday," Little Pal responded.

"They won't last the night without food. Is their mother with them?" The tall man focused on Little Pal.

"J-just us. Me and Scruffy and Big Dog. They were dumped out of a car and Big Dog dragged them to safety. Just like he saved Scruffy and me."

"All of you get in the transport craft."

"We said first come, first served," Ludovica protested. "There are many who have traveled a long distance."

The tall man looked at one of the other humans. "Charlie, can we make a second trip tonight?"

Charlie glanced at his watch. "That's taking a chance on being detected. But let's do it."

"Okay, load up quickly. Remember, silence can save us."

"Into the kennels first," Charlie said. "Then as many as will fit in the aisles. Puppies up front with Dr. Alek."

"Horace and I will stay here until the next trip," Maddie said as the dogs quickly and quietly loaded up. "That will make room for more of our canine friends."

"Are you sure?" Charlie asked. "If we don't make it back, you'll be stuck here until tomorrow night."

"Y-yes," Horace tried to be as brave as his adventurous wife.

"We might be raided by the catchers," Ludovica said. "Word is out on the street about our transports. We usually leave the area after the transport is gone."

"Maybe we can rent a suite in Costa Smeralda and sneak the rest of the dogs in," Maddie said with a mischievous grin. "We'll have time for a swim and a snack before the transport gets back."

"Bianca should be here to experience that." Ludovica's grin was as wide as Maddie's.

"Okay," Charlie said. "Horace, do you have a computer?"

At the older man's nod, Charlie continued, "Send us the new coordinates of where you want us to land when you get settled."

Chapter Thirteen

Street Dogs Get a Taste of Luxury

They called Ilaria Rossini, famous actress and owner of Greta the show dog, who used her connections to garner a private suite with a secluded outside entrance for Horace and Maddie at the resort.

As they checked in, Maddie requested lots of extra towels and a large buffet dinner sent to their suite. With nary a raised eyebrow, the staff quickly set about making this happen.

Behind the locked door of their suite, Maddie opened the back door and cautioned the dogs to be very quiet as they came inside. "You might as well get used to the dogdom routine. Into the showers before eating. No whimpering! Besides, this way you won't have to hit the showers when we get home."

"Home," one of the female dogs whispered. "It's been so long since I had a home."

"Quickly now so everyone has time to clean up before the food arrives."

"We won't have to go to sleep hungry?"

Maddie's heart hitched as the plight of these beautiful beings hit her full force once again. She straightened her hat and stated, "Everyone eats tonight."

All the dogs hustled through the shower, the last one bundled in a towel and hiding in the bedroom just as a knock on the door announced room service.

The man from room service sniffed as he entered, followed by several other staff.

"Is something wrong?" Maddie asked.

"I swear I smell wet dog."

"Oh. Well...that could be my jacket. You see, I miss my canine friends from home so much I spray my jacket with their scent before we travel. It's the only way I can bear to be separated from them."

With a toothy smile, the man nodded. "Yes. Yes. I understand pet owners can be very...devoted...to their pets."

"Devoted. Yes. We are very devoted to dogs."

The man bowed slightly as the rest of the staff finished the set up and walked out the door. "We will pick up the leftovers in the morning if that will please sir and madam?"

Not bothering to tell the man there would likely be no leftovers, Maddie handed the man a large tip and simply said, "Thank you."

As soon as the door closed behind the man, the dogs poured out of the bedroom–mostly in silence–and swarmed the food tables.

"Do you want us to save you some?" one of the dogs asked as he ate the last of the food on one plate.

"You go ahead. We ate before we left the dogdom."

For the next five minutes, the only sound in the room was slurping and burping.

"Oh man, I couldn't eat for another thirty seconds." One of the dogs rubbed his belly.

A slow smile claimed Maddie's face as the dogs drifted off to sleep on the beds, the divans, and the carpet.

"This is a good thing you are doing." Ludovica stared at Maddie and Horace thoughtfully.

"Doesn't begin to make up for the way other humans have treated our canine friends."

"It is a start, and perhaps others will learn from what you are doing."

A comfortable silence settled over them for a few moments, then Maddie asked, "When are you going to join us at the dogdom?"

Ludovica's sleepy eyes barely stayed open long enough to reply. "There is much work to do on the streets."

Chapter Fourteen

Hounded

Brutto snapped a long, black, snake-like whip across Cur's flanks. "Where are the *randagi*? You led us to nothing! A wasted night, you mangy beast. And government inspectors coming tomorrow to count the mutts we have in lockup. We still have not recovered the ones who escaped. You are worthless."

With a half-hearted snarl, Cur slunk off in the darkness to lick his wounded flank in private. He may have long ago lost his soul when he decided to sell out his fellow canines to keep from starving, but he still had a spark of pride.

Cur knew Brutto was looking for another mongrel who would rat out where the street dogs hid, so he had to deliver the goods–er, dogs, quickly. Where could they be hiding? It seemed as if *randagi* were simply disappearing off the streets.

He wandered toward the resorts in Costa Smeralda. The restaurants would be closing and *randagi* always scavenged through the garbage cans for scraps.

However, the streets were eerily quiet. Not a dog in sight. Something odd was indeed going on.

As Cur crept around the corner of the resort, a windstorm swirled violently around him. Terrified, he scurried for cover amid the garbage cans. Peering out between the slats of the fencing, Cur saw a line of dogs jogging stealthily out of one of the resort rooms and disappearing into thin air.

He rubbed his eyes with his paws and looked again. Ludovica!

No surprise she was involved in the disappearance of the *randagi*. She stood with two humans who waved and stepped back in the resort just before the windstorm erupted again.

Cur hunkered down to ride out the swirling wind, then crept close to the building, hoping to find out something that would make sense of what he had just seen–or not seen. Dogs couldn't just disappear into the air, could they?

~ * ~

Though Ludovica was sorely tempted after the luxurious night she had spent in Horace and Maddie's suite, she declined their repeated invitations to join them at the dogdom. She had vowed to save as many of her sister canines as possible from the streets before she retired in comfort.

Before Ludovica crept out of the room at dawn, Maddie told her they were having breakfast with show dog owner and famous actress, Ilaria, who had wonderful news to share about a fundraiser she was organizing to benefit the new dogdom and rescue even more *randagi*.

'Vica returned to the streets filled with hope, and perhaps not as watchful as she should have been. Cur jumped on her and pinned her on the closely cropped lawn before she left the manicured grounds of the resort.

"I saw you last night. How are you making the street mongrels disappear?"

Ludovica detected the scent of a fresh wound and whipped her tail hard against Cur's flank. As he jerked in pain, 'Vica kicked him off and sprang several feet away. "Dogs don't just disappear. Has Brutto been feeding you rotten meat that makes you hallucinate?"

'Vica didn't give Cur the opportunity to respond. She ran as fast as she could, disappearing into the scrubby hillside before the dawn gave away her location.

She was reluctant to return to the abandoned airport. Cur had probably led Brutto there, so the lair she had built with her ladies was no longer safe. In fact, they would probably have to find a different rendezvous point to transport dogs to the new dogdom.

She wondered if she had been foolish to insist all the girls go to the dogdom without her. As she trotted the streets alone looking for a new hiding place, memories of her early life on the streets returned to haunt her.

Mamma was pregnant when they dumped her on the streets, so being a randagi *is all I've ever known. Mamma begged for our food and many times searched the garbage cans for a few scraps. I watched her grow thinner and thinner as the four of us pups grew bigger. She seemed to shrink as we grew. Sacrificing herself so we would survive.*

I'm not sure why I watched while the others tumbled and played. Sat in the back doorway of a restaurant while the others begged from tourists on the street. That's where he found me the day Mamma got hit by a car. One of the few humans who showed any kindness to us street dogs. He left an extra treat for me on his way home from work.

"Ludovica, this is for you," he would say. "This will help make you strong. Make you a fighter so you can survive on the streets."

Then he would sigh and walk away, turning around at the end of the alley and shout, "I'll see you tomorrow, Ludovica."

So I waited for him and the next day he returned. When darkness came, he once again came out of the restaurant and left a special treat. Sometimes he told me, "I wish I could take you home..."

HIs eyes were so sad, I would lick his hand, trying to reassure him I would be okay. By that time, I had grown big. Bigger than my mamma ever was. And I had become a fighter, just as my human friend predicted.

But I also remembered how he had watched out for me when I was still a puppy. So I watched out for others who were smaller than me. Mostly other girls, and together we were stronger.

Now I miss them.

I wonder what happened to my puppy siblings from what seemed like a very long time ago? Maybe I will find them. Then I will go to the dogdom and leave the streets behind.

Chapter Fifteen

Welcome to Our Dogdom

The spacecraft whooshed to a halt inside the fortress walls atop the hill at the dogdom. While Dr. Alek hurried away with the box of puppies, the pilot named Charlie briefed those on board about what to expect.

"When you disembark from this transport craft, you'll go to the showers before eating–"

As whimpers of protest began, Charlie raised his voice. "Orders of the Canine Queen. Clean up or you don't eat. Enjoy your new accommodations, my friends."

The smell of food hurried the process of showers: wet down, shampoo, rinse, blow dry. Well, kind of. Little Pal tried to hide under Big Dog to avoid getting wet, but water sprayed up from underneath them also.

"Whoa!" Little Pal jumped, bumping against Big Dog's belly, who side-stepped and exposed Little Pal to a full drenching. He scrunched his eyes closed and hoped this would be fast.

When the shampoo squirted from all sides, Little Pal wrinkled his nose. He was going to smell like a girl! He just started into a full-body shake when the rinse water drenched him again.

This time Little Pal managed to shake his entire body, spraying water in all directions. Perfect timing as the next instant giant blow dryers came on, sweeping his hair back as it dried like a model's windswept hairdo.

Little Pal emerged from the dog wash with his eyes wide open in amazement, an expression reflected by many of the other dogs. He took refuge under Big Dog's belly again, glad that experience was over.

A human peered down at him and Scruffy, who had scrunched in beside him under Big Dog. "Would you like to go with other dogs your size?"

Trying to make himself even smaller, Little Pal shook his head.

"These are my brothers," Big Dog said. "Nobody messes with them."

The human smiled and pointed the way to the food line.

After eating, the most beautiful dog Little Pal had ever seen stood up with her front paws on a small table, and introduced herself as the Canine Queen. She told the story of their planet of Canid being destroyed and how their search for a new home led them to here. "The houses will be repaired to become our new dogdom, dedicated to allowing our dogizens to be as self-sufficient as possible and not have to rely on humans for our every day existence."

"We don't rely on humans anyway," Little Pal whispered.

Big Dog nudged him. "Shh. Listen to what she has to say."

"That doesn't mean starving on the streets and hiding from the catchers. We are honored to have humans devoted to our cause. They are repairing the houses in the village down the hill so every pack will have their own home."

"I don't want to be in a pack with no prissy dogs. I want my own pack." A scarred gray mixed breed swaggered his way toward the Canine Queen.

One of the Royal Canine Guards, Max, moved to step between them, but the Canine Queen stopped him with a paw on the arm. "All dogizens should also be aware that we will tolerate no fighting and no disrespect. This may be a new way of living for many, but is how our planet lived in peace for many years."

"But you're on our planet now, pretty one, and you get to play by our rules."

The gray dog continued to move forward and the Canine Queen sighed–just before she leaped over the table in a swirl of fur. Round and round the gray mongrel she spun, until his eyes crossed and he thumped to the ground on his butt, growing smaller and smaller.

When the Canine Queen's spinning stopped, a small silver-haired puppy sat in the place where the scarred gray mongrel had been moments before.

"Wow!" Little Pal stared at the Canine Queen with awe. "She looked like a spinning tornado with beautiful hair. And she can do magic too!"

"To the puppy compound?" Royal Guard Max asked.

"Yes. Perhaps with a different upbringing, our friend will make wiser choices as an adult."

Then the Canine Queen continued as if the interruption hadn't happened. "All dogizens should also know our new dogdom is a secret operation right now. We nearly lost a transport that could have shut down this entire dream because fellow canines lost their quiet over a cat–who has become our mascot, by the way, so no chasing. Quiet will be strictly enforced when necessary."

"I think everyone has had an eventful day, so we will show you through the portal to the temporary dorm rooms for sleeping. Please pick a buddy so no one gets lost. Any other questions?"

"Can we have two buddies?" Little Pal asked. "Me and Scruffy are used to being with Big Dog."

"Of course, two buddies would be just fine." The Canine Queen smiled.

As they made their way to the portal, Little Pal whispered to Scruffy and Big Dog, "Did you see that? The beautiful queen smiled at me."

"I think she likes you," Big Dog said.

Little Pal curled his tail over his back and strutted after his buddies.

Chapter Sixteen

A Doggone Big Dream

"Donations are pouring in since word of what happened to my Greta hit the media." Ilaria patted the poodle laying by her feet. The once lop-sided pom on Greta's head had been trimmed to resemble the shaved side, and the paint on her ribs was gone, so her fur was once more soft and white. "Profits from my latest movie will also benefit the dogdom."

"A dream come true. What a creative idea for an abandoned village. We want to be in on this." Chiara's friend, Gabby, from the rescue organization sat with several other dog lovers around the resort lunch table with Maddie, Horace and Ilaria. Gabby looked around and lowered her voice. "I've also heard you found Brutto's shelter and have plans to shut it down. That will be a godsend to all dogs."

Ilaria answered in a similar low pitch. "We don't want to just shut down the shelter, we intend to put Brutto out of business permanently."

"I've heard he's not just picking up *randagi*, but stealing show dogs and holding them for ransom." A well-dressed woman with black hair sporting a wide silver streak that perfectly matched the fur coloring of the Yorkie she held in her arms looked intently at Ilaria.

With a nod, Ilaria responded. "Several of my friends in the show dog circuit know of dogs who have been dognapped. Unfortunately, they seem to be tossed in with *randagi* at Brutto's shelter and soon lose most of the resemblance to the purebred champions they are."

"Putting Brutto out of business would do all of us a huge favor. What can we do to help?" A woman accompanied by a dog who looked strikingly similar to an African wild dog leaned forward and spoke with similar intensity.

"Besides closely examining any dog who comes to your rescues for clues they might be show dogs, we need humans in the dogdom who will stay in the village houses once they are repaired," Maddie said. "They will serve as dorm parents for the packs of dogs who will live there."

"What will be expected of these humans?"

"Not as much as pet parents usually do." Maddie glanced at Horace. "Thanks to the creative inventions of my brilliant husband, Horace."

Horace blushed as he explained. "The houses will feature many automations, like motion sensing doors and lights, as well as refrigerators with step-on pedals to open them and voice–or woof–activations for most appliances."

"But we want the village to seem semi-normal," Maddie said. "That is, occupied by humans. So keeping up that appearance will be the main job of humans, as well as playing with our canine friends and helping them with tasks their paws aren't able to perform."

"So this is kind of role reversal where humans are doggie servants?" The woman with the African wild dog lookalike asked.

"How is that role reversal?" Gabby asked. "I'm already at the beck and call of my own doggie pack."

Those around the table laughed and agreed.

Maddie sipped her coffee, wondering if she should tell these women the rest of their plans. She glanced at Ilaria, a question in her eyes. If Ilaria trusted these women, Maddie would also.

Ilaria nodded slightly. "Tell my friends about the secret missions."

"We are working on clearing the streets of *randagi*," Maddie said.

"All stray dogs off the streets?"

"Yes." Maddie sipped her coffee again and watched the others absorb this news.

Finally, one of the women spoke. "That's thousands of dogs. Where would you find room for all of them?"

"And food? And veterinary care?"

"All part of our mission," Maddie said. "If you want to be involved, there may be some risks. The pay-off will be an almost free house and food for a year's commitment, as well as the satisfaction of saving the street dogs."

"Wow. That's a big dream. I want to believe it's possible, but living the rescue life day to day..." The woman shook her head. "It's hard to remain hopeful."

"We're transporting about fifty dogs a day to the dogdom. Bathing is pretty much automated, but we need help with hair trims and especially vet care. Our one veterinarian is doing what he can, but quite frankly, we need more help from humans."

"My groomer is organizing her friends to have a cut and style day once a month," Ilaria said.

"Do you have a surgery site? Maybe we could organize a contingent of vets to do spay/neuter surgeries. Or rotate in one day a month to help your vet?"

"That would give Dr. Alek a much needed break."

"Alek Romano? We've been working with him on changing laws and running a spay/neuter campaign. If Alek is involved, count us in. That man is nearly a saint in the dog rescue world."

For the rest of lunch, the group talked about plans to spread the word among rescue organizations for those who might consider moving to the dogdom as well as ways to shut down Brutto's operations.

After lunch, Ilaria asked her driver take Maddie and Horace back to the dogdom, along with herself and Greta, of course, so she could see her dog friends. She especially wanted to see Ludovica, who wasn't there.

Disappointed, Greta convinced Ilaria to stay long enough to go on the transport run that night, hoping to convince Ludovica to come to the new dogdom.

Knowing Charlie was the pilot for these transports, Ilaria took little convincing to go along. She wanted to spend more time with this intriguing man and Greta would be able to see her canine friend.

"I love a man with his hands on the controls." Ilaria's finger traced Charlie's hand. Up the pinky finger and down the ring finger. Up the middle finger and down the index finger. Around his thumb, then down to his wrist and–

Charlie cleared his throat as he turned his hand over and stopped Ilaria's sensual movements. "We have a schedule to keep."

"Later then." Ilaria winked and shimmied as she settled into the co-pilot's seat.

Charlie completed his pre-flight check and announced lift-off. Within moments, the spacecraft settled on the cracked pavement at the abandoned *aeroporto*.

A contingent of anxious but eager canines looked at them hopefully.

"Where's Ludovica?" Greta asked.

"Not here," one of the dogs answered. "We weren't sure if the transport would come, but we waited..."

The eyes of several dozen dogs looked at the rescue team hopefully.

"We're here to take you home. Get on board."

With whimpers of relief, the dogs loaded up quickly and quietly.

Greta fretted all during the trip back to the dogdom and during the unloading and welcome process. "Something is wrong or 'Vica would have been at the airport."

Chapter Seventeen

Doggie Jail Reunion

Without her pack and a secure place to hide, Ludovica was vulnerable. And she had to face it, at four she was old for a street dog. Most *randagi* were lucky to live two years.

She knew Cur would seek revenge, but she didn't realize how dogged he would be. Members of his pack kept her on the move, showing up at her usual hiding places. She wasn't getting sleep and wasn't always able to get back to her restaurant friend with his steady supply of food, so she became weaker.

Finally, in desperation she returned to the abandoned airport. A number of other dogs were there, hoping for a transport to the rumored new dogdom on the hill. Ludovica told the dogs she would guide them there if they kept watch while she rested.

Unfortunately, Cur's stoolies alerted the catchers to the gathering of dogs at the abandoned airport. In the sweep, the catchers nabbed an exhausted and hungry Ludovica with several others.

'Vica had always sworn she would run in front of a bus before allowing herself to be captured and jailed, especially in Brutto's hellhole.

She stood in rotting feces and knew without a doggone doubt she had been right.

However, here she was, surrounded by whimpering and apathetic dogs waiting to die. Although many of them still managed to fight over the scraps of moldy food thrown into the cages. 'Vica quickly took charge of meal times, puffing herself up and growling warnings while distributing the food so everyone got a few morsels.

Brutto soon took notice of her and moved her to a kennel by herself. At least for a short time. Too soon he shoved another dog into the kennel and tossed in a chunk of meat. The other dog pounced on the meat and gobbled down part of it before Brutto dragged the food out of the kennel with a twine anchored in the middle of it.

"Kill!" He pointed at Ludovica and waved the meat.

"That human is making a fool of you." Ludovica dodged the other dog as he charged.

"I'll be a fool for food." The dog snapped at her and she sidestepped.

"Join our pack and we'll share food. Don't let the human use you."

The other dog lunged again, coming nose to nose with Ludovica. "Alfonso?"

"Been awhile, Ludovica, since you deserted the rest of us after that car hit Mamma."

'Vica dodged again. "Didn't desert you. I was getting food to share."

"You ran like a coward. You can't run now and I'm gonna make you pay." With another snarl, Alfonso lunged at her and scraped raw marks down her side.

Ludovica rolled away, curling tightly in a ball and protecting her head and ears as he tried to rip at her flesh.

"She's not fighting, boss!"

Brutto cursed and poked at her with a stick. With a mighty yank, she pulled the stick out of Brutto's hands. Off balance, he fell against the kennel.

"Throw her back with the sick ones! No bitch gets the best of me!"

Exhausted and sore, Ludovica tried to scrape a clean spot in the kennel where she could lay down.

"You could have taken him." One of the other dogs led 'Vica to a semi-clean spot.

"And been used for Brutto's next scheme? No thanks. I don't

want to die in a fighting ring for the amusement of humans."

I don't want to die at all, Ludovica thought, as a group of dogs she had shared food with settled around her in a protective circle. *Maybe I should have gone to the dogdom with the rest of the girls.*

Her rest was short but better than she'd had since the girls went to their new home.

"Here's a bit to eat." One of the other dogs dropped a crust of bread in front of 'Vica.

"Have the others eaten?"

The dog nodded. "We need you to be strong until they come."

"Who comes?"

"There's word on the street a rescue team is working to get rid of Brutto."

"Another of his like will just take over."

"Not this time. You know a dog named Greta."

Remembering the first time she had seen Greta with a lop-sided pom on her head and spray paint on her sides, Ludovica smiled slowly. "Turned out to be an okay girl. Went home to her fancy owner."

"Well, that fancy owner has some major clout, and she's got Brutto in her sights."

"No kidding? Who'da thunk our shy Greta had such powerful connections?"

"If we can just hang on till they get here."

"We aren't going to just hang on. We're going to help ourselves out of here." 'Vica felt energized again. With a rescue team plotting on the outside and the dogs plotting on the inside, they would be unstoppable!

~ * ~

"Alfonso said you'd be at the center of the trouble-making."

From behind hooded lids, 'Vica examined a doggie face that looked very similar to her own. "Who are you?"

"Sister number three. I was picked up at the same time as Alfonso."

"And our other siblings?"

"Angelica and Elena didn't make it. Crossed the Rainbow Bridge not long after Mamma did. Don't know where Jayda is. She disappeared the same time as you."

"Alfonso said I ran away."

"He is always looking for an excuse to be angry. I think deep down he's scared of the day he'll die, so he has to come up with some reason to keep fighting. The anger keeps him going."

Ludovica gave a doggie nod. "I can understand that."

"So what do you have planned to get us out of here?"

Chapter Eighteen

A Cur Turns Good Dog

Greta insisted they look for Ludovica. So Ilaria's driver took them–plus Charlie the Royal Canine Guard–to 'Vica's usual hiding places. She was no where to be found.

Finally they stopped by the restaurant in Costa Smeralda where the restaurant manager left special treats for 'Vica. A black, curly-haired dog named Diego lay in 'Vica's usual place.

"Where's Ludovica?" Greta growled.

"Don't know 'Vica."

"Then how do you know her nickname?" Greta narrowed her eyes and sniffed daintily at the other dog without getting too close. "Ew! You're one of Cur's pack."

Greta yiked and Ilaria came running, followed closely by Charlie and her driver bodyguard. "Get away from my Greta, you mongrel!"

Ilaria lifted a small cylinder toward the dog and sprayed. Flowery perfume and glitter poofed out, covering the head and face of the dog, destroying his tough-guy facade.

"Argh! I can't see and I smell like a human foo-foo girl. I can't go back to the guys like this."

"Tell us where Ludovica is."

"I told you–"

Another squirt of perfume-y glitter changed the dog's story. "She got herself caught. Ended up in Brutto's jail."

Greta gasped. "Mamma, we have to get her out of there. Brutto tortures dogs. Please, Mamma!"

Ilaria melted at the pleading look in Greta's eyes. "We can't just walk in and take her. We need a plan."

Then she looked at the other dog now half-covered with flowery-smelling glitter. "Since our stoolie here can't go back to his macho pack, perhaps he can be persuaded to help us."

The mongrel hung his head. "I'll be dog meat if I turn against Cur."

"There's a steak and a new home waiting for you if you do a good job."

"Truly?" A sad longing filled Diego's eyes. "I haven't ever had a steak. And I don't really remember what a home feels like."

~ * ~

With his laser gun set to stun and the camera on his lapel on auto-record, Charlie dropped to his hands and knees to follow Diego through a gap in the chain link fence and into Brutto's shelter for *randagi*.

They emerged near the incinerator, causing Charlie's stomach to churn.

"This way." Diego hurried through the nearby kennels of sick and dying dogs, which saved Charlie the embarrassment of upchucking on the camera.

"There she is." Diego pointed his nose to a large cage containing perhaps two dozen dogs, all of them watching the intruders with distrust.

"Ludovica," Charlie whispered. "I've come to get you out of here."

"Charlie? How did you get in here?"

"Crawled in on my hands and knees. Let's get out of here."

"Not leaving without my friends. And my sister." Ludovica put a paw on the shoulder of a dog that resembled her but was smaller.

"Greta insisted we find you, so we've been driving around. Not much room for passengers like in the spaceship transport."

"My friend, Greta, continues to amaze me." Ludovica grinned. "But I'm still not leaving without my friends and sister."

Charlie pulled the laser out of its holster and decimated the lock on the kennel door. "We can't take every one. Draw straws or bones or something to decide who is going to leave. Diego is going to give me a guided tour of the rest of this dump. When I get back, nine of you and Ludovica be ready to go."

"You trust that cur?"

"Bribed him."

"No *cajones* that one. I'll go with you on the tour. Make sure you see everything."

Charlie glanced at Diego, who had sunk to the filthy floor and let his head drop onto his paws. "Come on, Diego, we need you to show us around."

"She's right, you know. I am a coward. That's why I joined Cur's pack. Knew I couldn't make it on my own, so I let him bully me into ratting out my canine brothers."

"Now's your chance to change that." Charlie stared at the curly-haired dog expectantly.

"You think a tiger can change its spots?"

"Tigers have stripes, not spots." Ludovica blew out an impatient breath.

"So I guess if the tiger changed its spots to stripes, I can try to change too." As Diego pulled himself to his feet, 'Vica rolled her eyes.

"If you keep taking time to congratulate yourself, you'll be dining with the rest of us when Brutto's cronies throw moldy bread in the kennels at mid-day."

"I don't want to see that one." Diego shivered. "He scares me."

"Okay, 'Vica and Diego, let's get moving." Charlie said. "Nine of you be ready to go when we get back."

Though Diego tried to be brave, odd little noises made him jerk and whimper low in his throat. Closing his eyes in fright, he crashed into something left leaning on one of the kennels. When it fell on him, he panicked! Turning on the attacker with frenzied fright, he growled and gnashed his teeth, quivering the entire time. When the battle was done, the opponent lay in chewed defeat on the concrete floor.

"You saved us, Diego!" Ludovica peered around the other dog to look at the remains. "From a broom."

Diego stared at the chewed cleaning tool for a moment, then fainted.

"Well, he was very enthusiastic," Charlie reasoned.

'Vica picked up a chunk of the broom handle and poked Diego. "Come on, hero, rise and shine."

Diego wakened slowly and shook himself. "Is it safe now?"

"You have vanquished the enemy. Let's get out of here."

The trio made their way back to the kennel where Ludovica had been contained.

"Who's going with us?" Charlie asked.

Those in the kennel looked at each other. "Take the sick ones in the kennels by the death machine. We can hold out until you come back for the rest of us."

"What if we can't get back right away?" Charlie asked.

"At least we'll know we helped some of our fellow canines, like Diego did."

Diego pointed a paw at his chest. "Me?"

Those in the kennel nodded. "If one of Cur's pack can change and help those most in need, so can we. Those most in need are the sick ones who will probably die without human help. They don't even get the moldy crusts of bread like the rest of us."

"Okay, we'll take as many as we can and be back as soon as possible. Come on, Ludovica."

'Vica shook her head. "Take my space for one of the sick ones."

"You're all playing the martyr?"

"They're right." Diego sat on his haunches. "Let the sicker ones ride. The rest of us can sneak out in packs and make our way to the dogdom."

"Many humans are afraid of dogs in packs. Someone will report you to the *polizia* and you'll end up back here or worse."

"Not if we travel at night and hide out during the day." Ludovica added to the escape plan. "Don't you have a tracker thing like on the spacecraft that shows coordinates? Maybe one that can go on a collar or harness? You'll be able to find us that way and pick us up with the spacecraft."

"For the first trip, you'd better all ride so you actually know the way to the dogdom. Once we get there, we can fit you with tracking harnesses and bring you back in the spacecraft to transport others. We also need to figure out how many we can take before Brutto gets wise to what's going on."

"Yeah. 'Vica and me can be like guides for the other dogs," Diego said.

Ludovica raised a doggie eyebrow.

"Well, 'cause you know the way to the dogdom and I know how to avoid Cur's pack."

"Okay, limited partnership." 'Vica agreed reluctantly. "But we'd better hustle or Brutto's cronies will be here and no one will get out."

On their way past the incinerator, Charlie once more shivered as his stomach churned. The Death Machine. He aimed his laser at the control panel and zapped it. He might only be buying the dogs another day or two, but that would give time to save a few more.

Chapter Nineteen

Undercover Humans

"This is worse than I thought." Chiara turned away as the video of Charlie's trip inside Brutto's shelter replayed. "We have to get those dogs out."

"Or put our own people in place to actually take care of our canine brothers and sisters."

"We need someone to work undercover in these shelters."

"They know me too well," Chiara said. "And most of the volunteers who work with the rescues."

"They know Horace and me as well," Maddie added.

"We need someone who's not a local."

"My niece and her husband might enjoy a short stay in Sardinia," Maddie said.

"Of course!" Horace exclaimed. "MacGregor of Scotland Yard would be perfect for this assignment."

"You have connections with Scotland Yard?" Ilaria asked.

"Not actually," Maddie said. "There was a mix-up when we first met Ian–before he married my niece–and Horace thought he was from Scotland Yard. It became a family joke. He's an MP."

"Military police?"

Maddie nodded. "Though he wouldn't be acting in an official capacity, I'm sure his skills would be helpful in this situation."

"A movie script I read recently brings to mind a cover story. A detective poses as an intern for a large company. They entice their target with the possibility of a lot of money if they take part in a study."

"Brutto runs the shelter for the government money he receives and puts in his own pocket instead of using it to care for the dogs," Chiara said. "Would probably be a good motivator for him."

"How soon can your niece and her husband get here?"

~ * ~

"We represent the company, Quality Canines International." Ian MacGregor handed Brutto a business card. "Your dog shelter was recommended for a study of how government dollars are being used to care for stray dogs. Depending on what we find, the process may be replicated in other countries. There's also a bonus to shelters that take part in the study."

Brutto straightened at the mention of money. "What parts of the shelter do you want to see?"

"Eventually, all of it. Though if we find processes that are of particular interest, we could recommend those be adopted and the bonus money be paid before the study is completed."

This drew even more interest from Brutto. "How soon can you start?"

"My colleague and I can start as early as tomorrow. More team members can join us as needed."

"And the bonuses?"

"Can be negotiated."

Nearly rubbing his hands with greedy delight, Brutto rose and shook Ian's hand. "We'll be waiting for you in the morning."

As soon as Ian and Rissa were out the door of the shelter, Brutto gathered his cronies. "Get rid of the sick and dying mutts."

"How boss?"

"I don't care. Dump 'em in the furnace."

"It takes time to euthanize that many dogs."

"So just dump 'em in alive. They're gonna die anyway."

When Brutto left the room, his cronies looked at each other. "Who's gonna tell him the furnace don't work?"

One by one they shook their heads.

"Maybe we can just dump the mutts back on the streets."

"Or take 'em up in the mountains to dump 'em. They'll die before they make it back here."

"Yeah, that'd work."

~ * ~

As the rescue team in the spacecraft transport approached Brutto's shelter that night, they noticed some strange activity.

"Isn't that the truck the catchers use?" Charlie hit zoom on the monitor for a closer look as the cloaked spacecraft hovered over the shelter.

"But they're loading dogs into the truck rather than taking them into the shelter."

"Anyone getting a message from 'Vica about what's going on?"

"She doesn't know."

"So do we follow the truck or rescue dogs from the shelter as planned?"

"Won't be much of a rescue with Brutto's cronies around."

"Then we follow the truck."

In silence, the rescue team kept tabs on the truck for several miles.

"They're heading into the mountains. Toward the dogdom."

"Think they found out about it?"

"They're stopping!"

The team watched as two of Brutto's cronies opened the back of the truck and started urging the dogs out.

"They're just dumping those poor dogs. Some of them can't even walk."

Charlie landed the spacecraft a short distance away. "Lasers on stun."

The rescue team quickly incapacitated the two cronies and started talking to the dogs.

"We were in the back kennels waiting to die," one of the dogs said. "Brutto told his cronies to just dump us in the furnace. But the furnace didn't work, thanks to your handiwork the other night. So they drove us out here to die in the mountains."

"Well, that makes our mission to get you to the dogdom easier. We'll just drive you the rest of the way."

"Is this all of you Brutto wanted out of the shelter?"

"Not sure. All the sick and dying is what we heard. Might be waiting for the truck to take more of us away."

The rescue crew looked at each other. "Let's tie these guys up out here and make it look like the truck broke down."

~ * ~

"You call this a disguise?" Ian teased Rissa as he parked the rental vehicle by Brutto's shelter.

"If I remember correctly, khaki is what you selected for our bird-watching cover when we were trying to save Aunt Maddie."

"But matching shirts, not sweatshirts like these."

"These have a nice company logo on the pocket." Rissa favored Ian with a cheesy smile that quickly faltered. "I'm not sure I can face Brutto without doing bodily harm after spending the night with those poor dogs. Dr. Alek is doing a yeoman's job, but he can't save all of them."

"Just focus on the fact we're doing this for all those dogs. The faster we get Brutto out of here, the faster someone can come in who will actually take care of the dogs. Let's put Operation Dog Chef into action."

As Ian and Rissa stepped out of the front of the black cargo van with gold lettering on the doors that proclaimed, "Elite Chef to Delite Your Dogs."

"How do I look?" Buddy, one of the Royal Canine Guards, masquerading as the Elite Chef, pushed open the back doors of the van and strutted down the ramp, followed by two assistants. He paused and executed a pirouette to show off his chef's uniform, complete with toque on his head. However, in keeping with the Royal Canine Guards' color, Buddy's uniform was black instead of white as his assistants wore.

"Very chef-like."

Buddy grinned for a moment, then wiped the smile off his face and seemed to transform into a totally different persona. When Ian and Rissa walked toward the shelter, Buddy and his assistants marched behind them.

When they rang the buzzer to gain admittance, one of Brutto's cronies cracked open the thick metal door a couple inches and looked around suspiciously before hurrying them inside. Rissa jumped slightly as the door clanged heavily behind them.

"Not to worry," Ian whispered. "I have a grenade so we can blow our way out if need be."

Rissa smiled at him uneasily. "Like Uncle Horace's experiments–I hope this charade doesn't explode in our faces."

"Living with your uncle should more than prepare you for this assignment. It should be NWR–no weapons required."

Rissa's smile became a little more steady as she clenched her clipboard and ballpoint pen with the QC International logo.

Their guide–or perhaps guard–ushered them into a room where Brutto sat behind a desk on an elevated platform, rather like a king deigning to address to the lowly peasants. "We have made a number of the kennels available for you to inspect. I trust those will provide enough information to start the process for the bonus money."

"We'll also need access to kitchen facilities." Ian glanced at his clipboard, then smiled smoothly at Brutto.

Buddy strutted toward Brutto's desk, swatting the guard with a whisk when the man tried to stop his progress. "I am ze new chef for ze dogs. According to ze money you are receiving, each dog should have ze top quality meals two times each day. Where is ze kitchen and supplies for zes fur bebes?"

Brutto scowled. "No one said anything about a dog chef–"

"I am a chef for ze dogs, not a dog chef. A dog would need ze opposable thumbs to be a chef–"

"The rations for the mutts–er, dogs come already prepared and given out at mid-day."

"Zat cannot be. Ze fur bebes must have fresh to keep them healthy. I vill change zat immediately and order fresh from ze butcher." Buddy pulled out a cell phone as he walked away muttering.

"No one said anything about changing the food for the dogs." Brutto scowled at Ian and Rissa.

Ian leafed through a lengthy document on his clipboard. "Here it is on page twenty-seven of the agreement you signed. 'All dogs will be fed fresh food daily to keep them at optimum health'."

"The money we receive barely meets my–er, the dogs needs as it is. We can't take on any other expenses."

"Our company has a number of private donors already signed up to assist any shelter that meets our study requirements that should more than cover any additional costs."

"More money?"

Rissa could almost see the euro signs light up Brutto's eyes. *But you won't be around to see it, buster.*

However, as she and Ian agreed, she let Ian do the talking. This seemed to be their best shot to get rid of Brutto and truly make a difference in the lives of these dogs. She didn't want her anger at this creep to ruin that.

"Guido! Where's that lackey?"

Another crony appeared at Brutto's side. "Some trouble with the truck, sir."

If possible, Brutto's scowl deepened. "Show these people to the kitchen facilities."

One of the man's eye brows quirked up slightly.

"You heard me!" A vein stood out in Brutto's neck as he shouted the command.

"Yessir."

Rissa joined Buddy as he clicked off the call on his cell phone and fell into step behind this new crony.

"Did you like the accent?" he whispered to Rissa.

"A French chef might offend Italians who pride themselves on their cuisine. So maybe tone the accent down just a bit," Rissa responded in a low voice.

"But it was effective, right?"

"I think Brutto got the message."

Rissa and Buddy exchanged a smile. If feeding the dogs stirred

Brutto up this much, she couldn't wait until he heard about the groomers, veterinary staff, and 'round-the-clock staffing, as well as trainers who would be in next week. All paid from the government funds that had been going into Brutto's pockets, of course.

At midday, Ian and Rissa joined Buddy and his kitchen crew to feed the dogs, using the opportunity to take a head count of how many dogs were still at the shelter. Also, since Buddy's helpers were trained animal workers, they tried to get photos of each dog and make notes of their health conditions.

Any dog who was obviously in distress was flagged for transport to the dogdom with that night's transport.

With the arrival of a half dozen new staff in early afternoon, Ian informed Brutto of the requirement for 'round-the-clock staffing by humans dressed in dog suits. He didn't bother to mention these people were experienced security personnel with lasers set to stun to prevent Brutto's cronies from doing anything more with the dogs.

Seriously perturbed, Brutto insisted one of his cronies also be at the shelter. This played right into Ian's plan, as he had confirmed many of Brutto's cronies were criminals wanted in various countries. A simple jolt with the laser quickly incapacitated Brutto's crony and a rescue worker in a dog suit took his place. Then the unconscious crony was assisted in their perhaps subconscious desire to return to those countries and face what they had done.

When Ian and Rissa checked out for the day, Brutto didn't bid them farewell, but sat at his massive desk glowering at the papers in front of him.

Ian, Rissa and the rest of their team considered the day's work a success and handed their notes on which dogs needed the most attention to the night rescue team.

When the groomers showed up with the veterinarian staff the next morning, Brutto did indeed take it hard.

"Which way to the dog bathing facilities?" A massively muscled man wearing a pink apron with a pair of trimming scissors hanging from a chain around his neck glared at the crony who had unlocked the metal entry door for them.

The crony looked at Brutto, who had appeared to personally witness what Ian and Rissa came up with on day two of the study.

"We have no–" Brutto turned his suspicious glare from the groomer and his entourage of assistants to Ian. "Another part of the agreement?"

Ian consulted his clipboard. "Page fifty-six of the agreement."

"I suppose you have access to bathing facilities–at an additional expense, of course."

"We have donors–"

"Yes, I know. Lined up."

"The groomers have a mobile grooming salon, so if someone will let our grooming crew know where to set up?"

"Guido!"

"Are all his cronies named Guido?" Rissa whispered to Ian.

Ian shrugged. "Doesn't matter. We'll soon have them replaced."

When a person in a dog suit appeared instead of his crony, suspicion carved a frown on Brutto's face. However, he instructed the replacement to show the groomers to a possible location. The grooming assistants all had cameras to take before and after photos, which made it easy to add to their growing evidence of how dogs were really treated at the shelter to share with the public as they deemed prudent.

Of course, the after photos of the healthier dogs could also be used for adoption campaigns. Not that Brutto would be anywhere nearby to enjoy the happy tails of the dogs going home with loving families.

However, that was in the future. This day, Brutto was soon on the phone, talking with exaggerated gestures.

"How long do you think we have before Brutto stops cooperating completely?" Rissa asked Ian.

"Not long," Ian said. "We'd better implement part D for dog suit quickly."

Sure enough, when a person in a dog suit showed up at the shelter announcing all staff–not just the new staff–would be similarly attired, Brutto took a stand. "I have had enough. If Chiara Caddu and her rescue cronies are behind this so-called study, I want you to all clear out now!"

"Guido! Guido! Guido!" Brutto shouted out to his cronies.

However, they had all been replaced by doggie guards, one of whom zapped Brutto with a laser on stun. Quickly, the man stripped off the dog suit and began fitting it on Brutto.

"Did anyone think how hard it might be to zip an unconscious two-hundred-pound man into a dog suit?"

"Tougher than someone doing this willingly."

Several doggie guards grunted as they maneuvered the dog suit over Brutto's floppy body.

"There. Finally. Put the dog head on him and get him out of here. We have a country that has been waiting a long time for this criminal."

"Do you think anyone will suspect something?" Rissa asked Ian as two burly men dragged Brutto in a half-zipped dog suit to an armored vehicle.

"Naw," Ian answered. "From the stories Chiara told us, the locals will just think it's her causing trouble again."

Ian's prediction seemed accurate. Even days later when Brutto's absence was noticed by others in the *comune*, the replacement staff shrugged and said they heard rumors he was following up on a business deal with no mention of when he might be returning.

The man had simply disappeared as mysteriously as he had appeared.

Chapter Twenty

August, Five Years in the Future

Greta never went back to the show dog circuit and usually preferred a more casual grooming to relax at home. However, for this special grand opening of the Doggie Exchange Station–formerly called an animal shelter–she had allowed her groomer to trim her fur in the old Poodle pom style on her head and around the ankles of all four legs. This seemed to be a perfect complement to the pink winged sunglasses studded with rhinestones and the lei of flowers around her neck.

Though most of the dogs disdained costumes some humans thought were cute, Greta didn't mind putting on the dog for special occasions to please her human.

Tonight was indeed a special occasion. Greta's human, Ilaria Angelica Eleonora Rossini, world famous actress and singer, had tirelessly organized fundraisers and public awareness campaigns the past few years to change the attitudes of humans toward dogs and make this Doggie Exchange Station possible.

Greta and the Girls–Bianca and her last litter of puppies, now fully grown and all spayed–greeted human guests from all around the globe. All the Girls sported the latest grooming styles and seasonal accessories especially for this hot August night celebration.

After mingling with the crowd for a while, Ilaria opened the formal program by showing a video of the public awareness campaign that started several years before to change the public's attitudes about dogs. Big Dog and Little Pal's "fantasy" of dogs dropping off humans on the street and driving away, with the message "put yourself in their fur...adopt from a shelter." The clip ended by showing humans behind the bars of a shelter with dogs considering the humans' behaviors and training.

"We've come a long way," Ilaria said. "This would not have been possible without the efforts of you–dedicated dog lovers world-wide who donated your time, resources, and creativity to truly give dogs the lives they deserve.

"We no longer have thousands of dogs struggling to survive on the streets. They are safe and well cared for. The dogs from the show circuit who were dog-napped and hidden among other dogs in the shelter have been safely returned to their owners. The study by Quality Canines International that began as a means to rout out criminal elements seeking to profit from the suffering of our dog friends has become a model for ideal shelters all around the world. This study gave birth to what we now call Doggie Exchange Stations, where dogs who choose to live with humans can interview families who meet their requirements for a perfect life.

"So let's tour the exchange station and meet the dogs!"

Former show dog, Greta, met the visitors at the Doggie Health Center, where Ilaria explained some of the services available. "Greta's groomer leads a cadre of devoted humans who offer grooming, nail trims, and haute couture for dogs who want to be stylish. Our fur friends can also enjoy massage, energy healing, and acupuncture, as well as the therapeutic swimming pools."

The group watched as a Yorkshire terrier received a trim, ending up with a red bow around a topknot of hair.

"Omigosh! I want to adopt that dog," enthused one of the visitors.

"That's part of the reason behind grooming," Ilaria said. "To show our furry friends at their best."

While the visitor talked to an adoption representative with enthusiastic gestures, the rest of the group continued to the spay/neuter clinic. Dr. Alek greeted them and translated the doggie message of former street dog, Bianca. As she tilted her head proudly, Bianca's fur was indeed soft and white again. "Though not actually a favorite place of most dogs, I was the first volunteer. By having the spay operation, I don't have to worry what will happen to my puppies any more. Dr. Alek is the best and the recovery suites are quiet with soft beds and attentive humans who offer energy healing and massages of body parts that don't hurt."

"Is Bianca looking for an adoptive home?" one of the visitors asked.

"She is one of my beloved companions," Ilaria answered. "Like Greta, she is here at the exchange station to show what is possible when dogs and humans share a mutual love. And a love of play. Let's go to the exercise area."

A sleek and muscled Ludovica, former street dog and leader of the pack Ludovica's Ladies, offered her message through Aunt Maddie. "Our doggie guests can walk the paths or lie in the grass. Plus there are plenty of trees and bushes to mark for those so inclined."

In keeping with the beach party theme, staff had scattered blankets and picnic baskets filled with food on the grassy areas. The wading pools were surrounded by brightly striped canvas loungers shaded by umbrellas.

They paused by the bone-shaped wading and swimming pools. "On these hot August days–and nights–our water features are quite busy."

The visitors nodded in agreement, with several of them claiming a lounger or slipping off their shoes to try out the wading pools as the rest of the group moved on. "Any time of year, the digging pits with buried bone-shaped snacks are popular. We also have play days and events all year with human friends who enjoy playing ball and frisbee, or even dancing and agility with their canine companions."

"When tired, our dogs can climb aboard the automated cars and go snuggle with humans or go to the kitchens, which is your next stop." With a wave of her paw, Ludovica sat down beside Maddie and watched the guests climb into the vehicles.

At the kitchens, Big Dog and Little Pal with Buddy "ze French chef" offered cookies–healthy ones for both humans and dogs–to their guests, with plenty left for the two of them and their doggie friends.

"And now we arrive at the living areas." Ilaria paused at the entry to the pods. "These areas are climate-controlled for packs of four to six dogs. Quite a change from what used to be overcrowded cells often exposed to the weather."

As the group walked by, one of the dogs peeked out through the blinds.

"A dorm human stays with our canine guests around the clock, seven days a week to help meet their needs. This includes ordering meals from the chef's kitchen and advocating for whatever each dog in the pack needs. They also screen possible adoptive families, which includes a few lucky ones from this group who have been granted an interview to be adopted by a dog if you meet the requirements."

Excited conversations in a variety of languages erupted from the group at this announcement.

"If you have any other questions, please ask one of our human representatives."

From a back room where the tour group did not go, Cur curled his lip as he watched the humans fawn over the dogs in their fancy living areas. Never mind that his ultra-secure space was as luxurious as theirs. He railed against being neutered and held captive, when deep inside he longed to run free with his wolf ancestors and howl at the full moon, answering to no human.

Unknown to Cur, since most of the humans at the exchange station could communicate telepathically with animals, they knew of his desires and had finally located an isolated island where he could do this. Soon even Cur would have a fresh start.

As the celebration wound to a close and their guests departed, Ilaria and the other humans and dogs who had traveled from the dogdom said good-bye to the overnight staff at the exchange station. Then they entered a private room in the administrative offices that hid a portal between the exchange station and the dogdom, which had been name Sar-dog-nia.

As they stepped through the portal into the Tapestry House, they joined the Canine Queen and her mate, Reynaud, who were wrapping up the weekly meeting with the head of each dog pack from the hillside village spread out below the fortress.

"I believe we were very successful." Ilaria took off her hat and shook out her hair. "We received more donations, several invitations to talk to organizations about setting up exchange stations in their countries, and approved a number of adoptions. As soon as home visits are done, the dogs can be with their new families."

"Let's go celebrate the celebration at Ristorante Randagi!"

They walked across the castle courtyard lined with businesses that had been set up to serve the dogdom. In addition to Horace's automated bathing station, Greta's Groomers offered haute couture style for dogs with a fashion flair as well as their humans. For those not so much into culture, Missy Manners of the Canine Kind elevated skills such as butt sniffing and silent farting to an art.

Between the businesses, training and play centers for humans and dogs radiated out to the stone walls of the fortress. These included areas specifically for little dogs, others for rowdy players, pools for wading and swimming, and larger areas for playing ball and other games.

When they arrived at the restaurant, the owner himself greeted them. The former restaurant manager at Costa Smeralda took little convincing to pay a euro to live in one of the houses in the village. He brought his mother, who had suffered health challenges for years but was regaining her vitality, and he still set out a treat for Ludovica every night on her own special plate.

Other patrons–both dogs and humans–joined the celebration of the celebration, which lasted well into the night.

Finally, with everyone sleepy and sated with good food and friendship, they wandered to their own houses in the village down sparkling clean, narrow streets lined by freshly painted houses boasting window boxes overflowing with flowers. Inside each automated house lived a dog–er, make that a pack of dogs with a human companion.

Surrounded by Greta, Bianca and her grown puppies, Ilaria and Charlie walked arm in arm, planning their next space exploration to search for dogizens who might have survived the destruction of Canid. However, this would wait until after the yachting excursion around the island they had promised Bianca. They paused at the door of their home and waved good-night to the rest of the group.

Alek and Chiara continued home with Big Dog, Little Pal,

Scruffy and the four now-grown puppies who had been dumped in a box years ago and endured the journey to the abandoned airport. Older and still wise, Big Dog continued to protect the little ones and also comforted all the dogs who came to Alek's clinic.

As they opened the door to their house, Ludovica trotted by on the street, carrying the treat from her restaurant friend. Diego followed a few steps behind her, still trying to convince her they should be mates. A few houses away, she paused while the automated door slid open and allowed her to enter the house shared with her two sisters and their human. Then the door slid closed, leaving a disappointed but determined Diego outside. "I'll be back tomorrow!"

Arm in arm, Maddie and Horace continued to the village house they had purchased so they and their family could stay when they visited the dogdom. A pack of half dozen dogs welcomed them with wags and cuddles when they arrived.

The Royal Canine Guards, Buddy and Max, also had houses in the village when they weren't on duty protecting the Canine Queen, Reynaud, and their family. The Royal Canine Guards had expanded their ranks to include all the humans in the dogdom. Their wardrobe had also expanded. During cooler weather they wore jackets with a spiffy logo. At times like this hot August night, they had swimsuits to wear to the beach or in the swimming pools.

"Our dogdom is more than we ever envisioned." The Canine Queen and her mate, Reynaud, stood atop the fortress overlooking the village.

"Indeed it is," Reynaud said. "Let's go see what our offspring have been doing."

As they entered the portal into the underground city where most of the former street dogs lived, they paused at the Rainbow Bridge and looked across its arched form to a grassy area where Angel Dogs played.

Like every night when the full moon rose, the Angel Dogs began howling as their ancestors did. A few at a time, the dogs of Sar-dog-nia paused what they were doing and joined in, honoring those who were no longer physically with them.

After the chorus of howls, the Canine Queen and Reynaud

continued to their home to say good-night to their fully grown pups, who were deeply involved in coordinating operations of the dogdom.

While the Canine Queen's groomer brushed her long, silky fur, the pups briefed their parents on matters of the dogdom.

Reynaud considered the list of concerns as he continued to the basement laboratory Uncle Horace helped him set up. Using the improved robotic paw-hands, Reynaud became Horace's apprentice in inventions, communicating via computer when they were on different continents.

Back in the Tapestry House, the tapestry for which the house had been named seemed to magically transform with each house in the village that had been repaired. Now, the villas woven in the threads glowed with bright colors and flowers tumbled from window boxes, just like the real-life villas that marched in crayon-colored joy up the hill.

And in a room hidden behind ornately carved wooden doors, Destiny Rose was finishing up her latest weaving creation. This one featured herself with the cat mascot of Sar-dog-nia, laying out in beautiful woolen colors what their next adventure would be.

TWELVE DAYS TO LOVE
When Archer Steele shows up at Calanthe Durand's failing plantation with an alligator over his shoulder, Cali thinks she's never seen a more handsome man. During the war she had to defend herself and her servants from both union and confederate soldiers. Independent and self-sufficient, she vows to never marry. But Archer Steele has different ideas. The first time Archer sees Cali in town, he feels an instant attraction. He decides he will do everything and anything to convince the beautiful Miss Durand he is worthy of her love. During the weeks leading up to Christmas, he gives her twelve gifts in hopes she will fall in love with him.

BOOTS AND BLADES

An ancient evil from the old country has arrived in the high desert of Oregon. Gnome children are vanishing then re-appearing, showing various stages of traumatization. Tiamoon, warrior gnome, will put her skills to use alongside Killian, a handsome warrior, also in need of a cause.

CHRISTMAS PAWSIBILITIES

With their world destroyed and their space ship malfunctioning, the dogizens of Planet Canid have little choice but to crash land on Earth. They face tortuous experiments at the hands of the Geeks in Green...or they can trust an eccentric inventor and his zany family to deliver the Canine Queen's puppies and help them celebrate new lives.

Chapter One

Near New Orleans October 2,1867

"Sam! Close the shutters on the back landing. I'll get the front. Hurry. There's a storm coming." Calanthe Durand felt the small hairs on the back of her neck rise and shivers run down her spine. A big storm was on its way, probably a hurricane. Energy and fear poured through her like the pounding rain and flooding that accompanied high winds. Closing the house to the storm was imperative.

Cali took a moment to smile. She'd heard Sam grunt. He didn't talk much, but she wouldn't have survived the war or these last two years without Sam and his daughter Daisy. Both sides, the North and the South, had occupied their home. Daisy and Sam were family, the only family she had. She'd do whatever was necessary to protect them. Even with emancipation, life wasn't easy for blacks in the south.

"I've got them, Miss Cali." Daisy rushed past her and out the door. Wind whipped her hair and tugged at her dress. Branches torn from trees landed on the porch.

Cali followed, the storm swirling around her, her hair beating against her face. Her breath was ragged, and fast as her heart thundered. She pushed and tugged at her skirt, trying to detangle the fabric from her legs. "Get inside!" The tempest raging around them swallowed her voice.

"Not until we're finished here." Daisy fastened a shutter before moving on to the next one.

They worked together to protect the windows from the storm on the raised porch which stood five feet off the ground as wind howled around the eaves. A steady rain poured from the black sky, and lightning slashed the darkness.

Cali pushed dripping strands of hair that had slipped from her chignon away from her face. "I'll light the candles. It could get dark here pretty fast."

"Horses and livestock are safe for now." Sam stepped beside her. "Hope it's not a big one."

"Hello up there. Hello, bonjour, anyone home?"

Hearing the voice from below, Cali left the protection of the house to lean over the porch railing. Below her a man stood, with cupped hands to his mouth and a dead gator slung over one shoulder a quiver filled with arrows on the other. "Hello. Can I get shelter from the hurricane?"

"Don't know if it's a hurricane." Terrified of unknown men, Cali didn't want to do the charitable thing. She pursed her lips, thinking, but all that came to surface was memories of troops commandeering her home. Good lord but she'd had to hollow out a bedpost to hide her jewelry. The soldiers had taken everything they could see. Sometimes she felt as if the war had ripped her soul from her body.

"Maybe not a hurricane. Could be just a bad storm, but I don't want to be on the swamp right now. The water's rising." A loud roar and a thunderclap followed his pause. Behind him an old Cyprus tree crashed to the ground, uprooted by the wind.

"You can take shelter in the stable." Cali watched his back stiffen, while she swallowed hard, but she wasn't about to back down. The stable was good enough for some wandering man who she owed nothing. Besides, there was a tack room with a bed. No one slept there anymore, but she kept it clean and the moss in the mattress was fresh. Daisy had rolled it out two days ago. Yet a small niggling in the back of her head kept telling her this wasn't a traveling man but one of means. He was a man she should treat as a gentleman. She'd been taught better but the war had changed all that and the lessons she learned were not served to her with a silver spoon.

"Much obliged." He nodded before turning toward the barn. His natural swagger and broad shoulders sent a different kind of sensation through her. Warmth swept inside, swirling within and heating her frozen heart. For a moment he looked back, a strange expression on his well-chiseled face.

A tiny bit of guilt raced through her, but she wasn't going to change her mind. "What are you going to do with that gator?" Cali's stomach rumbled. Sam hadn't had much luck hunting the last few days, and a little meat along with the vegetables from the garden would be heaven sent.

He stopped, touching his hat. She didn't think he meant to acknowledge her question, didn't think he'd turn around. Seconds ticked by slowly. Rain sluiced off his clothes, pooling in the mud.

Her stomach rumbled, pushing her to ask him to come inside. Sharing a meal with this man couldn't be that horrible. After all, he was bringing the food not stealing.

Looking over his shoulder, he spoke. "Thought I'd eat it." Reaching out he tugged at the stable doors.

She waved a hand, frustration and anger urging her on. "Sir…ah…Daisy's a good cook. She can make gator taste like chicken."

While he turned again, tipping his hat, a broad grin forming. "I always thought it tasted like snake."

His smile made her step back, her hand to her chest. "Well, maybe, but why don't you come in? Sam will help you skin it."

"And Daisy will cook it. Sounds like a good idea, merci."

Before she could blink, the stranger was striding towards the house. The first level had been built on stilts, with decorative latticework in case of floods. A few times the overflow from the Mississippi and Lake Pontchartrain had kept them confined to the upstairs rooms.

"I'll go in the back way. Don't want to muddy up your parlor." He disappeared around the back of the house, not using the front steps to enter.

As Cali walked inside, she prayed this wasn't the wrong decision.

"No disrespect, but I was listening in on your conversation. You sure it's a good idea to invite this man inside, Miss Cali?"

"No, Daisy, I'm not sure, but now that he's here, it's up to us to cook that gator. Got any ideas?"

"We've got turnips in the cellar, carrots and tomatoes. Last of the crop."

"Flour and oil to fry the meat?"

"Yes, Mam."

"All right then, as soon as they finish skinning the animal, we can get started. I'll help with the meal, and Sam can keep an eye on…good lord, I didn't get his name."

"I know him. I've seen him in the swamp before. Town's folk call him Archer, but his whole name is Archer Steele. He's a carpetbagger. At least that's what some people think. They only know he fought for the north. He was born and raised in Louisiana so he can't be no carpetbagger. Hearsay is that he owns two ships…trades cotton and sugar and travels all over the world. Owns a sugar plantation a few miles from here. His family has French connections."

Cali had so many more unanswered questions. Just because a man owned a plantation and ships didn't make him a good man. She could think of a lot of men with money who were not good men. "Well, as far as I'm concerned he's got to prove himself. I don't care about pedigrees, even if they are a mile long."

"You aren't getting any younger, Miss Cali. Maybe it's about time you found a man. Besides, he's not from old money. He was born poor. Everything he owns he earned for himself by working hard."

True words, but Cali didn't think she wanted or needed to find a man. She was doing quite well living as an independent woman in her ancestral home. "Neither are you," she told Daisy.

"I know." Daisy wiped her hands on her apron. "Think I'll take a look at what's in the cellar."

"I'm sorry, Daisy." Cali reached out to stop her. "I know that wasn't nice." Good lord, when had she sunk so low? Daisy's beau was killed just before the end of the war. Daisy still mourned his loss, and there weren't that many men in these parts. Many who returned from the war just weren't the same.

"It's okay, Miss Cali. I started the conversation. It's just that I'd like to see you happy with a man to love and children to call your own." With those words said, Daisy picked up her skirts and whirling, headed for the cellar.

Her arguments hit home. Once upon a time that had been her dream. Once upon a time before her world fell apart and she learned few men were like her father, she had hopes for her future.

The lessons over the last few years were not pleasant, but they would stick with her forever. Believing in that fantasy again was not possible. Men would take what they wanted and give nothing in return. Her thoughts turned to Archer Steel. Would he take what he wanted and leave her with nothing? She stiffened her back and made a resolution to herself. Not if she had any say in the matter.

Puffing air, she blew a strand of hair from her face. *Quit the maudlin thinking and get to the task at hand.* A roar of wind shook the house, the windows vibrating.

With reflexes born from living through hurricanes, she clutched the counter top, hanging on until the gust died down. By now, the continuous roar impaired hearing.

"Cali..."

"Oh, you startled me. I didn't know you were there." Cali turned, her hand resting over her heart.

"Sorry, Miss Cali. The wind's mighty loud. Just wanted to say the gator's been skinned, and we've got alligator to cook." Daisy set the meat near the stove before gathering the flour and oil. "Going to fry this up."

"I'll pump the water for the vegetables."

"Miss Cali?" Sam stood in the doorway. "The horses have to be moved to high ground. Mr. Steele is going to help me. We'll be back as soon as we get the animals away from the rising water."

"You don't have to do this." Sam confronted the temporary houseguest. "It ain't none of your responsibility."

"Of course I do. I wouldn't want to take advantage. And taking me in is clearly not something the lady wanted to do." Archer had seen Calanthe Durand in town a few times. If one could believe in love at first sight, that's what happened to him three weeks ago. The moment he saw her, he knew she was meant for him. This trip into the swamp had not been a coincidence. The storm maybe, but he'd every intention of bringing her the alligator while hoping to share a meal.

Sam snorted. "You brought the meat. You don't have to do this. And Miss Cali is just trying to be cautious where it comes to strange men. She hasn't had it easy."

"A gentleman would lend a hand, and I intend to prove I was raised with manners." Even though he'd been brought up on a small farm in Louisiana, he'd learned a few things about courting a lady. Folks around these parts called him a carpetbagger, but he wasn't. Sure enough he'd bought his plantation with northern money, but he'd earned every penny. He meant to give back to the south, not take at their expense.

"All right then, keep up."

Archer chuckled to himself. It was just like Sam. The water had risen half a foot by the time they reached the stables. The horses snorted and moved restlessly as they rounded them up and led them toward higher ground. The wind thrummed constantly in his ears as rain pelted them.

What seemed like hours later, they reached a makeshift barn that sat in a semi-secluded area.

"They going to be safe here?" Archer and Sam hadn't spoken during the trek. Archer had serious doubts about this place.

"Hope so. Miss Cali would be devastated if she lost the horses, but with these winds one never knows."

"At least they won't drown." Archer wiped rainwater from his face while he studied the area. "Although, we might by the time we get back."

Sam chuckled. "Nope, the horses won't drown. That's the only good thing I can say about this. Now the horses are on their own. I'll come back for them as soon as the storm passes."

"Wish there was more we could do." Again, Archer studied the make-shift structure, sheltering the horses. He didn't hold out much hope for it to remain standing. If this storm was a full-blown hurricane, the refuge would most likely topple.

"We can't do anything else." Sam wiped running water from his face. "Let's head back before we drown or are blown away."

The walk from the high pasture to the old plantation was into the wind, every step harder than the next, but the winds didn't seem to be picking up speed. They were constantly fast with harsh wind gusts. Archer couldn't stand up straight against the pummeling storm, and Sam was bent over at the waist.

By the time they reached the house, water circled beneath, swirling into the basement and had risen more than a foot. They walked up the stairs and left their rain gear and boots in a room just outside the kitchen.

Sam disappeared for a few minutes and came back with clothes. "Think these will fit. You're about the same size as Monsieur Durand. He passed in the war—Gettysburg."

"Gettysburg you say... Well thanks for the clean dry clothes. I'll go change." The clothes did appear they would fit. Out dated, yes, but they'd keep him warm and dry. "Which way?" Thoughts of the war were seldom welcome and always brought back memories best left in the past. Thank God, he'd not been at Gettysburg. He'd heard her father had not made it home, but knew no details.

"Go through the kitchen and down the hall. You'll find a study where you can close the door for a bit of privacy. I'm going to change right here. The women folk won't come inside."

Archer stepped into the kitchen, closing the door behind him. He nodded at Cali and Daisy when they turned to see who'd come through the door.

"The livestock safe?" Cali dipped a flour-coated piece of alligator meat into the frying pan.

"As safe as they can be in this tempest. Just going down the hall to put on dry clothes. Sam said I could go into the study."

"Second door on the right. Daisy, why don't you go with him and make sure he has everything he needs."

"Yes, Miss Cali." Daisy dried her hands on a nearby dishtowel. "This way, Mr. Steele."

"There is really no need..."

"Don't be ridiculous." Cali put another piece of alligator into the pan. "Good God, broad shoulders, straight back, a woman would never get tired of admiring that sight."

"But."

Daisy waited at the door from the kitchen. Archer shrugged his shoulders, realizing no one listened to him. But he liked the women. Cali might be a bit shy when it came to relationships, but she seemed to be a woman who made up her mind. She was strong and independent. And, it seemed so was Daisy.

So, her father died in the war, and she'd maintained this property by herself. She kept the crops growing. Maybe not like it was in the best of times, but she must be making a living. If her father owned the house outright, all she would have to pay were taxes. But taxes were huge these days.

"The study is here." Daisy stopped and nodded for him to go inside. "After you change your clothes, you can wait in the parlor. Help yourself to the whiskey. It's on the sideboard."

He did as was told and after donning dry clothes, he made his way to the parlor.

"Thank you. Don't mind if I do." *So, a few hours ago, I was sent to the tack room in the stable. Now I'm drinking whiskey in the parlor. My prospects are getting better.* He poured another two fingers of brandy into his glass, swirling the liquid before sipping.

Daisy stopped at the door. "I saw the way you looked at Miss Cali. Don't be getting' any ideas. She's fragile, her heart, anyway. If you mean to court her, you best take it nice and slow. Do it the right way, if you get my meaning. You've got to win her trust before you can win her heart."

"I won't hurt her." How did this woman read his mind? Of course, he meant to win her trust.

"Words easy to say. You need to show her. That is, if your intentions are good."

He held up his hands. "I think we're jumping the gun here. Miss Cali isn't interested in me. The only reason I'm in the plantation instead of the stable is that she took pity on me because that structure is under water."

Daisy snorted. "Think what you want." She slipped out the door then let it close with a soft snick.

Archer mulled over Daisy's words. Was Cali Durand interested in him? She had a funny way of showing it. He made a slow three hundred sixty degree sweep of the parlor, stopping at pictures and knick-knacks he saw.

While he pulled off his sodden shirt, he strode to a picture of a man and woman. He assumed this was Monsieur and Madam Durand. Horrible thing to lose both parents. Well, they had that in common. A huge south facing window filled one side of the room. With the curtains open, it would let in light as well as a breeze. The furniture, while old, must have been expensive. The chairs showed signs of wear, some fraying around the edges, but this room gave off a good feeling.

He finished his inventory of the room and downed the whiskey. He'd entered the parlor through a huge door and into a room overlooking what he assumed would be a veranda. The shutters banged against the windows as the wind continued its eerie wale.

The sideboard with the whiskey was on an opposite wall. He helped himself to another two fingers, swirling it in his glass before tasting a small portion.

"Very good," he set the glass down, peering around the room, hoping to get a better idea of Cali Durand. But the room spoke of her parents, not her. Pre-war it must have been a grand place to live and visit.

Oh, the south had been so arrogant and brave. They'd thought they could fight the northern powerhouse and win. They had Robert E Lee and a host of other West Point graduates who were brilliant strategists. But in the end, they didn't have enough men, and they didn't have manufacturing plants. Hell, they'd even run out of shoes.

Brother against brother, uncles fighting nephews, what kind of country would put their citizens through such butchery. They were all Americans. He made his choices when he decided to fight for the Union, and he prayed he had never killed a relative or a friend. He was glad he'd never come face to face with someone he knew.

Daisy appeared in the doorway. "Dinner's ready. You can wash up in the kitchen."

Archer nodded and followed Daisy. A small table was set for four. China and silver at each place setting. He slanted Cali a glance, wondering how she was able to hang onto the silver.

She seemed to know what he was thinking and with a delicate shrug of her shoulders and an expression that seemed to say *I know a thing or two about pillaging soldiers*, she said, "I had an excellent hiding place."

"Well, that explains it." He pulled out a chair for Cali then Daisy. Sam sauntered into the room with a bottle of wine. Once again, he questioned her with a raised eyebrow. "Hiding place?"

One eyebrow rose before she picked up a napkin, spreading it on her lap.

He waited, wondering what he should do, what she would do.

"Would you say grace?" Her gaze held his and he felt sure she saw into his soul.

"Of course."

Rain pounded on the veranda surrounding them. Wind battered the closed window shutters. In unison, all four turned their attention to the fragile panes of glass.

"Hope they hold." Sam muttered, rising to look at the window as if he could fix anything from the inside.

"Sit down, Sam. You're not going anywhere. We've a meal that is hot and ready to eat. Mr. Steele is about to say grace."

He set his hands on the table, hoping they would all join hands. Cali clasped his in hers. Her fingers were long, delicate and he felt the fragility as well as the strength. Daisy took his other hand.

Clearing his throat, he began, "Dear Lord, bless this food and keep us and our neighbors safe from the tempest outside—"

Suddenly the shutter that had been rattling broke free and the ancient glass cracked, shattering into the room. Daisy shrieked, her hands rising to her face. Cali stood, knocking her chair down.

"Sam? Nails and hammer?"

"I'll get the broom—clean up the glass." Daisy headed for the broom closet.

Cali opened the outside door before Arched could protest. "Stay in the house."

She was outside in the middle of the storm. "I've always taken care of my home."

He heard the words and knew the truth. She'd been through hell, trying to survive. During the war, there had been no one to take care of her. He followed her from the house, Sam close behind.

Wind whipped her hair loose from its pins, the strands flying behind her.

"Oh my god!"

Sweet Misbehavin'
Book Three in the McKenna Clan Series

Cast adrift after fleeing the home of Jokul, the ice demon, Atantsi, a firestarter, grew to womanhood as she moved through time to keep the demon from finding her. Though stubborn and courageous, she was ill prepared to use powers she had not been taught. Her first sight of the intoxicating Carr McKenna left her breathless, and her second encounter gave her hope for a future she never thought she had.

A playboy, a second son and a shifter, a man who thought his life would be carefree, Carr McKenna was shocked to discover the woman he'd paid as an escort is a firestarter who is running for her life. He is the leader of all the McKennas around the world and that he has multiple powers. His passion for Margo and the need to defend her might cost him his life as well as hers.

Sweet Talkin' Sugar
Book Four in the McKenna Clan Series

Lyonesse McKenna, was dreaming or was she? From the instant Lyn saw Deacon McClain across a black jack table in a crowed Las Vegas casino the unmistakable attraction sent Lyn's senses flying into overdrive. Her family of shapeshifters believed in soul mates. She'd always been skeptical yet she couldn't help but question the way her heart sped when he looked at her.

When Deacon appeared in Las Vegas he knew his first job was to save Lyn from a Sea Demon, but the next order of business was to convince her he would someday mean more to her than she'd ever expected. But her stubborn nature and unbendable spirit consumed Deacon...and he had to chase away all the demons real and imagined in order to win her heart.

Sweet Surrender
Book Five in the McKenna Clan Series

Ripped from her family at the top of Infinity Cliff, Kimi McKenna finds herself thrust somewhere into the future. Dark elements threaten to destroy the earth unless Kimi can work together with the white witch to stop the destruction. Confused by her mate's role in the conspiracy, she refuses to acknowledge the connection. But amidst raging fire and attacks on the people she is coming to hold dear, she allows Maska O'keefe into her heart.

Maska O'keefe has loved the beautiful shapeshifter for years. Unable to save her life years ago, he vows to watch over her as he is given a second chance to convince her that even though he is a witch and not a shifter, they are indeed soul mates. Kimi's divided loyalties between her family and the cause she is now a part of will determine their relationship. Only the part she plays as the messiah can bring this to a conclusion in the final battle.

Dakota's Bride
The first book in the Lakota/Pinkerton Series

When Emma St. John received her brother's letter imploring her to escape her stepfather's vengeful scheme and to trust Dakota Barringer with her life, she was willing to chance it. But the handsome, brooding riverboat owner Emma found in Natchez a danger of another kind. For Emma soon found herself surrendering to an unrelenting desire.
Raised by the Sioux when his parents were killed, Dakota had been betrayed once before by a white woman. He wasn't about to trust another, especially one claiming that her stepfather, a powerful U.S. senator, had framed her as a murderess. But he couldn't let Emma's intoxicating effect on him. Now Dakota would risk his very life to protect the innocent beauty who had seduced him with her tender love.

My Angel
The second book in the Lakota/Pinkerton Series

A BEAUTY IN BUCKSKINS
When her father decided to send her to a finishing school back East, Angela Chamberlain refused to be confined to stuffy drawing rooms. Instead, the daring spitfire who could shoot like a man and ride like the wind longed for a life of adventure and romance—and she knew exactly who could give it to her. Devil Blackmoor was a hired gun with a dangerous reputation. But Angela was willing to go to the ends of the earth to capture the handsome devil's heart.

A DEVIL IN DISGUISE
He'd come to America looking for excitement, but Devil Blackmoor got more than he bargained for when he encountered a beautiful rebel who answered his kisses with a wild innocence that touched his very soul. Yet standing between them were more obstacles than either ever dreamed. For Devil had strapped on a gun for the wrong man. And that made Angela his enemy. Now he'll have to choose between his duty and the woman he loves more than life.

The Locket
The third book in the Lakota/Pinkerton Series

The year is 1894. Seeking revenge for crimes against his family, Misha Petrovich follows a path that leads straight to Ariel Cameron's boarding house in Mist Harbor, Oregon. A family heirloom in Ariel's possession leads Misha to believe she is guilty. The locket has been handed down to the oldest girl in the Petrovich family for generations. Ariel is innocent of wrong doing, but her father is not. Misha is torn by his feelings for Ariel and his need for restitution against her father. Knowing that the relationship between them is fragile, Misha does everything in his power to protect Ariel's father. His efforts are to no avail when her father is shot. Ariel comes to realize Misha's steadfast courage and determination to protect her and her father despite what has happened to his family. Ariel's love and devotion heals Misha's heart.

The Talisman
The fourth book in the Lakota/Pinkerton Series

Running from a marriage that lasted one night, Dr. Moriah McKeown discovers the land she has settled on is coveted by determined and lawless men. Yet the proud young woman who once vowed never to abandon her home has second thoughts when her adopted children are threatened. Her only recourse is to enlist the aid of a dark, dangerous gun for hire.
Haunted by the past and a betrayal he will never forgive, Ian Civanovich uses his fast gun and his reckless courage to forget the faithlessness of a woman in his past. He will trust no female—nor will he rest until the threat hovering over Moriah McKeown is put to rest.

Forever His
The fifth book in the Lakota/Pinkerton Series

Struggling to come to terms with the part she played in Jacob St. John's death, Etta Barringer resigns from Pinkerton Agency and seeks peace and solace in a Rocky Mountain Cabin.
Jacob has vowed to discover the reason Etta has betrayed him, sold him out to his enemy and left him for dead.
Isolated in their cabin, they discover their love for each other and learn to trust. But the trust is shattered when Jacob learns she is married to his sworn enemy; the man who left him in the desert to die.

Allura's Secret
Twelve Dancing Princesses Book One

Allura McClellan is horrified by her father's decision to take out an ad in the Times awarding her to the man strong enough and smart enough to win her hand and uncover her secrets. She's an intelligent young woman who takes great delight in the freedom allotted to her by her father. She's well aware that marriage would effectively curtail the adventures she's shared with her sisters and cousins.

Hunter Gray is nothing like the other men who've arrived to vie for Allura's hand in marriage and everything that goes along with it. However, he is the first to refuse to concede defeat and pursue her despite her attempts to disguise her true appearance. It's her temperament that is of more concern to him than her looks. Hunter has worked all his life with the hope of someday owning his own land. Now that it looks like there's a very real possibility that everything he's ever wanted is within reach nothing is going to deter him – including Miss Allura's disagreeable disposition.

Amorica's Wager
Twelve Dancing Princesses Book Two

Amorica Hepburn was sent to London to find a husband. Finding a man was the last item on her agenda. With her two cousins, Amorica wagers she can dissuade her suitor before the others. Despite her efforts she discovers a chemistry that cannot be denied. Suddenly she is the arrogant man's wife, pledged to a marriage neither desire. But swept off to his ancestral home above the Dover cliffs and into his strong embrace, Amorica is soon possessed by a raging passion for the husband she had vowed to despise...

Damian Andrews couldn't afford to trust the emerald-eyed spitfire who happened upon his secret. Amorica's hatred of all men of his kind only inflames the war that rages between them. Still, he can not control the intense desire his stubborn bride inspires, or make her surrender to his will until he has conquered the headstrong beauty on the battlefield of love...

Ravyn's Marriage of Inconvenience
Twelve Dancing Princesses Book Three

A REGAL BEAUTY
When the duchess decides to wed her to a wastrel and a fop, Ravyn Grahm takes matters into her own hands and declares her engagement to another man. Instead of fessing up and telling her great aunt what she has done, she goes through with the pretense. Aric Lakeland is the bastard son of an earl and has a dangerous reputation. But Ravyn is willing to do most anything to keep the duchess from discovering the lie.

A DEVIL-MAY-CARE SMUGGLER
He'd bought land in America, looking to put down roots and end his life of adventure, but Aric Lakeland got more than he bargained for when he encountered a beautiful heiress who made a promise she didn't want to keep. But the promise could not be undone and standing between them were more obstacles than either ever dreamed. Aric had made plans to spend the rest of his life in America and that was at odds with Ravyn's plan of living in England and running her father's estate. Now, he'll have to choose between his dreams and the woman he loves more than life.

Christel's Sunrise
Twelve Dancing Princesses Book Four

He Made Her An Offer...

Life has thrown Christel McClellan some experiences that could have devastated a less determined woman. Beautiful, self-assured and fiercely independent, she is trying to forget the loss of her stillborn child. But is the child alive?

She Couldn't Deny...

Life is carefree for Ryder MacLaren who loves to see what is on the other side of the sunrise. Laird of Clan MacLaren, he is wealthy, handsome and happily unencumbered...until stunning Christel McClellan enters his life. When he hears her story, he believes the child she thought dead has been sold to a wealthy buyer.

Storm's Passion
Twelve Dancing Princesses Book Five

SHE MADE A PROPOSAL...

Life strikes Storm Graham a shattering blow when she learns her father has bartered her to a man she detests. Storm is beautiful, self–assured and fiercely independent, and refuses to be a pawn in her father's schemes, yet she can find no way out of this bargain made in hell. Going on the offensive she asks the wealthiest man on the eastern coast of England to marry her, never believing she might fall in love.

HE TRIED TO REFUSE...

For Hadden Johnston life has provided everything he ever wanted, including a sanctuary for homeless children. He is wealthy, handsome and happily unencumbered...until stunning Storm Graham marches into his life and proposes a marriage of convenience. Yet this type of marriage to a woman who inflames his senses is far from acceptable. If he's going to be tied down, he will move heaven and earth to have this woman warming his bed.

Gotta Have Fayth
Twelve Dancing Princesses Book Six

A regal beauty with raven hair and piercing blue eyes, Fayth Graham is unwilling to parade herself in front of the wealthy Lords of England during the season. Seeking a means to dissuade any man wishing to wed her, she seeks a way to ruin herself for marriage. When she unexpectedly meets a man with sparkling gray eyes and an infectious grin, she decides this is the man who will keep her from agreeing to obey.

He returned from six months at sea, looking for a few nights of pleasure with a willing lass, but Jarret Kinsley got more than he bargained for when he met a beautiful debutant who responded to his kisses with a wild innocence that touched his heart. Yet the obstacles looming between them might rip them apart. Both had vowed never to marry, so when consequences of their dalliances got in the way, Jarret would have to choose between the life he's always desired and the woman he loves more than life.

Ella's Pleasure
Twelve Dancing Princesses Book Seven

A WHISPER OF PLEASURE

Ella Hepburn was an auburn haired debutant from the harsh Scottish coastline—a wild innocent to be seduced and tamed. A spirited beauty, she captivated Drake Montgomerie's jaded heart—while succumbing to the smoldering desire she felt for her unyielding suitor.

A WHISPER OF DANGER

In Drake Montgomerie's glittering world of money and privilege, young Ella discovered passion and desire could overcome everything she'd been taught to resist—entangling Drake, the heir apparent, in a lethal coil of aristocratic family intrigue. But grave peril would only nurse the sparks of a love that knew no limits and a magnificent ecstasy that would not be denied.

Eveleen's Seduction
Twelve Dancing Princesses Book Eight

A WHISPER OF SEDUCTION

A brutal attack on Eveleen Hepburn's cherished island off the Scottish coastline leaves her shattered and bewildered. Learning a man she once trusted can kill as easily as he can breathe even though the deed saves her life, creates questions that need answers. An innocent beauty, she enchants Logan Maxwell's cynical heart—giving in to the raging passion she feels for her mysterious suitor.

A WHISPER OF INTRIGUE

In Logan's Maxwell's world of espionage and privilege, young Eveleen discovers truths about herself she never expected, and a need for passion and love can overcome all her fears if she learns to accept certain truths. She finds herself entangled in a lethal battle for land that was once owned by French nobility, taken from them during the revolution and sold to Maxwell. But grave peril would unleash the flames of love that simmers, creating a magical union that cannot be refuted.

Tavia's Deception
Twelve Dancing Princesses Book Nine

WHISPERS OF DECEPTION

When her father decides to send her to London for her season, Tavia Hepburn resolves to see the world instead. The raven haired beauty decides to disguise herself as a lad and find employment on a ship bound for Barcelona as a cabin boy. But she never bargains on finding passion and love to a red haired sea captain who rescues her from certain death.

WHISPERS OF MURDER

For James Macmurra, the world is black and white until he meets a young debutante, who turns his world upside down. He's unable to deny Tavia's intoxicating effect on him. In a match tense with obstacles, unwillingness to divulge secrets, and unforeseen peril, irresistible desire and passion grows into undeniable love. James would risk his life to shelter and protect the innocent debutante who seduces him with her sweet love.

Larena's Fascination
Twelve Dancing Princesses Book Ten

WHISPERS OF FASCINATION

Fiery, free spirited Larena Graham never wanted to marry a duke. She is thrilled to be in love with the fourth son of an aristocrat, Gavin Broon. But when it seems Gavin ignores her, she set her sights on politics and bettering human life. Unsuspecting intrigue and a plot against her, she continues her dangerous plans despite Gavin's wishes.

Whispers of Trust

Gavin has every intention of properly courting the beautiful Larena until he must leave the city in order to put his affairs in order. Returning to London, he finds the woman he means to make his own is embroiled in political protests that could lead to a prison ship. Larena must learn to trust the handsome Scotsman whose most pressing mission is to protect her and keep her from harm.

Tira's Education
Twelve Dancing Princesses Book Eleven

WHISPERS OF EDUCATION

Learning how to build ships is Tira Hepburn's only dream until she meets Jamie Lundin and her world is turned upside down. With her raven black hair and vivid green eyes, she tempts Jamie and pushes him to defy his vows. She never bargains on finding an irrevocable love and a passion to a man who cannot fulfill her dreams despite his burning desire for her.

WHISPERS OF A BARGAIN

Arrogant and self-assured Jamie is brought up short when Tira captures his heart. All his carefully made plans are put to the test when he decides to teach her the art of ship building if she will spend a week with him alone on his ship. He is unable to deny Tira's intoxicating effect on him. When Tira leaves him behind unwilling to live with him without the benefit of marriage, he races after her. Jamie will risk everything to shelter and protect the innocent debutante who seduces him with her sweet love.

WHISPERS OF TRUST

Gavin has every intention of properly courting the beautiful Larena until he must leave the city in order to put his affairs in order. Returning to London, he finds the woman he means to make his own is embroiled in political protests that could lead to a prison ship. Larena must learn to trust the handsome Scotsman whose most pressing mission is to protect her and keep her from harm.

Aidan's Love
Twelve Dancing Princesses Book Twelve
Coming September 1, 2019

Twelve Days to Love

When Archer Steele shows up at Calanthe Durand's failing plantation with an alligator over his shoulder, Cali thinks she's never seen a more handsome man. During the war she had to defend herself and her servants from both union and confederate soldiers. Independent and self-sufficient, she vows to never marry.

But Archer Steele has different ideas. The first time Archer sees Cali in town, he feels an instant attraction. He decides he will do everything and anything to convince the beautiful Miss Durand he is worthy of her love. During the weeks leading up to Christmas, he gives her twelve gifts in hopes she will fall in love with him. Yet they are faced with challenges they must overcome before Cali can commit to a marriage.

Door to Heaven

Jessica Lawrence is the stepdaughter of a woman born in the twentieth century transported back in time to the year 1868. An acclaimed suffragette, she raises Jessica to believe in the equality of women. Jess Law believes everything she was taught, and when the time is right she becomes a private investigator. Courageous and impetuous, Jess finds danger in her quest to save all women from white slavery. Her passionate mission results in a wedding to Roc Newman, a man she knows can steal her heart...

Roc can't trust the sapphire-eyed spitfire who invades his home in search of secret papers and knocks him flat with her karate moves. Jessica's refusal to obey his wishes serves to inflame the war between them. Still, he cannot control the intense desire his reluctant bride inspires, or make her surrender her independence, until he has conquered the headstrong beauty on the battlefield of love...

Rebel Heart

HER REBEL SPIRIT DEFIED HIS OUTSIDERS SOUL...[SEP]She was velvet and silk, eyes the color of a summer storm and amber hair. Victoria DeMontville, because of a promise and a codicil to her father's will, was forced to marry one man to protect her from another. She hated Cameron Savage with a fierce passion. But to hold on to her genetic research and find a cure for the deadly Signe virus, she must pretend to love the enemy at her door, come with weapons of fire to melt her icy heart...

HIS OUTSIDERS TOUCH IGNITED RAGING PASSIONS...[SEP]He wore a mask, disguised as the Phantom, a true legend come to life. Even as war and debate over new genetic research engulfed them all, he would find his greatest adversary in the beauty who'd branded him an outsider and barbarian, the woman he was born to possess, his soul mate.

Safari Moon

Solo St. John, a wildlife photographer, is preparing for a trip to Alaska. Suddenly, Solo finds women of all sorts invading his privacy, his home and his office, all cooing nonsense words and blatantly throwing themselves at him. Solo doesn't know why, and he has no idea how to rid himself of the persistent women. He finally decides to beg a favor of his best buddy Nyssa Harrington.

In love with Solo for the past ten years and knowing he doesn't return her feelings Nyssa doesn't want to talk to Solo. She knows if she accepts his phone call, she will not be able to resist the temptation to hope again.

Straight to Heaven

Running from demons, Alexandra McMurdie stumbles into Forbidden Ground where up is down and elements of nature are contested. Though a strong independent woman in the twenty-first century' she is unprepared for life in the 1800s. Her first site of the formidable James Lawrence makes her heart skip a beat, giving her cause to reconsider her desperate need to find a way home.

Born with a silver spoon, James' life was torn apart during the War Between the States. Moving west he vows to put the life he once knew in the past. When he discovers a half-frozen woman near Gold Hill, his heart begins to thaw. His love for Alexandra and his need to keep her from a man who has pursued her through time might cost him his life as well as hers.

A Valentine's Anthology

The Lending Library-a fantasy by Christie L. Kraemer

Faeries try to fit into the human world when the forest where they make their home is destroyed by a mysterious enemy.

Chasing Rainbows-a contemporary romance by Genene Valleau

An eccentric aunt, an inventive uncle, a mother who wears poodle skirts, and a brother who wears pearls provide a hilarious backdrop for the courtship of a young woman who yearns for a "normal" family.

The Gift-an historical romance by Christine Young

A man and a woman on opposite sides of the Civil War get a second chance at love after one final battle returns soldiers to their war-torn homes to rebuild their lives.

A St. Patrick's Day Tale
by
Christine Young, C. L. Kraemer, Genene Valleau

Tumble through time…

…to Ireland in 1817, when tensions are high between Protestants and Catholics and faey people guide the fate of villagers. A lovely Catholic lass stumbles upon the weakly ritual fisticuffing between Irish lads. She falls into the lap of a handsome young Protestant. Family ties, grudges, and two conniving faeries threaten their budding love. But the faeries outsmart themselves when they hijack a time machine that has mysteriously appeared in their forest and are whisked to…

…Eugene, Oregon in the 20th century, amid a property feud between the local faeries and night elves. The conniving faeries from Olde Ireland try to stir up more mischief. However, a warrior gnome convinces the magic folk to control their own destiny, and forces the intruding faeries to take refuge in the time machine again, spinning their way toward…

…A modern day castle in western Oregon. An eccentric inventor is determined to reclaim his wayward time machine and save his beloved wife from her latest misadventure. If only they can travel safely past the black hole…

a May Day Anthology
by
Christine Young, C. L. Kraemer, Rosemary Indra, Genene Valleau

Highland Miracle -- Christine Young

HURTLED THROUGH TIME, Sean Michael Sterling, landed in the midst of a May Day celebration he didn't understand, assuming the role of Laird Sterling.

ILLIGITAMATE CHILD OF NOBILITY, Reagan Douglas searches for a way out of her half brother's house.

Defying the Odds -- C.L. Kraemer

The night elves on the hill aren't happy without their magic. They concoct a plan to punish those who were involved in the act that rendered them almost human. Meanwhile, Uther, the rogue night elf, has returned to woo the Librarian to be his eternal mate.

Love in Bloom -- Rosemary Indra

When childhood friends reunite it takes two fairies and a matchmaking daughter to help them admit their true love for each other.

No More Poodle Skirts -- Genie Gabriel

After drifting for years in the innocent age of the 1950s, a woman struggles to join today's world by finding a career and a new love, with some help from her zany family.

Once Upon a Christmas Moon
by
Christine Young, C. L. Kraemer, Genene Valleau

TWELVE DAYS TO LOVE

When Archer Steele shows up at Calanthe Durand's failing plantation with an alligator over his shoulder, Cali thinks she's never seen a more handsome man. During the war she had to defend herself and her servants from both union and confederate soldiers. Independent and self-sufficient, she vows to never marry. But Archer Steele has different ideas. The first time Archer sees Cali in town, he feels an instant attraction. He decides he will do everything and anything to convince the beautiful Miss Durand he is worthy of her love. During the weeks leading up to Christmas, he gives her twelve gifts in hopes she will fall in love with him.

BOOTS AND BLADES

An ancient evil from the old country has arrived in the high desert of Oregon. Gnome children are vanishing then re-appearing, showing various stages of traumatization. Tiamoon, warrior gnome, will put her skills to use alongside Killian, a handsome warrior, also in need of a cause.

CHRISTMAS PAWSIBILITIES

With their world destroyed and their space ship malfunctioning, the dogizens of Planet Canid have little choice but to crash land on Earth. They face tortuous experiments at the hands of the Geeks in Green...or they can trust an eccentric inventor and his zany family to deliver the Canine Queen's puppies and help them celebrate new lives.

Love in Bloom -- Rosemary Indra

When childhood friends reunite it takes two fairies and a matchmaking daughter to help them admit their true love for each other.

No More Poodle Skirts -- Genie Gabriel

After drifting for years in the innocent age of the 1950s, a woman struggles to join today's world by finding a career and a new love, with some help from her zany family.

Healthy Homicide

Two murders have occurred at the Barrel Springs Day Spa. Police hurry to find the method and reason before anyone else is murdered.

MANIC READER REVIEWS says: Healthy Homicide by C.L. Kraemer is an intriguing plot driven mystery. The plot is well written and pretty much carries the whole story...

Dragons Among Us

In a world full of anomalies such as the platypus and self reproducing Komodo dragon, is the human race willing to accept that dragons may be real?

Sapien Draconi-human-dragon shape shifters-all over the world face this dilemma every day. The question has become life and death as their species is plagued with unexpected and unwanted shifting in the most unlikely of places.

The Ancient Ones-full-blooded dragons-can offer advice, but few seem to put forward workable solutions to the problem.

The fate of the shape shifters hangs in the balance, and an answer must be found before the Homo Sapiens find, dissect, and hunt Sapien Draconi to extinction.

Dragons Among The Eagles

Aleda Sable faces the toughest decision of her life--to stay in dragon form, live as a two-legged or put one foot in the human world and one talon in the dragon world.

An urgent call from her newspaper editor sends Aleda to report on an accident whose driver appears to be a dragon. Authorities have the scene locked down and aren't allowing access to anyone. Television broadcasts flash pictures of scaly legs hanging from a crashed car. However, the bodies disappear into thin air. When the stations try follow-up reports, all they find are state highway workers busily tearing up the roads.

In determining the truth of the shifter disappearances, Aleda finds the truth of her own dilemma.

Shattered Tomorrows

Lucy Daniels has a secret--a deeply guarded secret.

Her life was going along just fine until she accompanied her best friend, Cassie, to her attorney's suite on top of the Equitable Building in downtown Salem, Oregon.

Once inside the lawyer's office, the world turned upside down and Lucy was forced to face a demon from her past. Thirty years ago, life had been different. Lucy had discovered Prince Charming and was headed to her happily ever after.

That's when the devil intervened and because of her brush with the devil, innocent people died.

Joker's Wild

Four brothers raised in the Northwest.

Two choose to stay and pursue life in Oregon. Two are seduced by the promise of Hollywood.

Life throws the Palmer brothers an ugly curve when two are killed in preventable accidents. Even more upsetting is the lack of justice in the trials of the perpetrators.

The remaining brothers will find justice using a shared passion of all the participants--motorcycle poker runs.

C. L. Kraemer

is also featured in these anthologies available at
Rogue Phoenix Press

A Different Kind of Valentine

A collection of four short stories:

Witness by k. J. Dahlen

When Colten finds an injured woman the police are looking for her, should he trust his own judgement about keeping her hidden from the law even if it means she might kill him?

The Prize by C. L. Kraemer

A computer geek learns valuable life lessons when he is given his dream car as well as a condo and the perfect job.

Crazy 'bout You by Clay Renick

Can a psychologist and a romance writer find true love in time for Valentines Day?

Time Changes by Nicolette Zamora

Laurie is just about ready to give up on love when she spies Rob Hender, her high school sweethearts older brother.

A St. Patrick's Day Tale
by
Christine Young, C. L. Kraemer, Genene Valleau

Tumble through time…

…to Ireland in 1817, when tensions are high between Protestants and Chatolics and faey people guide the fate of villagers. A lovely Catholic lass stumbles upon the weakly ritual fisticuffing between Irish lads. She falls into the lap of a handsome young Protestant. Family ties, grudges, and two conniving faeries threaten their budding love. But the faeries outsmart themselves when they hijack a time machine that has mysteriously appeared in their forest and are whisked to…

…Eugene, Oregon in the 20th century, amid a property feud between the local faeries and night elves. The conniving faeries from Olde Ireland try to stir up more mischief. However, a warrior gnome convinces the magic folk to control their own destiny, and forces the intruding faeries to take refuge in the time machine again, spinning their way toward…

…A modern day castle in western Oregon. An eccentric inventor is determined to reclaim his wayward time machine and save his beloved wife from her latest misadventure. If only they can travel safely past the black hole…

A Valentine's Anthology

The Lending Library-a fantasy by C. L. Kraemer

Faeries try to fit into the human world when the forest where they make their home is destroyed by a mysterious enemy.

Chasing Rainbows-a contemporary romance by Genene Valleau

An eccentric aunt, an inventive uncle, a mother who wears poodle skirts, and a brother who wears pearls provide a hilarious backdrop for the courtship of a young woman who yearns for a "normal" family.

The Gift-an historical romance by Christine Young

A man and a woman on opposite sides of the Civil War get a second chance at love after one final battle returns soldiers to their war-torn homes to rebuild their lives.

Other books by Genie Gabriel
Available at Rogue Phoenix Press

I Want to Have the Heart of a Dog

One woman's journey through several lifetimes of betrayal, abuse and violent deaths, coming to the present day realization that dogs are much more than furry companions. They are protectors, comforters, and teachers whose hearts contain the simple and miraculous knowledge of the Universe–if only we listen and learn.

Aunt Maddie's Doggone Misadventures

Exploding inventions, hilarious misadventures, zany characters and talking dogs are part of everyday life.

Chasing Rainbows–Book 1

An artistically eccentric aunt, an uncle who invents a mechanical dog, a mother who wears poodle skirts, and a brother who wears pearls provide a hilarious backdrop for the courtship of a young woman who yearns for a "normal" family. An artistically eccentric aunt, an uncle who invents a mechanical dog, a mother who wears poodle skirts, and a brother who wears pearls provide a hilarious backdrop for the courtship of a young woman who yearns for a "normal" family.

St. Batzy & the Time Machine–Book 2

An eccentric inventor is determined to reclaim his wayward time machine from the neighbor girl's dog and save his beloved wife from her latest misadventure. If only they can travel safely past the black hole...

No More Poodle Skirts–Book 3

After drifting for years in the innocent age of the 1950s, a woman struggles to join today's world by finding a career and a new love, with some help from her zany family and a talking dog.

Christmas Pawsibilities–Book 4

While former playboy Ryan Madison and elfenchaun Dori plan their Christmas wedding, a space ship carrying alien dogs crash lands into a neighbor's barn. When the evil commander of the Geeks in Green (GIG) wants to use the aliens for tortuous experiments, Aunt Maddie's zany family sneaks into GIG headquarters to foil this dastardly plan while the Blue-Haired Ladies stage a Nertz tournament as a distraction.

Aunt Maddie's Doggone Misadventures–book 5

Bernie's Legacy Series

Bernie O'Shea built a legacy as a street cop. Tough. Fair. Heroic. They say he was shot in the line of duty, leaving behind eight adopted children and a wife with secrets of her own. His children are determined to continue their father's legacy. But what happens when they get too close to the truth that killed Bernie?

The Rock 'n' Romance Trilogy

A fantasy encounter with a rock star ends in disaster, but Shannon and Geoff get a second chance a love if they can shake off mistakes from their past, outfox an overly protective Bodyguard who must vanquish his own demons to find another love, and maneuver around the comeback dreams of the Leader of the Band, who is forced to face his heart's true desire.

The Collie Chronicles

More Than Just a Dog
Book One

Three generations of independent women, driven in different directions by one man's anger. Until his death reconnects them with their mystical Irish ancestors and wonders beyond this limited human existence.

Trained in the shamanic arts by her Irish grandmother, Chessie Durand travels to alternate worlds to rescue animals in danger. Aided by her Chosen One, an angel dog and a mysterious merkaba necklace, she discovers powers unknown to most humans.

Ever practical, her mother provides a sanctuary for these alien and exotic species stall-beside-stall with barnyard creatures. And when their paradise is threatened by ignorance and poachers and unknown dangers beyond the stargates, Marlise loads her shotgun and joins the fight.

More than Just a Star Traveler
Book Two

To come back to Earth Three in his collie form, Chap agrees to go on Angel Assignments with his beloved human. Chessie Durand is sometimes amazed and sometimes frustrated as she learns how to use the powers of a mystical necklace given to her by a man who has loved her for many lifetimes.

Peter Stravel knows Chessie is his Chosen One when he travels through the stargate to her dimension. However, their love and their lives are threatened by those who want to destroy Chessie before she realizes her full power as the One who travels in the light of the merkaba.

Their survival depends on learning to trust their love and use their supernatural powers, as they team up with animals who play a special role in their lives.

**VISIT OUR WEBSITE
FOR THE FULL INVENTORY
OF QUALITY BOOKS:**
http://www.roguephoenixpress.com

Rogue Phoenix Press

Representing Excellence in Publishing

Quality trade paperbacks and downloads

in multiple formats,

*in genres ranging from historical to contemporary
romance, mystery and science fiction.*

Visit the website then bookmark it.

We add new titles each month

www.ingramcontent.com/pod-product-compliance
Lightning Source LLC
Chambersburg PA
CBHW061924170626
46813CB00006B/2294